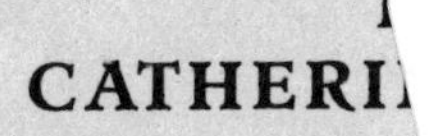

CATHERI[illegible]

"Anderson has a talent [illegible] characters."

—*Publishers Weekly*

"Ms. Anderson holds her readers spellbound."

—*Romantic Times*

. . . and CHRISTINA DODD

"Christina Dodd is a joy to read."

—Laura Kinsale

"Another winner from this talented author."

—*Romantic Times* on OUTRAGEOUS

. . . and SUSAN SIZEMORE

"An entertaining read."

—*Romantic Times* on WINGS OF THE STORM

"A rare romantic treat."

—*Affaire de Coeur* on MY FIRST DUCHESS

Other books by Catherine Anderson

Cheyenne Amber
Coming Up Roses
Comanche Moon
Comanche Heart
Indigo Blue

by Christina Dodd

Outrageous
Castles in the Air
Candle in the Window
Treasure of the Sun
Priceless

and by Susan Sizemore

My Own True Love
Wings of the Storm
My First Duchess

Available from HarperPaperbacks

TALL, DARK, ~ and ~ DANGEROUS

CATHERINE ANDERSON

CHRISTINA DODD

SUSAN SIZEMORE

HarperPaperbacks
A Division of HarperCollins*Publishers*

This is a work of fiction. The characters, incidents, and dialogues are products of the authors' imaginations and are not to be construed as real. Any resemblance to actual events or persons, living or dead, is entirely coincidental.

HarperPaperbacks *A Division of* HarperCollins*Publishers*
10 East 53rd Street, New York, N.Y. 10022

Cover illustration by Hal Frenck

First printing: September 1994

Printed in the United States of America

❖ 10 9 8 7 6 5 4 3 2 1

CONTENTS

Catherine Anderson
SHOTGUN BRIDE
1

Christina Dodd
WILD TEXAS ROSE
143

Susan Sizemore
ONE RIOT, ONE RANGER
265

SHOTGUN BRIDE

~ by ~

Catherine Anderson

In memory of Marliss Miller, my neighbor and friend,
who is surely tending the flower gardens in Paradise
and throwing Frisbees with the angels.

ONE ~

Oregon, 1887

Joshua Slade was dangerous, a godless man with an infamous reputation for speed and accuracy with a gun, a man who overindulged in drink, gambled at cards, and had absolutely no respect for decent females. Everyone in Juniper Hollow knew it. For that matter, everyone in Oregon probably did. Any woman who knocked on his door seeking help would be asking for trouble. Probably more trouble than she could handle.

The thought was deliciously exciting.

Charlie Masterson brought her wagon to a skidding halt and peered through the falling snow, which seemed to be coming down more heavily by the moment. Slade's ranch house was just up that wagon trail and over that pine-covered rise. His property stretched for several miles along each side of the main road.

Should she? Or shouldn't she?

Charlie fixed her gaze on the wagon ruts that led up to his place. Already the snow had nearly obliterated the tracks. In another ten minutes, the main thoroughfare might even be covered. What would she do then? Guess where to guide her horse and pray she didn't drive off into a ditch?

Under ordinary circumstances, there wouldn't have been a question. After living in this high-desert country all her life, Charlie recognized a blizzard in the making. She knew she should head for the closest house and hole up until the storm passed. But these weren't ordinary circumstances, not when the only house between here and town belonged to Joshua Slade.

If she sought his help, she might be stranded at his ranch for the duration of the storm, and then her reputation would be ruined. A preacher's daughter didn't put her good name at risk.

Charlie had seen Joshua Slade only from a distance. Dressed all in black from his hat down to his well-shined boots, he appeared to be devilishly handsome, tall, dark, and muscular. Rhoda Peck, the town flirt, claimed he had long-lashed, midnight blue eyes that fairly smoldered when he looked at her, and that a mere glance from him fairly melted her corset stays.

No one had ever melted Charlie's stays. No one had even warmed them up.

A shiver of excitement ran down her spine. Did she dare? It wasn't her fault that she had been out doing good works and was caught seven miles from town by inclement weather. Adventurous things always happened to people like Rhoda. Why not to her?

Because you're the preacher's daughter, her practical side scolded. *You're to avoid risky situations at all costs.*

But at the cost of her life?

Well, maybe that was exaggerating the conditions a bit much. But the snow *was* coming down rather heavily. Almost a blizzard. A prudent woman wouldn't try to make it. On the other hand, when one's virtue was at risk, death was supposed to be preferable.

What saint was it who had chosen death rather than be unchaste? Charlie couldn't remember, and a wicked little voice inside her head hastened to remind her that she wasn't Catholic, anyway, so what did it matter?

Until a few weeks ago, she had been so practical and virtuous, so dependable and constant. Now, suddenly, she found herself, more times than not, thinking like a pubescent girl.

Her problem was that maddening Orville Worscht, she decided. Four times he had come to dinner, and he still hadn't worked up the nerve to kiss her good-night. To finally have a beau, a real honest-to-goodness beau! Was it any wonder that sparking was on her mind a lot lately? Sweet-sixteen-and-never-been-kissed had passed her by a decade ago. Time was running out for her. Most women her age had been married by the time they turned seventeen and already had started their families.

It just wasn't fair. Wasn't God supposed to reward the dutiful? After her mother's untimely death, Charlie had stepped into her shoes and had made all the expected sacrifices, never begrudgingly, always with a smile. Her brothers were old enough to get along without her now, and there was no reason she couldn't continue to help Papa with his ministerial duties even if she married. She wanted her own life. Was that so terribly much to ask?

Darn that Orville, anyway. The man was a doctor, for pity's sake. A body would think he'd seen enough ladies in various states of dishabille that he wouldn't be shy. But, alas, he was, and painfully so. The bravest thing he had done so far was clasp Charlie's hand, and then his palm had been sweaty.

A blob of snow landed on Charlie's nose, and she crossed her eyes to watch it melt. She was out of her mind. That had to be it. Sitting here in a snowstorm, thinking about—About what? Mercy, in four years she would be thirty, and she still didn't know exactly what occurred between a man and woman behind closed doors. As the daughter of an absentminded preacher who had never even spoken to his four sons about such goings-on, she could very well go to her grave not knowing.

Getting to heaven by default didn't sound very glorious. She wanted a divine commendation. *Charlie Masterson was sorely tempted, but she persevered.* When an innocent young woman found herself in a compromising situation with a dangerous individual like Josh Slade, what might he do to her? All Charlie was absolutely certain of was that his palms wouldn't sweat while he did it.

Well, enough of this. She sighed and clicked her tongue at Molly, the family's trusty old mare. "Come on, girl. Let's try to make it home," she called as she gave the reins a shake.

As she passed the wagon road that led to Joshua Slade's house, Charlie lifted her chin a notch. It was just as well, she told herself. Dreaming about smoldering glances was probably a lot more fun than actually receiving one. As if the Joshua Slades of this world would give her a second look, anyway. Not likely. Unless, of course, it was to check out her bustle and wonder if her roundness at hip and fanny was the genuine thing or an illusion created by horsehair ruffles and padding.

Unfortunately for Charlie, *all* of her curves were genuine, and they seemed to be getting more and more genuine with each passing year.

She'd make brownies when she got home, she decided. The boys loved brownies, and so did her father, and it would be a perfect evening to bake them. She pictured how pretty the falling snow would look outside the ice-encrusted kitchen windows, imagined how cozy and warm the house would be once she got a fire built. She already had a nice rich soup sitting on the stove waiting to be heated for dinner so she would have plenty of time to whip up something special for dessert.

Brownies were not exactly exciting, and certainly not risky. But a woman had to warm her corset stays somehow, and piping hot brownies might be some consolation.

And who knew? Perhaps Orville would stop by this evening to pay his respects. Maybe afterward when she stepped out on the porch with him to say good-night, his watery blue eyes would begin to smolder. Maybe he'd be overcome with lust, grab her by the shoulders, and kiss her. Maybe he would—

A covey of quail, startled by the approaching wagon, *swooshed* up from beside the road, flapping right beneath Molly's nose. Caught daydreaming, Charlie had let her grip on the reins go slack, and when Molly bolted the leather slipped right through her fingers. The wagon lurched, and the horse broke into a wild, uninhibited run.

At first, Charlie wasn't really frightened. Molly was a sweet old mare and would respond to vocal commands as soon as her fright passed. All Charlie need do was keep her seat, which was no easy task when the wagon was lurching between ruts. She heard the two jars of blackberry preserves that Mrs. Harkland had given her clanking and bouncing around in the basket behind her. The wagon shocks creaked, groaned, and snapped beneath her weight.

"Molly!" Charlie cried. "It's okay, girl!"

As though Charlie hadn't spoken, Molly continued to gallop into the wall of falling snow ahead of them. *Mercy!* With a lump of fear rising in her throat, Charlie realized the mare truly was in a panic, possibly because the snow was blinding her, and she hadn't seen what it was that had startled her.

A runaway horse!

The same thing had happened to Melissa Stanger last spring, only Thad Jimpson had been near at hand to rescue her before an accident occurred. Jimpsy and Melissa had been married a month later.

Throwing a frantic glance at the sides of the road, Charlie saw no rescuer emerging from the blur of drifting snowflakes. And Molly showed no signs of slowing down. *Kerwhump!* The wagon hit a rut and was airborne. Charlie held tighter to her seat, growing truly alarmed now.

She prayed that Joshua Slade would suddenly appear. Maybe he was out in the storm—slim chance of that—and riding a fast horse. Maybe—*kerwhump*—

he would see the wagon hurtling along the road and rush to save her, plucking her from the wagon seat just in the nick of time.

Overcome with gratitude, she would forget herself and kiss him, and at the first touch of their lips, his midnight blue eyes would smolder. He would— The wagon wheel struck something large and solid, throwing the conveyance sideways.

"Oh, my goodness!"

Charlie felt herself part company with the wagon seat. A boulder? What was a blooming boulder doing in the road? The next instant, she landed full-length in the snow, plowed through it, and hit the rock-hard eastern Oregon clay.

With his black John B. Stetson tipped low over his eyes and his sheepskin collar turned up to shield his neck, Josh wheeled his horse to chase after a stubborn yearling.

"Yee-hah!" he yelled. "Get along there, you miserable rack of bones!"

The young steer bleated and veered right to avoid Josh's swinging lariat. Once that beast had been sent on its way to the upper pasture, Josh turned back to flush out yet another from the thick bitter brush. A juniper limb slapped him along the jaw, and he grabbed for his hat, tipping it back onto his head as his horse moved out from under the tree.

"Yee-hah! Get along!"

Damned storms, anyway. In this part of the country, if it wasn't one thing, it was another. In summer, it was drought and dust, snakes and mosquitoes. In winter a man froze his ass off trying to tend his stock, and still lost cows to the below-zero temperatures. This blizzard looked to be a pisser. It might blow for days. He had to get these strays in closer to the barn so he could hay them, or he'd lose every last one to cold and starvation.

"Yee-hah!"

A crashing sound caught Josh's attention, and he drew his horse to a halt. Squinting, he tried to see what was making the racket. The snow fell in a blinding curtain now, stinging his face as it slanted under the brim of his hat. Up near the road, he saw a hulking shape speeding along. Between clanks and rattles, he heard the unmistakable drum of hooves.

Josh dug in with his heels to send the stallion up the slope. A horse and wagon? He couldn't quite believe his eyes. And there was no driver. *Shit.* He lay low over his mount's neck and took off in pursuit.

The old mare that pulled the conveyance was already wheezing when Josh nudged his horse abreast of her. On the rocky, uneven ground, it was difficult to catch hold of her harness, but he managed. The mare slowly drew up, blowing clouds of steam, her sides heaving. Josh soothed her for a moment, then released her to check the wagon, hoping to find an unseated occupant. The bed was empty except for the strewn contents of a basket. Shattered glass and blackberries had splattered the wagon planks, the juice turning the blanket of snow inside a burgundy black. He rode a circle around the conveyance and noted that one wheel was broken.

Alarmed, Josh pushed his hat back and peered toward the road. A basket? *Jesus.* Surely no woman in her right mind would be out in weather like this. He tethered the mare so she wouldn't bolt again, then tried to follow the wagon tracks. The snow was falling so heavily that he soon ran out of lead.

"Yo?" he yelled. "Anybody out here? Yo! Holler so I can find you!"

No answer. Josh drew up his horse to listen. The hush that always came with thickly falling snow and cold temperatures hovered over the pine and juniper forest. He felt the freezing air tingling along his cheek. His breath plumed before his face every time he exhaled. If there was someone out in this, she wouldn't last the night.

TWO ~

Josh called out several more times in hope of hearing an answer, but there was none.

"Goddamn it, like I don't have enough troubles of my own."

There was nothing for it. He had to search the area. Better to end up with dead cows than to leave a person out in this weather all night. Setting off in a zigzag so he could cover more ground, Josh rode alongside the road, his eyes burning as he tried to see through the blinding whiteness.

His horse nearly trampled the woman before Josh spied her. Gray silk, a splash of fiery red hair, a pale hand splayed on the snow. His heart did a flip. Was she dead? She lay in an unnatural twist, torso turned sharply at the waist, arms flung outward, lisle-covered legs sprawled amidst a fan of ivory petticoats.

Josh leapt from his horse and knelt on one knee beside her. With the wealth of wet red curls framing her face in wild disarray and her cheeks pink from cold, Miss Charlotte Masterson didn't much resemble the snooty and missish preacher's daughter he had seen in town, but he recognized her nonetheless. Not by her face, because he had never seen her up close, but the red hair and plump figure were unmistakable. Josh's gaze had been drawn to the swing of those hips more than once. Old Deiter Friedlich, proprietor of the Shady Lady Saloon, claimed the activity under Miss Charlotte's bustle rivaled that of two spitting cats in a gunnysack.

"Miss Charlotte?" He lifted one of her hands and rubbed her cold fingers. Plump little fingers, the pads as soft as the underside of rose petals. "Miss Masterson?"

Alarmed, Josh bent closer, not at all sure she was breathing. He couldn't see any puffs of steam. He turned her onto her back and quickly opened the wool jacket of her walking suit, and then her silk under-blouse. More bosom than he had ever had the pleasure of unwrapping was pushed upward by her corset and spilled forth the moment the silk parted. Snowflakes peppered the fine lawn of her chemise and were quickly melted by her body heat. Once wet, the cloth of her undergarment went as transparent as onion skin.

At the sudden chill, her rosy nipples went instantly hard. Josh took that as a good sign. Pressing an ear over her left breast, he slowed his breathing. He felt a thready rhythm against his jaw. When he touched his own chest, the thud was far more pronounced. He straightened, wondering if the difference was due to her injury or the padding of silken flesh over her heart. He had pressed his cheek to a number of bosoms in his day but had never been listening for a woman's heartbeat while he was at it.

Christ. Gingerly he ran his fingers through her hair, feeling for head injuries. Nothing. Next he searched her arms and ribs for fractures. She moaned softly when he moved her left arm, but the bones there felt intact. Diving his hands under her skirts, he checked her legs from ankle to hip. The only irregularities he felt were where her soft, warm thighs bulged slightly at the tops of her garters.

At least nothing seemed to be broken. He prodded her neck, none too sure what to feel for. The vertebrae in her neck felt delicate in comparison to his own, but they all seemed to be in line.

Her long, reddish brown eyelashes fluttered against her cheeks. Josh suddenly found himself fixed by wide, startled green eyes. He could tell by her expression that she didn't know where she was, and that she was frightened. Not that he blamed her. He still had his hands curled around her throat. It would be unsettling to awaken and find oneself being touched by a strange man.

"It's all right," he said. "You had a wagon wreck. You may not remember me. Josh Slade? You've probably seen me in town now and again. Luckily, you had the accident near my place."

"Accident?" She gazed at the sky, batting her long lashes against the pelting snow. After a moment, she touched a hand to her bare cleavage. "Oh, my . . ."

Remembering her state of undress, Josh quickly tried to tug her blouse together. The silk was wet and had become slick. Covering her breasts was like trying to stuff ripe plums back into their skins. On top of that, he saw that in his haste he'd ripped away some strategic buttons. He settled for refastening her jacket.

"I'm going to lift you," he told her gently. "If it hurts anywhere, let me know."

Slipping one arm under her back and another beneath her knees, he started to pick her up. She was an armful, no doubt about it, and if not dead weight, still dazed enough to be close to it. As he tightened his embrace and tried to straighten, everything but her ass cleared the ground. Josh could see that he was going to need better handholds, and he set her back down. The question was, where could he grab her? Miss Charlotte was one hell of a lot of female, and every place he touched felt like forbidden territory.

Well, there was no help for it. He'd mind his manners later. For now, he had to get her up out of the snow. He slid an arm back around her ribs, this time snugly positioning his hand on her side, his fingers wedged under soft, heavy breast. He was thankful she didn't seem offended. Slipping his other arm under her thighs, he heaved upward. The muscles at the backs of his legs knotted with the strain.

"Oh . . . my shoulder!"

Her scream startled him so badly that his heart skipped. As carefully as he could, he dumped her back onto the snow. Her face was drained of color, and she clutched the left shoulder seam of her jacket. Nudging her hand aside, he said, "Let me take a look."

Through her jacket, he could tell little. He made fast work of unbuttoning it again and peeling away the wool. Modest, as one would expect a preacher's daughter to be, she tried to cover the upper swell of her bosom. It was a big undertaking for one hand, and she gave it up the moment he touched her shoulder.

Grabbing his coat sleeve with her right hand, she cried, "Ahhhhh!"

"Hurt pretty bad?" He started to rotate the joint. "It might be badly bruised, but I—"

"Ahhhhh!" She clenched her small, white teeth and hissed through them.

After further examination, Josh sighed. "Shit, I think it's popped out of socket."

With her hair pulled loose, damp, and wisping into a tangle of curls to frame her face, she was far prettier than he had been told. Plain and priggish was how the men who frequented the Shady Lady described her.

"I'm afraid that no matter what I do, I'm going to hurt you when I lift you."

She looked as if she might pass out just at the thought. "Oh, merciful Father, help me. Please don't move me."

Josh would be damned surprised if her merciful Father helped them out of this pickle. The snow was falling so thickly now that he couldn't see more than a few feet away. If he didn't get a move on, they could get lost out here less than a mile from his place.

"Miss Masterson, I have to get you up to the house before this storm gets any worse."

She looked into the snow, blinked, and then nodded. "Yes," she agreed weakly. "But it might be easier if I walk." A drawn smile flickered across her pale lips. "Easier on both of us."

"You're not that heavy." And she really wasn't. It was just a bit difficult to pick her up without handling parts of her he shouldn't.

"If you lift me, I'm afraid you'll hurt your back."

Masculine pride made him retort, "Bullshit. It'd take more than what you weigh to hurt my back."

She cast him a startled glance. Josh realized that he had used a profanity—and maybe not for the first time in her presence. She looked so scandalized he nearly apologized, then realized how absurd that was. They weren't at a church social, for Christ's sake.

He hated to move her again. There was no way he could pick up such an armful of gal without jostling her, but better she should suffer momentarily than freeze to death in a blizzard. Steeling himself against her low moans, he scooped her into his arms as gently as he could. As he straightened and shifted her against his chest, he accidentally wrenched her left shoulder. At the sudden pain, she gasped. Then she fainted, uninjured arm dangling, head lolling.

He stood there for a moment, not quite sure what the hell to do next. He was a big man, and stronger than most, but he couldn't mount a horse with both arms full. Not when they were this full, at any rate. *Son of a bitch.* There were days when he wondered if he shouldn't have stayed in bed.

He eyed his horse, Satan. The only thing he could think to do was drape her over the saddle, which was no way to treat an injured lady. But he had no choice. With a heave, he tossed her over the stallion's broad back, much as he might have a sack of grain.

Her hair, completely free of its pins, fell in a cascade of fiery ripples and nearly reached the ground. Not wanting it to drag and possibly be stepped on, he tried to tuck the heavy tresses under her jacket collar, but they wouldn't stay. Josh finally folded the length double and looped it into a loose knot.

It was slow going back to the house. Josh had to sense his way, and the terrain was rough. More than once, Satan nearly walked into a tree. Josh held Miss

Masterson on the saddle by grabbing a handful of her bustle. His knuckles pressed against lush softness. Not that he was surprised. If a man peeled away Miss Charlotte's outer clothing, he'd find woman, not fanny enhancers. Lots of woman. Enough to shade a man in summer and keep him warm in winter.

What the hell was he thinking? It was the freezing cold; maybe his brain was getting frostbitten. Josh forced his mind ahead to what he should do next. Once he got her to the house, building a fire was first on the list. Then he would have no choice but to leave her long enough to make his way back to the road and fetch her mare. Both horses would have to be safely put away in the barn before the full force of the storm struck.

He couldn't ride to town for the doctor, not in a storm such as this. He might not make it. Not that he wouldn't take the risk if need be, but a dislocated shoulder wasn't life threatening. He knew how to pop the joint back into place himself, and he had whiskey aplenty on hand to use as painkiller.

Josh smiled grimly at the prospect. Miss Charlotte, the prim and proper preacher's daughter, was about to experience her first drink.

THREE ~

Charlie awoke to a terrible pain. When she opened her eyes, she met the midnight blue gaze of Joshua Slade. With a start, she realized he was rolling her out of her unlaced corset. Horrified, she made a feeble grab at his large hands. She was too disoriented to be certain where she was, but acutely aware of the man looming beside her and the fact that he emanated masculine strength.

"What are you doing?" she asked weakly.

"I was hoping to put that shoulder back in place while you were passed out," he replied as he lowered her back onto the bed and tossed her corset aside. "I figured I should get the wet clothes off you first. The last thing I need is for you to come down with a bad case of catarrh. If it went into pneumonia, I wouldn't be able to go to town for the doc, not if this storm lasts like I think it might."

Charlie felt a wool blanket under her bare shoulders and arms. She glanced down and discovered her skirt, petticoats, and shoes were gone. All that covered her lower half were loose-legged, knee-length bloomers and stockings. She wore nothing on top but her chemise, which was damp. Her nipples pointed toward the ceiling, their pink tips clearly delineated. A blind man couldn't fail to notice them. A wave of humiliation washed over Charlie that was so intense her face burned.

"Mr. Slade!"

He drew the unused half of the wool blanket over her. "This is no time for false modesty, Miss Masterson. That shoulder needs tending."

"My modesty is not false." With her good hand, Charlie clung to the blanket. Her other arm lay useless beside her and ached so badly she was convinced it must be broken in several places. She clenched her teeth as she tried, without success, to move it. "Oh, goodness."

He rose from the bed. The thump of his boots resounded as he strode from the room. In too much discomfort to register her surroundings clearly, Charlie had a vague impression of log walls, open rafters, and cluttered wall shelving. On the bedside table, a lantern hissed, sending out an amber glow through its smoky glass chimney. When she turned her cheek against the pillow, the masculine scents of lemony shaving soap and special-blend tobacco assailed her.

This was *his* bed, she realized, where he laid his head each night.

When he returned to the bedroom, he carried a whiskey jug and two blue porcelain mugs. The mattress sank beneath his weight as he sat back down.

Dressed all in black, his ebony hair and bronze skin still wet from the snow, he epitomized all that was dark and dangerous. But Charlie was in no condition to appreciate the long-awaited moment of libidinous peril. That was a shame. Rhoda Peck would want a recounting of details.

As he set the mugs on the table and uncorked the jug, he asked, "You ever tipped the bottle?"

"Pardon?"

Those heavily lashed, dark blue eyes turned to her. "You ever had spirits?"

What sort of woman did he think she was? "Lands, no."

He poured two healthy portions of bourbon and set the jug on the table. Leaning toward her, he hooked a hand behind her head and pulled her up, then reached for a mug. "There's a first time for everything, I guess," he said, as he pressed the rim to her lips. "You'll need it for the pain. Forget every hellfire-and-damnation sermon your daddy every delivered. Don't taste, just gulp."

"My father doesn't give hellfire-and-damnation sermons," she protested. "At the wedding of Cana—"

"I know all about Jesus' first miracle, thanks. Drink up."

"Papa merely points out the perils of overindulge—"

He pushed the mug more firmly against her lips. "We agree your daddy's a saint. Now drink."

Charlie was hurting too badly to argue and did as he told her. The whiskey burned a path to her belly, and for just an instant, she thought it might come back up. But then the most delicious warmth spread through her. He lowered her back to the pillow, and she heard him pouring more liquor. He drew her up again and more or less poured the second measure of whiskey down her throat.

"We'll let that settle for a minute, then try some more," he informed her as he lowered her back onto the pillow. "Making your stomach roll?"

"No," she said. "It feels rather nice, actually. I'm surprised."

With a wry smile, he said, "That's one of the perils, no doubt: that it makes you feel nice." He reached for his own mug, raised it as if to toast her, and then tossed down the contents. After drawing a whistling breath, he bared his clenched teeth and said, "Medicinal for you, false courage for me." His dark blue eyes took on a twinkle. "I've put more than a few shoulders back in socket, but never a lady's."

The pain was so great Charlie didn't know if she could bear for him even to touch her. "I think perhaps I need Orville."

"Orville?"

"Doctor Worscht."

His firm mouth tugged at one corner. "Ah, yes. Orville Worscht. Sounds like a special blend of sausage the butcher mixed up."

Charlie had thought the same thing herself, but the humor was lost on her at the moment. Oh, tarnation, how her arm did hurt. Nothing had ever felt this bad, not even the time her youngest brother John had accidentally clobbered her on the head with the yard rake while trying to shake apples from a tree. "Would it be possible for you to go get Orville? He could give me something. Laudanum, maybe. Or a whiff of chloroform to put me out."

His mouth tightened. "I'm sorry, Miss Charlotte. But the storm is too bad. You're going to have to bite the bullet." He grabbed the bottle again and poured more liquor into her mug. "Besides, whiskey does a pretty good job of killing pain."

"It does?" This time she obediently drank when he put the cup to her lips. Her belly was beginning to feel hot, and the sensation kept working its way up her throat.

"Well, let's put it this way. If I hurt you, you won't remember much about it."

Charlie could see how that might be true. Amazingly, the heat in her stomach was beginning to make her feel deliciously warm all over. She even felt a little like smiling. But it didn't seem that her arm hurt any less. Her eyes widened slightly when he poured even more whiskey.

"How much must I consume?"

"You're a good-sized girl. A couple more jiggers, I would think."

A good-sized girl? If it were Rhoda lying here, he wouldn't be calling her good sized. What he actually meant was plump. "Does the effect of liquor alter with different body weights?"

He drew her up to fill her mouth with more whiskey. As she swallowed, he looked into her eyes. "In my experience, yes. Big men have to drink more to get inebriated, little men less."

She knew what he meant without his saying it: She was a big woman. Charlie wiped her mouth with the back of her hand. It seemed to her that the edges of the room were growing fuzzy. She glanced at the lantern, and its light now seemed to form a golden nimbus. She returned her gaze to Joshua Slade. His eyes weren't smoldering. Just her luck. Instead he looked worried. She gave a long, weary sigh.

"Feeling sick?" he asked.

"No, just disappointed." The moment Charlie spoke, she wanted to bite her tongue. She stared at his dark face, acutely aware that her own must be scarlet. "I mean disoriented," she said quickly.

He poured more whiskey. "One more dose, honey, then we'll wait for the happies to hit you."

"The happies?" Charlie gulped down the whiskey. "What are the happies?"

"The who-gives-a-damn happies. Get enough liquor under your belt, and all your troubles melt away."

Charlie was already beginning to feel untroubled. Her head was heavy. An awful pain still radiated down her arm, but she felt oddly separated from it, and she was no longer absolutely certain she could locate her shoulder if she tried to find it. She giggled at the thought, then swallowed the sound, afraid Mr. Slade might think her tetched.

Now that she wasn't sure where her shoulder had gotten off to, she could concentrate better on his face, and she decided it was a very nice one indeed. High brows, a thrusting nose, a square jaw, and stubborn chin. His ebony eyelashes were long and thick, lining his dark blue eyes in lustrous spikes. Charlie knew women who used burnt cork to darken their eyelashes, trying to get that look, and he probably didn't even appreciate it.

"You have beautiful eyes," she told him, then wondered where that had come from. Clearly her mind had departed along with her shoulder to places unknown. "I know women who would kill for those eyelashes." *Shut up, Charlie. The man will think you're crazy.*

The lashes in question swept low over his eyes, and

the crevices that bracketed his firm mouth deepened in a suppressed grin. "Oh, really?"

"Burnt cork doesn't actually work. I tried it once." She giggled again. "Instead of making my lashes look thick and dark, all it did was blur my vision and make me appear startled and runny-eyed."

He chuckled at that. "Your eyelashes are pretty like they are. The color of cherrywood and dusted with sunshine on the tips."

"Mud red and washed out," she corrected. But his description sounded prettier than hers.

"How you feeling?"

Charlie tried to concentrate on the question. "I'm not at all sure." With a bemused frown, she added, "However, I do believe you have given me enough spirits, if that's your worry. My nose feels numb."

"Good. Numb is how I want you."

Charlie sighed and gazed at the ceiling. "You have cobwebs."

"Yeah, well, I reckon I need a wife. The ranch takes up most of my time. I muck the house out every month or so, but it gets pretty bad in between."

She jerked her gaze back to his. "Then give up your wicked ways and go to church. There's an entire congregation of eligible young women there."

"I enjoy my wicked ways, and I avoid churchgoing women. I've never met one yet who didn't try to change me."

"And you don't wish to change?"

"I like my life just fine the way it is. Any woman I marry will have to accept that or make tracks."

Charlie was incredulous. "You can't continue to drink and gamble and womanize once you've married, Mr. Slade."

"Who says?"

He had her there. "It simply isn't done."

"That's what you women would have us men believe, anyway," he said good-naturedly.

With so much alcohol in her system, Charlie couldn't muster any indignation. Instead she only smiled. "You simply haven't met the *right* woman yet. When you do, drinking and carousing will no longer hold the same appeal for you."

"Is that so? She'll have to be one hell of a woman."

Looking into those beautiful, unsettling eyes of his, Charlie agreed. Joshua Slade's head would never be turned by anyone who was run-of-the-mill. There was still no smolder in those eyes when he looked at her, she noted.

Clearly uncomfortable with the personal turn their conversation had taken, he poured himself another measure of whiskey. He had wonderfully broad shoulders, she noticed. And when his biceps flexed, the bulging muscle stretched his rolled-up shirtsleeves taut. She made a mental note of that detail so she'd have something deliciously wicked to share with Rhoda when this was all over. The thought made her grin. For once, instead of Rhoda telling Charlie about something exciting, it would be the other way around.

As Joshua Slade sipped his whiskey, his gaze drifted to the window. Charlie sensed that he was waiting for the liquor she had consumed to take full effect, and she let her lashes fall closed, content to drift in the spirit-induced haze. The pain in her shoulder was now nothing more than an ache, she realized.

She heard his cup clink and knew he had set it aside. An instant later, he touched her hand, the left one. Charlie thought it rather odd that while all her other body parts seemed to have drifted away from her, the fingers he toyed with felt very much there. Expectant tingles should be crawling up her arm, but if they were, she was too numb to feel them. Still, he had warm, leathery hands, strong and ever so nice. His touch was firm. When she related all these facts to Rhoda later, she could embellish the truth a little and say she had felt tingles. It wouldn't really be a lie. She was surely tingling but too inebriated to feel it.

Her breath stilled. He was toying with her fingers as a lover might. Oh, dear. It struck her suddenly how vulnerable a situation she was in. Intoxicated and stranded miles from town with a handsome scoundrel. A handsome scoundrel who was caressing her. A handsome scoundrel who had absolutely no regard for God-fearing women. It was scandalous, particularly with her half-dressed. She wasn't sure how she should react. Should she open her eyes? Demand that he stop?

Definitely not. Nothing truly indecent was occurring, after all. If she made him stop too quickly, she would have nothing exciting to tell Rhoda. She was experiencing her very first perilous encounter. It was no time to be fainthearted. She wanted to savor every delicious second.

FOUR~

Joshua Slade slid his hand to Charlie's wrist and closed his steely, masterful fingers like a manacle. *Oh, my,* she thought dizzily. It was just as she had read in Rhoda's dime romance novels. And it was happening to *her*, Charlie Masterson. She opened her eyes ever so slightly to see if perhaps his gaze was smoldering. Not that she expected as much. She wasn't the type who usually elicited smolders. But she wasn't fussy. Even a glint of interest would make her happy.

He wasn't looking at her wrist. He was studying her arm. Through the liquor-induced haze, she suddenly registered the fact that he was trailing the fingertips of his other hand over her elbow. She should be feeling tingles galore. But she didn't. How very disappointing. Drat that whiskey.

He curled his fingers over her upper arm. Charlie's

heart hadn't raced like this since last winter when a mouse had run out from under the stove and up her bloomer leg. No man had ever touched her bare upper arm before, not even Doc Higgins, Orville's predecessor. It was ever so—

"*Ahhhhh!*"

Pain, a horrible, numbing pain, exploded in Charlie's shoulder, obliterating every other thought in her mind for a moment. Belatedly, she realized Joshua Slade had taken hold of her arm to *jerk* on it. In the blaze of agony, she rolled away from him to clutch her abused appendage.

"Oh, drat!"

"It's back in place," he said.

Charlie was hurting too badly to do anything but rock back and forth. "Why on earth didn't you tell me what you were about to do?" she cried. "So I could brace for it?"

There was a moment's silence. "I didn't want you to tense up."

Charlie exhaled a pent-up breath. She realized that the pain was quickly diminishing and that now her shoulder felt much better.

"Besides, what else would I have been about, if not to put your shoulder back in?" he asked.

What else, indeed? The question was as sobering as a bucket of icy water. Oh, she was a pitiful mess. So starved for attention from a male, any male, that she jumped to conclusions and looked for smolders in the eyes of a man who didn't even feel a spark.

Suddenly she wanted to cry. And, horror of horrors, she did so. In a rush, tears gushing, stinging in her nose, strangling her. It was absolutely disgusting. She never cried. Hardly ever, at any rate, and certainly not over some *stupid* man. It was the alcohol. That was the only explanation. No wonder her father spoke out so strongly against the perils of overindulgence. It reduced a person, made one incapable of controlling the emotions.

"Honey, I'm sorry. Let me check. Maybe I didn't get it back in place after all."

He thought she was blubbering with the pain? She felt his fingertips graze her shoulder. "Don't touch me," she cried.

"I'm going to have to. If it's not—"

"It's back in place!"

"Then why are you crying?"

That was a very good question, one for which she had no sane answer. "I don't know. Because I feel like it."

"The shoulder isn't hurting?"

"No." She said the word angrily. "It's much better."

"You're sure?"

"Of course I'm sure."

A momentary silence fell, which he ended with a low curse. "Don't tell me you're going to be a weepy drunk."

A weepy drunk? That was the killing blow to Charlie's foolish daydreams, not to mention her pride. She sucked in air, choked on an aborted sob, and stared at his wall, wishing she were anywhere but at his ranch. Anywhere . . . even lying in the snow. A weepy drunk?

"I really am sorry I had to do it like that," he said. "Catching you off guard, and all, I mean. But tense muscles make it difficult to pop the joint back in."

"I understand," she said, punctuating the words with a wet sniff. He didn't offer her a handkerchief.

Men never offered women like her their handkerchiefs. "And it only hurt for a moment, so please stop apologizing."

"Hurt like heck while it lasted, though, hm?" He gave her shoulder a comforting pat. "Luckily, you're a sturdy woman. No bones are broken. A more fragile female might have been seriously injured." Another pat. "Listen, why don't you get some sleep? I'll be in the other room if you need me."

"Yes. Some sleep."

Charlie felt as if she had two tongues, and both of them thick. As he stood, she felt the mattress lift. His boots tapped toward the door. She closed her eyes and felt a final wave of humiliation. *Oh, Charlie, Charlie, you're such an idiot.* She drifted into a drunken slumber wishing she were tiny and fragile. Oh, to have a visible collarbone and ribs, and maybe even hipbones. To have a man think of her as being delicate.

She would have settled for anything but sturdy.

Who would have thought it? And the preacher's daughter, no less?

Josh kicked back in his handmade rocking chair and gazed thoughtfully into the fire. He had run across some eager swatches of calico in his time, but none had tempted him quite so much as Miss Charlotte Masterson. She was in sore need of a man's attention, no doubt about it, and too artless to conceal it.

Charlotte Masterson? He grinned and shook his head. Well past her majority or no, her daddy would take a switch to her if he knew how eager she was to be compromised. Josh was sorely tempted to return to the bedroom and do the honors.

She was a lot of woman, but not nearly as stout as she appeared to be in those god-awful matronly dresses she wore. In an era when the ideal in feminine beauty was a sweet, girlish face and a full, womanly figure with a tiny, corseted waist, Miss Charlotte, who was naturally thus endowed, had fallen prey to the fashion of the day. She wore gowns cut to flatter far less shapely women, the result being that her already generous curves were amplified to the point of unattractiveness.

Under all those ruffles, poufs, flounces, and swags, Miss Charlotte was built like a goddamned Venus! Talk about hiding a light under a bushel. Josh had scarcely been able to believe his eyes when he had gotten her peeled down to chemise and drawers. Breasts as round as canteloupes. A naturally small waist. Nice, well-rounded hips. Plump, shapely thighs. It had been a heady discovery. And to top it all off, she was as pretty as a picture with her hair all loose in soft curls.

Hell, he wouldn't be a normal male if he didn't consider the possibilities. Stranded with her in a snowstorm, miles from town? He could have a field day. She was definitely a peach ripe for the picking. One look into those big green eyes had told him she was intrigued by him, and possibly even infatuated. With some smooth talking and a little more liquor, he could join her in bed and help himself to all that feminine softness.

He'd bet his last dollar she was a virgin, to boot, which would be a novelty. There wasn't a man alive who didn't want to be a woman's first, at least once in his life. Josh had been told there was no experience quite like it, that the tightness could take a man across the finish line before he got fully seated in the saddle. Personally, Josh had always preferred more experienced bedmates. but it could be that he didn't know what he was missing.

Those nipples . . . Like everything else about her, they were full and lush, their color the pink of strawberry juice and cream. Just thinking about them made his mouth water. Josh's jeans suddenly felt a size smaller than usual, and he propped a boot on his knee, tugged at the denim where it had begun to pinch, then curled a hand over his thigh. Thoughts like these were dangerous. If he so much as touched her, he knew he'd find himself saying "I do" at the unfriendly end of a shotgun.

Preacher Masterson had four sons, and they were all big boys, sturdy of build and rowdy for lack of discipline. Anybody who messed with Miss Charlotte could expect trouble from that quartet.

Josh sighed and pushed with his foot to set the chair into motion. No, sirree. Salivating over the dish was one thing, but helping himself to a taste would be crazy. The last thing he wanted was an entanglement with a preacher's daughter. Give her an inch, and she'd take a mile. Hell, she'd already alluded to his wicked ways, and that was just for starters. Given a chance, she'd be harping about his tobacco and liquor. She'd probably gripe about his going into town once a month to play cards and consort with the upstairs girls.

Why, she might even try to make him go to church!

During his lifetime, Josh had spent more hours on his knees than he cared to think about. The son of a fanatical preacher, he had grown up hearing terrifying sermons that shook the rafters, at home and at church. Quick with the rod and sparing with affection, his father had been a first-class bastard, not only with his children, but with his wife. It had been a harsh, joyless upbringing, and Josh had escaped the first chance he got, never looking back and never again setting foot inside a church, bending his knee, or opening a Bible.

He intended to keep things that way.

Charlie woke up ravenous. Remembering that she had made muffins yesterday, she sat up to go fetch a couple, along with a glass of milk. The slight tenderness in her shoulder made her freeze at the edge of the bed. Then she remembered where she was. She blinked and peered through the darkness. The lantern on the bedside table had been turned out, but firelight spilled in from the other room through the partially open door.

Charlie wondered where her outer clothing was. Finally, she settled for drawing the wool blanket from the bed and draping it over her shoulders. As quietly as she could, she crept to the doorway on stocking feet. Joshua Slade was stretched out on the floor in front of the hearth, his sheepskin jacket pulled over his shoulders for warmth. The soft, raspy sound of his snores drifted to her. She noticed that her clothing hung on nails at each end of the mantel, presumably to dry.

The door creaked when Charlie eased it farther open, and she hesitated. But hunger drove her. She hadn't eaten since breakfast the previous day.

The cabin's main room was a practical combination of kitchen, dining, and sitting area. No curtains hung at the windows, and the panes of glass looked as if they could use a good polishing, even in the dim firelight. Josh Slade was right; he needed a wife.

Charlie looked around the room, trying to picture what it might be like to live there. Unlike at home, there were no paintings or doilies or knickknacks to pretty things up. The roughly hewn plank table sported no lace-edged cloth, no vase of flowers, only a jug of Kentucky bourbon. The individual cross-buck benches had no cushions. A woman would have her work cut out for her here just to make things homey.

Her gaze trailed to the cookstove, icebox, and kitchen piano at one end of the room. Trying not to make the floor creak, she gravitated in that direction, hoping her host had some kind of food she might wolf down. Bread. Leftover meat. Anything that didn't absolutely have to be heated or cooked.

There were eggs in the icebox. No milk or anything else that looked palatable. Hoping he might have a tin of crackers, she moved to the kitchen piano and stealthily opened cupboards, drawers, and bins, feeling like a burglar. Flour, spices, lard, and baking ingredients. She sighed and looked toward the stove. A pan sat on the warming shelf beside a rusty flatiron. She walked over to it and rose on her tiptoes.

Ah . . . Cornbread. With eager fingers, she scooped out a piece, glad that he had already cut it into squares.

Charlie had never tasted such awful stuff. It was stale and dry. Wishing she had milk, she gulped down the bread and reached for a second piece. It was no easy task to swallow the dry globs. She picked up the coffeepot and swished the contents. Cold coffee wasn't exactly her favorite thing, but beggars couldn't be choosers.

Oh, what she wouldn't give for a cup of rich, piping hot chocolate and one of those brownies she had planned to bake. She grabbed a chipped mug from the hook over the dry sink, nearly losing her blanket in the process. Stuffing the rest of the cornbread in her mouth to free one hand, she turned back toward the stove.

"Hungry?"

Charlie nearly leapt out of her skin. Almost strangling on the cornbread came in as a close second. She turned and met Joshua Slade's questioning gaze. He was sitting up in front of the fire, clearly wide-awake. With her mouth stuffed full of cornbread that was too dry to swallow, Charlie found herself unable to articulate a reply to his question. Feeling foolish and more than a little embarrassed, she clutched her blanket with one hand, the cup with her other, and said, "Mmmmm." It was the best she could manage.

He stood up, stepped to the mantel to light the lantern, then turned back toward her, his shadow dancing in the sudden flare of kerosene light. "You should've woke me up. I've got food out on the stoop." Gesturing at the window, he added, "In these temperatures, there isn't much point in keeping ice for the box, so I keep my perishables outside in a trunk. I've got some leftover stew we could heat up. And raisin pudding. Sound good?"

Chewing furiously, gulping to swallow, Charlie nodded. He flashed her a friendly grin. "I like a woman with a hearty appetite. Most gals pretend food never touches their lips. You know damned well they eat, but they pick like birds. It's irritating as hell if you're paying the tab, I'll tell you."

Charlie finally managed to swallow the last of the

cornbread. "I think it was drinking all that whiskey. I seldom wake up hungry at night."

That was the biggest lie she had ever told. Mysteriously missing food had become a family joke at home. Her brothers always laughed and said, "Uh-oh, Charlie must have been walking in her sleep again last night." The truth was, Charlie woke up frequently in the dead of night, restless and craving something she couldn't quite put her finger on. She ate because putting something in her mouth made her feel better, especially anything made of chocolate.

"That much whiskey would give most folks a hangover," Josh said as he went outside. "Especially a woman unaccustomed to drink. You must have a cast-iron gut."

A cast-iron gut? Charlie wanted to shrivel and ooze through the cracks in the floor. Now she wished she'd stayed in bed and starved until daybreak.

Cold air rushed in the open door, and she could hear him rattling things around out there in the dark. A moment later, he reappeared, his black shirt dusted with snow, his dark hair wind tossed and lying across his forehead in unruly waves. Charlie noticed that he wasn't wearing his gun belt. Scanning the room, she saw it was hanging on a rifle rack, the pearl butt of the pistol shimmering in the lantern light. She supposed even gunslingers removed their weapons to sleep.

"Jesus, it's sure coming down." With both hands full, he had to shove the door closed with a lean hip and jostle the bar into place with his elbow. "I was hoping it might have let up so I could take you home in the morning. But it looks like we're in for a long hibernation."

Charlie pulled the blanket closer as his gaze met

hers. The heat that flared between them set her senses to reeling, and she nearly dropped the mug she held hooked over one finger.

She took a firm grip on the cup and on her imagination. The only heat in this room came from the fire, and she'd do well to remember it.

FIVE~

Trying to behave with Joshua Slade as she might have with one of her brothers was no easy feat for Charlie, but she was as determined as she was desperate. It simply wouldn't do for him to guess how her pulse skittered every time he looked at her. She had already humiliated herself once, and now she didn't have the consumption of too much whiskey as an excuse.

"I don't suppose you have any milk," she said. "I saw cocoa and sugar in the kitchen piano, and a cup of hot chocolate certainly would be lovely."

After stuffing paper and several chunks of wood into the stove's firebox, Josh closed the door and looked up at her with those fantastic, heart-stopping eyes of his. "A chocolate lover, are you?"

He had a grin that would light wet laurel. Charlie

tamped down her reaction. "I *love* chocolate. In any form. It's my one and only passion."

"And isn't that a shame?"

Refusing to let the remark hurt, Charlie tightened her hand on the blanket. After all, she had been teased about her stout build by four brothers for so many years she should be accustomed to it by now. "Yes, well, chocolate isn't good for the figure, I know. But I can't seem to help myself."

He gave her an odd look. As he straightened, his expression cleared. "I meant that—well, never mind what I meant." He gave her a slow appraisal, then chuckled and shook his head. "If you're any example, more of the ladies in Juniper Hollow should have a passion for chocolate."

Charlie stared at him, wondering what he meant.

"Most of them could do with a little more meat on their bones," he added.

Dumbfounded, she watched him pull cocoa and sugar out of the kitchen piano.

"If I bring in the milk, can you mix the chocolate while I heat the stew?" he asked.

"Surely."

Charlie took the saucepan and spoon he handed to her. While he worked at the stove, she stood at the piano, chipping sugar off the cone and crushing it into granules. Next she added cocoa, mixing and smashing. "I'm ready for the milk now."

He went back outside and returned a moment later with a full pitcher. "Make enough for me. I haven't had hot chocolate since I was a child, and not too often then. Only when my mother could sneak cocoa and sugar into the house."

"Your father disapproved of treats?"

"There wasn't much he approved of."

Though Josh delivered that statement with little expression on his face, Charlie was taken aback at the pain she recognized in his voice.

Her hands stilled in their task, and she looked at her host curiously. Not meeting her gaze, he set the pitcher on the kitchen piano, then turned away. Charlie could see that he regretted saying what he had, and she took her cue from that, not wishing to embarrass him by prying.

"If you don't drink hot chocolate, why do you have cocoa?" she asked with forced casualness.

He returned to the stove and began stirring the contents in a cast-iron Dutch oven. "Every once in a while I make chocolate gravy to go over hot biscuits."

"Chocolate gravy? I've never heard of such."

"It's a common enough treat in the South. I got the recipe off an old chuck-wagon cook when I first started wrangling as a child, and I've been making it ever since."

"You began wrangling as a youngster?"

"Thirteen years old."

"Goodness, I'm surprised your parents allowed it. That's dangerous work."

"Yeah, well, I ran away from home, and they didn't have much to say about it."

Charlie stiffened and glanced at him again. He had left home at age thirteen? Her brothers had still been babies at that age. Josh caught her staring and smiled slightly.

"The old man and I didn't get along," he explained. His light tone of voice was belied by the haunted expression in his eyes. "It happens like that in some families. After wrangling, I headed west to hunt gold.

It didn't take me long to see there was more to be found at gaming tables than in the digs. Eventually someone pulled a gun on me, I beat him to the draw, and got a reputation as a fast gun that was more exaggeration than fact. When I had saved enough to buy land, I came here. End of story."

Charlie hadn't a clue what to say, so she fell back on what they had been discussing earlier. "And now you make chocolate gravy on occasion?"

"I can't believe a chocolate lover like you has never heard of it. When it comes to the ultimate in chocolate treats, chocolate gravy has to be high on the list."

She smiled. "That good, huh?"

"Chocolate gravy over hot buttered biscuits? Honey, you haven't lived."

Until that moment, Charlie might have heartily agreed. But after seeing the pain in his eyes, she realized how blessed she had been. True, she had lost her mother at an early age, and the responsibilities that had fallen on her shoulders because of that had deprived her of a normal progression from girlhood into marriage. But she had never lacked for love.

She had a feeling that Joshua Slade had.

A pang of guilt went through her for the thoughts she had entertained right before the wagon wreck. There were far worse tragedies in life than being a spinster. Bone-deep loneliness, for instance. And being shunned by respectable folk when you moved into a new community, not because of anything you had done, but simply because of your reputation.

It struck Charlie suddenly that there was far more to this man than he allowed most people to see. Or perhaps it was that no one had bothered to look. Tall, dark, and dangerous, that was Joshua Slade, a man to fear and avoid. He fostered the illusion with his all-black clothing and the Stetson hat, which he usually wore tipped low to shadow his eyes. Those times when she had seen him at a distance in town, he had heightened the impression even with his walk—shoulders erect, arms relaxed at his sides so his hand was near his gun, his stride lazy and yet somehow challenging. *Don't try to be friendly to me*, that was the message he sent. Now Charlie realized that might be only a defensive tactic. He knew no one would try to be friendly, so he pretended he wouldn't welcome an overture if it came.

Her throat tightened, and she began stirring the chocolate mixture with brisk strokes. *Do unto others . . .* Her father had reminded her of the golden rule every day of her life, and she tried to practice it. Yet she had never once crossed the street to welcome this man to their town. Neither had any other decent woman in the community.

"Would you like to try some?" he asked.

Charlie was so caught up in her thoughts that the question didn't register. She blinked and focused. "Pardon me?"

He gave her a rakish wink. "Chocolate gravy. Would you like to try some? If you're not so hungry you can't wait, that is. The biscuits'll take a half hour because the oven's not heated."

The worst of Charlie's hunger had been satisfied by the cornbread. The hunger she saw in Joshua's eyes, however, was far from being appeased. Whether he realized it or not, he desperately needed a friend. From this moment on, she would be that for him. No more girlish daydreams about smoldering glances. No more foolish wishes for things beyond her reach.

She lifted her saucepan. "We can sip hot chocolate while we wait."

Josh had done a number of things in close quarters with females, but never had he cooked shoulder to shoulder with one. Oddly, he found himself enjoying the experience. Once she relaxed, Charlotte Masterson was engaging company. They were only halfway finished mixing the ingredients for biscuit dough before she had him laughing.

"Not *that* much flour," she cried. "Not unless you plan to add more lard."

"Get away with you. This is how I always make biscuits."

"Do you plan to shoe horses with them, or eat them?" she demanded, and nudged him aside. "I don't want to break off my teeth, thank you very much."

Josh watched her scoop flour from the bowl back into the bin. Then she began cutting in the lard.

"Jesus, how fine do you have to cut it?"

She cast him a saucy look, then glanced into the shadows behind her. "I didn't realize Jesus was mixing this batch of biscuits."

Josh narrowed an eye.

"I know!" she exclaimed. "He saw what a miserable mess you were about to make of things, took pity, and has appeared to perform a miracle!"

"I take it you disapprove of my language? If so, don't think to correct me. Better men than you have tried, believe me."

"How long have you needed spectacles?"

Bewildered by the question, Josh hesitated. "What?"

"You obviously can't see past your nose. I realize I'm no raving beauty, Mr. Slade, but you're the first person ever to mistake me for Jesus, or any man."

He chuckled in spite of himself, and the answering twinkle in her eyes made his mirth increase. After a moment, he sobered and registered the rest of what she had said. No raving beauty? Josh wasn't at all certain he agreed with that assessment. Her voice rolled over him like warm honey, and she had a sweet, musical laugh that filled hollow places inside him he hadn't realized were there.

She also had a deep dimple that appeared nearly every time she spoke and creased her cheek with every smile. Her green eyes were lustrous and had such a sparkle, he found himself wondering how she ever could have thought she needed to enhance them with darkened eyelashes. When she looked up at him, he got lost in those eyes of hers.

Taking her measure from a distance in town, he had believed her to be tall for a woman, but she wasn't. He supposed it was the way she carried herself, shoulders back, chin high. In reality she was a short but well-rounded female. A little too generously rounded for her height, perhaps, but damned if he didn't find that attractive. In gowns with more flattering lines, with her hair soft around her face, she'd be lovely.

Josh found himself wishing he could choose her clothing. He'd take her to the dressmaker's and order her a whole new wardrobe. No ruffles, very little lace, and none of those glittering jet beads and fringes she seemed to favor. She should wear unadorned gowns with soft gathers, fewer swags, and only a hint of a bustle. She also needed a bit of color around her face to set off her hair and eyes. He could almost picture how she might look. If she had half the potential he believed she did, every man in Juniper Hollow would be agog. Hell, they'd be kicking themselves in the ass for not grabbing her first.

No doubt about it. Even with the army blanket draped around her shoulders, Charlotte Masterson was far lovelier than she had a right to be, especially after taking that tumble from her wagon. The green wool set off the flaming brilliance of her hair and brought out the emerald color in her eyes.

As she poured in milk, stirring with her left hand, Josh saw her mouth tighten and remembered her injury. He wrested the spoon from her fingers. "You pour while I mix," he said. "That shoulder of yours must be tender."

"I'd almost forgotten. It scarcely even hurts."

"You know one can go to hell for lying," he reminded her.

She set aside the pitcher and rotated the injured joint. "No, truly. It's a bit sore, but hardly at all considering how it hurt before you fixed it. Orville better beware. You'll run him out of business if word of this gets out."

At that suggestion, Josh's guts knotted. If word of this got out, Miss Charlotte's reputation would be shot all to hell. Right about now, everyone in Juniper Hollow was probably worried sick about her and praying for the snow to stop so a search party could be organized. When he finally got her back to town, it wouldn't take a genius to figure out where she had weathered the storm, or with whom.

Josh wasn't exactly a pillar of the community. Vicious tongues were bound to wag, and speculation would run rampant. He hated to see his unsavory reputation rub off on such a nice lady. Not that it would have mattered whom she was with. People's views were just that rigid.

Josh knew that a decent man would be thinking about these consequences and ways he might prevent them, with marriage at the top of the list. Even a proper young woman like Charlotte Masterson could be ostracized by polite company if she spent time with a man unchaperoned.

He wondered how he felt about that and sneaked another glance at her as they moved in unison to the stove. Not glancing up, she immediately went to work dropping biscuit dough by the spoonful onto the prepared baking sheet. He studied her as she turned the dollops to coat them on all sides with melted lard. She had a streak of flour on her cheek, and her hair was a wild mess of tangled curls. He stared at the spot beneath her ear and wondered if her skin would taste as sweet as it looked.

The man who married this lady would be one lucky fellow. It was a pity it couldn't be him. The last woman on earth he would ever tie up with would be Preacher Masterson's daughter.

She bent to open the oven door and tossed in a pinch of flour to see how quickly it browned. The heat turned her cheeks pink. Seemingly satisfied that the baking temperature was right, she placed the sheet of biscuits on the rack. As she moved, her blanket slipped.

From his vantage point, Josh was treated to an enticing view. The scooped neckline of her chemise gaped, and the pink tips of her breasts were clearly visible. He glanced away, but not before his maleness snapped to attention. He turned slightly so she wouldn't see the welt of hardness that had sprung up inside his jeans.

Stirring the stew with more force than he intended, he slopped some broth onto his wrist and burned himself. At his curse, Charlie leaned around to see what the problem was.

"Oh, dear, are you all right?"

He clamped his mouth over the stinging spot and gently sucked. A mistake. After seeing what he just had, he immediately imagined having one of those delicate pink nipples at the mercy of his tongue. Lips still on his wrist, he stared blankly into those innocent green eyes of hers and began to feel like a low-down skunk. Her blanket was once again modestly in place, and he could tell by her expression that she had no idea what he was thinking.

"Here, let me see."

She drew down his hand and moved close to examine the red place on his wrist. It had been a hell of a long time since a woman had touched Josh so gently or showed such genuine concern for him. He stood there for a second, tangled in his own emotions, one part of him wanting the moment to last, another almost frantic to break the contact. The way she made him feel was dangerous, a caldron of churning reactions that couldn't be isolated or controlled.

"A bit of butter might help," she said.

The blanket was slipping again. Josh couldn't look away. Those swells of creamy flesh. That dusky cleavage. He swallowed hard. "I'm fine."

"Without something on it, it might blister."

He jerked free from her grasp. "It won't," he said more brusquely than he intended.

She drew the blanket close again and looked at him worriedly. Then she smiled. "Just like my brothers, afraid a little mothering will make a sissy out of you."

Mothering from her was the last thing on his mind. Josh wheeled away from her, feeling as though the air inside the room had gone suddenly thin. Blood pounded in his ears. What in the hell was the matter with him? He took care of his physical needs regularly with the upstairs girls at the Shady Lady so it wasn't as if he was desperate for female companionship. Being around a woman, any woman, didn't usually have this effect on him.

He sat on one of the cross-bucked benches, putting the table between them. Gazing across the narrow expanse, he studied her disheveled appearance and assured himself that she wasn't all that pretty. Why, in addition to being plump, she had a smattering of freckles across her nose. He had never been a man who went for freckles.

After putting the bread in the oven, she set about cleaning up their mess. Her no-nonsense manner appealed to him, and he also liked the fact that she didn't seem uneasy. Most females reacted to Josh in one of two ways, with wariness or flirtatiousness.

When the biscuits were nearly done, he started heating the chocolate gravy. A few minutes later when he spooned the rich mixture over butter-smeared, hot bread, the expression on his guest's face made him smile. Shoving a plate toward her and keeping one for himself, he took a seat across from her and watched her take her first bite. A beatific glow came over her face, and she tipped her head back and moaned. She looked for all the world like a woman on the verge of having an orgasm.

"Mmmm . . ." The tip of her tongue darted to each corner of her mouth, then made a sensuous sweep across her pouty bottom lip. "Oh, Mr. Slade, this is—well, it defies description. I've never experienced anything so—so heavenly."

Josh realized he sat frozen in rapt attention, his fork halfway to his mouth. She scooped up another bite and touched her tongue to the chocolate. His guts twisted in reaction.

"It's so good it's almost sinful, isn't it?"

Josh shoved his fork in his mouth. Damned if he could taste a thing, and the only sinfulness he had on his mind at the moment was of the carnal variety.

If this wasn't a hell of a mess, he didn't know what was. He wanted Miss Charlotte Masterson so badly he was trembling. So badly he was tempted to throw her over his shoulder, carry her to the bedroom, and forcefully kiss the chocolate off her mouth while he tore away her underclothing. He wanted to see that glow of satisfaction come cross her face as he buried himself deeply inside of her.

The thought made him disgusted with himself. A blind man could see she didn't intend to be seductive and that her pleasure was purely innocent. For so many years he had lost count, Josh had distrusted females and their motivations. He considered them all, from puberty to old age, to be devious and self-serving, and the only truck he had with any of them was to slake his physical needs.

Charlotte Masterson deserved better than that. She was the kind of woman a man should respect. The kind of woman who should be sheltered and protected . . . from men like him.

Josh hadn't prayed in nearly eighteen years, not

since his father had stood over him with a razor strop and forced him to. But he found himself praying now—for the storm to subside quickly so he could take Miss Charlotte Masterson back to town where she belonged. Back to her family, where she would be safely beyond his reach.

He had an awful feeling his prayers wouldn't be answered.

SIX ~

Shortly after dawn the next morning, the storm abated, and despite the deep snowdrifts, Joshua Slade wasted not a minute in getting Charlie delivered safely back to town. Once they arrived at her house, he made short work of getting Molly put away in the barn and Charlie deposited on her front porch. Because he seemed in such an all-fired hurry to be rid of her, Charlie was surprised when he hesitated before remounting his horse.

"Charlotte." A dark flush crept up his neck, and he swept his hat off. "Miss Charlotte, I mean." He glanced away, apparently uncomfortable with whatever he wanted to say. His gaze settled on the storefronts along the main street of town, which lay a short distance from her house. "Sometimes . . . well, when things like this happen—"

He was having such difficulty getting the words out that Charlie found herself straining to help him. "Yes?" she prompted.

His dark blue eyes settled on hers, and she thought she heard him swear beneath his breath. "There isn't a polite way to put this," he finally admitted. "So I'll just say it. The people in town—they're likely to say things occurred between us last night that didn't, and if that's the way the wind starts to blow, I don't want you to feel shy about coming to me. I'm no prize. I realize that. But if need be, I won't turn my back on you."

Charlie's throat went tight as she understood his meaning, and she hadn't any idea what to say. Most times, men caught in compromising situations had to be forced to marry the woman at gunpoint. Yet Joshua Slade, the town's blackest scoundrel, was offering, should that prove necessary.

"I, um—" Charlie laughed suddenly. "Perish the thought, Mr. Slade!"

His gaze sharpened on hers, and she could see that he didn't know whether to smile or feel offended.

"Don't misunderstand me," she hastened to explain. "It's a gallant offer, and I'm touched. But what sort of person would I be to expect that of you? You saved my life, and then you opened your home to me." She waved a hand. "And on top of that you gave me the recipe for chocolate gravy!"

His tension seemed to ease, and a slow grin touched his mouth. "If you have trouble with lumps, remember to add more butter."

"I shall make a note of that."

On impulse, she stepped off the porch, then immediately regretted the move, for the snow was deep. He stepped forward to catch her arm. "What're you—?"

Charlie cut him off by rising on her tiptoes to plant a quick kiss on his jaw. Embarrassed by her own brashness, she quickly moved away but caught his hand as she did. "And tell me, Mr. Slade, if I learn to make chocolate gravy without lumps, will you join us some Sunday for breakfast?"

"Breakfast?" He looked as if he'd never heard the word. "With you and your family, you mean?"

"I'm a very good cook, and my father and brothers are entertaining company. We'd enjoy having you, and I'm sure Papa would like the opportunity to thank you in person for all you've done."

"I don't think—"

"Please? At least think about it."

His hand tightened on hers. "I'm not much for polite conversation."

"Stuff and nonsense. I enjoyed our conversation last night immensely."

"Your father's a preacher. What would people think if I—"

"My father cares little about what people think. He's far too preoccupied with heavenly concerns to be aware of what mere mortals have to say."

"Well, maybe."

"When the weather clears a bit?"

He flashed a white-toothed grin. "I'll think about it."

It was more than Charlie had hoped for, and after giving his hand a quick squeeze in farewell, she trudged back through the deep snow to gain the porch. He had mounted his horse by the time she found solid footing on the steps and turned around.

Tipping his hat to her, he said, "I meant what I said. You know where to find me."

The lump in Charlie's throat prevented her from

answering, so she only nodded. With a nudge of his heels, Joshua Slade wheeled his horse in a tight circle to leave the yard by way of the open picket gate. Charlie remained on the porch, watching him until he disappeared from sight.

As silence settled around her, she smiled sadly. His eyes never had smoldered when he looked at her. Not even once. In the brisk wind, the stays of her corset bit into her ribs with icy coldness. She lowered her gaze to the spotless drifts of snow, and it seemed to her in that moment that the vast void of whiteness epitomized her life. She would have nothing exciting to share with Rhoda Peck, she realized. Not this morning. Not ever. It was time she turned loose of her girlish dreams and accepted that.

No, indeed. She would have no exciting stories to tell. But wasn't the truth much better? Joshua Slade was not only a decent man, but a gentleman. It was time the town gave him the friendly welcome he should have received months ago.

When Charlie entered the house, she was perplexed to find it empty, and none of the beds appeared to have been slept in. Putting two and two together, she realized her father and brothers had probably paced the floors all night, worried sick about her. Now that the storm had subsided, they were undoubtedly over at the church trying to muster a search party. Anxious to ease their minds, she quickly went back outside and struggled to cross the yard. Before she got too far she heard voices and glanced toward town to see her four brothers coming up the street, their progress slowed by the deep drifts the wind had deposited between the rows of buildings.

"Yoo-hoo!" she called out.

"Charlie!" they cried in relief. Matthew yelled, "You're safe! Praise God!" Another one said, "Charlie, we thought you might've frozen to death!"

Charlie hugged herself against the chill and watched with a fond smile as the four approached. Unlike her, they had all been born after her father entered the ministry, and each had a biblical name. At twenty-three, Matthew was the eldest. Next came Andrew, who was twenty, then Luke, nineteen. John, the baby, had just turned seventeen and had started shaving last summer. Charlie was as proud of them and loved them as much as if they were her own, which really wasn't strange since she'd practically raised them.

When they drew near enough to hear her clearly, she said, "As you can see, I'm fine. Where is Papa?"

"Old man Oakley took to the bottle again yesterday, and Papa went out there before the storm hit to settle him down. Needless to say, he got stranded." Matthew stomped his feet to shake the snow from his trousers, then jerked off his hat and muffler. Red hair in a tangle, he hooked a strong arm around Charlie's neck and hauled her roughly against his chest. "Oh, Charlie, how I worried about you! Praise Jesus you're okay. The storm came on so fast!"

"Tell me something I don't know!" she murmured against the damp wool of his coat.

"No one expected it to blow like it did. It was so bad we couldn't even go searching for you, and all night long, I pictured you stuck out there someplace, freezing to death."

Before Charlie could reply, all four boys began firing questions. "Where did you stay?" "Is Molly okay?" "Where's the wagon?"

Making the rounds to give each of them a hug, Charlie said, "Molly's in the barn, safe and sound. The wagon has a broken wheel." She quickly recounted the details of her wreck and how Joshua Slade had rescued her. "All's well that ends well, yes?"

After nearly squeezing the breath from her, her youngest brother, John, said, "I'd better run tell the sheriff you're home safe and sound. All the men in town are getting ready to go out looking for you."

Matthew agreed. "Hurry back, John!" he called. "Until Papa gets home, I want all of you where I can keep an eye on you!" Turning back, he gave Charlie a quick once-over. "Let's get you in the house and warmed up. You can tell us exactly what happened in front of a fire." Touching her cheek, he asked, "You haven't taken a chill or gotten frostbite? How long has it been since you've eaten?"

His questions drove home to Charlie how worried the boys had been about her. Now that she studied Matthew, she saw the lines of exhaustion on his handsome face and the shadow of whiskers along his jaw. It struck her suddenly that he had not only grown old enough to take care of himself but that he had matured into a man who, as the eldest brother, felt responsible for her. After so many years of being the family caretaker, Charlie was amazed.

Where had all the years gone? It seemed only yesterday that Matthew had been a frightened, grieving six-year-old, clinging to her for comfort. Now he loomed over her, with his broad shoulders, and his eyes reflected the maturity of an adult. Glancing at her other two brothers, Charlie realized they had become young men as well. It seemed to be a morning for revelations, a time for her to reassess and see things as they actually were.

"I'm fine. Truly," she assured them.

As they started for the house, Charlie began relating the events of the previous afternoon in more detail. She kept up the monologue in the kitchen, automatically starting breakfast because her brothers had big appetites and were undoubtedly hungry. With the clatter of pots and pans to fill in when she drew breath, it took her several moments to realize the boys had gone unnaturally silent. She turned to find the three of them frozen in their tracks, their green eyes fixed on her, their expressions horrified.

"What is it? Papa? He is okay, isn't he?"

"You spent the night with Joshua Slade?" Matthew asked softly.

"Yes." Charlie grabbed her apron from off the towel rack and quickly tied the sash at her waist. "Andrew, fetch some firewood from the box for me, please? Luke, would you lay the kindling?"

Neither one moved. Charlie looked at each of the three, smiling and expectant. "Well? I can't fix breakfast without a fire, boys."

"To hell with breakfast," Matthew shot back.

The profanity so shocked Charlie that she blinked. "Matthew, for shame."

"My God, Charlie, the shame isn't mine. Don't you understand the ramifications of this? Joshua Slade?"

Beginning to understand, Charlie waved her hand. "Don't be silly, Matthew. He's not nearly as bad as his reputation paints him. He was a perfect gentleman."

"Yesterday you didn't think so. Now you're defending him?" Luke said. "The man is a blackguard of the worst sort."

"He was a perfect gentleman, I tell you!" Charlie cried, beginning to feel vexed. "Now stop with this nonsense and get the fire laid."

For the first time in her memory, her brothers didn't hop to mind her. Cursing under his breath, Matthew tossed his hat and muffler onto the table.

"That will be quite enough of that kind of language in this house, young man," she said.

Matthew swung to face her. "Did you or did you not just say that Joshua Slade gave you whiskey for painkiller and then put your shoulder back in place?" Before Charlie could answer, he went on. "If he found you in the storm, your clothes must have been soaked. How'd he get them dry? And what of your shoulder? How did he tend to your injury with you completely dressed?"

"Well, he . . ." Charlie's voice trailed away. "Matthew, nothing unseemly occurred."

"Nothing unseemly? The blackguard got my sister drunk, removed her clothing, and had his hands all over her person. Not to mention the fact that you spent a night with him. Nothing unseemly, Charlie? Dear God, are you so innocent you don't realize what the bastard has done?"

"Don't be absurd, Matthew. I'm twenty-six years old. I would certainly know if I had been compromised."

Striding toward the fireplace, Matthew said, "Somehow, I doubt that." He drew the shotgun from the rack and began loading it. Then he tossed it to Luke and reached for the Henry. "Tell me the bastard didn't disrobe you."

Charlie's heart had begun to bump hard against her ribs. "What in heaven's name—Matthew, put that rifle back this instant."

"Did he remove any of your clothing?" Matthew demanded.

"Well, yes, but—"

"Did he give you liquor?"

"I told you he did, but it was only to ease my—"

"Did he put his filthy paws on you?"

Charlie started to wring her hands. "Matthew, the man saved my life."

Matthew fixed glinting green eyes on her. "And now he's going to save your good name, so help me God!"

Charlie felt as though she were having a nightmare. Nothing she said seemed to make a difference.

John returned from his mission and added kindling to the blaze. "You should've seen the look on everybody's face when they heard where Charlie spent the night!" That was all Matthew needed to hear, and the other three boys rallied behind him.

Charlie grabbed Matthew's arm only to have him shake her off. "At least wait until Papa gets home!" she pleaded. "Matthew, this is crazy! Come back here this minute! Do you hear me?"

Before Charlie could think of anything she might do to forestall them, the four brothers had left, slamming the door loudly behind them.

"For the love of God, don't do this!" she wailed. "After all he's done, Joshua Slade deserves your thanks, not your anger!"

She was speaking to an empty room.

SEVEN~

Josh had faced unfair odds a number of times in his life, and he usually used his side arm as an equalizer. But when the Masterson boys came calling, madder than hornets and determined to take it out of his hide, spilling blood was out of the question. For one, Josh sympathized with their outrage. If his sister had been dishonored, he would have gone after the culprit loaded for bear, and he couldn't blame Charlotte's brothers for doing the same. For another, Matthew being the only exception, the boys were still young and hardly a match for a man of Josh's experience. He couldn't in good conscience harm any of them.

By the same token, Josh had to defend himself. He had no intention of getting his ass peppered with lead or letting four brawny young men use him for punching practice.

With his temper under firm rein, Josh met the vengeful quartet in his snowy dooryard, informed them that only cowards needed weapons to settle a dispute, and took off his gun belt. As enraged as they were, the Masterson boys had been raised with a strict sense of right and wrong, and they promptly set aside their own guns, climbed down from their horses, discarded their coats, and rolled up their shirtsleeves, clearly determined to whip his ass and ask questions later.

"Is there any chance at all of our discussing this?" Josh asked.

"Not a chance in hell!" Matthew responded. "We know exactly what you did to our sister. She told us. After we beat the tar out of you, Slade, you're gonna go back to town and do the honorable thing by her, or so help me God, I'll know the reason why."

Josh zeroed in on one point. "Your sister told you what I did to her? Would you care to elaborate on that?"

"You compromised her, you miserable son of a bitch!"

Josh could scarcely believe what he was hearing. "She told you that?"

Matthew's answer was a fist in Josh's mouth, and from that instant on, Josh lost his grip on his temper. He wasn't a man to shirk his responsibilities. He had offered to do the right thing by Charlotte Masterson, and instead of coming to him as he had asked, she falsely accused him of wrongdoing and sent her brothers in her stead. Marrying a woman of his own free will was one thing, but to be forced at the end of a shotgun? Just the thought made him see red.

With little compunction about fighting dirty, Josh made short work of the four angry young men. When they were all sprawled in the snow around him, he wiped the blood from his lips, checked his mouth for loose teeth, grabbed his side arm, then went to saddle Satan. When he returned to the yard leading his stallion, the youths were staggering to their feet, their expressions ranging from shame to anger.

Still rigid with rage himself, Josh mounted his horse. "Get your sorry asses in the saddle," he ordered. "We're going to pay a visit to your sister and get to the bottom of this."

With jerky indignation, Matthew brushed the snow off his coat before donning it. "The only thing I want you saying to my sister is 'I do,' Slade. Her reputation is ruined, thanks to you. She'll never be able to hold her head up again."

The truth of that was borne out when the five rode into town a little later. Josh couldn't miss the accusing looks that were cast his way by the people on the boardwalks. The news of where Miss Charlotte had weathered the storm was clearly the hottest topic of gossip, and it didn't take a genius to see that the worst was being said about her.

The possibility of this happening had occurred to Josh last night, and he had already decided then that he would do the right thing, which was to marry the girl. Only a low-down skunk would stand aside and watch her be crucified for circumstances beyond her control.

But to be forced into marrying her? Josh would do what was necessary to solve the problem, but, by God, he'd do it on his own steam and in his own fashion, not because four young pups tried to force him or because a man-hungry old maid told outrageous lies to snare herself a husband.

The more Josh thought about Charlotte's lying, the angrier he became. By the time they reached the Masterson house, he was livid. He wanted to give her the paddling of her life, which he felt she richly deserved, then shake some sense into her. Was she so naive that she didn't comprehend the possible consequences of this sort of treachery? Once married to her, a mean-hearted man might beat the holy hell out of her for pulling such a stunt. And once he took his anger out of her hide, he might and most probably would do exactly what she had accused him of, being none too gentle in the process. There would be nothing to stop him from exacting his revenge, that was for sure. A marriage document gave a man carte blanche when it came to how he treated his wife.

In his anger, Josh found that thought had a certain appeal.

As they drew up in front of the house, the treacherous Miss Charlotte threw open the door and came out onto the porch. Still dressed in the gray silk dress from yesterday, which was rumpled and water-stained, she put Josh in mind of a plump-breasted, mottled pigeon whose feathers had been badly ruffled. In addition to the unflattering dress, she had pulled her hair back into a god-awful bun, which gave her a squint-eyed appearance. If Josh hadn't seen her stripped down to chemise and drawers with her hair loose around her creamy shoulders, he wouldn't have believed there could be a pretty woman hidden under that severe coiffure and all those ridiculous ruffles.

After taking a long look at the bloodied and bruised countenances of her brothers, she went pale and looked at Josh accusingly. Her green eyes flashed like polished emeralds.

Having already decided what had to be done, Josh didn't intend to waste time on conversation. Nor did he plan to be overly pleasant. "Get your wrap," he ordered tersely.

Her eyes went wide with dismay. "Why?"

"Don't ask questions, just do as you're told."

"Now, you wait just one minute," Matthew said. "It's not necessary to talk to my sister that way."

"A man can talk to his wife any damned way he pleases," Josh replied icily, "and that's just what she'll be within the next few minutes, my wife." To Charlotte, he repeated, "Get your wrap."

Josh wasn't expecting the flush that crept up her neck, though why it took him by surprise, he couldn't exactly say. With that flame red hair and those flashing green eyes, Charlotte Masterson had the coloring of the Irish, who were famous for their tempers.

"I'm not marrying you or anyone else."

"Now, Charlie," Matthew cut in. "I'm sure Mr. Slade didn't mean that exactly the way it sounded." Glancing at Josh, he went on, "He just forgot to say please."

At that, Josh lost what little remaining patience he had. "*Please?* This young woman is trying to railroad me into marriage, and less than an hour ago, you four yahoos came calling at my house toting guns. 'Please' isn't a word in my vocabulary at the moment."

"None of this is Charlie's fault," Matthew said.

Josh flashed him a glare. "Well, I sure as hell didn't ask her to have a wagon wreck near my place, so it isn't exactly mine, either." To Charlotte, he said, "Are you going to get your wrap and go with me to see the justice of the peace, Miss Charlotte, or do I light out for home and leave you to face this mess alone?"

"Over my dead body!" Matthew interjected.

"That can be arranged," Josh replied in a dangerously soft voice.

At that, Charlotte's face went even paler, and she shot a frightened look at her brother. "Matthew, mind what you say. One can't forget Mr. Slade's reputation with a gun."

Josh thought her concern on that score came a little late but he refrained from saying so. The more anxious she was for her brother's safety the less trouble she was likely to cause Josh, and since he was already feeling somewhat less than accommodating, that suited him fine. If he was going to marry the damned woman, he wanted to get it done and return to his ranch. It was beginning to snow again. The last thing he needed was to get stranded there in town away from his livestock.

Charlie couldn't believe any of this was happening. Last night and earlier this morning, Josh Slade hadn't seemed frightening, but now he scared her half to death. Sitting astride the large black horse, his dark face taut with anger, he looked capable of murder. His midnight blue eyes, she noticed, were finally smoldering, but only when he looked at her brothers, not at her.

Beset by a rising panic, Charlie cried, "Th-this is insane, Matthew. I can't marry this man. I scarcely know him."

Mr. Slade seemed to take perverse pleasure in saying, "You should've considered that before you told him all the lies you did."

"I told him nothing but the truth."

"Really?"

"I do *not* lie!"

"Right. And pigs can fly."

His audacity struck her speechless. While she sputtered for a comeback, he forestalled her from saying anything by adding, "If you're bent on stirring up more trouble, Miss Charlotte, don't hold me responsible for what happens. I held my temper once, but if these boys come at me a second time, I make no guarantees they'll walk away from it."

The threat wasn't lost on her. Right now, her brothers were angry and there was no telling what they might do if Josh Slade tried to ride away. Making one last attempt to defuse the situation, Charlie said, "Gentlemen, couldn't we at least discuss this over a cup of coffee?" She cast a pleading glance at Matthew. "Papa will be home soon, surely. If there *is* to be a wedding, I'm sure he would wish to officiate, and if not, then perhaps he might make sense of this mess and—"

"I'm not saying words in front of any goddamned preacher," Slade interrupted, "and to hell with coffee and making sense of any damned thing!" He drew off his black hat and slapped it against his thigh to rid it of white flakes. "I don't have time for nonsense. I've got a ranch to run and livestock to tend."

"I appreciate your sense of urgency," Charlie replied. "But, as the old saying goes, Mr. Slade, marry in haste, repent at leisure. It seems to me we should at least—"

"If one of us repents, Miss *Charlie*, it's going to be you, not me. That's how things come about when a foolish young woman connives to trap herself a husband."

"Connives? You flatter yourself, sirrah! And your implications that I've told lies to my brothers are not appreciated in the least. I will remind you that I am a good Christian woman!"

"I wouldn't give you a plug nickel for a whole church full of sanctimonious Christians, female or otherwise." His eyes narrowed. "As for you not lying, did you or did you not tell these boys that I gave you liquor?"

"Well, yes, but—"

"And did you tell them I disrobed you?"

"Yes, but—"

"And that I put my hands on you?"

The heat that Charlie felt flooding her face was no longer due to anger. At her flush, Slade drew his mouth into a thin, bitter line.

"I think that says it all, doesn't it?" he said. "And now the damage is done. It's marriage or a bloodbath, your choice, but I warn you now, if you choose the latter, it won't be my blood that's spilled."

EIGHT ~

Charlie's sense of being trapped in a nightmare increased with each passing moment over the next two hours as a grim-faced and resentful Joshua Slade escorted her up the street to town, searched out a justice of the peace, and insisted they be married with no ado. Scarcely having assimilated that, Charlie was hurried back to her childhood home by her surly new husband and ordered to pack her belongings.

"Don't leave anything important behind," he said. "If we never darken this doorstep again, it'll be too soon for me."

By the time she entered her bedroom to pack, Charlie was close to tears. As she drew her neatly folded clothing from the drawers, her hands began to tremble. From what she gathered, Joshua Slade didn't plan to allow her to visit with her family. What had her brothers done? She was married to a man who had every reason to despise them, and her as well. He clearly didn't cotton to religion and probably wouldn't let her attend church. In a matter of hours, her whole life had been turned topsy-turvy.

Once all her clothing was laid out on the bed, she realized she had no trunk in which to transport her things. She'd grown up in Juniper Hollow and seldom traveled. While she stood there pondering her predicament, Joshua threw open the door.

"The snow is coming down heavier by the minute. Is there a problem?"

Unnerved by his tone, Charlie turned to face him. "Yes, as a matter of fact. I haven't a trunk or portmanteau."

"It's just as well because we're a one-horse show and I couldn't haul one anyway." With that, he took three brisk strides into her room, swept her neatly organized possessions off onto the floor, and began stripping the bed. After spreading out a sheet, he tossed most of her things onto it, then drew all four corners into a tight knot. The remainder of her belongings received similar treatment on the other sheet. Before tying up the second bundle, he glanced at her. "Anything else?"

Too upset to reply, Charlie could only stand there and stare at him. If his utter disregard for her possessions was an indication of how he might treat her, she was in big trouble. For an instant, she entertained the notion of refusing to leave the house with him. But then she remembered her brothers. She couldn't risk a confrontation between them and this man. He'd probably kill one of her brothers without so much as an instant's hesitation.

His gaze went to her chest of drawers and the

knickknacks atop it. Before she could stop him, he stepped across the room, pushed all her things to the center of the dresser scarf, and knotted its ends around the lot. Charlie flinched when he tossed the bundle onto the sheet. Her only photograph of her mother was in there, and if he broke the glass face, the image might be damaged in transport.

"Is that it?"

Charlie felt the blood drain from her face as she met his gaze. His eyes no longer smoldered; they were ice cold and chilled her wherever they touched.

"Yes, that's all I have," she replied shakily.

As she said the words, she realized how horribly true they were. This man meant to deprive her of her family. Aside from her loved ones, all that she had left in the world was inside those two sheets.

The return ride to Joshua Slade's ranch was torture for Charlie. The entire way, she continued to ask herself how this impossible situation had come about and what she might have done differently to prevent it. She had *tried* to restrain her brothers, and she had *not* maligned Joshua Slade's good character. Not that he was likely to believe that even if she were disposed to explain. Which she wasn't. No one had ever accused Charlie of lying, and his doing so was so offensive she refused to credit it by defending herself.

Riding double on the stallion in deep snow was not Charlie's idea of how to spend the morning. She rode in front, snugly tucked between Joshua Slade's thighs and the projection of the saddle horn. His arm at her waist was punishing in its hold, his hand positioned indecently close beneath her breasts. Charlie felt so self-conscious she could barely breathe. Whenever he moved his hand, her heart skipped a beat.

Oh, dear heaven, she was his *wife*. Legally bound to him. Whether she liked it or not, he could touch her wherever he chose. She supposed she could protest, not that it would do any good. Within the hour, they would arrive at his ranch, which was remote, and then the two of them might become snowbound together. If that happened, she would be stranded out there with him, completely at his mercy, if indeed he had any. Somehow, Charlie doubted it. He was rigid with anger. She could feel it in every line of his body. Angry men weren't usually inclined to be kind.

Agonizing over what he might do to her, Charlie swallowed her pride and made an attempt to explain what had happened. "Mr. Slade, about the things I told my brothers. I truly—"

"What you told them, or why, doesn't count for much now."

Charlie supposed that was true. "Yes, but—"

"Having regrets, Charlie?" His fingers curled more firmly over her ribs. "That is what your family calls you? Charlie?"

"Yes." Frantically searching her mind for a way to convince him of her innocence, she said, "Mr. Slade, a woman would have to be extremely foolish to trap a man in marriage."

"You got that right, real foolish."

"Well, I am certainly no fool."

"Excuse me, but from where I stand, you don't strike me as the smartest thing ever to come down the pike."

Her voice going shrill, Charlie cried, "The situation got out of hand. Can't you understand how that could happen? One minute, I was answering my brothers' questions, and the next—well, they went off half-cocked before I could talk sense to them. The next thing I knew, the five of you were at the door, and not a one of you would listen to a thing I said!"

"The way I figured it, you had already said enough."

"It wasn't like that!"

"Pardon me for saying so, but I don't really give a damn."

"So no matter what I say, you will continue to make me as miserable as you possibly can at every opportunity?"

"Is that what I'm doing?"

"Yes."

He gave a harsh laugh. "Honey, you haven't seen miserable yet."

When they reached the ranch, Slade dumped Charlie and her bundled possessions unceremoniously onto the porch. With a curt order for her to start dinner, he went to the barn to unsaddle and rub down the stallion.

Charlie dragged her things inside and stowed them along one wall, then returned to the porch to rifle through the foodstuffs he had in the trunk. On such short notice and having no idea where his meat, potatoes, or canned goods were kept, Charlie made do by fixing biscuits and reheating the remainder of the stew he had served last night.

When Joshua came in from the barn, he gave the stew a disgruntled look and said, "You *can* cook, I hope."

"If I have the ingredients to cook with," she replied

with mock sweetness. "The moment you show me where everything is, I'll prepare a more creative meal."

His expression dark and sullen, he sat on a bench at the table, avoiding her gaze as she served the food. Not waiting for her to join him, he filled his bowl and began slathering butter on three large biscuits. Charlie noticed his sleeves were turned back over his broad wrists, that the dark hair there looked damp, and decided he must have washed before coming indoors. Stiff with tension, she took a seat across from him, folded her hands, and bent her head. Acutely aware of his broad expanse of shoulder and the glowering darkness of his countenace, she found it difficult to concentrate. A sudden, unnerving silence fell.

"Let's get something understood," he said sharply. "I don't cotton to praying, and if you hope to turn me into a holier-than-thou Christian by acting pious, you can forget it. As for you praying at my table, it spoils my appetite."

"I always bless my food before regular meals."

"Then do it without making a big show."

Charlie met his gaze. "A big show?"

"The reverent, saintly act."

Charlie's throat tightened with anger she didn't dare vent. In as mild a voice as she could manage, she said, "My reverence is not an act, Mr. Slade."

"Josh," he corrected. "And it sure as hell must be an act. The sun hasn't even set on that pack of lies you told your brothers about me. As I recollect, one of the commandments is not to bear false witness."

"I told you I did *not* tell lies about you."

He laughed softly and gave her a mock salute. "I have to give you credit where it's due, sweetheart. You sure have the innocent look mastered. Last night, you had me completely fooled. You ever considered a career on the stage?"

"I will say it once more, then never again. I didn't tell any lies about you."

"Right. And out of gratitude to me for saving your life, your brothers paid me a call, guns loaded for bear."

Her appetite destroyed by the disgust she read in his eyes, Charlie set her spoon back down beside her bowl. Apparently not caring if she ate or not, Josh dove into his meal. In the silence, the sounds he made seemed explosive. Each time he chewed, his jaw popped. He slurped his milk. After he took a bite of biscuit, butter smeared his upper lip. Last night his manners had been better, but then so had his mood. Charlie had a hunch he was deliberately trying to shock her.

"You got a problem?" he finally asked.

"For some reason, I'm not feeling very hungry, that's all."

"A blind man could see you don't usually lack for appetite. If you hope to make me feel guilty by not eating, forget it. A woman like you has enough meat on her bones to survive missing a meal or two."

That remark stung so badly that Charlie stood up from the table. As she pumped water into the kettle to heat for dishes, she could feel him watching her. Her cheeks burned with humiliation as she went over to the stove. She found the wood box was empty when she lifted the lid.

"The woodpile's out back," he said.

Refusing to be baited, Charlie let herself out the back door. To her dismay, the woodpile, convenient though it was to the stoop, had been buried under snow. Her hands ached from the cold by the time she had unearthed and gathered an armload of logs. Then, on the way back to the house, she was unable to lift her skirt and tripped on the hem. The next instant, she and the wood went tumbling. As she fell full-length in a deep, powdery drift, one of the logs jabbed her in the side and sent a sharp pain knifing through her ribs.

"Charlie, you okay?" he called from the back stoop.

Angry and frustrated, she sat up and brushed snow from her eyes to glare at him. "Fine, just fine!" Too furious to ask for his assistance, she attempted to stand by herself only to be hampered by her skirts. Perilously close to tears but determined not to show it, she jerked impatiently at the wet folds of silk tangled around her legs. "I've never been better!"

"Here, let me give you a hand up."

"Please, don't trouble yourself."

Finally gaining her feet, Charlie bent to regather the wood. A large brown hand closed over her wrist. "I'll get it."

Charlie refused to loosen her hold on the length of split log. In the end, he prized it from her grip. Trembling with anger, Charlie became even more incensed when she glanced up and saw that he was grinning.

"Do you find it amusing when a woman falls down, Mr. Slade?"

Eyes dancing, he shook his head and bent to pick up the remaining wood. "Not at all."

"Then may I inquire as to why you're laughing?"

"I'm not laughing, I'm smiling. And if you're smart, you'll be glad of it."

"You did tell me to get the wood myself."

"When I told you that, I wasn't thinking of how deep the drifts are."

Once all the wood was balanced on his forearm, he straightened. Before Charlie guessed what he meant to do, he brushed the snow from her hair with his free hand, loosening her pins while he was at it. She reached up to tidy the mess only to be stopped once again by his grip on her wrist.

"Don't. It looks pretty, loose around your shoulders like that."

Startled by the husky gentleness that had entered his voice, Charlie met his gaze. As if he suddenly remembered he was supposed to be angry, his mouth hardened even as he smiled.

"You *are* my wife," he added silkily. "From here on out, it's your duty to please me. Correct? I like your hair down." His gaze slid over her in slow assessment. "We'll deal with your clothing later."

"My clothing?" Charlie glanced down. "What's your complaint about my clothing?"

"It'd be quicker to list what I like about it, which is nothing."

Completely bewildered, she looked back up. His eyes had gone cold again, and a shiver went down her spine.

"Don't worry your head about it now," he said softly. "For the next few weeks, a proper wardrobe for you will be the least of my concerns. Or for that matter, yours."

"The next few weeks?" she repeated.

"During our honeymoon," he explained, delivering the words with cutting emphasis. At her shocked expression, he smiled again, but there was no warmth in it. "That's what marriage is all about, Miss Charlie. Fleshly pursuits. Did your preacher daddy forget to tell you that?"

Charlie felt as if her legs might fold. She couldn't look away from his glittering eyes.

"If you're inexperienced, you needn't worry," he added acidly. "With weather like this to keep me indoors, I'll have plenty of time to teach you how to perform your wifely duties. From dawn to dark, and then all night. When I think about it, I should thank you for telling your brothers all those lies. I was in need of a woman to do the domestic work around here anyway, and sooner or later, I'd have been forced to go wife hunting. Not to mention that long winters usually drive me insane. Now I'll have a female at my disposal to keep me entertained."

Before she could respond to that, he headed for the house.

NINE~

The afternoon flew by as if on winged feet, and before Charlie knew it, darkness had fallen. When Josh came in from outdoors, she jumped with a start and turned from the stove, flinching each time he stomped his boots to rid them of snow. His mood was clearly not much improved. His dark face was still taut with anger, his eyes glinting each time he glanced her way.

As he took off his coat and stepped to the fire, Charlie saw that he still wore his gun belt. The pearl handle of his Colt shimmered in the firelight as he moved. She wondered how many lives he had taken with the weapon and glanced away, afraid of him as she hadn't thought to be last night.

Over the course of the afternoon, she had located his food storage, and a nice meal awaited him at the table. Charlie could only hope the tender steaks and mashed potatoes with gravy would take the edge off his temper. He didn't look impressed as he sat down to eat. Without a word or glance for her, he dished himself a plate and started stuffing food in his mouth.

When she didn't join him after a few minutes, he finally looked up. "Going to skip supper?"

The truth of it was, Charlie felt too nervous to eat.

When she said nothing, he shrugged. "Suit yourself."

He went back to his meal, shoving a large piece of steak into his mouth. "You don't set a bad table." He eyed her speculatively. "If you aren't going to eat, you may as well put the kettle on to heat. The quicker you get the dishes washed, the quicker we can start enjoying our cozy little wedding night."

Charlie knew very well what he meant by that, and as she set about the task of cleaning up the kitchen, she felt as though she might be sick with nerves. All too soon for her, he finished his meal and the last dish had been washed, dried, and put away.

Her voice quavery, Charlie said, "Well . . . I suppose I should get ready for bed?"

Standing at the hearth with one arm propped on the mantel, Josh looked up from the flickering flames. In the unsteady fire glow, he looked satanic and heartless to Charlie. She wanted to run, but there was nowhere to go. With the snow blowing as it was, she'd never make it back to town, not even if she stole his horse.

"Yeah," he agreed in an oddly thick voice. "Get ready for bed."

Charlie escaped to the bedroom, then leaned against the closed door, her heart slamming. It took her several minutes to calm down enough to think clearly. She eyed the window speculatively, then discarded the thought as childish. She was an adult, and as impossible a situation as this was, nothing the man chose to do could possibly be so bad that she should risk life and limb in a snowstorm to escape him.

Assuming a calmness she didn't feel, Charlie opened her bundles, located one of her flannel nightgowns, and quickly donned it. Inside the knotted dresser scarf, she found her brush and gave her hair its nightly one hundred strokes. The single mirror in the room hung over the washstand, a small, cloudy oval. When she looked into it, she saw a white-faced woman with frightened eyes staring back at her.

A hysterical urge to laugh struck her. This was her dream come true, wasn't it? She was finally married. And waiting outside that door was a man who could give her the babies she had yearned for. No matter that he detested her. No matter that he probably wouldn't take her with gentleness. All her wishes had finally been granted.

Stiff with fear, she turned toward the door. It took all her courage to open it and step into the other room. Josh still stood at the hearth, one shoulder pressed to the rock face of the fireplace, one booted foot crossed over the other. He looked big and powerful and lethal, more man than Charlie knew how to handle. She gulped and came to a stop in the middle of the room, pinned by his gleaming gaze.

That gaze covered every inch of her with agonizing slowness. Then he snorted. "Is *that* what you call getting ready for bed? To sleep, maybe. But that isn't on our agenda."

"I haven't any other nightwear."

"Then I'll settle for nothing at all."

Charlie couldn't believe she had heard him correctly. "Surely you aren't serious. Nothing at all?"

"Nothing at all," he repeated with exaggerated clarity. "Come now, Charlie. Surely you're not feeling reluctant at this late hour. If you were going to entertain second thoughts, you should have done so before you sent your brothers out here."

Charlie was tired of defending herself, so she let the accusation pass. "I know you're very angry with me," she said shakily. "And I don't blame you for that, truly I don't. But to punish me in this fashion is cruel."

He raised one dark eyebrow. "I could do worse. Shall I make you a list? For starters, I could slap you silly. Or beat the sass out of you. That's what a lot of men would do if you pulled a trick like this on them."

Charlie bent her head. What he said was true, and she knew it. As a preacher's daughter, she had seen the best and the worst of human nature, and not all men were as gentle and loving as her father.

"Come here," Josh ordered in a low voice.

On feet so numb she could scarcely feel them, Charlie moved toward him. At a distance of about two feet, she drew to a stop, unable to make herself step closer. With her head down, all she could see was his legs, but they seemed to stretch forever, hard and muscular, encased in tight black denim.

"Are you going to take that gown off? Or should I?"

Charlie lifted shaking hands to the line of tiny buttons that ran from her chin downward. She unfastened several, enough for her to pull the gown off over her head. As she tugged the garment upward, she prayed with every breath that he would stop her at the last minute.

He didn't.

Charlie had never been naked in front of a man, not even her father, and as she drew the gown off and let it slip from her fingers, she wanted to die of shame. She could feel him staring at her. For the life of her, she couldn't force herself to meet his gaze. This wasn't how it was meant to happen, she knew. Without a kind word. Without so much as a touch to ease the tension.

Her breath caught when his warm hand curled under her breast. A leathery thumb rubbed the crest of her nipple, making it turn hard. The shock of sensation that shot from there to the pit of her stomach made Charlie's head reel. Before she could recoup, he made another teasing pass. It felt to her as if every nerve ending in her body had congregated in that hardened projection of her flesh. She shivered.

"Ah, you like that, do you?" He flicked her with his nail and laughed softly. "Is this what you've been wanting, Charlie? If so, why in hell didn't you just ask?"

Charlie was no longer certain if the sick wash of heat flowing over her was from humiliation or some other, darker sensation. He had the practiced touch of a man who had known many women. Her breast responded to him, the nipple swelling to his fingertips. Never in her life had she felt so helpless or so ashamed.

He moved suddenly, and before she realized what he meant to do, his hot mouth closed over her other nipple. With a sharp pull, he drew all of her in and laved her with his tongue, the entire while teasing her other breast with his hand. Even as her body shuddered in reaction, tears filled Charlie's eyes. She didn't know which stung her pride more, the hunger he created within her or the sense of degradation.

In her mind's eye, she saw herself as he must, a

homely, desperate woman so hungry for a man that she would stop at nothing. A woman whose body had ached to be touched like this, night after lonely night, making her pace the floors and console herself with food. A plump, homely woman no man wanted.

His teeth closed around her, and Charlie gave an involuntary moan, hating him as she had never hated anyone. The tears in her eyes slipped over her bottom lashes onto her cheeks.

"Tell me what you want," he whispered against her skin. "This?"

With that, he flicked her with his tongue. Charlie started to tremble. To feel so much, and to feel it so intensely. And to know he was laughing at her. She squeezed her eyes closed and wished she were dead.

He drew back suddenly, She didn't know why. She only knew that the torture had momentarily ceased. A fingertip touched the wetness on her cheek. Then she heard him swear under his breath. The next minute, the tattoo of his boots echoed in a path across the floor. Leather rustled. A rush of cold air swamped her. Then the door crashed shut.

Charlie opened her eyes to find herself alone in the room. Feeling as though she might be sick, she collected her gown and ran to the bedroom. After pulling on the flannel garment, she slipped into the bed, drew the covers over her head, and lay there, huddled against the misery.

Her breasts throbbed from his touch, and deep in her belly, there was an ache of longing. Charlie didn't lie to herself. This yearning she felt was lust, pure and simple. Had she no dignity? He had been mocking her. Mocking her! And still her body had responded to him. How pitiable he must think her.

The slamming of the door echoed inside her mind, and every time she relived hearing the sound, her shame grew. To stand naked before a man, his for the taking, and then to have him turn away. The humiliation of it eclipsed every other slight she had ever suffered at the hands of men. Never being asked to dance at socials. Having her picnic baskets bought by the older men in her father's congregation only because they felt sorry for her. Charlie Masterson, the plain, plump, dowdy one. The girl no one had wanted, now the old maid no one wanted.

Charlie turned her face into the pillow and made fists in the ticking. In the morning, she would go home if she had to walk. Nothing the townspeople said or did could be worse than living with a man who found her revolting.

Josh buried the toe of his boot in a hay bale. Expending some of his frustration didn't help much. With a muttered curse, he sank onto the bale and dropped his face into his hands. His stomach turned as he remembered the pallor of Charlie's face and the glisten of her tears in the firelight.

The rage that had simmered inside him all day was gone, and in its place was self-disgust. Jesus. Why had he carried things so far? To get his pound of flesh? The girl had lied, yes. But since when was he so damned self-righteous? Lord knew, he had told a number of lies himself over the years.

Maybe he was more like his father than he wanted to believe.

Josh swallowed hard. Dear God. He had never laid a hand on an unwilling woman in his life. Nothing

Charlie had done excused him for doing so now. The look on her face. If he lived to be a hundred, he would never forget it. And he had been the cause.

Josh straightened and pressed his back to the rough planks of the wall behind him. Staring into the eerie brightness of the snow-swept night, he discerned familiar shapes and concentrated on them to clear his mind. The art of observation. It was a trick he had learned long ago, a way to thrust aside emotion and grow calm. In a gunfight, the ability to set everything else aside had saved his life more than once.

Taking slow, deep breaths, Josh sat there for several minutes, not allowing himself to think. Then he slowly let his mind turn back to the problem of Charlie. He examined his earlier feelings of rage and could finally see them for what they were, more hurt than anger. Last night and this morning, he had truly believed she was as sweet and artless as she seemed. And he had let himself hope they were becoming friends.

Josh Slade, the man everyone avoided like the plague, with a friend. When she had invited him to her home for a Sunday breakfast, he had felt warmed clear through, and for the first time in years, he had felt good about himself. He had even been ready to trust a woman again. And she had thrown that trust back in his face, betraying him with the most treacherous sort of lies.

He had been betrayed by women before, dozens of times by his own mother, then again by the only girl he had ever loved. To fall for Charlie's innocent act and then realize he'd been duped had brought all his old anger to the surface. Over the course of the day, every time he took a shot at Charlie, he was actually getting revenge for wrongs done to him years ago by women who had nothing to do with her.

Josh tried to think how he meant to go on from there. They were married. That was a fact neither of them could escape. Did he mean to make her pay for that with every breath she drew for the next several days? It wasn't as if he hadn't been willing to marry her, after all. He guessed that was what burned him most of all, that instead of coming to him and simply asking, as he'd told her to do, she'd sicced her brothers on him.

The girl didn't have sense enough to fill a thimble. Any idiot could understand that telling falsehoods to trap a man was no way to begin a marriage. Victims struck back.

Funny, that. Charlie didn't seem a stupid woman. Naive, maybe. But no dummy. Surely she must have known how furious he would be, and that he would vent his anger on her once the deed was done.

The thought crystallized in Josh's mind and hung there like the frozen moisture in the night air. Hell, yes, she must have known how he'd react. And if so, why had she taken the risk when she could have accomplished the same end by simply requesting his cooperation?

With his mindless anger set aside and cold reason beginning to assert itself, he suddenly felt sick. What if she had been telling him the God's honest truth all day? What if she *hadn't* told her brothers a pack of lies?

TEN ~

That thought brought Josh surging to his feet, and suddenly he knew he was dead right. Remembering the look of shame on Charlie's face and her tears when he had touched her, he groaned aloud. He thought of all the terrible things he had said and done since their wedding ceremony. Getting even with her for something she hadn't even done. Dear God. He had made a few bad calls in his time, but this one took the prize.

He imagined her inside the house, crying her eyes out and probably terrified that he might return any moment to finish what he had started. After all, he hadn't given her a reason to think he might have any compunction about raping her. If his assessment of her last night had been correct, she was a virgin and undoubtedly scared half to death of what he might do to her. It also followed that she was every bit as sweet and uncomplicated as he had believed her to be before rage clouded his judgment.

This was an unpleasant revelation, standing apart and seeing himself without blinders. When had he become so embittered and vengeful that he could threaten a defenseless young woman and take perverse pleasure in her fear of him? When had the hatred inside him become so overwhelming that all other emotions were swept aside? Charlie had tried to tell him the truth, but he had refused to listen. And why? Because years ago two other women had nearly destroyed him with lies, and on that evidence, he had condemned Charlie as guilty without giving her a chance to defend herself. Josh knew how it felt to be judged unfairly. Yet he had done it to Charlie without a qualm. He owed her a heartfelt apology, no two ways about it. He could only hope she didn't follow his sterling example and refuse to listen.

Before Josh could get his feet to move, he heard the snort of a horse out in the yard. Satan whinnied in answer, assuring Josh that his ears weren't playing tricks.

Suddenly alert, he stepped to the barn door and looked out. A short, stockily built man was dismounting from a swaybacked horse.

Preacher Masterson.

Josh set his jaw and walked out to greet his visitor. When the older man detected his approach, he turned and peered through the silvery gloom with an owlish expression on his face. "Mr. Slade?"

"Reverend." Josh stopped several feet away and planted his hands on his hips. "What brings you out this way with a blizzard threatening?"

The older man smiled slightly. "Well, as I understand it, we have a devil of a mess to untangle."

After carrying things as far as he just had, Josh didn't think there was much hope of that. And now that he was starting to get his head on straight, he wasn't at all sure that was what he wanted. There were worse fates for a man than finding himself married to a woman like Charlie. This thought no sooner came to him than Josh had cause to question his sanity. After all, she was still a preacher's daughter.

Josh studied Masterson closely. There was no censure in the older man's manner, and unlike so many of his calling, he didn't seem to be full of himself.

"If by 'untangle' you mean to undo the marriage, I'm not sure that's still an option," Josh said. "At least not one that would be in Charlie's best interests. If tongues were wagging before, they sure as hell will be now."

Masterson shivered and rubbed his arms through his coat sleeves. "What say we discuss this inside?"

Carrying on the conversation in front of Charlie probably wouldn't be a wise move, but the night was so bitterly cold, Josh didn't see a way around it. As he led the way up the steps and opened the door for his guest, he couldn't quite believe what was happening. A preacher inside his home? Josh's aversion to the profession was so strong that just being near a minister made his skin crawl. For some strange reason, Masterson didn't make him feel that way, though.

Not quite sure what to expect, Josh was relieved not to see Charlie in the room when they entered. He carefully opened the door to the bedroom and tiptoed in. Streaks of moonlight cut swaths through the darkness. Huddled like a frightened child beneath the quilts, she was sound asleep. His heart caught when he bent close and saw the trails of dried tears on her pale cheeks. She was wearing her nightgown buttoned to her chin—flimsy armor against him, but it was all that she had.

If she was still there in the morning, he would have some fences to mend. Josh sighed and drew the quilt higher. She made a soft sound, half sob and half sigh. He touched her hair lightly, wishing he could slip into her dreams and tell her he was sorry for being such an ass about everything.

Remembering her father, he straightened and crept back out of the room. Masterson stood at the fire warming his hands. As Josh closed the bedroom door, the older man turned and asked in a low voice, "She's asleep this early?"

Josh debated with himself about how frank he should be. Something about Masterson made him decide on honesty. "I think she cried herself to sleep. I'm afraid I let my temper get the upper hand, and I was pretty rough on her."

The preacher bent his grizzled red head and gazed at his wet boots. After a bit, he met Josh's gaze with kindly green eyes. "I'm not going to insult you by pursuing that. I trust she's all right."

"Physically." Josh realized he was standing before the other man like a child called onto the carpet. It was no more than he deserved. He raked a hand through his hair. "I, um—" He broke off, closed his eyes, and said, "Jesus. I know it's no excuse, but I was so damned mad this morning, I couldn't think straight, and the mood stayed with me all day. When those boys of yours showed up, they said that Charlie had accused me of compromising her, and I didn't doubt the truth of it until just a few minutes ago." He forced himself to look into Masterson's eyes. "Before I dropped her off at your place this morning, I offered to marry her if there was gossip. When your sons showed up packing guns, I saw red."

Masterson smiled slightly. "They were wrong to do that, and tomorrow all four of them will be out here to apologize. They're good boys at heart, but collectively, they don't have the common sense to scratch where they itch when their tempers get riled."

Josh sank onto the rocker, then remembered his manners and sprang back to his feet.

"Young man, is it my imagination, or do I make you nervous?"

Josh sighed. "You could say that, yes. I don't much cotton to preachers. My father was a man of the cloth, and a meaner son of a bitch never lived."

Where that had come from, Josh didn't know. Startled at his own candidness, he felt a flush creep up his neck. Preacher Masterson merely nodded. "I've met that sort. It's a shame they're allowed to wear a collar, but nothing is inviolate to the dark side of humanity, including organized religion."

Josh had expected an argument. Now he studied the preacher through new eyes. "Living in my father's house was a nightmare. I've got the scars on my back to prove it. I ran away at thirteen, and I've never been on my knees since. I never plan to be again."

"A man can pray standing."

"Not me."

Masterson chuckled. "My daughter has her work cut out for her, I see."

Josh stiffened. "Does that mean you don't want the marriage annulled?"

"Well, that's a decision we must make, isn't it? Is the marriage consummated?"

Josh hesitated. "I came close."

"Close is only good in horseshoes."

Josh wasn't sure he could force his next words out. "Let's put it this way, sir. I didn't take it all the way, but if those boys of yours showed up here packing guns tomorrow, I did enough that I should probably let them shoot me."

Masterson sighed and pinched the bridge of his nose. "None of it was Charlie's doing, you know. She tried to talk sense to them, and they were so fired up in defense of her virtue and reputation, they wouldn't listen."

"I realize that now. Unfortunately, I didn't realize it soon enough."

In a tight voice, the older man asked, "What, exactly, did you do to my daughter, Mr. Slade?"

Trying his best not to color the truth in his own favor, Josh recounted what had occurred. A long silence fell after he finished speaking.

Finally, in a voice that shook with anger, Masterson said, "I've never wanted to strike a man quite so badly as I do you at this moment."

"I have it coming, so take your best shot."

For a tense moment neither man spoke or made a move.

"There is no sweeter, kinder young woman alive than that girl in there," Masterson whispered softly. "Her mother passed away when she was only nine, scarcely more than a baby herself. But she stepped into her shoes, caring for her brothers, making sacrifices at every turn, and never once complaining. She's never done a cruel thing to anyone in her life, as far as I know."

"I'm beginning to understand that."

"Your understanding came a tad too late for my daughter."

Josh took a shaky breath and slowly exhaled. "It isn't too late. It's never too late to right a wrong, and that's what I plan to do. That is, if you'll give me the chance."

"After what you've told me, you expect me to leave my daughter here?"

"What's waiting for her in town if you take her home?"

Josh could see he had him there. Masterson made an agitated gesture. "Better to live with gossip than suffer abuse from you. If you were of a more decent cut, I might trust in your good intentions and hope some sort of fondness might develop between the two of you. But to condemn Charlie to marriage with a man who has so little respect for females that he'd—" He shook his head. "No. I think not. I'll just gather up my child and take her home."

Josh had known that was coming, but as perverse as it was, he found himself resisting. "I'll treat her good. I promise you that."

Masterson muttered under his breath.

"I can't say I love her," Josh continued. "We haven't known each other long enough for that. But I can tell you this. If it's in me to have deep feelings for a woman, it would be for someone like Charlie. If you take her home, no other man will ever marry her. This episode had ruined any chance she has for that, and you know it. What's the harm in at least giving me a chance? If she's miserably unhappy here, and decides she wants to leave, I won't stand in her way. You've got my word on it."

The preacher seemed about to say no.

"Please," Josh said hoarsely. "Not for my sake, but hers. Take her out of here tonight, and what happened between us is going to stay with her for the rest of her life. At least give me a chance to undo it if I can."

Masterson finally nodded. "On one condition. If she wants to come home in the morning, I want your word you'll bring her, no argument."

Josh nearly agreed to those terms. But then he remembered the shattered expression on Charlie's face. "I need a week."

"A week?"

"After what I did, of course she's going to want to go home in the morning. I need a week to mend my fences with her, no interference from you or your boys. I swear I won't mistreat her during that time, and I won't touch her unless she's willing. Just a week. Even if she hates every minute, seven days won't kill her, and it sure as hell can't do any more damage to her reputation."

For a moment, Josh thought Charlie's father would refuse. But then he nodded in agreement. "All right, seven days, then. Though why a man who was so all-fired angry about having to marry a woman would fight an annulment so hard is beyond me."

Josh couldn't explain his reasons; he didn't understand them himself. All he knew was that Charlie had given him a glimpse of things that were sorely lacking in his life, and he wanted a chance to examine them more closely before he tossed them aside.

ELEVEN ~

After Masterson left, Josh sat in the rocker and stared into the fire, on the one hand congratulating himself for a battle well won, but wondering on the other what the hell he felt so smug about. He had acquired himself a wife he wasn't in love with, and who was a sanctimonious Christian and the daughter of a preacher, no less. Yet he was as happy as a clam? Ever since finding Charlie in the snow, he had been feeling unlike himself.

No matter how he looked at it, he wasn't making a lick of sense. But being sensible and constantly guarding his heart against another treacherous female had led him to the age of thirty with no wife, no children, and no plans to remedy the lack. It was a lonely way to live. And lately, his Saturday nights at the Shady Lady were no longer taking the edge off of that loneliness. Having weekly sex with a woman whose only concern was getting paid handsomely for it got old after a spell. As crazy as it sounded, even to him, he yearned for a little affection sometimes. When he sacked out at night, he missed having someone in the bed beside him. And he was damned sick and tired of eating meal after meal by himself.

What it boiled down to was that he wanted a wife for far more than her domestic skills. He wanted a partner, someone to talk to, someone who would share his dreams. Eventually he wanted children, a passel of them. A man couldn't have any of those things if he stayed a bachelor.

As reluctant as he was to consider the possibility, Josh couldn't help but wonder if someone up there wasn't watching out for him. If left to his own devices, he might never have worked up the courage to start courting a decent woman. Now the choice had been taken out of his hands and Charlie had been dumped in his lap. Maybe they were meant to be together. Maybe it had been fate that led her to have that wagon wreck near his place, fate that he had been the one to find her. Twenty years hence, he might look back on the events of the last three days and thank his lucky stars.

Josh's eyes grew heavy, and he sank low in the rocker. Within seconds, he drifted off to sleep, ever aware that Charlie with the laughing green eyes and dimpled cheeks slept in his bed only a few feet away. He felt rather like a hungry cat that had cornered a delectable little mouse and had no intention of letting her slip away.

Sometime shortly before daybreak, a slight sound woke Josh, and he straightened in the chair to glance over his shoulder. In the dim glow from the dying fire, he saw Charlie coming out of the bedroom, taking great pains to be quiet, her bundled possessions dragging along the floor behind her. She wore a god-awful dress the color of cow manure with capped sleeves and a yoke of wide ruffles that made her appear heavy breasted and unattractively thick through the arms and shoulders. At the waist, the dress ballooned out into more ruffles, swags, poufs, and flounces, creating the illusion that she was broader than she was tall.

She wore her hair skinned back into a plain bun at her nape, a severe, matronly style that added years to her countenance and minimized its delicate lines to the point of appearing nondescript. Blinking to wake up, Josh sat straighter and combed his fingers through his hair.

"Good morning."

She leapt as though she'd been stuck with a pin and whirled to stare at him, her eyes wide with alarm. Though he knew he had it coming, Josh's heart caught at that look. "Charlie, I know I haven't given you much cause to believe this, but you have no reason to be afraid of me."

As she positioned her bundles side by side, he saw her throat convulse. Perching stiffly on one of the benches at the table, she turned toward the window and folded her hands primly on her lap. "The snow has slacked off. As soon as the sun comes up, I'll be leaving. The moment I get home, I shall see to it this marriage is annulled. Please accept my heartfelt apologies for having inconvenienced you as I have."

The speech was so well-rehearsed it bordered on expressionless, and Josh pictured her awake most of the night planning it. A good thing, for she was clearly too nervous to string that many words together except by rote. She was shivering, and in hopes of chasing away her chill, Josh quickly built a fire, adding on logs until the blaze was roaring.

Satisfied that the room would soon be warm, he lit the lantern and turned toward her. "Charlie, we need to talk."

"We've nothing to discuss."

"Sure we do."

"Like what?"

He could see she had no intention of making this easy for him, not that he blamed her. "Well, for one, I'd like to apologize for the way I treated you last night. I behaved like an ass."

She threw him a wary glance. "Think no more of it, Mr. Slade. I shan't."

Josh sighed. "Charlie, can you possibly find it in your heart to forgive me?"

Two bright spots of color flagged her pale cheeks. "A man can't be blamed for his tastes, Mr. Slade. There is nothing for me to forgive."

As if keeping a constant vigil might make the sun rise more quickly, she went back to staring at the window. Josh considered what she had just said but was unable to make sense of it.

"My tastes?"

Her cheeks grew more flushed, and she bit her bottom lip. Even in the dim light, he could see tears shimmering in her eyes. Her meaning finally struck him, and he took a hesitant step toward her only to freeze, afraid to go closer.

"Oh, hey, wait just a minute. I think you misinterpreted—that wasn't why I left the house."

She squeezed her eyes closed. "Don't, please . . . I just want to pretend the whole thing didn't happen."

"But it did happen. Charlie, look at me."

"No, thank you."

Josh closed the distance between them and crouched in front of her. "Honey, look at me. Please?"

No response.

It was wicked of him, he knew, but he wasn't above using her religious convictions against her. "It's not very Christian of you to refuse to look at me when I'm trying to apologize."

She sniffed and opened her eyes.

"You're a beautiful woman," Josh began.

At his words, she shot up from the bench, swept around him, and went to stand at the window. He pushed to his feet and followed, the guilt he had felt last night increasing a hundredfold. Instead of terrifying her, as he thought, he had made her feel ugly. Nothing could be further from the truth, but how could he convince her of that? The fear he had caused her would eventually become nothing more than an unpleasant memory, but the same was not true for lacerated self-esteem. The wounds had a way of crusting over and festering, sometimes for years. No one knew that better than he.

The light from the fire and lantern threw their reflections against the glass. Measured against his darkness and height, she looked like a little mud duck. From his conversation with her father last night, Josh gathered that her mother had died when she was very young, leaving her without a woman to teach her how to choose flattering clothing or arrange her hair. Preacher Masterson seemed to be a nice enough fellow, but he was clearly too preoccupied with his ministerial duties to worry overmuch about worldly things, especially something so unimportant as his daughter's wardrobe. Only, of course, it wasn't unimportant. Josh doubted Charlie had any idea of how lovely she actually was. Unless someone forced her to see herself as he did, she might never realize it.

That was an issue he would address in a moment.

"Charlie, please try to understand how angry I was yesterday. I thought you'd lied to your brothers about me, and that really hurt." Josh's throat went suddenly dry. Stripping his feelings bare wasn't an easy thing for him to do. "While we were stuck here alone together in the storm, we started to become friends. At least I thought we did. Maybe that's not of great significance to you, but it doesn't happen very often for me."

He paused and ran a finger under his collar. It wasn't buttoned, but he felt a choking sensation, nonetheless.

"When I bought land here, I had high hopes that I'd be accepted by everybody, that maybe no one would judge me by my past. That didn't happen. I know everyone gossips about my weekly visits to the Shady Lady, but that's the only place I've been made to feel welcome. The women there are the only females in town who don't snub me."

He saw her close her eyes and began to hope that maybe he was getting through to her.

"Until you came along, that is." A rush of words crowded into Josh's throat. He prayed they would come out the way he intended, for he was no master at eloquence. "You made me feel good about myself, Charlie. You even invited me to breakfast at your house. I left for home feeling like you thought I—well, that I was fit company for decent folks, and it was the first time I'd felt that way in so long I can't remember when. The next thing I knew, your brothers were in my yard toting guns. It wasn't just a slap in the face. I felt like a goddamned horse had kicked me."

She made an inarticulate noise under her breath. He went on.

"I was wrong to take what they said at face value. I realize that now. But at the time the hurt I felt was so bad I couldn't reason my way past it. Does that make any sense?"

She nodded almost imperceptibly.

"I acted like a skunk. But you've got to believe my walking out last night had nothing to do with your looks, or with whether or not I wanted you. I stormed out of here because I made you cry. Seeing that—well, it was like a splash of cold water in my face, and I realized what an awful thing I was about to do. I had no right to treat you that way, no matter how many lies you'd told, so I walked out. Can you understand that?"

She said nothing.

"You're beautiful, Charlie. Trust me. I don't think you have an inkling of just how lovely you really are."

"Stop it," she finally whispered. "You've apologized. I forgive you. Now leave it alone."

"And let you leave as soon as the sun comes up, believing I walked out of here last night because you're undesirable? No way, sweetheart. I've done you a heap of hurt already without adding that to the list."

She gave a wet little laugh. "Mr. Slade, it isn't as if last night was the first time I realized my homeliness."

"Homely? Honey, you're as far from that as a woman can get."

In a thin voice, she cried, "Would you stop it? I *know* how I look."

"Oh? And how is that?"

She sighed in exasperation. "I'm short, fat, and plain." She hugged her waist. "I know you mean well, but it's more humiliating to hear you go on, saying things you can't possibly mean, than it would be if you said nothing at all. I wish you'd just—"

"Fat? You're not fat, Charlie. Pleasingly plump, maybe."

He was unprepared for her reaction to that. Green eyes flashed at him. "Pleasingly plump! Lord, how I hate those two words. People have been saying them to me all my life. What they really mean to say is that I'm fat. Why color it?"

Josh clamped his hands over her shoulders and forced her closer to the window glass. "You're not fat, goddamn it."

In the back of his mind, he knew what he was about to do was outrageous, and with any other woman on earth, it would be inexcusable. But extraordinary situations sometimes called for extraordinary measures. He started jerking pins from her hair, taking perverse delight in destroying that god-awful old maid bun she persisted in wearing.

To keep her distracted, he demanded, "Show me where you're fat. Go on! Look at yourself in the glass and show me some fat, dammit."

While he combed his fingers through her hair, she touched a trembling fingertip to her jaw. "Slender women have hollowed cheeks."

"Skinny women have hollowed cheeks. Since when is skinny the be-all of every man's existence? Did it ever occur to you that some men prefer women with meat on their bones?"

"I have a double chin."

That was absurd. Josh glared at the body part in question as he began unbuttoning her collar. "That isn't a double chin."

"What is it then?"

"It's—well, it isn't double. Soft and round, that's what it is."

"Soft and round? Who ever heard of a soft and round chin?"

She blinked and focused on her reflection. Then she gasped in outrage. Apparently she had just noticed that he was unfastening her bodice. But he already had the task nearly completed, and he was determined that the damned dress was coming off if he had to take his knife to it and remove it, piece by piece.

TWELVE~

Charlie grabbed his wrists and cried, "Wh-what are you doing?"

Josh continued his task. "I'm going to show you the difference between fat and pleasingly plump."

"Oh." She gasped again when he jerked the sleeves of the dress down over her arms. "Wait a minute. You're—stop this. I'm not going to stand here and let you—you're trying to undress me!"

"No 'try' to it." He jerked at her bustle and petticoat ties. "Horsehair ruffles, Charlie? And a tiered petticoat four layers thick? A beanpole would look fat under all this shit you wear."

He tugged the garments in question down over her hips to puddle on the floor around her feet along with her manure brown dress. Next he attacked her corset laces, no easy feat with her trying frantically to stop him. She might have succeeded if she could have made up her mind whether to seize his hands or cover what they had already laid bare. As he hoped, her more immediate concerns about modesty won out.

Stripped to her chemise and bloomers, she hunched her shoulders, crossed her arms over her breasts, and shivered. "You're crazy. If I go back to town and tell on you, you could be arrested."

"For what? Undressing my wife?"

"I'm *not* your wife. I'm annulling this marriage, remember."

"Maybe."

"What do you mean, maybe?"

Josh clasped her wrists and applied a bit of strength to draw her arms from her chest. "Don't be embarrassed, Charlie."

"Don't be embarrassed?"

"I saw all there is to see last night. Besides, I have no intention of looking at you that way."

"What way?"

He nearly chuckled at that. "In the obvious way. For now, I just want to point out a few things to you, as one friend to another. Will you let me do that?"

"Absolutely not."

"What can it hurt? Like I said, I saw more than this last night. You can still run home to Daddy and get the marriage annulled afterward. I promise. But first let me show you something."

"There's nothing new you can possibly show me."

"Not true, because you've never really looked. At least not through my eyes."

"It's your eyes I'm concerned about, sirrah."

Josh applied more pressure and forced her arms to her sides. She promptly shut her eyes. "Charlie, the idea here is for you to see yourself the way I do. Would you cooperate and look?"

"You let go of me. If you don't, I'll tell on you, I swear."

He did chuckle at that. "Then I may as well enjoy myself, hm?" He surveyed her reflection in the glass. "Charlie, just look at yourself. Without all that material bunched in the wrong places to make you look stout, you have a glorious shape."

She cracked open one eye, then quickly closed it. "Oh, mercy. I'll never forgive you for this."

"Name me one place where you're fat."

"You will notice that I have no collarbone."

"Collarbone?" he echoed drily. "My lovely young woman, who needs a collarbone with that glorious a chest?"

She gave a thin little squeak.

"Why in hell do you think so many of the women in town wear bosom pads, for God's sake? Because they have 'skeeter' bites instead of breasts, that's why. And all those ruffles? Those were designed to make them look fuller in the bust."

"Stop it. This is indecent."

"I won't stop. You've got about the prettiest bosom I've ever run across, and it's time you appreciated how lucky you are."

"I'm sure a man of your ilk has run across his share of bosoms, and in all shapes and"—her face flushed crimson—"conformations."

"Not like yours, I haven't. Jesus, Charlie, you're a man's dream come true." Josh heard his voice growing thick and wanted to kick himself. "And look at that waist. You don't need to wear a corset. Nature shaped you beautifully."

"I've no ribs," she said.

"Ribs?" he repeated blankly.

"You can't feel my ribs."

"Ah." He smiled in spite of himself, pleased by what he did feel. "You're soft and—" Josh released one of her wrists to settle a hand on her waist. Her well-rounded hip flared under the heel of his palm, warm and femininely fleshy. In a purely male response to her softness, he tightened his grip and bent his head to better enjoy the flowery scent of her silken hair. "Charlie, there isn't a man alive who gets passionate over ribs and collarbones," he said in a dangerously husky voice. "Trust me to know."

Oh, God, did he ever know. He shouldn't be doing this. He had thought he could handle it, but now that he had plunged in too deep to turn back, he found he couldn't resist that sensitive spot below her ear. Not a second longer. He touched his lips there, ever so lightly.

He half expected her to stiffen, but at the contact, she seemed to melt against him. Then, to his amazement, he heard her breath catch. The softness of her fanny connected with his thighs, so tantalizing that he yearned to bend his knees and come in behind her with a long, slow grind of his hips.

"Charlie . . ."

She tipped her head to better accommodate his searching lips, a blatant invitation if ever he'd received one, but Josh didn't know if she intended it thus. He seriously doubted it. Intentional or not, though, her body was sending out very encouraging signals.

A peach ripe for the picking.

Only she wasn't a piece of fruit to be devoured. She was a sensitive, wonderfully warm young woman. He should stop this. Now. He knew that. So why was he nibbling at her throat and running both hands over her hips?

With a shock, Josh realized he had released both of her wrists, yet she was doing nothing to make him stop. Instead she was leaning against him as though her legs no longer had substance. He knew then that she was his for the taking, as starved for his attentions as he was eager to give them. It would be such a simple thing to carry her to the bedroom.

As if controlled by a will of their own, his hands slid up to her waist, then higher over the wonderfully soft tapering of her sides. No ribs. He smiled at the thought even as his palms homed in on what he sought. The thin lawn of her chemise scarcely more than a tease over them, her nipples went instantly and wonderfully hard when his fingertips grazed them. The soft mounds of her flesh rested heavily in his hands. Ah, Charlie. Plump, yes, and oh, how pleasingly so. The kind of woman a man might never get enough of. Her skin smelled as sweet as a honeysuckle vine. He wanted to nip and taste. He gave in to his earlier urge and bent his knees to press his hips hard against her.

"Oh, God, Charlie, for two cents I'd carry you to the bedroom and love you until you begged me to stop."

He was breaking all the rules, taking advantage. She was a simmering little honeypot of unsatisfied sexual need, and he was using the expertise of long practice to stoke her blaze. It was unfair. Charlie was in way over her head.

Finally Josh clenched his teeth and forced his hands away from those tempting breasts. Gripping her waist, he stood behind her, rigid with a longing he couldn't in good conscience slake, his guts afire with need. He prayed she wouldn't move. That she'd do them both a favor and just stand there until he regained his control. Otherwise, he was going to do something he'd regret. If he took her—no, when he took her—he wanted it to be special for her, not a tawdry joining of bodies that meant nothing.

In a thready voice he could barely discern, she said, "I have two pennies in my reticule."

As her words sank home, his brain froze. He couldn't have heard what he thought he had. A hard swallow and a deep breath later, he finally managed to say, "Wh-what?"

"No one else has ever wanted me," she whispered. "No one."

There was so much pain in that statement that a fist seemed to close around Josh's heart.

"It's highly probable that no other man ever will." She stirred slightly, and Josh heard her drag in a quavery breath. "Is it so horrible a thing for me to want someone to love me? Just once? Do you think I'm awful?"

"Oh, Charlie, no."

"I'll never tell. When it's over, I'll go home. I won't make you stay married to me. I swear it. And I'll be good as gold for the rest of my life. But just once I want to experience what other women are fortunate enough to take for granted."

Josh breathed in the scent of her. "Ah, Charlie, you don't know what you're asking. Once is never enough."

"For someone like me, once will have to be."

For someone like her. It was those words that pushed Josh beyond bearing. No one had ever wanted her? He couldn't believe that. Were all the men in Juniper Hollow eunuchs, or just blind?

Not allowing himself to think beyond the moment,

he bent to sweep her off her feet. In a flash, he remembered the last time he'd lifted this particular armful. A fragile flower, Charlie was not. But in Josh's estimation, that just meant there was more of her to love. With a grunt and jostle, he got her positioned in his arms.

"What are you—put me down, Joshua! You'll hurt your back."

He met her startled gaze and felt as if he were drowning in emerald swirls. "Oh, I'll put you down, darlin'. But not here. The bed's where I'm headed."

She kicked one foot to toss off her petticoat, which had hung up on one of her shoe buttons. "I'm too heavy!"

Ignoring the strain that lanced up his thighs, Josh managed, a little breathlessly, to say, "You hardly weigh a thing." As he turned and strode with her toward the bedroom, he smiled at the fib. A man could go to hell for lying. On the other hand, he might pave his way straight to heaven. "Don't wiggle, for God's sake. I don't want to drop you."

She hugged his neck. "Don't you dare!"

Josh had never been able to resist a dare. He loosened his hold and chuckled as she fell, squealing, onto the bed. He seized one of her feet and began unlacing her shoe. After jerking it off, he sent it flying and reached for the other one. Once she was unshod, he straightened and saw the uncertainty in her eyes.

"Second thoughts?"

"No," she said weakly. "Except that—well, if you don't want to do this, I shall certainly under—"

"Oh, I want," he assured her, planting a knee on the mattress. "All I've got is one question. Do you prefer the version I reserve for ladies, or do you want me to love you until you can't think? Your choice, but be prepared for a few shocks if you opt for the latter."

"There are different versions?" Her eyes went even wider.

"Very different."

She caught her bottom lip in her teeth, looking uncertain. "Well, if things were different, I might choose to work my way into things slowly. But this is probably going to be my one and only dangerous encounter."

"Dangerous encounter?" Josh couldn't help but grin. She had no idea how dangerous.

"With a man," she added. "And since that is the case, I believe I shall request the act in its entirety, if you please."

Going down on one elbow to hover over her, Josh whispered, "The lady's wish is my command."

She lowered her chin to follow his gaze, hers darkening to jade with sudden wariness. "Joshua . . . is this procedure going to hurt?"

Procedure? Looking down at her upturned face, he felt a wave of emotion hit him. The intensity of it rocked him. A man couldn't fall in love in three days, especially not a man who considered that state to be more fiction than fact. But, dear Lord, she was sweet. So incredibly sweet and unspoiled. A woman to cherish. When this was over, she wasn't going home. Over his dead body. Miss Charlie was staying right here so he could embroil her in dangerous encounters for the rest of her life.

"Yes, it'll hurt," he admitted. "And the God's honest truth is, I don't know how bad." At her look of worry, he quickly added, "But I don't believe it's an excruciating sort of pain. More of a discomfort."

"Perhaps I should partake of a little whiskey first?"

Josh pressed his face closer to hers. "No whiskey, Charlie. Trust me to take care of things."

He settled his lips lightly over hers to end that particular line of questioning. Answers would be forthcoming soon enough.

But not too soon . . . First he had to make certain Miss Charlie experienced this "procedure" in its entirety.

THIRTEEN~

Joshua was absolutely right, Charlie reflected a few moments later. She was shocked. Rhoda, for all her vast experience with dangerous encounters, had never mentioned that these sorts of things transpired between ladies and gentlemen. Perhaps that was because this was not the ladies' version.

Charlie gasped and made fists in his black hair, staring in wide-eyed fascination as he caught her nipple sharply in his teeth. She was about to protest and change her mind about which version of this procedure she preferred when he rolled the captured flesh with his tongue. A jolt of sensation such as she had never experienced zigzagged into her stomach.

"Joshua?"

In response he growled, actually *growled*. Charlie

tingled clear to her toes. When he glanced up at her, she saw that his midnight blue eyes were smoldering. Really and truly smoldering. The kind of smolder to melt corset stays. Only she wasn't wearing any. And from the feel of things, she would soon be divested of her drawers as well.

"Joshua, I think—"

He clearly didn't want her to have a clear thought in her head, for in response to that he took firm possession of her other nipple with a leathery thumb and forefinger. Charlie's mind went into a spin, and she arched her neck to wail, completely overset.

Oh, gar. This was beyond her wildest imaginings of a dangerous encounter. She was beginning to think it might prove the death of her. It was—oh, my, it was—Charlie groped for a way to describe it. Only Joshua was groping, too. And his groping was ever so much more interesting. There went her drawers. His hard hand cupped her between the thighs, and he parted her with a relentless fingertip.

Something had gone awry down there, Charlie realized. She was hot and slick. That was not her usual state, and embarrassment swamped her. She struggled to dislodge his hand, but he kept hold with the tenacity of a bronc rider.

"Joshua!"

"It's all right, Charlie. Trust me, sweetheart."

Trust him. An odd sensation filled her lower portions, part ache, part tingle. And then the sensation exploded. Charlie bucked to meet the thrusts of his hand, crying out again as burst after burst of tingles radiated through her. It was the most wonderful feeling. Nothing else he might do could surpass it, she felt sure.

Joshua soon proved her wrong on that score. Before she quite realized what he was about, he found an exterior sensitive spot and pressed his thumb lightly against it. Charlie couldn't breathe, couldn't think. She was vaguely aware that he had angled himself up on one arm beside her, and that he was watching the expressions that crossed her face. It was rather humiliating, but she had no control and couldn't separate herself from the feelings he evoked.

More and more tightly, the sensations knotted her belly, the ache growing sharp and trilling up through the center of her. She heard herself panting. Joshua bent to kiss her, catching her short breaths, nibbling softly at her lips, his thumb driving her ever higher with gentle sweeps. Charlie cried out and gave herself up to the jagged streaks of lightning.

Joshua. Somehow, his shirt disappeared, and he rose over her, a figure of rippling muscle sculpted in bronze, his black hair falling in damp waves over his forehead. His dark blue eyes glittered into hers, not allowing her to look away as he nudged her legs apart and knelt between her thighs. Grasping her hips, he moved forward, and she felt the hard yet silken length of him nudging for entry.

Just when his invasion began to hurt, he bent down to her, taking her lips in a sweet, patient kiss. "Hug my neck, Charlie."

She did as he asked and closed her eyes, tensed against the pain she knew would come.

"I'm sorry," he whispered.

With that, he impaled her. Charlie gasped and then moaned, digging her nails into his skin. She felt as if he had ripped her asunder, and for an instant, she nearly panicked. He held perfectly still, allowing her to grow accustomed to his presence inside her. Then, slowly, he began to thrust.

The pain melted away, replaced by a glorious heat that soon combusted. Charlie clung to him, her only anchor, as he drew her into a soaring funnel of feeling. Higher and higher. The sensation wiped out her awareness of all else. To the pinnacle, he swept her, and then mercilessly forced her over the edge into a swirling vortex of multicolored flame.

The little death, the French called it. Charlie knew that from reading Rhoda's romantic novels. But never had she imagined how accurate a description it might be. Afterward, she felt completely boneless and separated from reality, as if she floated on clouds with angels. Joshua drew her close to him and positioned her head on his shoulder, whereupon he began to stroke her hair, making her feel cherished and loved.

Charlie drifted, savoring that feeling, for she knew it would be all too brief. And she was right. Soon after, Joshua's breathing altered and his arms went limp around her. Then he began to snore softly.

Taking care not to wake him, Charlie sat up and collected her discarded underthings, which she quickly donned. Before she left the room, she allowed her gaze to rest on Joshua for a moment. A deep sadness filled her, and tears stung her eyes. Oh, how she wished she could stay here, that the tenderness she had imagined in his touch could have been real. In sleep, he looked charmingly boyish—not at all as dangerous as his reputation painted him. She itched to smooth his tousled black hair with her fingertips. Long, dark lashes swept his high cheekbones, like spidery etchings on bronze. She gazed at his large hands for a moment, remembering how gentle yet strong they had felt on her.

In that moment, she knew the memory would remain with her always, and she forced herself to smile. A promise was a promise. At last she had experienced a dangerous encounter, and he had made it an absolutely extraordinary one. Now it was time for her to keep her part of the bargain.

When Joshua awoke, the slant of sunshine outside his window told him it was well into afternoon. He stretched to yawn and then stiffened, suddenly aware of the empty place beside him on the bed. Charlie . . . He smiled sleepily and sat up, groping for his trousers.

"Charlie?"

Silence echoed throughout the house. Jerking on his pants, Josh nearly ran out of the bedroom. Charlie's bundled possessions no longer sat near the table, and the house had an empty feeling that he had come to know too well.

She was gone. He couldn't quite register it. His place was seven miles from town. It would be a long walk at the best of times, and in deep snow it would be a trial. He went back to the bedroom and stared incredulously at the bed, wondering if he had dreamed it all. Something on the bedside table caught his eye. He turned and stiffened. Two neatly aligned pennies rested there.

His breath caught when he saw them, and an ache filled his chest. He picked up the coins and held them on his palm. Like his life, they felt cold and hard, so unlike the precious woman who had left them there.

* * *

As Charlie prepared supper for her father and brothers that night, she couldn't help listening for footsteps on the front porch. It was foolish of her, she knew. But a part of her clung to the silly hope that Joshua would come to collect her, that he would insist she was his wife and that she should go home with him.

But, of course, he wouldn't. At this moment, he was probably thanking his lucky stars that she had kept her word and returned to her family, no strings attached. Such was her lot in life, and all that she could reasonably expect. A handsome man like Joshua couldn't be blamed for wanting a wife as fine in looks as he. What had she to offer him?

For that matter, what had she to offer anyone?

Charlie tried to smile brightly as she set the meal out on the table and called her family to eat. She avoided looking directly into her father's eyes and tried to keep the conversation light. Gloomy and ashamed of their actions the day before, the boys didn't help on that score, and she found herself chattering nervously, her sole aim to make noise.

Her father ate in silence, his expression thoughtful. Her brothers picked at their food. Charlie had no appetite, not even for dessert. Later, as she cleaned up the mess that always followed a large meal, she accepted what she should have known all along.

She wouldn't hear footsteps on the porch that night because Joshua wasn't coming. He never would.

She had touched a rainbow. But such beautiful moments were, by their very nature, short-lived.

* * *

For Charlie, the next two weeks were the most difficult of her entire life. She began the proceedings to get her marriage to Joshua annulled. Now all that was left to be done on that score was for Joshua to visit her attorney's office to sign the papers. Unfortunately, putting an end to the marriage did not end the gossip. For the first time in her recollection, Charlie noticed people staring at her and whispering about her behind cupped palms. When she went about her business in town, it seemed to her that the other ladies were no longer as friendly as they had once been. She had become a pariah.

For that reason, Charlie was feeling particularly gloomy one afternoon as she walked along the boardwalk with a list of errands to run for her father. It had been two weeks since her dangerous encounter with Joshua Slade, and she hadn't seen hide nor hair of the man since. Yet the townspeople acted as if she were trysting with him on the sly.

Their behavior made Charlie angry. If they wished to ostracize her over the scandalous things that had happened two weeks ago, she could accept that. But to have everyone watching her every move as if they might catch her sneaking to meet her disreputable lover? Her life wasn't nearly that interesting.

What upset her the most was the effect all the vicious gossip was having on her poor father. He was looking pale and drawn lately, and his eyes were constantly shadowed with worry. Charlie knew he was concerned about her and how all this was making her feel. She tried her best to hide her pain behind a cheerful facade, but a man of her father's profession wasn't so easy to fool. He knew her heart was breaking.

So preoccupied was Charlie with her musings that she nearly didn't hear Mrs. Butterworth, the local dressmaker, call her name.

"Charlie! Miss Charlie?" the fashionably dressed seamstress hollered. "Can you be a darling and step into the shop for a moment?"

Perplexed, Charlie made her way across the muddy street, taking care not to soil the hem of her gray silk gown. As she gained the opposite boardwalk, she questioned Agnes Butterworth with her eyes. "Your husband isn't ailing again, I trust?"

Mrs. Butterworth waved an elegant hand. "Oh, no, not that at all." Pushing the door to her shop wide, she said, "Do come in, dear. I've a surprise for you."

The surprise, Charlie soon discovered, was an array of beautiful new gowns in brilliant colors. There was a twinkle in Mrs. Butterworth's eyes as she displayed each for Charlie's approval. "It's not often a gentleman turns loose of so much coin to buy a young lady a new wardrobe. Luckily I had record of all your measurements and was able to fill his order without ruining the surprise."

Charlie blinked in amazement and touched the emerald green skirt of the dress Mrs. Butterworth held up. "My father can't afford these gowns."

Mrs. Butterworth blushed slightly. "Yes, well . . ."

"It *was* my father who ordered these?" Charlie could almost see him doing such a thing in hopes of cheering her up. Bless his heart. But the cost of all these dresses and accessories must have been substantial. "His income doesn't allow for expenditures such as this!"

"The gentleman who bought these insisted he remain anonymous because he feared you would be concerned over the expense. He is obviously *very* fond of you. It would be ungracious to refuse the gift."

Recalling the worried expression in her father's eyes, Charlie knew that to be true. Her father was not only fond of her, but terribly concerned. He must have hoped to help her out of her mood slump, and ordering her some new dresses had been the only thing he could think of to do. Even if the purchases strapped their budget, the damage was already done, and there was naught for Charlie to do but accept this madness with good grace.

At Mrs. Butterworth's insistence, she donned each gown to check the fit. The styles, cuts, and colors were much different from those she usually favored. To her pleasure, she saw that the simpler lines flattered her figure. With fewer ruffles, her shoulders and bust no longer looked quite so substantial, and in their simplicity, the gowns showed off her waistline and complemented her well-padded backside instead of magnifying it.

Why, she actually looked curvaceous!

"I never dreamed he had such an eye for fashion," Charlie murmured.

Mrs. Butterworth chuckled. "He's a man, isn't he?"

"Yes, but a rather distracted one."

"Well, my dear, *you* have clearly caught his attention. Enjoy it."

With more than a little awe, Charlie ran her hands over the hint of swag across her hips. She felt as if she had been a lump of clay that a master had sculpted into a beautiful figurine.

"I can't believe it," she whispered.

"Truth to tell, I'm amazed, too. And humbled." Mrs. Butterworth shook her head. "Let this be a lesson to me. I should never get so caught up in current fashion that I fail to see that some styles are completely wrong for certain figure types. You don't need bustles and flounces and enhancers, my girl. Nature gave you all the padding you need, and now that you're wearing a flattering gown, I can see that it's in all the right places."

After Charlie had divested herself of the dress, Mrs. Butterworth beckoned her into the consulting room and directed her to a chair. "When your benefactor ordered the new wardrobe, he also enlisted my aid in regards to your hair."

"My hair?" Charlie saw that the woman had picked up a comb and a pair of scissors. "What's the matter with my hair?"

"Too plain," Mrs. Butterworth assured her. "With all those lovely new dresses, you need a coiffure to match, don't you agree?"

Before Charlie could protest, the woman was unpinning her tresses.

"Nothing drastic," Mrs. Butterworth said to reassure Charlie. "A few tendrils to curl about your face and at your ears. And an arrangement of curls at the crown. You'll love it. Trust me."

An hour later, Charlie felt as if she had been transformed into a different person. Mrs. Butterworth had insisted she wear a new blue serge shirtwaist with a matching short jacket that sported minimized leg-of-mutton sleeves. Its lapels featured soft gathers instead of the popular pleats, and the color brought out the flame in Charlie's hair and the green of her eyes.

"You're lovely," Mrs. Butterworth said with a softly indrawn breath as Charlie turned before the mirror. "Truly lovely, Charlie. I've never witnessed such a transformation."

FOURTEEN~

As she left the shop, Charlie struggled to keep her feet firmly rooted in reality. It simply wasn't possible that a new ensemble and coiffure could bring about the incredible transformation that Mrs. Butterworth claimed. Charlie knew she wasn't lovely. Not even close. Still she felt wonderful as she went up the boardwalk to finish her errands, and she couldn't wait to stop by the church to model the shirtwaist and jacket for her father.

Bless his generous heart. Tears stung Charlie's eyes when she thought of the money he must have spent. But she quickly shoved the thought aside. What was done was done. Since he had spent the much-needed funds, she should enjoy the gifts in proportion to the gesture.

"Miss Charlie?"

The masculine voice was laced with a note of

incredulity. Charlie turned to see Orville Worscht walking along the boardwalk toward her. He stopped a few feet away and simply stared.

"Is that you?"

Charlie couldn't help but feel flattered. Orville's eyes were actually bugging, and never before had he looked at her in quite that way.

After exchanging pleasantries with the young doctor, Charlie stopped in at several shops and received much the same reaction from the proprietors. No one seemed to recognize her, and once they did, they stared in amazement. It was rather unsettling for Charlie, who had spent most of her life receiving about as much attention as a stick of furniture. But she also had to admit it was deliciously fun. Especially when she noticed gentlemen stopping on the street to gape at her.

In the end, though, it was the reactions of her father and brothers that Charlie thought she would always remember the most vividly. When she stepped into the church, her father caught one glimpse of her and dropped his Bible. Her brothers froze in motion.

"Charlie?" they all cried in unison. Then her father whispered, "God help me, for a moment I thought you were your mother."

Charlie's mother had been a lovely creature, and never before had her father hinted that Charlie had inherited her looks. Turning in a full circle so the men in her family could admire her ensemble and new coiffure, Charlie said, "Oh, Papa, I know we can't afford it. But, weak soul that I am, I couldn't resist wearing this one home. Thank you so much. I'll make it up to you, I swear."

Her father nodded as if dazed. "How much did you spend?"

Charlie halted in a twirl and stared at him. "Not a penny. Mrs. Butterworth said you paid in full when you made the order."

"What order?"

It hit Charlie then, and for a moment, she felt as if the floor disappeared. Now she realized that each dress was designed in the style Joshua Slade had told her she should wear. Her heart caught, and then joy welled within her. A pure, radiant joy. He hadn't forgotten her after all! On the heels of that thought, Charlie's spirits plummeted. It was as plain as the nose on her face that Joshua had ordered these clothes for her only because he felt sorry for her, and possibly guilty for what he had done.

"Oh, dear!" she cried, and quickly related what had occurred at the dressmaker's. "I should have realized it was he who bought them." She looked down at her beautiful new shirtwaist and wanted to weep. A lady couldn't accept such expensive gifts from a man not her husband, especially not personal items such as clothing and underthings. "Oh, Papa. What an idiot I am. And I've paraded all over town wearing this. If the gossips had a field day before, they surely will now."

With that, Charlie fled from the church, blinded by tears. She was still weeping an hour later when her father came home and found her in her bedroom. He sat on the edge of her bed and put a hand on her heaving shoulder. "Charlie, honey, I think we need to talk. You love him, don't you?"

The pain that lashed Charlie at hearing those words was nearly unbearable. "What difference does it make when he doesn't feel the same way toward me?"

"I'm not so sure about that. Why else would he have bought you new dresses, not to mention all the time he must have spent choosing the colors and styles? A man doesn't do that for just any woman."

"I haven't even seen him since I left his ranch."

Her father chuckled. "And neither has anyone else, namely the folks over at the Shady Lady. For the entire year he's lived here, his horse has been tethered in front of the saloon every Saturday night. These last two weeks, it hasn't been. The man has changed his ways, and it could be because some young woman has gotten a corner on his affections."

Charlie rolled onto her back to stare at her father hopefully. "Oh, Papa, do you truly think—but if that's the case, why hasn't he come calling?"

Her father grew thoughtful. "I'm not sure what took place between you two, and I shan't ask. But I'd bet my pulpit he has his reasons."

"What should I do? About all the clothing, I mean? If I keep it, the people in this town will surely talk."

Her father smiled. "Honey, your reputation can't possibly suffer any more than it already has. If I were you, I'd accept the dresses as they were obviously intended, as a gift. At the moment, you're still married to the man. It really isn't such a bad thing to let him dress you."

"Still married?" Charlie frowned. "But what of the annulment?"

"I stopped by the attorney's this morning to check on that, and it's at a stalemate. He went out to Slade's ranch to get his signature on the documents, and Slade refused to sign them."

"He did? But why?"

"I can't tell you that. Perhaps when you see him, you can ask."

"If I see him," Charlie added bleakly.

* * *

Charlie was still wondering the same thing the following Saturday evening as she walked toward the community hall to attend the monthly church social. The route from her house led past the Shady Lady, and as she walked by she saw a familiar black stallion tethered outside the notorious establishment. Her heart felt as though it dropped to her toes. Her father, who was escorting her, cleared his throat and tightened his grip on her elbow.

"Appearances can be deceiving," he reminded her. "Judge ye not."

Charlie couldn't speak, but even if she had been able to, there seemed nothing to say. Joshua Slade was once again patronizing the Shady Lady. If he remembered her at all it would be to draw unfavorable comparisons between her and the more desirable women there who peddled their wares in the upstairs rooms.

Charlie caused such a stir when she entered the community hall that she promptly set aside her concerns about Joshua's plans for his evening and began to worry about how she might survive her own. Every woman in the place seemed to be whispering, and Charlie hadn't a doubt she was the topic of their conversation. She was wearing a new black velvet skirt and a shirtwaist blouse of handkerchief linen with mock pleats at the bodice, which she felt was appropriate for the occasion. The reaction to her entrance made her touch the small eyelet bow at her collar with nervous fingers.

Beaming proudly, her father took her short emerald green jacket and matching rabbit-lined muff. "You look lovely," he whispered. "Hold your head high. They're all just jealous."

Charlie gave him a startled look. "Jealous?"

"You don't see the men whispering, do you?"

Charlie looked and saw that indeed they were not. Each one was watching her instead. Even the married ones. Her cheeks grew warm, and she threw her father another nervous glance.

"Tonight, Charlie, my love, I warrant you'll dance till the soles of your slippers wear out," he said with a smile.

As the evening progressed, Charlie saw that he was correct. Maybe the women were shunning her, but the men definitely were not. For the first time in her life, she was the center of masculine attention, more sought after for dances than even Rhoda Peck. Charlie could only assume everyone believed her marriage had been annulled, and she was having too much fun to disabuse them of the notion.

It was time.

Josh tossed down the remains of his whiskey and left the saloon. He had given Charlie most of the evening to bask in the warmth of masculine admiration. Now he intended to claim his wife. If one night wasn't enough to convince her of how desirable she was, so be it. He'd spend the next fifty years reassuring her.

He didn't doubt for a second that Charlie would be the belle of the ball tonight. He had seen her pass the saloon on her father's arm earlier, and her appearance in the new clothing and styling of her hair surpassed even his expectations. Properly turned out, the girl was breathtakingly lovely and would undoubtedly be the envy of every woman at the social—despite the scandal on everyone's lips.

Josh smiled to himself and repositioned his gun belt as he neared the hall, tucking his coat behind the holster so the pearl handle would be visible. This was one time he was glad of his reputation. There wasn't a man in town who would dare dispute his claim on Charlie.

Heads turned when he entered the brightly lit hall. He had no difficulty spotting Charlie's flame red hair in the swirl of dancers. To Josh's way of thinking, Orville Worscht was holding her too closely to be considered proper, but Charlie was smiling as if she didn't mind.

Josh had come prepared to act as if he were jealous. It came as a surprise that the anger lashing him now was genuine. He didn't appreciate seeing Charlie's breasts flattened against another man's chest. As a matter of fact, he didn't like it at all.

"Good evening, Mr. Slade."

Josh turned to see Charlie's father. "Preacher Masterson," he said through nearly clenched teeth.

Masterson gazed out at his daughter on the dance floor, his expression pensive. "I want to thank you for this," he said softly. "Too often in love, we take and seldom give. I always hoped that Charlie would eventually find a man who'd not only appreciate her but understand her. You've proven that you do, and with an intuitiveness that humbles me. Look at that smile. She's fairly glowing. If I had half your eye for fashion, I would've bought her flattering dresses years ago. Tonight has boosted her self-confidence. It was good of you to stand aside and allow her the experience."

Since the minister had obviously read the situation correctly, Josh didn't bother to argue. But goddamn it, he didn't want Charlie to glow for anyone but him. He bunched his fists, resisting the urge to storm out onto the dance floor. "I'm glad to see the new wardrobe did the trick," he finally managed to say.

Masterson chuckled. "Are you? By your expression, I'd say you're feeling a little green."

"Nonsense. I wanted this to happen. As you said, she had so little self-confidence, and I—" Josh felt a flush creeping up his neck, and he had the good grace to grin at his father-in-law. "It looks like my plan worked a little *too* well." They shared a chuckle at the truth of that. Then Josh added, "Now the question seems to be, how do I claim my bride? Hell, from the look of it, she can take her pick of the bachelors. She may no longer think I'm such a great catch."

Masterson's eyes twinkled with amusement. "Is there a woman alive who doesn't dream of making the man she loves jealous? After doing all this to make Charlie feel desirable, my good man, don't pass up the perfect opportunity to finish the job."

Josh laughed in spite of himself. "If I make a scene, tongues won't stop wagging for a year."

"I doubt they will anyway." Masterson arched an eyebrow. "Just don't hurt poor Orville. When my back goes out, he always pops it back in to get me going again. I can't get along without him."

Charlie froze midstep when she caught sight of Joshua shouldering his way across the crowded dance floor. He was glowering, and the muscle along his jaw was ticking with anger. Charlie threw Orville a warning glance, but he was so preoccupied with executing the waltz step that he didn't notice. Josh caught him by the shoulder, jerked him away from Charlie, and fairly roared, "Get your hands off of my wife."

The color drained from Orville's face, and his blue eyes bulged. He looked down at Joshua's gun and began to stammer. Charlie stepped between the two men, appalled at Joshua's behavior. "See here—" she began.

Josh gently swept her aside and leveled a finger at the quaking doctor. "Nobody dances that close with my wife and gets away with it. Nobody. Do you understand? If you want to rub bellies with a pretty woman, find yourself another dance partner."

Charlie gasped in outrage. Rub bellies? She felt her face go hot, and she grabbed Joshua's sleeve. He truly did look angry. No, furious. And she was suddenly afraid he might harm Orville, who was half his size. "Joshua, please. You're overreacting."

"Overreacting? I come in here and find my wife with another man, and you think I'm overreacting?"

Charlie tugged on his arm. "Dance with me."

Shooting poor Orville another glare, Joshua did as she requested, albeit with obvious reluctance. As he swept her into a whirl across the floor, Charlie noticed that everyone else on the floor had stopped dancing to stare, and she closed her eyes in embarrassment. "Oh, Joshua, how could you?" she murmured. "I shall never live this down. What were you thinking? You can't come in here yelling that I'm your wife and expect to get an annulment. Everyone thinks it's a fait accompli."

"Good." He half lifted her off her feet to execute a smooth glide. "I don't want an annulment. I never did want an annulment. If you hadn't run off before I woke up, I would have made that clear."

Charlie lowered her gaze to the buttons of his black shirt, acutely conscious of the breadth of his shoulders.

Even encased in thick sheepskin, his arm around her felt hard and wonderfully strong, so unlike Orville's. But then it wasn't really fair to compare the doctor to Joshua. When it came to strength or attractiveness, Joshua won hands down.

It was shallow, Charlie knew, but she wanted this man, and one of her many reasons was that he was so attractive. So attractive that just looking at him made her legs feel weak. She wanted desperately to believe him when he claimed he didn't want his freedom. But she couldn't forget that he had been at the Shady Lady earlier. The smell of whiskey lingered on his breath, and she could detect the sickeningly sweet scent of flowery perfume.

The violinists ended the dance number, and Josh led her off the floor, as though a confrontation hadn't just taken place. Charlie wasn't nearly so adept at hiding her emotions, and in her agitation, she tripped on an uneven floor plank. Joshua caught her and kept her from falling, his gentle grip reminding her of another time when he had touched her.

"Charlie, will you step outside with me so we can talk privately?" he asked politely.

Unable to meet his gaze, afraid she might weaken if she did, she shook her head. "Joshua, it's best this way. Let it be, please, for both our sakes."

"Best?" He leaned closer. "Charlie, look at me."

When she refused to do as he asked, he hooked a finger beneath her chin. As their gazes met, Charlie forgot they were in a roomful of people. There was just the two of them, and the memories.

"I'm falling in love with you," he whispered. "Tell me what I can do to convince you, and I'll do it. But come home with me where you belong."

"Oh, Joshua. I wish I could. But it would never work. We're too different. I might grow accustomed to your drinking whiskey, but I could never countenance your—well, your other women."

"My what?"

"The other women—over at the Shady Lady."

Raising his voice slightly to be heard over the hum of conversation around them, he said, "Charlie, those days are finished. I swear it. I haven't touched another woman since you, and I won't. I promise you that."

"You were over there tonight. I can smell perfume on you."

"Only because Dora issued me an invite, followed up with a hug, which I didn't return. I refused the invitation, Charlie."

She tapped her toe, longing to run so she wouldn't feel torn like this.

"Come outside with me," he urged. "Please, Charlie. Just for a few minutes."

"I'd better not."

He swore under his breath. "I won't set foot in another goddamn saloon."

"You say that now. What about in a few months?"

"What'll change in a few months?"

Charlie swallowed, wishing she were anywhere but there. "I don't know. Things."

He took her arm and gently steered her toward the doors. Charlie avoided the curious glances from the other couples they passed. Behind them, she heard the squeak of a violin as the musicians began warming up for the next selection.

The cold night air washed over them as they stepped outside, making her wish she'd taken her jacket. Seeing her shiver, Josh drew off his coat and settled it around her shoulders. The pile lining was warm from his body and heavy like the man himself. Charlie recalled his embrace, his lovemaking, and tears stung her eyes. He led her away from the doors, then turned to regard her, his dark blue eyes shimmering in the moonlight, his harshly carved features cast into shadows.

"Will you give me a chance? Just a chance, Charlie?"

"Why? What have I to offer you? Why are you suddenly so bent on our staying married? I'd think you'd be glad I'm not pressing you." She watched his face. "It's not as if you're in love with me. We're ill suited, for one, and for two, you haven't known me long enough."

He glanced away. "Ill suited? Why? Because I drink whiskey now and again? And because I don't attend church? I'm not good enough for you. Is that it?"

When he looked back at her, Charlie saw the pain in his expression, and her heart caught. Until that moment, she hadn't believed, wouldn't allow herself to believe, that he might truly care. "That's not it at all."

"Then what?" he whispered. "You want me to say I love you? Those are only words, Charlie. Empty words if they're not sincerely meant."

"But, Joshua, for a woman like myself, those words are everything," she told him gently. "If a man doesn't care deeply for me, how else shall I hold him for fifty-odd years?"

He gazed down at her for a long moment, then slowly shook his head. "It was all for nothing, wasn't it? The clothes, and these two weeks." He jabbed a thumb toward the hall. "You've got every damned man in there drooling, and you still see yourself as you've always seen yourself, a woman no one wants. I thought that you might—" He broke off and pinched the bridge of his nose. "You know what the problem is, Charlie? The real problem? It just struck me. You can't believe that I or any other man could possibly admire you, because deep down you don't admire yourself. In your eyes, you're a plain, plump old maid with nothing to recommend you, and you'll cling to that vision until hell freezes over."

Unable to defend herself on that point, Charlie bent her head. "Thank you for the clothes, Joshua. They have made a difference. Truly, they have. It's just—"

"Just what?"

"They're just that, clothes. Remove them, and what will you have? The same old Charlie. One can't fashion a silk purse from a—"

"Don't you dare say it!" As he spoke, he grabbed her arm and jerked her roughly toward him. His anger came so suddenly it startled her. "You want the words, is that it? Fine. I swore I'd never say them to another woman, but for you, I'll break that promise to myself. I love you, Charlie. And, by God, don't tell me I haven't known you long enough. What has time to do with it? You make me laugh. And you make me feel—" He broke off and dragged in a bracing breath. "I'm not very good at this. You make me feel wonderful inside. Warm and happy for no reason. When you smile at me, I dare to dream again. If that's not love or something very close to it, what do you call it?"

Speechless, Charlie stared up at him.

"As for clothing and what you are when it's removed? You're a beautiful woman, that's what. Making love to you that day—it was the best I've ever had, barring none. All I hear from you is what you're lacking. Well, dammit, what about all your fine points? Physical and otherwise? They don't count? I say to hell with that."

"Joshua—"

"No arguments. You've got two choices, going home with me where you belong or back inside to that puny, lily-livered doctor. If you choose the second, I swear to God I'll break him in half. The same goes for any other man who gets near you. You're my wife, dammit. This marriage has been consummated. If I have to, I'll shout it from the rooftops."

She gasped. "You wouldn't!"

"I sure as hell would." In a louder voice, he said, "I've been compromised! You used me, and then you took off without a by-your-leave. And all in hell I've got to show for it is two measly pennies. Well, I want more. I want you in my arms at night, and I want to see your face beside mine on the pillow in the morning. I want someone to share my life with, someone to raise a family with, someone I can love and who'll love me."

"Joshua, please lis—"

"You say we're not suited? I don't much cotton to church. I admit that. But what's to say you won't change my mind about that over time? I like your father. He's nothing like mine, ranting and raving and threatening everyone with perdition. I might even enjoy his sermons. But are you willing to fight for that? Hell, no. You're calling it quits before we start."

Smothering a smile, Charlie hugged her waist. "Say it again."

"Say what again?"

"That you love me," she whispered.

"So you can throw it back in my teeth?" He glared

down at her. "My luck with women hasn't been exactly great, Charlie. If my mother betrayed me to my father once, she did it a thousand times, and every time he treated me to another lashing with his razor strop. My own mother, dammit. He whipped me until I bled, and she stood there and watched."

"Oh, Joshua . . ."

"I lit out when I was thirteen, and I never looked back, never wrote her, nothing. I loved her, and she kissed that bastard's boots, selling her own son down the river to stay on his good side. When I left there, I swore I'd never love another woman, that I'd never make myself vulnerable again. But I did, damned fool that I was, and the first time I turned my back on her, she went straight into the arms of my best friend." His gaze held hers, relentless in its intensity. "Then you came along, and that very first night, I found myself starting to trust you. I didn't want to. God knows I didn't. But I couldn't help myself."

"And then you believed I'd told lies about you," she said sadly. "Oh, Joshua, no wonder you grew so angry."

"But I got past it. Now here I am practically begging you to come home with me."

Tears nearly blinding her, Charlie stepped forward and hugged his waist. His jacket slipped from her shoulders onto the snow, but she scarcely felt the cold. "You needn't beg, Joshua. All you ever had to do was tell me that you cared."

As if he was afraid to believe his ears, he encircled her with trembling arms. "You'll come back to the ranch with me?"

"Of course," she whispered. "If you'd come and asked me to that first night after I left, I would have jumped at the chance. I waited and prayed to hear you on the porch, but you never showed up, and I thought you were glad to be rid of me."

"Glad? It was all I could do to stay away. But I wanted to give you tonight first. I thought maybe—"

"I know what you thought," she said softly. "And it was a wonderful gesture, truly it was. However, it was rather a waste of time. You were the only man I really wanted to notice me. The others were just frosting on the cake. The experience was sweet but not truly important. All I've been able to think about these last three weeks is you. If it hadn't been for Papa, I might have given up hope entirely. He insisted you wouldn't have gone to such trouble and expense for a woman you didn't care about."

He gave a shaky laugh. "I'm beginning to suspect that your papa is a very wise man. In case you haven't guessed, Charlie, my father was a minister. I've got a heap of bad memories to get past before I become a churchgoer. But I will promise that I'll drive you into town so you can attend services, and I'll never object to your taking our children."

Children. The word was music to Charlie's ears. She leaned her head back to look up at him. She remembered that day the snowstorm hit and all her fanciful imaginings about him. Now Joshua Slade was holding her as though she were made of glass, and he was offering to make all those wonderful dreams and wishes come true.

She felt his lips graze the side of her neck and closed her eyes, moving closer to his heat. *Joshua*. She loved the feel of him all around her.

"Let's go home," he whispered. "I never finished letting you experience a dangerous encounter in its entirety. Maybe we can work on that tonight."

"You mean there's more?" she whispered in amazement.

"You needn't worry. We have the rest of our lives to introduce you to all facets of the procedure."

The rest of their lives. As Charlie fell into step beside him, she thought she had never heard sweeter words. Smiling, she glanced up, and what she saw made her miss a step.

His eyes . . . It might have been the moonlight. Or maybe it was the product of wishful thinking. But she could have sworn his eyes were smoldering as he looked at her.

WILD TEXAS ROSE

~ *by* ~

Christina Dodd

ONE ~

West Texas, 1882

"It's our dance, Rose."

Seated in a chair against the wall of the ballroom, Rose Laura Corey froze.

That voice. That insolent, laughing male voice. How long since she'd heard it last? How many years had it haunted her guilty dreams?

You're going to be mine someday.

Thorn Maxwell hadn't said it now, but the memory of that eight-year-old promise reverberated in her brain, and its vitality had never diminished.

The plate of barbequed ribs wobbled in her grasp. Pinning a smile to her lips, she willed her racing heart and shaking hands to stillness and raised her formal gaze to her nemesis.

As she well knew, he stood six foot four inches in

his stocking feet—and he wasn't wearing just stockings. His black leather boots added another inch to his height, and the long sweep of his blue denim shrink-to-fit Levi's made him look taller yet. A starched, ironed blue chambray shirt covered shoulders now strengthened by maturity. His bandanna, Rose noted with fastidious disapproval, drew the eye like a magnet. It was red, the color of fire, temper, and lust—an appropriate shade for an inappropriate man.

He was not noticeably discouraged by her disapproval as he loomed over her with the arrogance of a man sure of his welcome. "You promised this dance to me," he insisted.

"What are you doing here?"

She spoke in a low, ladylike voice, hoping desperately to keep this encounter from becoming the talk of the party.

A hope doomed to failure.

By virtue of his size, his outgoing nature, and most of all, his notoriety, Thorn made them the focus of all eyes. Glancing around the big ballroom in righteous surprise, he repeated, "What am I doing here? Why, I've come to Pogue's annual roundup party, just like everyone else."

All the old women seated in the long row of chairs beside Rose thrust their long necks out, like curious fowl, for a better view. Utilizing his considerable charm, Thorn smiled and bowed to them, transforming them, Rose thought scornfully, into a giggling flock of silly geese.

"That's not what I mean." She sounded prim and outraged, as withered as the old ladies and stern where they were not. "What are you doing back in Presidio County?"

"I can't hear you when you talk so low." He said it in the clarion tones of a town crier, and the ladies settled back in their straight-backed chairs, glad of their front-row seats. "What am I doing in Presidio County? I came for the dance you promised me."

The heels of the dancers drummed on the floor, the music sang a waltz, but the sounds of conversation faded as the whole county paused to watch this unlikely combination of spinster and scoundrel.

Sue Ellen Pogue, hostess of the party, biggest gossip in west Texas, and Rose's dearest friend, cut sharply into the silence. "You've been gone eight years, Thorn. When did she promise it to you?"

With a slight bow, Thorn acknowledged Sue Ellen, but his gaze remained on Rose, devouring her.

Jabbing Rose with one sharp elbow, Sue Ellen said, "Everyone's watching you, Rose. He's been gone eight years. When did you promise it to him?"

Rose, too, ignored Sue Ellen, preferring to mark the transformation of Thorn from boy to man. His face had changed from the pure, exquisite handsomeness of youth. The artistically arranged curl on his forehead had given way to a plain comb-back that left his features stark and unadorned. The sun had marked his smooth, juvenile skin, burning lines across his brow and creases beside his mouth. His clean-shaven chin looked blue-black in the ever-present shadow, and he sported a close-cut mustache that endowed him with a desperado's appearance.

Yet the brilliant blue eyes were just the same: hot, demanding, seeing more of her than any other person could. The arrogance was just the same: proud, sure, knowing what Rose wanted without asking.

She was relieved. Of all the nightmares she'd suffered,

the greatest had been that Thorn Maxwell's magnificent spirit would be crushed by the labor, indignity, and cruelty of prison.

He snapped his fingers beneath her nose, then presented her with his broad, creased palm. "You promised me this dance, and I have reason to know you always keep your promises."

Rose looked at his hand, then at him. "I am not a dog, to be summoned by a snap of your fingers." She placed the fork across her plate. "But you are right. I did promise you this dance, and I will fulfill my promise."

"Well!" Sue Ellen absorbed the remarkable admission as a sponge absorbs water. "I never!"

Thorn's smile softened, and he spoke only to Rose. "Ah, Rosie, my beautiful darlin', how I have missed you."

Rose ignored the flattery. In the most humiliating of circumstances, she had discovered it to be false.

Shoving her plate into Sue Ellen's hands, Rose said, "Give this to one of the servants. I can't eat any more. And for pity's sake, stop gaping. You look like you're catching flies."

Sue Ellen snapped her mouth shut and took the plate, but her jaw dropped again when Rose placed her hand in Thorn's. He pulled her onto the dance floor at arm's length, making a production of the simple act of beginning a dance. He did it to attract attention; he had always done everything to attract attention.

And he succeeded.

The other couples edged away, leaving them a clear circle within the dancers, and the creases around Thorn's mouth deepened in satisfaction. He was enjoying himself a little too much, Rose decided, but before she could protest, he did the expected.

He gathered her into his arms.

His forearm slid across the middle of her back, his fingers spread across her waist. She might not have been wearing the worn silk dress, the corset cover, the corset, or the chemise, for all the protection they afforded her. The heat of his palm burned right through the layers to her skin. When she would have caught at his hand, he pulled her even closer to his body and sensation overwhelmed her.

They fit well together: the thin, spare ranch woman and the muscled convict.

They always had.

The music hadn't stopped—only they hadn't moved. They stared into each other's eyes like two lost souls who glimpsed home. The brazen bad boy disappeared, leaving the man tender with remembrances. Her strict, controlled facade dropped away, and she knew only that he was the iron, she the fire, and together they were forged of steel.

He touched her cheek with one finger, rough against soft, and whispered, "Rose, you have the most beautiful eyes of any woman I've ever seen."

Flattery. Lies.

She stiffened. "Are we going to dance or talk?"

He threw back his head and laughed—loudly, joyously, making them even more of a spectacle than they already were. "For a minute there, I thought we were going to make love." She tried to jerk away, but he pulled her back and around in a tiny circle. "We'll dance."

The arm across her back weighed heavily. When he took her hand, she carefully tensed her muscles, tendons, and bones into one long line from elbow to fingertip. It symbolized resistance, courage, dignity—those qualities that she prized so highly.

He seemed unimpressed.

Rose suspected they gave the appearance of two matching porcelain figures. Her blue bengaline evening gown had been turned twice to disguise its age, but despite her efforts it had faded to the color of his shirt. The cut of the gown bared her arms and a modest proportion of her chest, but her own dislike for lace and frills resulted in an almost masculine elegance—a counterpoint to Thorn's hard-bitten grace. Although he was tall, she was, too, and if she'd laid her head against him, her cheek would have fit in the hollow of his shoulder.

They traveled the floor slowly, out of step with the beat; she watching her step and carefully keeping her skirt and bustle out of the way, he staring over her shoulder—as stilted as two people posed for a daguerreotype. The other couples, at first goggle eyed, began to lose interest, and a few dancers joined them on the floor. More joined those until finally Rose lost the sensation of being on display.

As the noise around them returned to normal levels, Thorn murmured in her ear. "You dance mighty fine for a woman with a stick up her back."

Well, she couldn't complain of flattery now. "I did warn you I couldn't dance."

"So you did. Ten years ago. And I promised I would teach you." They twirled in a stiff circle. "You'll find that I, too, always keep my promises."

You're going to be mine someday.

"I can live without learning." She didn't mean dancing.

"That's not living. That's just existing." He didn't, either.

She tried to take a deep breath, but the whalebone

of her corset obstructed it, and she gave serious thought to fainting. But she'd never fainted before, and feared making a fool of herself.

She'd already been a fool about so many things.

"The first thing you have to learn," he said, "is to loosen up."

"I wouldn't know how."

"Why, darlin', I can teach you"—he glanced around at the big room made bright with kerosene lamps—"but not here."

"That's enough dancing for one night," she said, and gave him a firm push on the chest. He let her go, and she reflected smugly that he could be handled, if treated like a refractory horse. "I have some visiting I must do."

"Selling horses to the ranchers, Rosie?"

She fell off her cloud of superiority and hit the ground with a thump. "How do you know what I've been doing?"

Rocking back on his booted heels, he tucked his thumbs into the top of his faded denim jeans. "It's the talk of the party. Miss Rose Laura Corey has been breeding those horses since she was seventeen years old, and now that she's . . . what? Twenty-five?"

"I'm seven months younger than you are, as you well know, Thorn Maxwell."

His blue eyes twinkled. "That's right. I'd forgotten. Twenty-six just two weeks ago. October eighteen. My, my, how time flies."

"Horses," she prompted.

Glancing at the surrounding couples, he asked, "Do you really want to discuss it with me here?"

"I don't want to discuss it with you anywhere else."

"Your distrust wounds me deeply, Rose." Like a

naughty boy brought to justice, he hung his head and sighed. "Deeply."

"Horses."

He peeked up at her and grinned. "Couldn't ever make a fool of you, could I?"

"No one else ever made such a fool of me."

Hard experience and her own innate dignity had taught her to keep emotion from her voice, but he seemed to hear more than she wished. Straightening, he said, "Word is that, womanlike, Miss Rose gave up trying to raise good cutting horses and has concentrated on ladies' horses. Nice, gentle mounts for a matron to ride. Horses with enough spirit for a girl to ride. Talk is, the men might be willing to take a look at your horses—just to keep the womenfolk happy and to help you out."

"Is that what this batch of self-righteous cattlemen are saying?"

"Yes, ma'am. That's what they're saying."

It meant they would buy. It meant she would make enough money to keep her land and maintain her beloved horses until she could breed and break some more. It meant she would survive. Yet triumph mixed with fury, and she snapped, "Help me out? My parents died two years ago, and this is the first time any of those charitable ranchers have spoken of helping me out."

"This is the first time any of those ranchers laid eyes on Goliath."

"Goliath?" Her focus returned to Thorn. "What do you know about Goliath?"

"He's the best-looking stallion this county has ever seen."

"Texas has ever seen." Her correction was automatic.

But something about Thorn's innocent drawl didn't ring true, and she scrutinized the place on his belt where his holster normally rested. The worn, scraped leather bore mute testimony to constant wearing and constant use.

Why? His muscled, fit body told her—and every other woman—that he'd been living hard. His brown, tough skin and watchful demeanor certified an existence on the edge of civilization.

What had he been doing? And whom had he been doing it with?

With the word *outlaw* whispering in her mind, she stepped close to him again and lowered her voice. "Didn't you just get back into the county?"

Putting his arm around her, he drew her close. "Why, Rose? Are you afraid I've been seeing other women? You know there's no one for me but you."

"You, sir, could sell a furnace to the devil—and probably have." She freed herself in a flurry. "But you can't sell flattery to me."

The safety of the chairs beckoned, but as she reached the edge of the dance floor, his whiskey-warm voice hailed her. "Rose!" There was such promise in his tone that the band stopped playing and the dancers halted in their tracks.

She didn't want to turn around. She recognized mischief when she heard it. But as always, when Thorn presented temptation, she heeded its siren call. Pivoting on her heel, she glared at him. "What?"

He kissed his fingertips, then flung the kiss with open-handed generosity across the floor. "Later, darlin'."

The gusty sigh from the widows and spinsters nearly knocked her over.

If Thorn Maxwell had any decency, he would have turned away and laughed, making it clear to all that he was making fun of skinny old maid Rose Laura Corey.

He had no decency.

He seemed to lust after her like a hawk after a field mouse.

It was a good act. It fooled every soul in Presidio County.

It even fooled her.

Rose might have stood there forever, malleable clay in the hands of Thorn, the master sculptor, but Sue Ellen tugged at her elbow and asked, "Do you suppose Thorn has spent the last eight years in jail?"

TWO~

Rose turned her dazzled gaze on Sue Ellen, and the smaller woman repeated, "Do you suppose Thorn has spent the last eight years in jail?"

Thorn was standing where Rose could see him, leaning against the wall with the assurance of a man who knows the boards are privileged to support him. She snapped out of her wistful stupor. "I doubt it, since he was only sentenced to one year of hard labor. Besides"—she imitated his bold sweep of her own figure—"he looks too robust for a man who's spent eight years in jail."

Sue Ellen hauled her backward to an open space against the wall. "When did you promise that dance to him?"

Rose sagged. She should have remembered. Once Sue Ellen latched onto a thing, she hung on like a bulldog with lockjaw. "Before he went to prison," she finally answered.

"What else did you promise him?"

Rose gathered the shreds of her dignity about her. "I did not promise him another thing."

Sue Ellen snorted. "Maybe I should ask what he promised you."

You're going to be mine someday.

Blushing, Rose stammered, "W-why?"

"By chance," Sue Ellen continued, "are you bothered by a draft?"

Rose tried to face her, but Sue Ellen, with all the effort of her tiny body, held her in place against the wall. "What are you talking about?" Rose demanded.

"Half your hair pins are gone, and your bun's coming loose."

As if on command, the severe chignon at Rose's neck slithered down her back. With the instinct of a lady at her toilette, she caught it before it uncoiled completely to reveal her knee-length, chestnut-colored, unmanageable locks.

Across the room, Thorn watched with the appreciation of a man invited into a woman's boudoir.

"And the back of your dress is unbuttoned right to the top of your chemise."

A judicious exploration proved Sue Ellen was right.

Thorn lifted his drink in salutation and Rose glared, but it didn't matter how angry he made her. All that mattered was that moment between the breath going in and the breath going out, between fear and flight—that silence wherein only their two souls could speak.

"Do you see the way he watches you?" Sue Ellen edged behind Rose and buttoned as quickly as she could.

"I imagine everyone sees how he watches me," Rose answered dryly.

"I'm frightened for you, Rose. He wants to give you saddle rash."

"Yes."

"You're certainly taking this calmly!" Taking the ribbon out of her tumble of sausage curls, Sue Ellen looped it around the heavy rope of Rose's hair and, with the inborn ability of a coquette, fashioned a new style. "You live alone, and now you've got a man who's taking off your clothes and letting down your hair in public. He had this whole county whispering about you eight years ago, and now he's a hardened criminal. He's probably raped thousands of women—"

"Oh, Sue Ellen!" Rose chuckled. "He's never had to rape anyone. Every widow with an itch in her drawers is intent on raping *him*."

Sue Ellen tried to hold it in, but she couldn't. She giggled, and her bustle waved behind her like the sting of an excited honeybee. "Some women have no shame, especially when it comes to a man like that." Flipping open her fan, she eyed him over the top. "Look at the way he fills those jeans. And look at the women gathering around him! And—oh, isn't that rude?" She fanned herself in vexation. "Jeanette stepped right between us and I can't see him anymore."

Rose couldn't see him, either, but she didn't care. She couldn't care.

"She's flirting with Thorn, and her a married woman. Isn't that disgusting?"

"You flirt all the time, Sue Ellen, and you're married to one of the wealthiest ranchers in west Texas."

"But it's different flirting with a convict. Why"—

Sue Ellen drew an excited breath—"Thorn might be dangerous."

The growing crowd of women around him parted, giving Rose a glimpse of the smiling, hard, and handsome face. "I would almost guarantee it."

With exaggerated care, Sue Ellen adjusted her already low chiffon bodice and moire-taffeta cap sleeves to display more of her bosom. "In that case, perhaps I should sacrifice myself for my dear friend."

Rose caught Sue Ellen's bustle before she had taken more than one step to join Thorn's admirers. "Sue Ellen, don't do this."

Sue Ellen had tugged the velvet out from between Rose's fingers when Sonny Pogue bellowed, "Sue Ellen!"

Jumping like an indentured servant at her master's call, Sue Ellen abandoned her planned flirtation and hustled toward the portly, perspiring man she had married.

Rose turned her head away. She couldn't stand to watch them together—Sue Ellen cloying and sweet, Sonny demanding and tyrannical.

Staying close to the wall, Rose moved to the door and stepped out on the porch where tin lanterns provided flickers of light through their lacy clefts. She thought she was unobserved, but Sonny bellowed again. "Rose, you're not leaving?" His bulk blocked the light. "You must stay the night."

Patient with Sue Ellen's husband as she had never been with plain old Sonny Pogue, Rose answered, "I can't. I've got those horses to feed."

Sonny dragged Sue Ellen through the opening like an extra appendage cemented to his arm. "Don't you have any ranch hands left?"

"I have Patrick."

"That old Irishman?" Sonny curled his lip. "You know what I think of the Irish. Thieves and drunkards."

Irritated at the criticism of her friend, Rose said, "Patrick's good with horses and he's good to me."

"Well, you don't have to snap!" Sonny protested. "Just like a woman to resent a little advice."

"I didn't realize it was advice." Rose took a step off the veranda. "I thought it was faultfinding."

"No, no." Sonny put on his jovial persona. "I wouldn't criticize you. Why, I've known you since we were children. We grew up together, me and you and Thorn. 'Course, you and me turned out to be decent, law-abiding folks, and Thorn was always the bad seed. He made a fool of you, pretending to love you, but you fixed him when you—"

Sonny jumped. Rose thought Sue Ellen must have pinched him.

Even in the dim light, Rose could see his ruddy face flush redder, and irritation made him react nastily. "Patrick can't be too good a hand, or you wouldn't be losing horses."

"What?" Dismayed, Rose stopped her retreat.

"You wouldn't be losing . . ." He cleared his throat, obviously uncomfortable and sorry he'd spoken. "That is, we heard rumors someone was stealing your horses."

Rose had hoped that nobody knew. She had thought this latest threat to her land and her income a secret no one could possibly suspect. Now, sober with dismay, she asked, "Where did you hear that rumor?"

"Now, Rose, a man can't reveal his sources." Sonny may have been mean spirited, but he wasn't stupid. He peered at her. "But I guess it's true?"

Rose watched him steadily but said nothing. The

years had taught her that Sonny used words as both shield and weapon, and only silence could break him.

As she expected, he began to sweat, then stammer. "I have my cowboys keep an eye on your place. Kinda because I feel protective, and kinda because I figure it's going to be mine someday."

"And why do you think that?" Rose asked.

"Ah, face it, Rose. You haven't got a chance. It's a man's country and cattle country, and here you are, a woman trying to raise horses. I told you when you sold me those extra acres I'd be first in line to take the rest, so I figure—"

Of all of Sonny's irritating idiosyncrasies, this one annoyed Rose more than any of them. "You bought my land for no more than a fair price, Sonny, and I only sold it to you because I couldn't run cattle on it. I don't owe you anything."

"Goddamn, Rose!"

"Don't swear."

"You're so prickly"—Sonny searched his mind for an insult, and produced one in triumph—"no wonder you're an old maid."

"Sonny!" Sue Ellen sounded sincerely shocked.

As defiant as a rude little boy, Sonny insisted, "It's true." He went on as if Rose weren't there. "She's not that bad looking—a little worn down from working so much, and so skinny she's only got one stripe on her bedgown, but she's got brown eyes as pretty as any heifer's and a smile that makes a man wish for the nearest double bed. In fact, if she smiled at the men as often as she smiles at her horses, they'd be buzzing around her. And if she came to this party in a new dress instead of that made-over thing . . ."

"Sonny Pogue, if your mama could hear you now!" Sue Ellen scolded.

"Don't you bring my mama into this." Sonny sniffed and rubbed his sleeve across his nose.

"She'd be ashamed."

Sonny sniffed again, and subsided. But not for long. Nothing could subdue Sonny for long—he was too vulgar to keep his thoughts to himself. "Say, Rose, that stallion you rode here. That Goliath. He's a pretty horse, but too big for a lady to ride. I'd take him off your hands for three hundred dollars."

Behind his back, Sue Ellen winked at Rose. "That's real neighborly of you, Sonny. Especially since Bubba von Hoffmann offered five hundred already."

"What?" Sonny said. "He's throwing his money around."

"He likes what I've done with my breeding program," Rose answered coolly.

"But I'm your . . . we're your friends," Sonny whined.

"When my daddy bought me my first stallions nine years ago, everyone laughed. You laughed hardest, Sonny." She descended the last steps to the ground. "I'm not giving you Goliath, Sonny."

"I'll say five hundred dollars."

"I'm not selling him. To anybody. Goliath is my horse, as I am his master. We know each others' minds and hearts, and he'll allow no one else on his back."

Sonny had mined the bedrock of her resolution, and he seemed to recognize it, for he backed off.

Allowing herself a smile, Rose said, "But I've got one of his foals I've broken to ride—as pretty a mare as I've ever seen. Sue Ellen would look mighty elegant on her."

Sonny stopped, and his eyes narrowed. "Mares aren't worth as much as stallions."

"Star Bright is the first foal off that English chestnut mare you admired last time you were out at my place."

"Don't have the money to be throwing around on a horse for Sue Ellen."

Rose nodded judiciously. "That's true."

"That's funny. Rose told me that Royal Lewis said the same thing," Sue Ellen said, lying through her teeth.

"Yes, until he saw . . ." Rose tried frantically to finish the tale, but she'd had no practice with telling falsehoods. Lamely, she finished, "You're not interested in that."

She strolled toward the stable and heard Sonny's boots as they struck the stairs behind her. "Wait just a minute. Just a minute. What did Royal Lewis do?"

Rose halted, started again, halted, providing just enough tension to set the hook, yet not knowing what to do with the fish she'd landed.

But Sue Ellen knew. She moved to the edge of the porch and wrapped her pale, soft hands around the rail. "Why, he bought one of Rose's mares for his wife to ride. Ana Marie Lewis has been gloating no end, but I told her to just never mind. I told her my husband didn't have the time or the money for such frivolities. I told her—"

"Damn it, Sue Ellen! You told her a damn sight too much. Just like a damn woman."

Sue Ellen shrugged in a coquettish, well-practiced gesture. "If you can't hunt with the big dogs, Sonny, stay on the porch. Royal Lewis made a wagonload of money on his cattle this year."

Belligerent, Sonny insisted, "No more than me!"

"And he can afford to pay four hundred twenty-five dollars for a good horse for his wife. So don't you go bragging you're worth so much when you can't ante up."

"Four hundred twenty-five dollars." Obviously, Sonny hadn't heard a word beyond the price. "Four hundred twenty-five dollars. For a horse. For my wife."

Sue Ellen seized upon his daze. "For me?"

"What?"

Sonny started to straighten, but she reached out and massaged his beefy shoulders. "You'd buy Star Bright for me?"

"Now, Sue Ellen . . ."

"Oh, Sonny." Clasping her hands, Sue Ellen leaned over the rail and gave him a clear view of her snow-white bosom. "Do you mean you'd pay four fifty for Star Bright for me?"

Shrewd as Sonny might be, he was a healthy male animal who did his best thinking with his glands.

"Four twenty-five," he said, but his resolve was failing.

"But Sonny, Star Bright is a better horse than that cheap thing Ana Marie Lewis got." Sue Ellen's fingers fluttered, captured Sonny's hand, and brought it to press on one of her breasts. "Won't you pay four fifty for Star Bright?"

Mesmerized by Sue Ellen's cleavage and the feel of her in his palm, Sonny nodded up and down, up and down. "Never paid as much for a horse before, but I'll do it for my little sugarkins."

"Sonny, you are the sweetest thing." Sue Ellen brought his hand to her lips and kissed it, then shoved it back at him. "You go inside and tell Royal and Ana

Marie Lewis that you bought the best horse in Texas for me, and don't you let on you know anything about Ana Marie's horse. It'll be really funny if they pretend they don't know a thing."

Still stunned with lust and his own extravagance, Sonny did as he was told. Sue Ellen watched him fondly. "If there's one thing that man loves better than dancing the matrimonial polka, it's bragging about his possessions. And right now, he could strut sitting down."

"You weren't the belle of three counties for nothing," Rose observed, amused by Sue Ellen's wholesale manipulation of Sonny. "You put that training to use even now."

"Did you think he got it all his own way?" Sue Ellen observed Rose shrewdly. "You did, didn't you? I know Sonny's a bully and a shyster sometimes, and I know his family had a reputation for branding other people's cattle, but I keep him on the straight and narrow." Moving down the steps, Sue Ellen added, "At least he's not a ruthless criminal."

Quickly and defensively, Rose protested, "We don't know that Thorn is, either."

"Why else didn't he come back when he got out of prison?" Sue Ellen asked. "I never heard that he even came back to visit his mother or his brothers and sisters."

Rose looked away from Sue Ellen's sober gaze. It was one thing for her to suspect Thorn of heinous crimes, but Sue Ellen had arrived at those suspicions unaided. It lent Rose's distrust a validity she'd refused to bestow on it, and made Thorn's presence here a challenge in itself.

"I want you to stay the night," Sue Ellen added.

"Even if I wanted to, I couldn't." Rose placed her

hands over Sue Ellen's and pressed lightly. "Thanks to you, I've sold a horse—"

"Two horses, after Sonny talks to Royal Lewis."

"—and I've had an opportunity to get away from the ranch. But it's true what Sonny said. I don't want it noised about, but someone *is* making off with my horses. And you think that maybe"—Rose struggled with the concept, and found that even the articulation of it caused her pain—"Thorn is the thief?"

Sue Ellen burst out, "Oh, to hell with your horses!"

"Don't swear."

"Rose, it's *you* I'm worried about. He's after you. He's hot as a two-dollar pistol on Saturday night"—Sue Ellen shook Rose by the shoulders—"and he's hot for *you*."

Remembering the wild youth Thorn had been, and remembering even more his feelings for her, Rose couldn't be alarmed. "He's not going to hurt me, and I'm too worried and harried to be seduced."

"Ha!" Sue Ellen clearly didn't believe it, but she tried another tack. "You can't catch the bandit by yourself."

"I know." The smile that charmed even Sonny broke across Rose's face. "I don't want you to repeat any of this—in fact, I want you to shut Sonny up about the thieving—"

"Done."

"—but I sent for a Texas Ranger."

"A Ranger? You sent for a Ranger?" Sue Ellen seemed stunned by Rose's audacity. "When?"

"A couple of months ago, when the thieving first began. Patrick tries to help, but he's too old to do more than train horses and sneak off to Fort Davis to play cards when he thinks I don't notice."

Shivering, Sue Ellen rubbed her arms. "There's a chill in the air tonight. Must be winter coming on." She took a restless turn around her well-tended flower bed, and came back to stand in front of Rose. "Are they sending somebody?"

"I received word they'd send a Ranger as soon as one was free."

"That should be soon," Sue Ellen said to reassure herself. "There's not much to do now that the Indians have been subdued. But in the meantime, Thorn's back."

A thrill rattled Rose, and she hoped Sue Ellen hadn't noticed.

But there wasn't much Sue Ellen didn't know about men and women, and now she looked both sorry and embarrassed. "You're one of the most upright, Christian women I know. You don't swear or drink, and you certainly don't fornicate. But you don't tell falsehoods, either, and you told me you couldn't be seduced."

"No."

"Not even by Thorn?"

Rose hesitated. Had her abstinence been nothing more than lack of temptation? Had temptation presented himself tonight?

It was possible. More than that, probable.

Sue Ellen took her silence as an answer. "The trouble is, Thorn doesn't want you forever, for marrying—he wants you for revenge. Rose, he's been in prison, and your testimony put him there."

THREE~

Rose took a deep breath of the chill night air, and smelled it.

Freedom.

Freedom from overbearing ranchers, from insincere pleasantries, from business discussions that pointedly excluded the lone concerned female. Freedom from the worry of the ranch, the horses, their disappearance. For just a few moments, just until she reached home, she could pretend she was carefree again, riding the rises and dips of the Davis Mountains without a thought beyond the moment.

Leaning down across Goliath's neck, she spoke softly, encouraging him, and he leapt forward. Stretching his neck out, Goliath mouthed the bit and seemed to sense her need for flight, her sheer pleasure in his motion. With polished responsiveness, the intelligent horse monitored their progress, watching for the tumbleweeds that might entrap him, the gopher holes that might trip him. The night wind urged them along. The stars shone; the moon trickled a thin white light over the oak-studded landscape. Together, Rose and Goliath frightened a mule deer from its cover. Together, they heard a coyote crying its lament.

Freedom. Perfect, mindless freedom.

You're going to be mine.

Rose never swore, and right now she regretted it. Why, when she released the restraints from her thoughts, did Thorn always appear? He *was* a thief, for he stole her sense of freedom and replaced it with guilt.

Guilt that she'd sent him to prison, although she knew it had been the right and proper thing to do. Guilt that she'd been too cowardly to go to his mother and apologize for sending her son away. Guilt that he had been humiliated enough to steal that saddle in the first place.

Yet when Rose saw him tonight, eight long, guilt-ridden years had vanished, swept away by a swagger and a wink. He *did* want her. It was there, in his confident smile, his brash claim, the press of his body against hers. But did he want her for revenge, as Sue Ellen claimed? Or did he want her horses, as she feared?

Surely not. As a boy, Thorn had always been fearless and brazen and quick-tempered, but he'd always been kind—and more than kind. Passionate, generous, dedicated to her and their love.

But she didn't know him anymore, did she? Perhaps prison had changed him. Perhaps he really had run with the wolves for the last ten years, and she imagined she heard a lonely howl. She imagined she heard the distant drum of pursuing hooves, and she felt the prickle of awareness as someone's gaze followed her progress.

She whispered encouragement to Goliath until the canyon arms dropped their embrace, and she rode into the broad, mountain-ringed valley of Corey Ranch. The clapboard house stood on a rise above the stream, its broad porches commanding a view of the stables and the fenced area where the less valuable horses grazed and dozed.

All looked peaceful.

Yet anxiety clawed at her as she swiftly rode to the corrals. One, two, three, four . . . twenty-four horses were in the enclosure, exactly the right number. Hurrying on, she went into the dark stable, leaving the great door open for a bit of light, and again counted. Twenty stalls. Eighteen horses. Just as it should be, with one stall left for Goliath and one left empty for any unexpected guest.

Letting the peace of the dark, warm, familiar stable enfold her, she realized nothing was out of order. Nothing was amiss.

As she led Goliath to his stall, she spoke softly to the horses that reached out with neighs and nudges to greet her.

She loved them all. Wily, gentle, affectionate, high-spirited—the horses were more than just a living to her. They were her family now.

Tying a clean apron over her dress—it was her best bengaline dress, for all that she'd turned it—she removed Goliath's saddle and wiped him down. Grooming him, she noted the sculpted muscularity of his neck, shoulder, and leg, his firm belly, his strong croup, buttocks, and thighs. No other creature on earth was blessed with such a combination of intelligence and strength.

No other creature except . . .

It had been a near thing eight years ago. She'd been visiting her horses in the stable. Thorn had been visiting her. Two young people who had been unlikely friends their whole lives. He'd brought out the merriment in her. She subdued the streak of wildness in him. No one had thought, when they were children, that they would become mates, but by the time they were sixteen, everyone saw the attraction that drew them together.

Her mother had talked to her, seriously, about the importance of maintaining a pure body and mind. But she didn't address the desire that Thorn created in Rose with his impudent grin.

Her father had talked to her about Thorn's wild ways, his increasing penchant toward mischief, and his lack of repentance for his deeds. But he didn't address Thorn's uncanny comprehension of her needs and thoughts.

Her parents—staid, upright, Christian people—couldn't understand the heat between Thorn and their daughter, but they felt it, and in their plain way imagined that their words could dampen the fire.

And naive little Rose believed what they believed.

So when Thorn touched her that afternoon in the barn, she hadn't expect to tumble into the straw like some weak-kneed easy woman.

But she had.

He'd been sitting there on the rail, watching her groom her first colt, and when she stepped out of the stall, he'd jumped down beside her.

"Rose, honey, you know what I'd like?" he had asked.

She'd shaken her head, smiling up into his serious face.

"I'd like to rub you all over, just like you did that colt."

Her smile faded. Something about his tone, and the way he towered over her, made her want to soar like a hawk on the wind.

A dangerous pursuit, but irresistible.

"I'd like to stroke your back"—his hand rubbed her spine—"and your waist and your breast"—his voice quivered a little—"and your legs all the way up . . ."

The updraft caught her, she opened her mouth to gasp in excitement—and he kissed her. Kissed her face and neck as if he wanted to swallow her whole. His lank body shivered with need, and he muttered, "I think of you, Rosie, all the time. All night, all day, wanting you, dreaming of you . . . Goddamn it, Rosie, please . . ."

"Don't swear," she admonished as she took him by the wrist and led him to the empty stall.

She had to take his hands and place them on each of the points he wished to touch, but once she gave him that permission, he took liberties she'd never imagined. The heel of his palm massaged her nipples and she'd liked that. But then he pushed aside her bodice and chemise and put his mouth there—and she nearly flew right off the straw and into the air. He laughed—even in his youthful rush, he was wickedly happy—and he whispered, "Tell me I'm not alone in this. Tell me you dream about me, too. Rosie?" He pushed her skirt up around her waist and struggled until he had his pants pushed down to his knees.

"Yes. Please. Yes. Thorn!" She half screamed when

he opened the slit in her drawers and pushed his finger inside her.

"Hush. Quiet, now," he warned, but he grinned into her face, inviting her to share his delight. "God, you're ready for me. You're slick. It won't be so tough. I won't hurt you much, and then you'll be mine. Tell me, darlin'." He was coaxing as he positioned himself. "Mine."

Then the stable door slammed open.

They both jumped, shot out of flight in midair.

"Miss Rose!" Patrick's Irish brogue sounded sharp as a razor. "Where are you?"

Thorn rolled away from her, tugging his pants up while pulling her skirt down. She fumbled with the buttons on her dress.

"Miss Rose?" Patrick's boots stomped across the wooden floor.

"Don't!" Thorn and Rose exclaimed together, and the boots paused.

"What's going on in there?"

Patrick sounded mean enough to tangle with a cougar, but Thorn bobbed up, brushing the straw from his hair. "Nothing, sir."

Looking up at Thorn, Rose despaired. His shirt was in a tangle, his Levi's were buttoned wrong, his face was red and scared and frustrated. He looked just like what he was—a young cowboy who'd been interrupted during his roll in the hay.

Patrick's explosion proved it. "Ye worthless young half-wit, what have ye been doing with Miss Rose?"

Frantic, Rose added her protestation to Thorn's. "Nothing, Patrick."

"Nothing? Then how come ye're staying out of sight? Haven't got yerself buttoned up yet?"

She withered with embarrassment, trying harder to get her buttons closed.

Thorn said, "Don't you talk to her like that! She didn't do anything. I did it."

"I never doubted that for a moment. Ye're nothing but a hoodlum, a no-good half-pint thief and skirt-chaser who's been after Miss Rose like a stallion in rut."

"Oh, yeah?" Thorn stepped out of the stall. "My mama says you've got quite a story in your background, too, so who're you to judge me?"

Rose heard the crack, saw Thorn fly backward and hit the stable wall. She cried out as Patrick yelled, "Brat!"

He stomped out of the stable and she ran to Thorn. A bruise puffed his lip and blood trickled out of his mouth. He sat immobile, staring at the empty doorway.

"Let me get you a wet rag," she said.

But he pushed her away and stood.

She was unsure of his mood, but she knew she didn't like the savage fury that gathered on his features. "Thorn?"

"Brat?" he muttered. "Hoodlum? *Thief?*"

"He didn't mean it, Thorn. He's been like an uncle to me, and he—"

"Doesn't think I'm good enough for you. I know what he thinks. What everybody thinks." He wiped blood off his chin with the back of his hand, and his gaze fell on her father's best tooled leather saddle.

"Thorn?" She scrambled to her feet. "Don't do that."

He laughed, a harsh and reckless sound. "How do you know what I'm going to do? You think you know so much about me, but you didn't know I was a hoodlum, did you? A thief, just like he said."

"You don't steal things—especially not a saddle that's worth more than any horse in the stable."

He turned on her, grabbed her arms, and shook her. "I have. I've stolen corn out of the fields and pies off a windowsill."

"Thorn!" She was shocked. As shocked as if he'd confessed to cattle rustling. "Stealing is wrong!"

Perversely pleased, he said, "And one time I stole a book from the traveling teacher."

"Oh, Thorn." She covered her ears, not wanting to hear more. "How could you?"

"It's just so damn dull here, Rosie. So damned"—he went and lifted the saddle off the sawhorse—"dull."

"Please." She stepped toward him, palm extended. "Please, Thorn."

"That's what you said in there." He jerked his head toward the stall, and repeated, "'Please, Thorn. Please.' But that was before you knew I was a . . . a half-pint skirt-chaser." He weighed the saddle in his hand and looked at her with a crooked smile. "Someday you're going to be mine. No matter what I do or what I am, you're going to be mine, and proud of it."

"Don't take it."

He looked at the saddle as if he didn't know what it was, then at her. "Mine."

He hadn't meant the saddle, she knew, but he hadn't returned it, as she prayed, so she'd done what had to be done. She had turned him over to the sheriff, and testified at the trial that sent him to jail.

The fact that his mother had testified that she'd found the saddle in his room—that his own mother had helped send him to prison—meant nothing to Rose. Rose felt totally responsible for his incarceration, and she hadn't been able to look the woman in the eye since.

She'd done what was right, but at a cost that sometimes seemed too great. When she was alone at night, or when she saw her friends' children, or when she caught sight of a man who stood with a kind of insolence . . .

No, she wouldn't think about Thorn now. No strange horse stood in the empty stall. No strong male body waited to renew acquaintances in the hay.

Odd, that she'd let Thorn spook her so.

She turned to hang up the brushes, and jerked back from the broad male figure that blocked the entrance of the stall. The blood raced in her veins, and if she'd been the screaming type, she'd have let loose a loud one.

Then he spoke, and she felt only foolish.

"Miss Rose? Did I startle ye?"

"Patrick." She half laughed, half gasped. "Yes, you did! You should have made some noise."

"Same as normal, Miss Rose, but ye were muttering something about spooks and didn't hear me."

Rose blushed, glad of the darkness. But she didn't need light to see the bandy-legged son of Ireland who tended her ranch. She knew every line and angle of Patrick O'Brien, keeper of her horses, foreman of the ranch, gambler par excellence. As a man of fifty, he had left Ireland and everything he had there and taken a ship to Galveston. From there he'd found his way to the Corey Ranch, where he'd worked for the last twenty years.

Now, as Patrick pulled a lucifer from his shirt pocket and scraped it across the sandpaper, she said, "I sold Star Bright tonight."

The lucifer flared with fire, and its rotten-egg smell filled the air. Patrick stared at her, his sagging, hound-dog face astonished. When the match had burned down to his fingers, he gave a pithy oath, blew it out, and stomped it into the floor. "Ye sold me darlin' filly?"

"To Sonny for Sue Ellen." Lighting the lantern herself, Rose fixed him in the beam. "For four hundred and fifty dollars."

She gloated as Patrick staggered back, clasping his hands at his breast. "Four hundred and fifty dollars? From that skinflint?"

"There's one way around Sonny, and that's to tell him Royal Lewis bought a horse for his wife."

"But he didn't!" Realizing he might not know the whole story, Patrick asked, "Did he?"

"No, but when Ana Marie Lewis gets done with him, he will."

Patrick cackled. "Ye're a wicked one, ye are, and I've long tried to teach ye the way of such dealing." He cocked his head, his bright eyes gleaming. "But I thought ye'd said 'twas dishonest to tempt people by appealing to their envy."

Feeling abashed and uncomfortable, she confessed, "Well . . . actually, it was Sue Ellen who did it. I tried—I really did, but I couldn't think of a story to tell Sonny that would make him buy that horse."

"No, ye'll never get the way of it. Ye're too honest for yer own good, ye are." He grinned. "But I'll raise a glass to Sue Ellen when next I'm in Fort Davis."

"You do that, for now we can put up the stable before the first norther comes through," she said with satisfaction. "I'll order the lumber and call the neighbors, and we'll have a barn raising. Nobody can steal those horses once they're padlocked inside."

"Mother of God. That's the truth. I hadn't realized." Patrick scrubbed his fingers through his thick, gray hair and tugged the ends. The pain seemed to wake him, for he gave her a hug. "That'll be a relief, for sure, for sure. Think we'll be for doing it by Christmas?"

"I think we'll be doing it next week. Now that the train comes through, we can get the lumber right away."

Patrick nodded sagely. "Ye've been looking tired lately. Have ye been keeping vigil for this bastard—"

"Don't swear."

"—for this horse thief?"

"Just occasionally. Just at night when I can't sleep, anyway. You can't watch all the time, Patrick. I worry about you."

She *did* worry about him, more than she could say. When her father had been alive, Patrick had had to keep his drinking and gambling under control. Now he staggered more often than she liked to see, and came back from Fort Davis all sad and bedraggled. The burden of watching for horse thieves and doing a good portion of the work had aged Patrick. Yet regardless of his faults, she couldn't forget his loyalty. When her parents died, he'd put his whole faith in her, refusing to seek greener pastures. In staying, he took the biggest gamble of his life—that her success would provide for his livelihood.

No one had been prouder or more astonished when she'd sold her first four-year-olds, just last spring, for two hundred fifty dollars apiece. Now, with Sonny's disdain for Patrick still pealing in her mind, she added, "You taught me to ride, you taught me to love horses, and you've given me the benefit of all your experience in fine Irish stables. I don't say it often enough, but you're my dearest friend in the world. You know that."

She guessed he was embarrassed by her affection,

for he ducked his head and shuffled through the straw toward the exit. "Did ye count the horses outside?"

She accepted his change of subject. "They're all here."

"They were all here when I went to bed, too. Maybe I scared that bas—that horse thief away last week when I chased after him. Maybe I wounded him when I shot."

Closing Goliath into his stall and taking the lantern, she kept her voice even. "I hope he dies of lead poisoning."

"Lost eleven good horses to that"—he paused significantly—"horse thief, and he's not satisfied yet. I've started sleeping in the hayloft, Miss Rose, to keep an eye on the stable."

"But he hasn't stolen from the stable," she said automatically.

"The best horses are in the stable." Patrick jerked his thumb toward Goliath and Star Bright. "And a clever thief can pick any lock. He'll come around, I wager, but I'll be after him straight off. Ye can count on it."

"Don't chase him," Rose said, feeling cold with the threat to her prizes. "Shoot him where he stands."

"Miss Rose!" Patrick protested, sounding sincerely shocked. "A lady should never think such violent thoughts."

"This lady—" She broke off, struck by the vision of Thorn falling, shot, dripping blood, dying.

A shudder rattled her, and Patrick said, "See? Ye don't mean it."

Straightening her shoulders, she said, "But I do. Better to shoot a horse thief than to hang him."

Now Patrick shuddered. "Hanging's a cruel way to die, Miss Rose."

"Yes." They stepped outside and strolled to the corral,

and Patrick draped himself over the rail while she stood erect and unsupported. Unable to help herself, she again counted the horses, then gave in to her appalling curiosity. "What did this horse thief look like, when you saw him?"

Watching the horses with a keen eye, Patrick ignored her query at first. "I think Lady Hypatia ought to be bred to Goliath next. With their lines, the foal will be a handsome thing." Then he rolled a cigarette, licked the paper, and lit it with another lucifer. "Couldn't tell what that . . . villain looked like. He was on horseback, fleeing from me."

Fidgeting with the five-foot length of thin hair rope hanging on the post, she demanded, "Short or tall? Thin or fat?"

"Tall, with broad shoulders. A cowboy, probably, by the way he sat the saddle."

"A good horseman?"

"Born in the saddle. He wore a dark hat and he smiled at me, like he was taunting me." Patrick warmed to his subject, and lowered his voice dramatically. "Even in the dark, I could see the flash of his teeth."

It was a description that fit a hundred men in Presidio County.

And a description that fit Thorn.

She had to warn Patrick. She didn't want to, for Patrick knew a good sight too much about her and Thorn and their early, silly passion, but it wouldn't be fair if she didn't. Abruptly, she said, "Thorn is back."

Patrick almost swallowed his cigarette. "The Maxwell boy? Here?"

"He was at the dance tonight." Lowering her gaze, she watched her hands as they formed a noose in the end of the rope. "I wondered if he was our horse thief."

"No, I'd heard rumors he—" Patrick stopped. "How long has he been back?"

"He wouldn't tell me. He sidestepped the question."

"I'm surprised he hasn't visited ye here yet."

Rose glanced at the house, and thrust the rope into her capacious apron pocket.

"Ye did send him to prison, Miss Rose, and him thinking ye were so sweet on him ye'd let him take what he wished. And he does have a history of thieving." Patrick puffed until the cigarette tip glowed, then blew a lungful of smoke across the corral. "Stealing the horses, heh?" He nodded. "Ye might have a point, Miss Rose. Ye might have a point."

Rose bade Patrick good-night and, feet dragging, made her way to the house. It didn't welcome her as the stable had. It hadn't been more than a place to stay since her parents died—a spinster's home, a barren place.

But tonight it seemed different, almost as if a fresh breeze had blown through and wiped the musty air away. She lifted the lantern and glanced around, trying to put her finger on the difference, but nothing was out of place. Nothing, except . . . the hair lifted on the back of her head.

Her bedroom door. Her inner sanctum. The place where she dreamed a girl's dreams and wept a woman's tears. She never closed it, yet now it was shut tight. Moving toward it, she clasped the doorknob in her hand and felt the vibration, the presence of a foreign being.

She almost backed away, but nothing could make a coward of Rose Laura Corey. Prepared to fight, she flung open the door.

FOUR~

The door bounced against the wall, rousing the figure that rested on her bed.

"Rosie, darlin', you don't have to be so rambunctious," Thorn rebuked her, pushing his dark hat back off his eyes. "I would have woken up for you regardless."

Rose stared at him, grim, frustrated, and trembling. "What are you doing here?"

His long figure covered the bed from headboard to footboard. His broad shoulders obliterated the pillow. "Why, Rose, you're whispering again. You got a cold or a sore throat?"

"Patrick is out there, and I don't want him to know you're in my bedroom."

"Ah, you've still got Patrick, do you?" His face twisted in distress. "Is he still as nosy as ever?"

"Yes. So just"—she pointed toward the window—"get out."

He pouted. "You sure are unfriendly considering the favor I just did you."

"Favor?" Remembering the dance and the gossip that would result, her voice rose, but he lifted his finger to his lips. Dropping her voice again, she repeated, "Favor? What favor?"

"I rode all the way here just to protect you."

"You followed right behind me?"

"No, I stayed back a ways. Didn't think you'd want me intruding on your fun."

"What fun?" she demanded.

"Riding so wild and fierce, like a goddess in some pagan tale." Lifting his head from the pillow, he tossed his Stetson aside and ruffled his dark hair. "You really need a breastplate and a Viking helmet with horns. That'd scare the wolves off your track."

She recalled her own heady excitement. The knowledge that she'd been observed left her feeling raw and exposed. "I have no doubt it would take something more substantial than a breastplate and horns to dislodge the largest wolf."

"You mean me?" His wide eyes and tangled hair might have looked innocent and boyish on another man. But on the hard-bitten, rough Thorn, they signified only danger. "Why, I'm not a wolf. I'm a gentleman. I couldn't let a lady such as yourself come so many miles alone. There are ruffians and thieves out there. Desperate men who would seek to strip you of your dearest possession."

In her mind, Goliath reared up, slashing his hooves as he fought to avoid capture. "And what is that?"

He blinked in feigned astonishment. "Why, your virtue, of course. You *do* still have your virtue?"

She wanted desperately to give a scathing retort, but before she could articulate a word, he nodded. "But you *do* still have your virtue. That's obvious to every man who danced with you tonight."

"But you—" She stopped.

"Yes. I was the only man who danced with you tonight." Propping one pointed boot on the other, he studied the pattern stitched into the leather. "But then, you were the only woman I danced with."

"No!" she cried. "You didn't."

"Didn't what?"

"You didn't make me the talk of the county by ignoring every other woman—"

"I wouldn't say I *ignored* them."

"—practically undressing me on the dance floor—"

"Your clothes were restrictive."

"—then leaving as soon as I left."

He turned a sad, lovelorn expression to her. "Did you think I could dance with anyone else after I danced with you—the most beautiful woman there? Why, compared to you, those other women could charge to haunt a house."

With a muffled groan, she flounced away, and her train swept the floor with satisfying elegance. Perhaps the dress was old, but it made her feel stylish and womanly—and that ignited her temper. Why should she feel any different, just because Thorn was watching her?

"You seem mighty put out, Rosie, and I would think you'd be ecstatic. Didn't you just sell a horse called Star Bright to Sonny Pogue for a vastly inflated price?"

The man could ruffle her feathers without even half trying. "That horse is worth every cent. She's a combination of the best Irish racing horses and the toughest wild Texas horses, and she'll make Sue Ellen a superb mount."

"Sure thought it was funny when I heard you were breeding mounts for ladies. When I knew you, you were interested in only the bravest, fastest horses to be had. What happened?"

She smiled a crooked smile. "Life happened. I was breeding the bravest, fastest horses and trying to sell them to the cattle ranchers, and the ranchers were patting me on the head and telling me that a pretty little thing like myself shouldn't be trying to breed a *man's* horse. Only men could breed a man's horse. So I got mad, and then I got even."

"What did you do?"

She was talking too much. She knew it. But he acted so interested and seemed so caught up in her tale. Perhaps she was only starved for attention, but she couldn't resist boasting. "If only a man can breed a man's horse, then only a lady can breed a lady's."

"Ah." He followed her mind with the expertise of a detective. "So you took the horses you were raising for the ranchers and broke them for the ladies."

"Not at all. I took the horses I was raising for the ranchers and broke them just the same as I would have for the men." She tilted her nose up into the air. "The ladies in Texas ride just as well as the gentlemen."

"Then . . . I don't understand. What's the difference?"

"I *told* all those patronizing ranchers I was breaking them for the ladies."

She chuckled as the confusion slowly cleared from his face, and he wiped the back of his hand across his forehead. "God, there isn't a man in Texas who can match wits with you."

"Thank you, kind sir." She bobbed him a curtsy.

"There's a lot of money in Texas right now. There's a train that runs clear across it. And when Miss Rose Laura Corey gets done, no lady of high station will be without a horse from the Corey Ranch."

He eyed her with respect. "You're creating a bunch of snobs."

"No. They're already snobs. I'm just selling them horses that tell the rest of the world they're superior."

"Superior?"

"At least rich."

He laughed as if he found pleasure in her acumen, laughed as loud and as long as he had at the party.

"Hush," she scolded. "You hush up. Patrick will hear."

"What do you care? If Patrick hears, he'll know you've got an uninvited guest and come and rescue you. Isn't that what you want?" She glared at him, and he watched her with more than normal curiosity. "If your venture is a success, why do you seem so worn out and angry? You got a problem you want to tell me about?"

Instantly cautious, she asked, "What do you mean?"

"Seems like with your horse-selling business making money, you'd be a little more kindly to your old friend, Thorn Maxwell." He smiled and patted the bed beside him. "Why don't you sit down and talk to me? Maybe I can help with your problem."

"Everyone has problems," she said shortly. But she was tempted. So tempted.

"There are a lot of rich and not-so-rich bastards in this county who'd stoop pretty low to get their hands on your land. Might even sabotage your operation." He rubbed the quilt as if it were her thigh. "Might even steal your horses."

Horrified, she wondered if this were proof that everyone in Presidio County knew her troubles . . . or proof that Thorn was the culprit. "What makes you say that?"

"Come and talk to me."

"I think I've talked enough." She paced toward the door, then back. "How did you—"

"Get in?" He pointed at the window, which was open to the breeze that blew her lace curtains. "I just pushed it up. You never locked it."

"No. That's not what I wanted to ask. How did you get here so quickly?"

"I was ahead of you, darlin'"—he flashed her a smile—"all the way."

She knew what he meant. She heard the significance beneath the words. But nothing could induce her to acknowledge it. She stalked to her dresser and placed the lantern beside her neatly arranged brush and comb. Using a thin stick, she transferred the flame to the glass kerosene lamp and looked in the mirror. Her appearance appalled her. Sue Ellen's ribbon had disappeared in the ride, and her hair had snarled around her shoulders. The wind had turned her cheeks pink, and her brown eyes looked at least as wide as any heifer's, and twice as confused.

"Where's your horse?" she finally asked.

"I tethered it on the other side of the house. I didn't want him . . . disturbing you when you rode in."

"You mean you didn't want me to know you were here."

"I suppose some suspicious people could interpret it that way," he admitted.

"No one could move faster than Goliath."

"My horse is a good one, just like yours." He relaxed back on the bed and closed his eyes. "Good lineage, well broken, comes straight from an Irish stable."

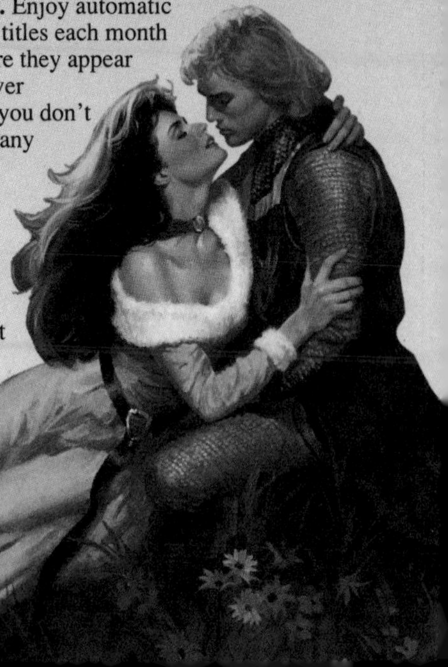

She flinched, and although he shouldn't have been able to see it, he came up as if her wedding-ring quilt had bugs. "Why, darlin'," he crooned. "What's the problem? You act like I stole that horse."

Lifting the brush, she applied it to the tangles. "Did you?"

His fingers closed on her bare shoulders, and she jumped and dropped the brush.

"You're strung tight as a bowstring." His breath caressed her neck as he spoke. "Why don't you lie down on the bed and relax?"

"That's it!" Her elbow connected with his solar plexus before he could react, and she heard a satisfying gasp. His hands dropped away, but she caught him before he could stumble backward. In one efficient move, she brought the noose out of her pocket, looped it around his wrist, and tightened it. His other hand came up to tug at the cord, and she wrapped the rope over it with the expertise of a cowhand—which she had been in her day.

Like a fractious calf, he jerked back, and she used the motion to set the knot.

"Damn, woman!" But while his astonishment was genuine, his eyes twinkled with tiny blue sparks, and that made her madder. Hooking her heel around his knee, she knocked him off balance. He stumbled backward, but without his hands to break his fall he hit the puncheon floor. Before he could react, she wrapped the length around one booted ankle. She jumped away from his free foot and reflected that her performance would rate well in a rodeo.

With one foot connected to his tied hands, he couldn't stand with ease, nor do more than roll and sit. But he tried. Oh, yes, he tried. When he'd proved the strength of her knots, he complained, "You have me trussed up like a Sunday roast at a potluck dinner."

Keeping one cautious eye on him, she knotted the end of the rope to the foot of her brass bed frame.

"Darlin', if you wanted me at your bedside this bad, you should have just whistled. I'd have come."

"Humph." The man should have looked like a disobedient mongrel. Instead he looked like a bright, chipper, well-groomed purebred.

It had been too easy.

She should never have been able to hog-tie Thorn Maxwell.

It had been too, too easy.

"What are you going to do with me now?" he asked.

What *was* she going to do with him? It had been a stupid, if undeniable, impulse. "I'm going to"—she groped for inspiration—"call the sheriff first thing in the morning and have you hauled off."

"To jail?" He lifted one quizzical eyebrow. "*Again?*"

"Again."

"I won't be there long. Coming into your house by the window is hardly the equal of stealing your daddy's best tooled-leather saddle."

"No," she admitted.

"But it's a damned sight more interesting." He chuckled and shook his head. "What kind of rumor do you suppose that will start, when the sheriff finds me tied to your bed?"

"I'm not interested in rumors." But she was, especially in this one, and he knew it.

"I've been dreaming about seeing you in your nightgown, Rose." Never taking his gaze off her, he rolled into sitting position and braced his back against the post. "I guess this is my chance."

"Your dreams are no concern of mine." She eyed the knot holding his wrists together. It looked firm. The knot around his leg was stupid—he might be able to get out of it by taking off his boot. She wished she had another length of rope or the nerve to hit him on the head and knock him unconscious.

"Why are you staring at me like I'm a bull you're about to make a steer?"

He asked, but clearly he knew. She wanted to tie him in knots so he couldn't escape—and in fact, the thought had its appeal for more than one reason.

"These ropes are unnecessary. You know I'd never hurt you."

"No, you wouldn't." She agreed without even thinking about it, and didn't notice the complacency that creased the corners of his mouth. "Not physically. But maybe . . ."

"Maybe?"

"Maybe you'd do something worse."

She was thinking of horse stealing.

He was not. "What I want to do to you isn't worse. It'll be the best time you ever had."

No matter what she said or did, he came right back to the same thing. The way he talked, it was the only thing on his mind—just as it was the only thing on hers. "You are the most frustrating man."

"And you are the most frustrated woman," he teased. "But I can cure that. Come here."

"I must appear to be a fool."

He looked her over carefully before he answered. "No, ma'am. You look like the sweetest woman this side of the Pecos."

She couldn't help it. She laughed as she thought of the back-stepping caution she and her ambitions generated among the ranchers. "You're the first man to see *that*."

Drawing out the words as if he savored them, he said, "That's because you're only sweet on me." He crooked a finger. "Come here."

"No."

"I need you to roll me a cigarette."

"You don't smoke."

"You're one observant lady." He shrugged his shoulders. "I have an itch in the middle of my back."

"Scratch it on the bed."

"Heartless ladies have no fun." He hung his head. "I may as well tell you the truth. You tied my hands too tight."

He wiggled his fingers, and she almost groaned. Was it possible for a man to lose his hands from lack of circulation? No, surely not. She hardened her heart. "I'm sure you've experienced worse."

"They're getting cold."

Although it was hard to see by the light of the single lamp, his fingertips did look white.

"If I promise not to touch you in any undignified way, would you come here?"

Against her better judgment, she moved closer and knelt down. "I can't loosen the knots."

"Of course you can't." He smiled. Not his smirky, superior smile, but as kind a smile as she'd ever seen. "But you can kiss 'em better."

She tried to jump back, but his bound hands caught her with more strength than she could have imagined.

"Just a kiss," he coaxed. "I want to show you something."

"And I know what it is," she muttered, trying to

twist free—from him, and from the impact of his body so close to hers.

"Why, Rose. Your mind has truly sunk to the depths."

He sounded as if he were marveling, but at what? At her crudeness? Or at the attraction that flared with the power of their vanished adolescence, and with the hunger of long denial?

She didn't want to look into his eyes. She knew she shouldn't, for if she did . . .

Blue sparks, *his* sparks, lit the fire in her. The same conflagration he'd created eight years ago, and nothing had ever extinguished it. Somehow, he looped his arms over her head to pull her close, and she sprawled across him in wicked abandon. "Thorn." She whispered his name, but she could have been shouting, for it betrayed her loneliness—and lust. Bawdy, heart-thumping, wicked, delightful lust.

She clasped the hair at the nape of his neck with both her hands, holding a willing man captive as she tried to remember all the ways they'd kissed once upon a time.

She remembered. He remembered. And they discovered a few new ways for lips and tongues to meet and mate.

She'd never kissed a man with a mustache before—as a youth he'd been clean-shaven, not prickly and tickly. She'd never kissed a starving man before—as a youth he'd been intent on seduction, not honest about his need.

"Rose," he groaned. "Closer. God, Rose, harder."

An imp, one she thought long slain by suffering, raised its mischievous head. "Pull your hair," she murmured, "harder?"

He grinned at her, his mouth still wet, his lips softened with pleasure. "You are a sly and scarlet woman. I do love a scarlet woman." He slid lower and arranged her on him, so she lay on him chest to chest, stomach to stomach. Then, raising his free leg between both of hers, he pushed her against his thigh so she rode him like a stallion. "Harder—like that."

The pressure melted her bloomers and layers of petticoats, sending such a surge of sensation through her that she bucked to escape—or get closer. He chuckled and groaned, seeming to luxuriate in her enjoyment as much as his own. "When you make those little whimpering noises, you make me want to bust my buttons." Then he gave her no time to worry about which buttons, but kissed her until she ran out of breath.

She drew back to gasp, to learn something new, to give some more pleasure, but he wouldn't suffer her to move away. He came after her, and his mouth found the skin of her shoulders.

Closing her eyes, she braced herself for the memories that would sweep her.

But they didn't come. This was too immediate, and so much more delightful than before.

His head dipped, and he followed the lace across her bosom to its lowest point. With his chin he nudged at the material, but her rigid corset thwarted him, and he whispered, "Dammit, take that instrument of torture off."

"Don't swear," she rebuked automatically as she reached for her buttons—and rapped her hand against rigid whalebone and stiff satin. The corset, she realized, was more than an undergarment. It was a call to sanity and decency.

He realized it, too, and glared into her face. "Don't think. Stop thinking! Don't remember the facts—

remember only the sensations, the glory. There's no other two people in the world like us. Don't"—his arms tightened—"think."

Filled with despair, she just looked at him, wishing she could do as he demanded.

"Too late," he whispered. "That brain of yours is working."

He took a deep breath, a breath he seemed to need. He, too, had been willing to deprive himself of air for their kiss. But no sense of decency could cure disappointment and desire, and he knew it.

A grin, crooked but satisfied, slashed his face. He whispered still, as if this matter was for the two of them only. As if it were too intimate to confide even to the breeze. "If you must think, think of this. My hands are tied. I'm almost helpless. But you're helpless, too. Even when you could have run, you stayed to kiss me, not because you wanted to, but because you had to. I had to come back here, Rose. Sooner or later you knew I would. I had to fulfill that promise."

She pushed his arms over her head and wiggled away, and he lowered his knee and let her go without any attempt to keep her. It was as if he knew he held a lasso looped around her or a corral built to keep her close.

"Remember," he urged. "Remember. Someday I'm going to make you mine."

A chill ran up her back. The words were the same. The tone was the same. But the audacious boy had grown to a man, with a man's determination and a man's confidence.

And her doubts were no match for his arrogance.

"I'm going to lay down now," she said.

He covered his eyes with his clumsily arranged

fingers, then peeked as he said, "I won't watch as you undress. I promise."

"Listening to your promises is about as useful as spitting into the wind. I'll rest just like this." She moved away from him in much the same manner as she would move away from a threatening rattler. "I'm a light sleeper—I've had to be." That much was the truth, she comforted herself. Anything woke her these days, for anything might be a threat to her horses. "So don't try to escape."

"You still don't understand," he said. "I'm never going to escape from you."

No. She'd never sleep now.

But for some reason—a false sense of security?—she did sleep, and when the discomfort of her corset woke her two hours later, he was gone.

So were two of her horses.

FIVE~

Goliath and Star Bright. Gone into the night.

Rose stared numbly at the empty stalls. They were gone, Thorn was gone, and Patrick—

"Patrick. Patrick!" She clawed her way up the ladder to the loft where he said he'd been sleeping. Scattered throughout the hay, his belongings testified that he had been there, but now he, too, was gone.

Like the horses. Like Thorn.

But she didn't have the time or the inclination to mourn. She ran across the yard to the house and into her bedroom. Stepping over the rope, which was laid flat on the floor without a knot in it, she put on her oldest, most serviceable riding habit. In her bag, she packed some day-old bread, the barbeque Sue Ellen had insisted she take, and a cup for dipping water out of the water holes. Finally, from her father's rifle cabinet, she removed two Colt six-shooters with the belt holster that held them, and a Winchester .44 carbine.

Shorter than a rifle, the carbine was easier for her to handle—and she did know how to handle it. She knew how to handle all firearms. Not too long ago, the territory had been Indian country, and every man, woman, and child west of the Pecos knew how to shoot.

But she'd never had to kill a man before. As she loaded the holster belt with cartridges and strapped it on, she realized she'd never been angry enough to kill a man before.

Now she was.

Back in the stable, she selected Rooster, a six-year-old sorrel with stamina, patience, speed, and a unflappable nature. All qualities she needed, both for tracking and in case the . . . the criminal tried to ambush her.

In the light of the moon, the hoof marks shone like beacons leading away from the stable. It surprised Rose that the thief had left so clear a trail through the grass—he never had before. What did it signify? Had he been in a hurry? Or was he planning an ambush?

No matter. Her daddy had taught her some tricks he'd learned from his stint with the Texas Rangers. Tricks the Comanches used. No man would get the drop on her.

The trail led north, deeper into the mountains, and it soon became clear that, once away from the ranch compound, the bandit felt the need for caution. He made numerous attempts to disguise the trail—riding down creek beds that trickled with water from the fall rains, cutting across ash flow tuffs where hoof marks scarcely showed. Rose had to stop frequently and scour the ground for clues.

The night added a surreal sense to her mission, cloaking her in darkness, yet also cloaking anyone who might threaten her. She moved stealthily from shadow to shadow, from ponderosa pine to gray oak, avoiding the open places where the moon betrayed all movement. About two hours before dawn, she was rewarded by the sound of two horses moving toward her. Leaving Rooster on the flat, she took her firearms and scrambled up the shadowed side of the canyon. Just in time, she crouched behind a boulder that had tumbled free of the palisade cliff. She quivered with strain: her eyes, her muscles, her nerves anticipated action. Yet her stomach churned like a rock in a stream.

Then, as casually as if he were riding down a Dallas street, Thorn came around the bend. He was leading Star Bright on a tether and whistling under his breath, and his offhand manner replaced Rose's apprehension with a spitting rage. Cocking the lever to feed a cartridge into the breech, she rose, fit her carbine into her shoulder, and stepped out from behind the rock, taking aim with the care of a sharpshooter.

"Don't!" Thorn's command echoed back and forth across the columnar walls, and he brought his horse up short. On the leading rein, Star Bright wasn't so cooperative, and Thorn struggled with her for a moment. When he had control, he looked up at the place where she stood in the shadows and begged, "Darlin' Rose, don't shoot me."

That voice. That whiskey-smooth, coaxing voice. How many times had she done as he asked? How many times had she been sorry?

Jolted from her first, burning rage, she hesitated an instant too long and felt the rush of blinding fury fade. "You dirty thief. How did you know it was me?"

"I've been watching for you—although I didn't expect you quite so soon." He pushed back his hat so she could see his face, and grinned so wickedly her trigger finger itched. "I'll have to see what I can do about helping you sleep."

Same song, different verse. Did the man think of nothing else? "You're mighty bold for a man who's about to have lead fired into his heart."

"Are you as good a shot as you ever were?" he asked.

"Better." It wasn't a boast. It was the truth.

"Then you'd better do it now, before you lose your nerve. Here"—he brought his horse around, presenting his broad chest—"this is a better target."

She sighted down the barrel, held her breath, settled her finger on the trigger, tried, tried to squeeze it—and couldn't.

In as gentle a tone as she'd ever heard from him, he asked, "Darlin', would you believe me if I told you I didn't steal your horses?"

"When I've caught you red-handed?" With her trigger hand, she wiped at the film that fogged her vision. "Hardly."

He muttered, "I was afraid you wouldn't."

Steadying the carbine, she tried again, remembering all her daddy's strictures, bracing herself for the recoil.

The recoil that wouldn't come, because she couldn't get herself to pull the trigger.

Thorn shook his head, and compassion colored his tone. "Rose, there was only one moment you could have killed me, and that was when you stepped out from behind that rock, all mad and righteous. You can't do it now, woman. Put the carbine away."

"I'll do as I like," she retorted, as petulant as a child.

"Put it away."

His voice lashed her with authority, and before she could think, she'd lowered the carbine.

"That's better." His patronizing approval almost brought the gun back up again, but he continued, "You'd feel damn remorseful when you killed me and the thieving didn't stop."

"Not much chance of that." She gestured to the horse. "What are you doing with Star Bright?"

"I stole her back for you."

She laughed and heard the resentful, hysterical edge in her merriment. "Then where's Goliath?"

He pointed north. "About five miles ahead in a junction of two canyons. The thief built a corral, and there's four other horses in it. They're all yours. They all have your brand on their flanks."

"And how did you just happen to find them like that?"

"I followed the thief when I heard him take the horses from the stable. I would have caught him, too, but I was . . . er . . . all tied up." He grinned. "Once I got those knots untied—you're damn good with a rope—he was too far ahead for me to do more than track him, and when I found the corral, no one was there except the horses."

"So you just whisked in and stole Star Bright."

"Yeah, but even that was pushing my luck. Now, you want to tell me what's happening? I'd help you if you'd ask me."

"Help me? Help yourself, more likely. What's the matter with you?" Indignant and upset, she started down the slope, slipping on the loose dirt and gravel. "Stealing my horses. That's a mean-spirited revenge, not at all like the Thorn I used to know."

"Lower the hammer on your carbine," he warned, sliding out of the saddle.

"And taking Star Bright the night I sold her. That's just plain ugly, depriving me of that income. I need that money. You want me to starve?"

Thorn met her before she reached the flat. "Put the safety on your carbine before you discharge it accidentally."

Leaning down, he tried to do it for her, but she jerked it away. "I'll do it!" She clicked the safety. "Are you afraid I'll shoot you accidentally, like I couldn't on purpose?"

"No, I'm afraid you'll shoot yourself, and I haven't waited eight years for you for nothing."

He didn't sound sweet or cajoling or wicked or kind then. He sounded stern and concerned, like father and lover in one, and her indignation tasted twice as bitter at his false devotion. Poking her carbine barrel in his chest, she asked, "What are you going to do when you run out of my horses? You going to go steal someone else's? You going to keep at it until someone sees you who isn't afraid to shoot you?" She poked at him again, and he stumbled backward down the slippery slope. "Or until someone recognizes you and you get strung up by the neck? You know how long it takes a man to die by hanging?"

"Longer than the victim likes."

"Patrick's told me. He saw it done in Ireland. About forty-five minutes to die. If you're lucky, somebody'll come along and jerk on your feet and break your neck. It shortens the agony." The image of a struggling, gasping Thorn swinging from a tree flashed before her eyes, and she poked him again. "Is that what you want?"

"Let me show you what I want." Grabbing the carbine by the barrel, he jerked it out of her hands. He broke open the barrel, levered the cartridges into his hand, and shoved them into his pocket. Then he turned the carbine sideways and tossed it back into her arms. Before the weight of it could make her stagger, he grabbed her and jerked her forward. The whiplash flung her head back, and that seemed to suit him just fine, for he used the opportunity to press a kiss on her.

She kicked at him, but the high tops of his boots eased the blow while he attempted, by the coaxing of his lips, to ease her ire.

He let her take a breath, and she snarled, "You have just proved that there are more horses' rumps here than there are horses."

"And you have just proved that you haven't been kissed enough," he snapped back.

He kissed her again, massaging her back while feeding her delight through her mouth. The taste of pleasure made her stagger, but nothing could halt her declaration when he again lifted his head. "You're nothing but a suck-egg mule."

"And you're just stubborn enough to be my mate."

This time the embrace contained enough mutual invitation to bring her ire down from its all-time high. As her knees and elbows went limp, the carbine slid slowly toward the ground, eased by the press of their bodies.

He caught it at the last moment, too much the Texan to allow a Winchester to hit the dirt. Weighing it in his hand, he asked, "You're not going to kill me, are you, darlin'?"

Watching him between slitted eyelids, she thought, and thought hard. She had a choice. She could kill him—or could turn him over to the law. She'd done it before. It had broken her heart, but her mama had taught her right from wrong, and stealing her daddy's hand-tooled leather saddle had been wrong.

She'd warned Thorn not to do it. She'd warned him that she would turn him in, but he'd thought her so infatuated she wouldn't, and he'd reacted to the admonition as if it were a dare.

A dare that had cost him dearly.

But it seemed he'd learned nothing from his stay in prison. Only how to steal bigger and better things. And everyone—both the law and the vigilantes—hanged horse thieves, without remorse or a second thought.

So it was up to her to convince this varmint to follow the high road. He could do it. He had a mama on a ranch not far from here, a lovely woman of high morals and a credit to the community. He had two brothers and three sisters, and every one law-abiding citizens. So Thorn could be, too.

By God, Thorn would be, too.

"There's nothing lower than a horse thief," she finally said.

"No, ma'am."

"Unless it's a dead horse thief, six foot under."

"Yes, ma'am."

"So you are going to promise me"—reaching up, she grabbed his ear and twisted, bringing him to his knees as successfully as their old schoolmarm—"that you'll stop stealing horses."

"Rosie," he gasped. "For God's sake, Rosie, let go!"

She twisted a little harder. "When you promise."

He could have grabbed her wrist and squeezed it hard enough to make her release him. Instead he whimpered like a helpless calf, which he ill resembled. "Ow ow ow! What makes you think I'll keep the promise?"

"I don't think anything." Releasing him, she took a handful of hair on his forehead and lifted his face to hers. "I only know that I will kill you if you betray me again."

Looking up at her, he seemed to see things in her face. Things no one else ever saw. Things like—she'd wanted him all her life. Things like—she'd never lied or stolen or cursed, saving herself for this one big sin. The sin of loving Thorn without benefit of wedlock.

"Rose?" He wrapped his arms around her knees. "Rose?" His broad hands burned a path up her thighs, pressing the heavy, gray material of the riding skirt into her flesh.

And she received the weight of his hands, the heat of his demand with avid greed. Somewhere in the dark and the chill of a Texas night, her resolution had hardened. She would kill him if he stole again—as she would take her pleasure of him tonight. Sinking to her knees, she pressed her lips to his urgently, half-afraid that the need to pillage would overtake him before he taught her the meaning of pleasure.

He opened his lips to her search, but when she tried to press him down, he refused. "Not here. Not now." He looked around at the rock-strewn landscape. "You deserve better than this."

"This is Texas. There's nothing better than this."

He chuckled. "I want to treat you like porcelain, like a delicate southern lady, and you always remind me that you're as solid and as lasting as good Texas stone. At least"—he stood and swung her up in his arms—"let me remove you from the dirt." Still holding her, he kissed her until her whole body clenched and his shirt was wadded in her fists. Laying her across the top of the waist-high boulder that had previously hidden her from his sight, he said, "Let me take off your clothes. Let me do everything for you."

"No." Proudly, she pushed him away and sat up. Beneath her fingers, her buttons sprang apart, revealing only her chemise beneath her jacket. She was a working woman and wore her corset only for social occasions, but he seemed jolted. He seemed shocked. He also seemed unable to tear his gaze away from the flesh she revealed as she shrugged out of her jacket and unlaced her chemise.

"Oh, honey."

She didn't know if he was calling her a sweet name, or making a sweet compliment. She only knew that his callused fingers reached out to touch her breasts with a little reverence and a lot of experience. Bracing herself against the stone, she flung her head back, accepting the homage as her due, and reveling in his wonder.

Yet he had his revenge when he put his mouth to her nipples and suckled. She stiffened, then in a low voice that she scarcely recognized, she murmured, "You do that mighty well for a big, fat liar."

"Rosie?"

"Hm?"

"I'm not fat."

His mouth slid lower. He cupped the weight of her breast in his hand, tasting her in open appetite, and she lay back. Cool rock supported her. Warm hands roamed over her. The stars spun overhead and the moon bowed off the sky stage as the first sunrays hinted at dawn.

When Thorn stepped back, she cradled her head in her arm and looked at him. He still stood beside the boulder, scrutinizing her as if she were a pecan pie and he a starving man. But he was still fully dressed. "I bet," she mused, "you are one fine-looking man without those clothes on. And I bet if you took them off nice and slow and pretty, I'd give you a reward."

"Yes, ma'am!"

She could see his eyes shining as he nearly tore the buttons off his shirt, and she reprimanded him. "Slow. Nice and slow."

He ripped his shirttails out of his denim pants. "Or what?"

"Or I won't. . . ." Her riding boot clattered to the ground, and she reached one leg out to rub her foot on his crotch.

Did she say slow? The sun brightened the sky faster than the man removed his clothes. She watched as he tugged off his boots, as he unbuttoned each riveted button from his jeans, revealing a stomach well rippled by muscles and a skin shadowed by coarse hair. "If my horse venture fails," she mused, "I think I'll go into Fort Davis and open a saloon for ladies."

He peeled off those skintight jeans and proved he always carried his pistol. "That's stupid," he said. "Ladies don't frequent saloons."

"They would if I hire you to strip for them."

He glanced toward the east where predawn revealed him. "Rosie, you're embarrassing me."

"Is that what that is?" She leaned out and trailed one finger down his stomach, down as far as she dared. "You must be mighty embarrassed."

Beneath the finger, she felt a rush of heat. Was he blushing? Or was he just . . . hot?

He lifted her hand away from him and pressed it to his lips. "Promise me you're not like this with anyone else."

It stopped her, that he would be thinking such a thing. "I've never been with anybody, not even with you. You stole that saddle before—"

"That's not what I meant. I just meant . . . you're so prim and solemn, and you don't cuss or drink secretly or indulge in gossip. But when you ride your horses, you get that barbaric look about you, and men like to speculate. Are you ice all the way down? Or are you fire beneath?" He scraped his feet in the dirt, and watched them as if they were entities separate from himself. "You're fire and joy, and I want all that fire and all that joy for myself."

Touched by his avowal, she sighed. "Thorn . . ."

Prosaically, he added, "You've got a bawdy sense of humor, woman, and I'd be irked if you used it with anyone else."

She sighed again, but for a different reason. He was embarrassed by the very emotions that she delighted in. She tried to think of a way to respond to his confession, but he was a man with his feet firmly planted on the ground—literally—and if the words meant love to her . . . well . . . the act meant love to him.

So she would perform the act, and he would understand. If anything could bind the wild man that he was, it was love. Physical love.

Unfastening her holster, she said, "I don't think I'll need these."

"No, ma'am." He took the belt, stuffed with ammunition and cradling her two Colt six-shooters, and reverently laid it aside. "I'm not taking anything you don't give me."

As she loosened her riding skirt, she assured him, "Sue Ellen and I talk bawdy, but then, she'll be my first customer in the saloon."

"Great," he muttered as he helped her rid herself of both the skirt and her remaining boot. "I've escaped the bullets all these years so Sonny Pogue can shoot me." Stepping back, he looked her over as carefully as she'd done for him.

She didn't mind, even though the light grew stronger with every moment. She'd been waiting for this for eight years.

Hoarse with passion, he said, "If you'll let me peek up your skirt whenever I want, Miss Rose, I'd be honored to dance in your saloon."

Scooting down the curved rock face until her head was level with his, she wrapped her arms around his shoulders. Her feet would have dangled, but with bent knees she braced them on the rock. Her weight rested on her rear, but as she leaned forward, more and more of her body met Thorn's. More and more of her body warmed and tingled, and when he stepped between her legs, the whole of her, from head to toe, flushed red with heat.

It was, she decided, a most glorious embarrassment.

Adolescent passion. Mature longing. They mixed and melded when his lips touched hers. He wanted . . . she wanted instant gratification, a crazed rush toward climax. Yet . . . they'd waited so long. They'd imagined so much. Now they had the reality, and they savored each other. Cherished each other. Cherished until she trembled with need, with desire, with now.

"Dear God, Rose." Thorn touched the inside of her knees, the inside of her thighs, and, skirting the very place she wanted him to touch, the milky skin of her abdomen. "You're as fine and soft as silk, yet underneath"—he stroked the long line of her muscular arm—"you're as strong as one of your horses."

"You're strong, too." Imitating his motions in reverse order, she rubbed his arm and then his thigh. But she couldn't reach his knee, so, giving in to her curiosity, she substituted one body part for another.

He jerked, just as if he were a telegraph wire and she the electric current. Grabbing her, he begged, "Slow down. Please, slow down. I want to make you happy."

She smiled at him, carefree and young as she had not been for too many years. "You already have made me happy."

He pushed her back, as serious as she was carefree. "I'm the expert here, and I can assure you, you're not nearly as happy as you're going to be."

Sunrise approached, but not nearly as rapidly as her fulfillment. When he finally braced his feet and fitted their bodies together, she knew exactly what he meant. If happiness was frustration, she was happy. If happiness was crying aloud with no thought to a listener, she was happy. If happiness was sweet agony, then she was happy.

But nothing had ever made her as happy as his slow slide into her. It was the answer to a demand and a prayer. It was pain and it was pleasure. It was the beginning of the best ride she'd ever experienced, and when he paused to ask, "Are you hurting?" she lifted her head and glared.

The sun broke over the canyon wall and lit his face, his chest, and his slow, delighted, wicked grin. "I'm happy, too."

She hadn't noticed before, but it was cool and the sun had not yet warmed the boulder she lay on or the air striking her naked body. Turning her head, she looked around, wondering where Thorn had gone. Wondering how he ever discovered the energy even to walk. All three horses, she saw, were unsaddled and tethered to a bush. In some vague corner of her mind, she was glad they hadn't wandered away, untended as they were. Hearing movement behind her, she rolled over wearily.

Using branches and an Indian blanket, Thorn had made a bed in a notch under the cliff. The saddles, supplies, and firearms were tucked behind the bed for safekeeping. Thorn wore his jeans and his boots, but his chest and shoulders were still bare. Still beckoning. And she wanted to start all over again.

His warm chuckle pulled her gaze to his face. "Don't even think about it. You'll be riding sidesaddle as it is." Gesturing to the bed, he asked, "Think we could sleep here for a while? I don't know about you, but I'm tuckered out."

"We need to go get my horses." But a yawn interrupted her.

"They're not going anywhere until the next train comes through." He came over and pressed a kiss right in the middle of her back, then lifted her over his shoulder and carried her to the bed. Fussing like an old maid with a guest, he inquired about her comfort, formed a pillow for her head, and when she had been placed to his satisfaction, covered her with another blanket. "Now"—he lay down and wrapped an arm around her—"who knows you sold Star Bright?"

"Just about everyone, I would guess. Sonny would have told everyone at the party. Didn't he tell you?"

"I heard it before I left," he admitted. "Before I came along and you had somebody to be suspicious of—who were you thinking might steal those horses?"

"Somebody who didn't like me or my parents."

"Everyone likes you. Everyone liked your parents."

She kept her head pressed into his chest. "Except you."

He ignored that. "How about Sonny?"

"How about Sonny?"

"Didn't you ever think of him?"

She sat up and asked incredulously, "Sonny?"

Two cynical lines set themselves into Thorn's cheeks. "When I lived here, every rancher in the area knew he'd better get his calves off the range fast, or his cows would have no calves, and Sonny's cows would suddenly all have twins."

"That was Sonny's father."

"Yeah, and Sonny never did it?"

She didn't answer.

Thorn shook her a little bit. "Who stands to get your land if you fail? Who's got the resources to have cowboys watch your place night and day and pick off your horses when the time is right?" She didn't answer, and he added the clincher. "The corral with the stolen horses is on his land."

"Oh, no!" She thought of Sue Ellen and her blatant assurance that she was keeping Sonny on the straight and narrow.

"I know you don't want to believe it, but my money's on Sonny Pogue for horse thief."

Slowly she lay down.

"Just think about it," he coaxed. "When you wake up, the answer will be right before your eyes, I'm sure."

The answer? Right before her eyes? The only thing that would be right before her eyes was . . . Thorn.

He kissed her forehead and cuddled her, murmuring love words and assurances, and before she knew it she slept.

When she awoke, it looked to be about noon, and she was alone. She heard Thorn talking in a low tone—to the horses, she guessed. Was he answering the call of nature? Was he moving the horses into the shade?

Or was he leaving, like the thieving liar he was?

Embarrassed by her suspicion, but unable to quiet it, she rose, peeked around the corner—and saw him. He was fully dressed, his guns strapped on, his hat pulled over his eyes, and he was leading his horse away.

Away! After what had happened, after the pleasures of the night and the promises of the morning, he was going away!

She collected her carbine from behind the bed, swiftly reloaded it, and set it into her shoulder. Stepping out into the sunshine, she caught him just as he fitted his boot into the stirrup.

"This time, you bastard"—she cocked the lever—"I really am going to kill you."

SIX ~

Jumping Jehoshaphat, Rose was nude! Not a stitch on! Bare beamed and buck naked! In the open, in full daylight, without a shred of self-consciousness or guilt.

Thorn gulped. What a woman. What . . . a . . . woman.

Was that a rifle she was holding? Oh God, it was. She had her Winchester, and her hands were mighty steady. And she'd called him a bastard—the first curse word he'd ever heard her use. Deep in his gut, he had the ugly suspicion she would, without remorse, shoot him through the heart. He'd better think fast.

But she was naked! Nothing on but skin and hair!

And she was magnificent. The sun shone full on her flesh, lighting every curve, every muscle, every part that had never seen the sun before. It shone on the hair of her head, creating a glossy halo.

God, how he loved her.

Unfortunately, that same sunshine shone on the carbine—on the black, well-greased barrel, on the warm brown stock, on the cold, empty mouth that would spit death at him.

Too bad he didn't have the brains to be scared, but all his sense seemed lodged in his pants.

She spoke, and he almost couldn't hear her for the pounding of his heart. "Get away from the horse," she commanded. "I wouldn't want him hurt if the bullet goes all the way through your nonexistent heart."

"Now, Rose." Thorn tried to free his boot from the stirrup, and found his coordination had disappeared with his eloquence. Maybe it was the fact he couldn't take his gaze off of her. "Now, honey . . ."

She gestured with the barrel. "Get away from the horse."

"Yes, ma'am." With a series of hops, Thorn managed to extricate himself, although he behaved so oddly even his stallion turned his head and watched him in amazement. "But before you kill me, I think there's something you should know."

The blank eye of the barrel followed him as he moved carefully away from the horse and toward a boulder. He thought he might be able to leap behind it—if she shot before he explained. The location placed the sun up and behind him, so it might mess up her aim—if she shot before he explained. Most important, it kept the light full on her, so his last sight on this earth would be Rose—if she shot before he explained.

Might as well die happy.

"There's a reasonable explanation for what I've done," he said.

"Yeah, and I bet you're trying to think of it right now."

Tilting her head, closing one eye, she sighted down the barrel. She looked as ruthless as any killer he'd ever faced, and twice as mad. Her anger inspired him to say the right thing—just as the sweetest couple of teacups he'd ever seen on a woman inspired him to stay alive. "You know your daddy always warned you your temper would get you in trouble."

Her knuckles tightened on the rifle, and he thought he was dead for sure. Then she lifted her head. "So?"

"You're not thinking straight. You're thinking I'm abandoning you when that's the farthest thing from my mind."

Her gaze cut to his saddled, travel-ready horse, then back.

He waved his hands in what he hoped would appear to be innocence. "Now, now—there's a reason. A really good reason, and if you'll let me—"

He reached for his jeans pocket, and every one of the muscles in her body tensed. She looked like a woman facing death, and he froze.

She suspected he would pull a gun on her. She thought he could kill her.

My God, what kind of a man did she think he was? He'd been trying to do what was best for her for years, and she thought he'd *murder* her?

He didn't understand women. He didn't understand them at all.

Easing his hand away, he said, "My wallet's in my pocket. You know that's where I keep it, and you know I didn't have any little guns hidden on me last night." He tried out his patented, charm-their-bloomers-off grin. "Only keep my big gun in my pants."

Neither the grin nor the joke worked. In fact, her cold gaze got colder, and sweat broke out on his forehead.

In his most soothing tone, he said, "I want to show you what's in my wallet. If you'll just let me get it out, I'll toss it to you and you'll understand everything. I swear I won't move while you examine it. I know you're not feeling too kindly toward me right now, but try and remember that you said you trusted me not to hurt you. Not even when you thought I was a horse thief. Not that you don't probably think I'm a horse thief now, but—"

"Get the wallet."

"Yes, ma'am." He'd been babbling, he realized, but how could he do anything less when faced with her totally unclothed figure—and that gun? "Right here, ma'am." He managed to dig his wallet out of the tight pocket and toss it toward her. It landed close and skidded right to her foot, just the way he planned it.

Thank God his aim hadn't deserted him, too.

Tucking the carbine under her arm, keeping a careful eye on him, she scooped up the wallet. She opened it, and he knew what she saw.

Nestled in the worn brown leather was a five-star silver badge, stamped with the imprint of a five-peso Mexican coin—the badge of the Texas Rangers.

The Texas Rangers. A band of law enforcers unique to Texas and the wild frontier.

That badge told Rose everything she needed to know about him—although he half expected her to accuse him of stealing it.

In fact, he saw suspicion swoop over her features, but her mind grasped the facts before she could voice them. "You're the Ranger I sent for."

He almost collapsed with relief. Everything would be all right now. She'd welcome him with open arms now. She'd understand the sacrifices he'd made for her sake now. "Yes, ma'am, and I was just going to get on that horse and go do my job. I wasn't abandoning you. I couldn't do that." He lowered his voice into a sexy growl. "Not after last night."

But she didn't even notice, for she was still staring at the star. "You've been a Ranger for a long time."

"Since I got out of prison in '75."

The carbine drooped. "Are there a lot of shady characters in the Rangers?"

He didn't much like the tone of her voice. "A few. If a man is good at rustling, it stands to reason he'd be good at catching rustlers."

"Is that why you joined?"

He didn't like the way she was staring at the badge, either, or the way she wouldn't look at him. "Major John B. Jones was my captain. He met me while I was serving my time, and offered me an early out if I'd throw in with his troop to fight the Indians."

Carefully, she shut the wallet. "So you did, of course."

Had she been waiting for him? Had she expected him to return after his prison term was over? He'd come back seven years ago—she hadn't known it, but he had.

He remembered the way she had looked. Even from a distance, he had seen too much for his battered heart. Her hair had been flying, her face had been lit by a smile. She had looked content, happy.

He remembered the way he had felt then. Cold, alone, almost . . . betrayed.

God knew she hadn't sent him a message through his mother. According to his mother, Rose could barely look her in the eye when she saw her, and had made a point of avoiding everyone in the Maxwell family. She'd wanted nothing more than to forget him, and she'd probably tried. Just as he'd tried to forget her.

Obviously, that had proved impossible for both of them.

"It was my patriotic duty to join. We fought Kiowas and Comanches and Apaches until we herded them to Oklahoma in '77. Then we chased thieves and killers on the frontier." He couldn't keep the pride from his tone. "Caught 'em, too."

"Yes." Turning away, she presented him with a view of her long, strong legs, rounded buttocks, and straight—too-straight?—spine as she returned to the campsite. "The Texas Rangers are famous for taming the frontier."

He followed, but kept a wary distance. "I'm a captain." That would impress her.

But all she asked was, "What brought you back here?"

She laid the carbine down on the ground by the bed, and he chose to take that as a tacit surrender. He'd been keeping the frontier safe for her, so she could raise horses or whatever she wished. By God, he'd been one of the heroes of Texas, and she should be honored that he'd taken the time from his life to do that.

Of course, she didn't look honored. She looked mean enough to go bear hunting with a switch.

Feeling much like the bear, he said, "Major Jones died last year, and I was going to resign, anyway. The law is in place, for the most part, and it's getting damn dull policing a territory that doesn't need policing. When your letter came in, asking for a Ranger, they called me in because they knew I . . . knew you. I'd, uh, talked about you some."

She looked over her shoulder. Just a look, but it spoke volumes, and he hastened to explain, "Not in an ugly way. Just mentioned that I had a girl back home who . . ." He trailed off. What should he say? A girl who was his life? A girl who had turned him in to the law? A girl he'd given up because he thirsted for adventure and she hungered for stability?

Profiled against the stone, she opened the wallet and gazed again at the badge. "Why didn't you tell me?"

The clean outline of her body chased the last lingering bit of reason from his mind. "When?"

Her slashing glance told him what she thought of him.

"You mean last night at the party?" Bringing his attention back to the conversation, he shrugged, trying to project suave indifference. "I'm here on a mission—to discover who stole your horses. It's easier to nose around if no one knows I'm interested."

"You've been in the county for weeks. Isn't that right? Why couldn't you have come to the ranch and told me before?"

Funny. He hadn't thought he might have trouble explaining why he'd pulled the wool over her eyes. The men of the Rangers were known for their honesty, and for their contempt of deviousness—yet he had been devious with her, and for no good reason.

At least—it had seemed a good reason at the time, but faced with a naked, outraged woman, it was obvious that any reason that kept him from her bed, even temporarily, was stupid.

Impatient with his silence, she demanded, "Why didn't you tell me last night in my bedroom? Or later, when I pulled the gun on you? Or after we—?" She gestured furiously at the boulder.

He could have sworn he discerned burn marks on that rock. It had been the night he'd dreamed of for years. It had been, for him, their wedding night. For her, too, he supposed. He hoped. And if last night was their wedding night, today was the first day of their marriage, and he owed her honesty for now and forever.

Mustering his courage—more courage than it took to face her carbine—he said, "I didn't tell you because I wanted revenge."

She repeated the word with a clipped enunciation. "Revenge?"

"For sending me to prison."

"I thought you were stealing my horses for revenge."

"No." He was shocked and righteous. "That would be dishonest."

She muttered . . . something. Had she called him a bastard again?

Defensively, he said, "You did send me to prison for stealing your daddy's saddle. I know I deserved it, and I know that saddle would cost a month's wages, but it seemed like fooling you—just for a little while—wouldn't be . . . ah . . . too terrible a thing."

"Fooling me," she repeated. She clutched the wallet tight in one hand, and balled the other hand into a fist.

She had mentioned that before, he remembered. That he'd made a fool of her. Trying to placate her, he stammered, "Now, sugar. Now, listen. It's all over. No harm's been done." It didn't matter how much he sweet-mouthed her, rage still emanated from her every pore. And even enraged, every one of her pores looked just fine to him. In fact, her whole body looked fabulous to his whole body, and his button-front fly felt as though it had been struck by lightning.

He wanted her. He wanted her bad—or good, or any way he could get her. And he couldn't imagine that she didn't want him. She'd always wanted him. Their mutual desire had been the thread that drew them together, even as their different ambitions had pushed them apart.

But now they wanted the same thing, for he had changed. He wasn't the green boy who had stolen a saddle, or the youth who, after he was released from jail, had come back to see his love.

Nor was he the youth who had ridden away from that love, wiping his streaming nose on his shirt. He'd grown up, he was ready to settle down—and, truth to tell, he didn't feel that strong anymore. He had done as he promised. He had made Rose his own, and he couldn't let her go again.

He spread his arms wide and flung his head back in a mighty gesture of conciliation. "It doesn't matter about the past. All that matters is that I'm here now. Come and take me. Love me until I can't bear to leave you." He dropped to his knees, proposing to her as he'd dreamed of doing a hundred times. "Marry me and stay with me for the rest of my life. I won't be a happy man if you don't."

"You conceited jackass!"

A projectile hit him square on the breastbone. "What the—?" He grabbed at it as it glanced off and flew past his nose.

His wallet.

"Are you crazy?" He yelled, although more from amazement than pain. "My badge is in there!"

"Marry it and stay with it for the rest of your life." Savage in her disdain, she mimicked, "You won't be a happy man if you don't."

"I . . . you . . ." He hefted the wallet in his hand. This wasn't going the way he had imagined. "That silver star is heavy. You might hurt someone!"

She rotated her throwing arm and massaged it with her hand. "I am not so lucky."

She appeared to be serious. But she couldn't be. "Dammit—"

"Don't swear."

Standing, he dusted off his knees. "Is that any way to respond to a proposal of marriage?"

"No, but I can't shoot you. It's against the law to kill a Texas Ranger."

He gaped, but she seemed to have no more attention to spare for him, and when he came racing up the slope, she simply ignored him. "Why are you acting like this?" he demanded.

Calm as you please, she picked up her chemise and slipped it over her head.

"You can't get all het up just because I proposed."

"I'm not the one who's het up." She tugged the drawstrings in the front so tight it puckered from waist to chest, then pulled on her riding jacket and buttoned it all the way to the neck.

"There's a lot of women out there who . . ." Her legs, her hips, her waist. Damn, what had he been talking about? "A lot of women out there who'd like me to propose to them."

"So do it."

Her hose and garters accented the curve of her calf and made him aware that he'd just said the stupidest thing a man could say to the woman he loved. He had thought he always knew the right way to woo a woman, but Rose was different. Rose was important. And how could he concentrate when faced with her half-clothed figure?

Desperately, he tried to salvage lost opportunities. "I don't want to propose to anyone else. You're the only woman I could spend my life with. The only woman I've ever even considered spending my life with."

She stepped into her drawers, then her riding skirt. She braided her hair, coiled it, and pinned it close against her head. She settled the hat on her head and belted the holster around her waist. Then, facing him, she asked, "Should I be honored?"

Her feet still peeked from beneath her skirt, and above her feet were her legs, her hips, her chest, and every last, luscious inch between. "I'm not a bad catch," he answered absently, wondering how to get her clothes back off.

"Not a bad catch?" She chuckled bitterly and jammed her feet into her boots, depriving him of his last suggestive view. "Not a bad catch, if I don't mind being the object of laughter for my husband."

He caught her around the waist. "I don't laugh at you."

She let him draw her forward until their bodies met, then leaned back and looked him in the eye. "You've made a fool of me for the last time, Thorn Maxwell."

"I never made a fool of you." But he faltered, because, in some ways, he had.

"No, I guess not. I made a fool of myself." She smiled scornfully. "I suffered agonies when I testified against you. I haven't been able to look your mother or your sisters or your brothers in the face since I did it. Then, when your prison time was up, you didn't come back. You didn't send word or let me know if you forgave me for sending you to prison. I haven't known for eight years where you were, and then you come waltzing in, sweep me off my feet, making sure that everyone in the county knows your game."

"It wasn't a game. I've never been more serious in my life."

He might as well not have spoken, for all the attention she paid him. "Even I knew your game, but I thought I knew you, too. I remembered the smart, restless scrapegrace, and I remembered the kindness he always tried to hide. Well, I guess you hid it long enough that it disappeared. Your flattery may be warm and it may feel good, but I'm still smart enough to know when you're wetting on my leg, and I don't want any of it!"

SEVEN~

Funny. Rose had looked happier when she thought he was a horse thief. When she learned he was a Texas Ranger, she'd gotten plumb unreasonable. Didn't she like law-abiding men? Thorn had known women who got a thrill from a brush with a scoundrel, but he hadn't imagined Rose was one.

In fact, he'd thought she was the woman who only got a thrill from him. Maybe he'd been deluding himself. Maybe last night had been a dream. A hot, sweaty, magnificent delusion.

He narrowed his eyes at her upright figure in the saddle atop Rooster.

Yeah, it must have been a dream, because now she was cold enough to freeze a fire. You'd never know it was early afternoon, and kind of warm down there where the canyon walls provided shelter from the wind.

He scanned the rocky rim for the tell-tale flash of gunmetal. Every thicket and every tree, every rock and every rise could shelter a bandit, and Thorn kept his rifle loose in its saddle holster.

The way Rose was acting, only her horses mattered. She had insisted on going with him to the hidden corral, and when he suggested they wait until dusk, she'd been scandalized. She refused to leave Star Bright behind, and one would have thought the still-imprisoned Goliath was her dearest friend in the world. And where did that leave Thorn?

Derisively, he answered his own question. It left him riding toward a stash of stolen horses under a sky filled with thin clouds, trying like hell to make his woman happy when he knew she ought to be at home tending her tatting.

Their horses' hooves clomped too loudly in the dirt for his comfort, and the rock walls rising on either side of them relentlessly revealed the two riders to any watching eye. Their vulnerability started an itch down his spine, and he projected his voice to reach her ears, and no farther. "Let's stop here. It's not far to the corral. Around this bend, we'll intersect with another canyon, and just beyond there's a notch in the wall where the horses are fenced."

She glanced at Star Bright. "Then we can go and get the horses at once."

"No."

"What?"

He had to draw the line somewhere. "*We're* not going anywhere. I'll scout around. See what I can find. If there's no one out there—and I imagine Sonny has someone posted to watch the horses—then we'll let Star Bright loose to wander over to the corral."

"Are you crazy? You steal Star Bright back for me and now you want to return her? I want my horses!"

"And I want the thief."

"I want Goliath."

"You'll get Goliath. As soon as I discover who's behind this."

She glanced around as if expecting a posse to appear. "You don't mean you want to capture this thief by yourself?"

Remembering the fixes he'd gotten himself out of in the last seven years, he almost smirked. But he didn't want to upset her more, so he said simply, "Why not? I've intimidated a cattle camp full of drunken cowboys. I can certainly capture one horse thief."

She paled.

Hastening to reassure her, he added, "Besides, I'm not by myself. I've got you."

She turned white.

He knew it wasn't from cowardice. He wished it was, but the woman had more courage than sense. Still, she'd had some shocks over the last few hours, and maybe some hidden delicacy caused that queasy look on her face. Concern made him gruff, and he said, "Dammit, Rose—"

"Don't swear."

"Are you getting sick?"

"No."

"Because I don't like having a woman along on a mission, especially not my woman—"

"I'm not your woman."

Exasperated, he grabbed the bit in Rooster's mouth and brought the horse close beside him. Leaning clear out of the saddle, balanced on one stirrup, he kissed Rose, hard and fast. Then he let her go, and she backed

Rooster away from Thorn as if he were nuttier than a peach-orchard pig.

He inspected her face. "That brought the color back, anyway." Her hand flew to cover her cheek, and he declared, "You're my woman, all right. You just have a bad case of the peadoodles. After you get used to the idea, you won't be so nervous about it."

"I don't plan to get used to the idea."

God, she looked haughty as only Rose could look, and that made him grin. That, and the fact that she'd liked the kiss. "You mean you're already used to it."

"No, that is not what I mean. You are presuming too much on the basis of a single"—she stared between her horse's ears—"kiss."

"A kiss?" He chuckled and dismounted. "A single kiss? I recall a little more than that."

Smoothing Rooster's mane, she said, "No matter what happened, you would still presume too much. You are a presuming type of man."

He led his horse to the shade against the rock wall and tethered it to the branch of a ponderosa pine. "I guess I am. I guess when a woman demands that I take my clothes off nice and slow—"

"Thorn!"

"—and offers me a job stripping in her saloon if I'll stop stealing horses—"

"You hush." She looked around as if the Ladies' Aid society was going to hop out of the bushes.

"—and after we melt a solid Texas boulder down to glass and I tell her I've never stolen horses . . . well, I *presume* she's going to be happy, and I *presume* she's my woman." He cocked his head and studied her. "I told you I was going to make you mine."

"Well, you did." As stiff as she was, she must have starched her face. "And I hope you enjoyed it."

Remembering the night, he rumbled, "Yeah, I did. Never had so much fun with a rock before. Beats skipping 'em any time." He held Rooster's bridle and looked up at her. "Didn't you enjoy it?"

He held his breath and waited for her to lie. But he should have remembered. Rose didn't lie. "Very much." She clipped her words like a goddamn Yankee. "But I have no intention of repeating the experience."

"Too bad, 'cause it just gets better. When a woman and a man—say you and me—get into a bed with clean white sheets—say your bed at your house—they push the quilt all the way to the bottom. Then they take off their clothes—nice and slow, the way you like, or nice and fast the way I like—and the man—that would be me—takes hold of the woman's feet—your feet, Rose—and starts kissing from the toes up." He grasped her boot at the ankle, and she jumped violently. Working his way up under her skirt, he massaged the sensitive skin behind her knee. "By the time the man—me—gets this far, the woman—you—is making those little whimpering sounds like you did last night. And when I kiss the inside of your thighs—" His fingers skated up, and Rose did whimper, just a little. Quick as a minnow, he slipped his hand out. "But you're not interested in that."

"Thorn!"

"Let me tell you what I want you to do. We're going to walk into the canyon to the corral, and—Rose, are you listening?"

He could have answered the question himself. No, she wasn't listening. She was looking . . . right at his button-front fly. Trouble was, he couldn't spend much time around Rose without that conspicuous bulge, and he sure as hell couldn't discuss the hours he planned to spend in her bed without mimicking a stallion in rut.

But she could play the casual game as well as he could. "You said you thought Sonny was behind the horse rustling."

Wondering what she was getting at, he agreed. "Yeah."

"And Sonny has a whole flock of cowboys at his command."

"So?"

"So you're not trying to bring in one horse thief. You're trying to bring in an army."

She had a point, but she just didn't understand. "Honey, haven't you heard about the Rangers all your life?"

She nodded.

"About Jack Hays and how he was the first to fight Indians with the Colt six-shooter in 1840? About Rip Ford and how he chased that rebel Cortinas into Mexico in 1859?"

She nodded again.

"And don't you know the Rangers avenge their own? I've got the legend behind me. When I show my badge, it'll be like a whole squadron of Rangers riding to the rescue. Come on, I'll help you out of the saddle."

She looked doubtfully at his outstretched hands, but she slid down and he caught her by the waist. Holding her in front of him, he assured her, "Those cowboys won't dare go up against me. In the end, it'll be just Sonny and me."

"As long as those cowboys don't shoot first," she said.

"There's that." Canny as a treeful of owls, he said, "You'd best accept my proposal. That way I'll go down a happy man."

Unimpressed, she answered, "Let's just do our best to see that doesn't happen."

"That I go down, or that I'm happy?"

"Both," she said, but her mouth had white lines around it.

Was she worried about him? He thought so, and rejoiced at the idea. Afraid she'd see his delight and more afraid she'd think he was laughing at her, Thorn took Rooster and tethered him beside his own horse. "I'll stash you and Star Bright as close as I can get you to the corral without putting you in plain sight. I want you to stay where I put you, quiet and still, until I've scouted the area. If nobody's watching, I'll call and you let Star Bright go. She'll go to the corral—"

"How do you know?"

"Because Goliath's her leader, and she'll come when he calls." He took her hand and kissed it. "She's a smart female. You could learn a lesson from her."

Her control faltered, and Rose snatched her hand away, but he glimpsed anger and hurt in her face. Wanting, needing to give comfort, he reached for her. She stumbled back to avoid him, and he asked, "What's wrong, darlin'? We've come so far, we can't give up now."

"I'm not giving up. I'm going to get my horses." Steadfastly, she ignored both his outstretched hand and his true meaning, and got her carbine from the saddle holster. "What do we do after Star Bright finds Goliath?"

"If you don't trust me not to laugh at you, how come you trust me to direct the rescue operation?"

"You're the Ranger. You're the expert at catching thieves, and I'll do as you instruct for that reason." Composed once more, she folded her hands in front of her, in effect posting a no-trespassing sign by her posture and her prim mouth.

He hated no-trespassing signs, and he thought about ways to rumple her composure. A mere kiss wouldn't do it this time. It would take more . . . specific action. "I'm the expert at loving you, too, Rose."

She blushed crimson.

"That's a pretty color," he approved, glad to see she *had* shared that dream with him last night. "Goes nice with your gray riding suit. Shows you're thinking about that wedding proposal."

"Are we going, Mr. Maxwell?"

"After you, Miss Corey." He bowed as she swept past. "You want me to take Star Bright?"

"I can take care of my own horses, thank you," she said, crisp as a pair of starched bloomers and just as scratchy.

"Yes, ma'am."

He stood still, watching the swing of her hips and the outline of her legs beneath the velvet, wondering if he could scorch her skirt with his regard.

"Mr. Maxwell!" She hadn't looked back, but she sounded as incensed as if she'd felt his hot gaze.

Well. Maybe he *had* scorched her skirt. Feeling cocky, he got his rifle and hurried to catch up. "After Star Bright goes to Goliath, we wait." He lifted one hand when she would have objected. "There'll be somebody along soon to water the horses, if nothing else. When the thieves see Star Bright out of the corral, it'll be like ants to honey."

"What am I supposed to do while you're intimidating the cowboys with your shiny Ranger badge?"

"Getting a little testy, aren't you?" He didn't wait for a reply. "You're to sit in your cubbyhole, and if I need help, you're to start shooting. Can you do that?"

"I don't know." Rummaging in her sleeve, she pulled out a handkerchief and dabbed her nose. "I couldn't kill you."

"For which I am deeply grateful."

"And you deserve it more than the cowboys who are just doing as they're told."

He sighed in exasperation. "You just can't stand to let me heal up and hair over, can you?"

The wind kicked up as they neared the junction of the canyons, and in typical Texas capriciousness, it contained the first taste of winter. Thorn saw Rose shiver and check the sky, and he noticed the clouds streaming in thin wisps on some lofty wind.

"We'd best kick it in the rump," he added, "or that norther'll be on us and we'll be out in the cold."

"Yes." She sounded subdued, but he saw she was straining to look ahead, wanting that first glimpse of the horses.

He took her hand, and she let him, almost as if she were unaware of him, or as if she needed the comfort of his touch. Keeping close against the wall where the tumbled boulders provided shelter, they rounded the corner where one dry creekbed merged into another. There the wind blew stronger, carrying on it the high complaints of an unexercised stallion. "Goliath," she whispered. Her hand squeezed Thorn's, and she walked on tiptoe. Torn between watching her and watching for trouble, Thorn found a sheltered place for Star Bright, and took the halter from Rose.

She tried to keep it, but he gave her a little shove and pointed at the top of a rise. "The horses are on the other side. If you keep your head down, you can take a look."

She scrambled up the grade, hunkered down when

she reached the top, and peered over. He knew when she had her first sight of the horses, because she wiggled like a puppy whose ears are being scratched. Thorn found himself grinning and wishing happiness was always so easy to provide. She would have stayed there forever, he guessed, but he finally called to her, and she reluctantly crept back down.

"They're there," she said unnecessarily.

"Yes, ma'am." He transferred Star Bright to her custody by taking both Rose's hands and wrapping her fingers around the bridle. Then he leaned over her, and before she could draw back, said, "Last chance."

"For what?"

"To accept my proposal. I might get killed out there."

"Unfair," she murmured.

"Yeah." Unrepentant, he kissed her, savoring the taste of her indignation and her passion. The silly woman might not like him right now, but she sure did want him.

She stood there and let him kiss her, enjoying his expertise even as she deplored it. The man had no shame, but he did have a way of using his lips and tongue that had nothing to do with sweet-talking and everything to do with sweet loving.

"Rose," he whispered. Like a gunslinger's hands above a holster, Thorn's hands hovered above her arms, waiting for the signal to touch.

She didn't give it to him. She couldn't. She'd already given him too much and bought herself heartache in the bargain.

He didn't grin as usual, but watched her solemnly, then drew his Colt and slipped away.

She watched him disappear around the bend and wished she had him back—had him back so she could throw him off her land and order him never to darken her door again.

Knowing him, he'd just climb in the window.

All those years, thinking of him in prison, imagining him as a thief or a gunslinger, imagining him shot or hanging for his crimes—and he'd been a Texas Ranger. He could have come back for her any time. He could have at least let her know that he was safe.

And he hadn't.

You're going to be mine someday.

It had been a boy's promise and had become a man's threat. But she'd been too infatuated to care. She'd imagined an eternal love where there had been only lust and, for all he denied it, a desire for retaliation. After all, she had put him in jail, and she'd spent years feeling guilty about it. Even now he could be laughing up his sleeve, remembering her passion with a smirk and his proposal as a joke.

And if he were serious? Heavens, that was even worse. If he were serious, if he really wanted to marry her, then she'd been put in her place with a vengeance. She wasn't Rose, the love of his life—she was Rose, the woman he remembered when the excitement of his life had died down, when he had nowhere else to go and nothing else to do.

So be it. She didn't need him around, she'd proved that. She could make a living with her horses. She could keep her land and her pride, and he could go find another woman who'd be satisfied with being a tiny part of Thorn Maxwell's life.

Rose already hated that woman, just as she hated the flattery that had made her think she was special to Thorn. More than that, she hated her own susceptibility.

She'd been a fool again. A fool for Thorn.

Star Bright tugged at her halter, and Rose soothed her, petting her nose and making soft, horsie sounds. But Star Bright would not be comforted, and Rose finally realized why.

The horses over the rise were restive and their neighing rose in ever increasing volume. Star Bright wanted to join them, and Rose did, too. What was happening? She glanced around. Where was Thorn? He wouldn't approve if she went to look—he liked his own way far too much—but perhaps she should. Just as a precaution.

After all, if Thorn was scouting around, he couldn't be watching the corral.

Pleased with her justification and smug about defying Thorn's orders, Rose tied Star Bright to a bush and, cradling her carbine, crept up the rise once more. As she neared the top, she lay down flat in the dirt and grass and, feeling like an accomplished crime fighter, crawled the rest of the way to the summit. Then she lifted her head to look.

A man stood down by the corral, and it wasn't Thorn.

Shocked, she ducked down again. With trembling fingers, she examined the carbine, assuring herself it was ready to shoot while praying she wouldn't have to pull the trigger.

But she could, she assured herself. Her horse thief stood below.

And Thorn was at risk.

Then, in the corral, Goliath stretched out his neck and called, and Star Bright responded. Rose heard the sound of shredding branches and brittle foliage as Star Bright ripped herself loose from the bush that had tethered her. Rose felt the thunder of hooves as Star

Bright headed up the hill, and she glanced back to see the mare running straight toward her. A vision of her own savaged body flashed through her mind, and she reacted instinctively by rolling down the slope.

Just in time. The mare thundered over the rise without a glance at her mistress, and in the corral, Goliath welcomed Star Bright with a triumphant whinny.

Rose lay with a hand on her thumping heart. That had been close—and what would Thorn say now? She'd lost their bait before Thorn was in position, and she'd almost gotten herself run down.

Perhaps getting trampled wouldn't have been such a bad idea. It might have beaten facing Thorn.

Did she dare peek at the corral once more, or would Star Bright's arrival bring the horse thief's caution to the fore?

But the man at the corral called out in familiar tones, "Star Bright! Where have ye been, me darlin' girl?"

The lilting Irish accent, the gruff voice, the familiar welcome . . . it was Patrick!

Patrick was down at the corral. Patrick had traced the horses here, and was now recklessly exposing himself to the thief.

Rose grabbed her carbine, scrambled to her feet, and waved her arms at her foreman, but Star Bright stood between them. Starting down the hill, she risked a cry. "Get down! Patrick, get away."

Caught by surprise, Patrick dodged behind Star Bright.

"Patrick," Rose called again, and he hopped around the horse, stopping to peer from behind Star Bright's neck.

When he caught sight of Rose, his face crumpled in

horror, and he croaked, "Miss Rose! What are ye doing here?"

"We found the horses, just like you did, and we're trying to catch the thief. You've got to get away"—she tugged at his arm—"or you'll be shot."

He glanced wildly around and with one hand clutched at the pistol at his hip and raised the rifle he held in the other. "Shot? By who? Who's we?"

Another tug, and she jerked him into motion. "Thorn and I. He found the horses—"

"*He* found the horses?"

"—and I wanted to free them, just like you—"

"Yes, that's what I wanted to do." He panted harshly as she dragged him toward a sheltering stand of gray oaks. "Free the horses."

"—but Thorn insisted we find the thief first, so he's out scouting for signs." Reaching the trees, Rose pulled Patrick down into the grass.

"Mother of God." Alarm painted his face in shades of green, and his mouth hung open, then worked uselessly as he tried to speak.

"Patrick?" She shook his shoulder, trying to free him from the paralysis of terror. "It's all right. We should be safe here."

"Miss Rose, I . . ."

"We've got our rifles." She lifted hers and pointed to his. "And Thorn's out there. He'll protect us."

"Thorn . . ." Patrick stuttered, and tried again. "I've been . . . making inquiries about Thorn. He's wanted for . . . horse rustling in . . . Crockett County."

True, those had been her suspicions less than twelve hours before, but now they sounded so ludicrous she giggled. "No, he's not."

Grasping her hand in his cold one, Patrick stammered, "Yes, he is. He'll shoot us dead when he sees us."

"Patrick!" She was amazed at his fear and his conviction. "Thorn is a Texas Ranger."

"Saints preserve us."

"I saw the badge."

Squirming like a worm on hot ashes, Patrick said, "He stole it."

"No, Patrick, I'm telling you." She tried to be patient, but he was so terrified she didn't know if he even understood her. "Thorn Maxwell is a Texas Ranger and has been since he got out of prison."

Patrick's next words struck at her with the venom of a roused rattlesnake. "He's a liar! Don't ye understand? He's a liar and he always has been. He's taking advantage of yer affection for him and using ye, just like he did before, and ye're letting him, just like any floozy. Just like before. Haven't ye any pride?"

Stunned by his vehemence and angered by his invectives, Rose cried, "Thorn isn't a liar! He's not using me. Why, he's been in these parts for weeks, scouting out the horse thief. He knows who it is."

Patrick's eyes rolled until she saw the whites. "I'll not be hanged. I've got to get out of here."

Abandoning his rifle, Patrick lurched to his feet, and for all her fury, she couldn't let him get himself shot. She caught his leg. "Patrick, wait! You'll expose yourself to gunfire. You can't . . ." He tried to shake her off. "You mustn't . . ." She dodged a blow from his hand, but she couldn't dodge the ugly suspicion as what he said finally hit her with its telling force. "Patrick, you . . . dear God, Patrick, you've been stealing my horses."

EIGHT~

Aiming the pistol with care, Thorn pulled back the hammer on his Colt, and the quickening wind almost drowned the metallic click.

Almost, but not quite.

The figure on the ground froze in its low crawl and cautiously turned its head.

Thorn smiled but without a bit of warmth. "What're you doing here, Sonny?"

Dirt stained Sonny's wool vest across the belly and he'd knotted his bandanna so tight his eyes bulged. His Levi's were new, scarcely bent at the knees and baggy in the seat. He had a Remington Frontier .44 in his grip and a new tan Stetson on his head, and when he crawled toward the edge of the cliff to look down on the corral, he rolled like a Conestoga wagon on the move.

He didn't look the part of a horse thief. He scarcely looked the part of a cattle rancher.

"What am I doing here?" Sonny glanced around him in fake surprise. "This is my land. The question is—what are *you* doing here?"

Thorn said, "Let me tell you about the rules, Sonny. The man who has the drop on the other man asks the questions. Put that pistol down real slowlike and tell me—what're you doing here?"

Sonny's quick examination of Thorn confirmed that he did, indeed, have the drop on him. Loosening his grip on the Remington, Sonny placed it carefully in the dust. Without a pause, he fell back on the weapon that had proved so successful for him. Bluster.

"I'll tell you what I'm doing here. I'm taking a look at that corral down below. It's got horses in it. Miss Rose's horses, I bet, and I bet you know all about it."

"Good bet, Sonny. And I bet I know who stole them and stashed them there."

"Yeah."

Sonny narrowed his piggy eyes, and together the men said, "You."

"Me?" Sonny yelped, struggling to sit up. "Not me."

Thorn straightened his arms and pointed his Colt at Sonny's head. "Lay back down."

Sonny hit the ground.

When they were boys, Sonny had been taller, bigger, and a bully. But after they passed their seventeenth birthdays, Thorn grew tall and Sonny filled out, acquiring fat where Thorn acquired muscle, and the balance of power had shifted. Now Thorn tried to subdue the niggling thrill he felt at having Sonny grovel at his feet. In his strongest Texas Ranger voice, he said, "It's your land, Sonny, and you're always bragging you know everything that goes on on your land. You going to tell me you didn't know about this corral and Miss Rose's horses?"

"My cowboys just told me."

Sonny's whiny denial infuriated Thorn, and he snarled, "Or your cowboys built it for you, stole those horses for you, and have been shipping them off for you while you ply Miss Rose with phony concern."

"I wouldn't do that!" Sonny didn't make the mistake of trying to sit up again, but he writhed on the ground in protest.

"Your family's been branding new calves since the Dead Sea was only ill, and stealing Star Bright from Miss Rose is a damn sight better business than paying for her."

"I *didn't* do that." Sonny looked as agitated as a mule with a bee up its butt. "My Sue Ellen would skin me alive. Why, Rose is her best friend, and if you think I'm going to make my life a living hell over a lousy horse or a few lousy acres, you're missing a few dots on your dice. My men have been watching Rose's place, and I knew her horses were disappearing, but I didn't know why until you came back. It's you who're stealing those horses, goddamn it. You!"

"Don't swear." Thorn answered automatically, but Sonny's protestations shook him. He'd seen Sonny lie before and knew Sonny's methods well. Sonny got all slick and smiling like some big butter-and-egg man from the East. He sure didn't turn red and get righteous, and act like some sour-bellied lizard on a hot sand bed.

Thorn had been so sure it was Sonny, he'd never given thought to another explanation. Trouble was—

if Sonny hadn't taken the horses . . . well, who had?

Carried on the wind, Rose's lament lifted the hair on Thorn's head as cleanly as if he'd been scalped.

"You! How could you?"

Thorn waited, but heard nothing more. Running to the edge of the cliff, he saw her facing off with a squat cowboy, her carbine dangling uselessly in her hand. "Would you look at that?" Sonny stumbled to Thorn's side, and Thorn indicated the woman below with an exasperated gesture. "She'll point that damn thing at *me* for doing my duty, and all she's doing now is scolding that damn horse thief."

Thorn headed down the steep, gravelly trail, mumbling to himself. "Damn woman. Won't stay where I damn well put her. Gotta go face a damn horse thief on her own. Get herself damn well—" His litany failed him as the image of Rose, blasted by a shotgun and lying in a pool of blood, surged into his mind, and he concentrated on his booted feet, afraid that one wrong step would lose him time. Then he'd be too late. Too damned late.

Anxiety threatened his attempt at balance, but as he rounded the last corner, he drew his Colt—and saw them. Rose and . . . he squinted. Patrick? Wasn't that man Patrick, the ranch hand who'd caught them in the hay and soundly humiliated them eight years ago?

Still dumbfounded, he said, "Patrick?"

The two figures before him whirled around, and Rose looked almost as dismayed as the quaking Irishman.

"Mother of God!"

Patrick grabbed for his holster, but Thorn was too quick. His Colt appeared in his hand like an extension of his arm, and his aim never wavered.

"Now, Thorn." Rose walked to Patrick just as if he weren't on the verge of blind, total panic. "There's nothing to get excited about."

"Get away from him!" Thorn barked.

In a soothing tone, Rose said, "Patrick's not going to hurt me." She put her hand on Patrick's shoulder, and the old man nearly jumped a foot in the air. "I've been talking to him about this, and he knows—"

Speaking slowly and clearly, Thorn commanded, "Get away from him, Rose. He's liable to do something stupid."

"I just want to make sure *you* don't do anything stupid."

She was still using that soft voice, the one she used to curb fractious stallions, and Thorn ground his teeth so hard he didn't know if he could speak.

"This is a personal matter between Patrick and me," she said, "and we don't need you to interfere."

But Thorn could yell. "*Interfere?* The man's been stealing your horses, and you don't want the law to interfere?"

Wide-eyed, Patrick shook his head.

Rose, too, shook her head. "The law would be too rough on him."

"The law—"

"Don't you worry about the law, Miss Rose." Sonny stepped out from the pile of stones beside the trail and pointed his Remington right at Thorn. "I'll take care of this for you."

Thorn's jaw dropped to his chest. "What the hell? . . ."

"Drop the Colt, Maxwell. I've got you covered."

And Sonny did have him covered. Two cowboys stepped out from behind him. One stepped up on the cliff and aimed his rifle. Another stepped over the rise.

"Godda—" Thorn stopped and glanced at Rose. "Dognation, Sonny, can't you see what's happening here?"

"Sure can." Sonny smirked like a fat pony in high oats. "You're pointing your fancy Colt Peacemaker at Miss Rose and her ranch hand. *Drop it!*"

The crack of Sonny's voice sounded too much like the crack of gunfire, and Thorn dropped his Colt. "Sonny, listen to me," he began.

"The other one, too."

Sonny was excited and scared—a dangerous combination, and one Thorn diagnosed as potentially disastrous. He eased his other pistol out of its holster.

"Sonny, you idiot!" Rose's irritation bubbled up into her voice and her face. "Thorn is doing his duty, asinine as that sounds. He's a Texas Ranger."

"He's a"—Sonny giggled nervously—"what?"

"A Texas Ranger," Thorn answered. "Wanna see my badge?" He heard the cowboys murmur among themselves and knew a strong sense of achievement. Just as he'd told Rose, the mere mention of the Rangers had its effect on the men.

It had no effect on Sonny. "Your badge? You mean you stole a badge?"

"He's been a Texas Ranger since he got out of prison." Rose said, walked toward Goliath. The big stallion came to her eagerly, and she petted his nose. "I mean, think about it, Sonny. Look at him—at Thorn, I mean. He's either been an outlaw or a law keeper, and the fact is, I sent for a Ranger when someone started stealing my horses."

Both Patrick and Sonny squawked like gospel birds

on Sunday, and she turned on them impatiently. "Did you think I was going to roll over and let some . . . dishonest person—"

Thorn grinned. She couldn't stand to hurt Patrick's feelings.

"—steal my horses and ruin my livelihood? Not even for you, Patrick—"

But Patrick had slipped his pistol out of its holster, and he had it pointed right at Thorn.

Just as Thorn had predicted. The Irishman had panicked. Panicked to the point of having his brain scrambled. Deliberately, Thorn started backing toward Sonny his hands open and extended. "This isn't the way to do this."

"Patrick, you put that away!"

This time Rose's voice was sharp with command, and Thorn's was soothing. Neither seemed to have its effect on Patrick, for although he was shaking all over, he kept the pistol pointed at Thorn.

"What's going on here?" Sonny demanded, pompous to the end. "I've got Thorn covered, Patrick. There's no need to get ugly about this."

Patrick laughed, loud and high. "Ugly? He's going to hang me. Ye're going to hang me. I might as well do what I can—"

"Patrick, no." Rose started toward him.

"Get away!" Patrick swung his gun at her.

Thorn jumped toward Sonny. Patrick swung the gun back toward them. Thorn grabbed Sonny's hand, gun and all.

"Patrick!" Rose leapt and collided with Patrick just as Thorn pressed his finger into the trigger and fired. Patrick and Rose flew backward in one tumbled heap under the impact of the bullet.

"Rose!" Thorn knocked Sonny aside and ran. "Goddamn it, if I shot you . . ."

He knelt by her side and she muttered, "Don't swear."

Relieved, but not enough, Thorn ran his hands over her. "Where are you hurt? Where did the bullet—"

Beside them, Patrick shrieked, "I'm dying. I'm dying, and I'm going straight to hell."

"Serves you right," Thorn snapped, still seeking the bullet wound on Rose.

She pushed his hands away. "We've no time for that. Let me up." Crawling to Patrick, she crooned, "Where are you hurt?"

"My shoulder," Patrick said, holding out a blood-stained hand. "It's blown clean away."

"That's the least of your problems." But Thorn crawled over beside her and examined Patrick's wound. "Bullet went right through," he pronounced. "It won't do you much good at your age, but it won't kill you, either."

Patrick set up a wail to wake the Indian spirits. "Then I'll hang. I'll hang for horse stealing."

Sitting down in the dirt, Thorn took off his hat and fanned his face. The steadily increasing wind wasn't enough, he realized, to cool the sweat of fear that covered him. This shivering, whimpering, wounded old Irishman had almost gotten Rose killed. Had almost made Thorn shoot her himself. When Thorn thought how close he'd come . . . He fanned harder. "If you didn't want to be hanged, what'd you steal 'em for, you stupid old man?"

"Gambling."

"I need something to stop the bleeding," Rose announced.

Thorn took off his bandanna and handed it to her. "What do you mean, gambling?"

With a guilty, sideways glance at Rose, Patrick said, "I've been going to Fort Davis and gambling with the troops, and sometimes I . . . lose a little more than I should."

Sidling up in time to hear, Sonny admonished Rose. "I told you he wasn't worth a damn. I told you Irishmen were nothing but trouble."

"Shut up and give me your bandanna," she said.

"No, he's right, Miss Rose. Ye've been nothing but good to me. Ye and yer folks, and this is how I repay ye." Patrick winced as she wadded one bandanna over the wound, then tied it on with the other. "Yer pa knew about me. He knew I got chased out of Ireland with the threat of a rope around my neck."

"For what?" Rose asked.

Thorn stared at her. How dare she act so calm, as if all was well? Didn't she realize she'd almost been killed? He was still as nervous as a long-tailed cat in a room full of rockers.

"For gambling and thieving." Patrick wiped his nose on his sleeve. "Just like here."

"I knew you were in trouble." Rose, too, took off her hat and fanned her face. "But I never thought to tell you you couldn't go to Fort Davis." Wisps of hair escaped from her braid and chased each other in the breeze, and dirt streaked her face.

Thorn thought she'd never looked better.

Patrick nodded, then moaned as if the motion caused him terrible pain. "Ye didn't tell me I couldn't go. I was like yer uncle, Rose, and I took advantage of it. Once I got in deep, I didn't know how to pay my debts except with the horses. But my luck was just about to turn. Just about. I only wanted to make some money to help ye."

Thorn looked at him sharply, but Patrick appeared to be sincere.

"I kept thinking if I could just bring in a little more cash, we'd be for having the best stable in Texas right away." Patrick's faded blue eyes sparkled for a moment, then faded with a sheen of tears.

"We *are* going to have the best stable in Texas."

No edge of doubt marred Rose's expression, but Patrick shook his head. "That we are, but Miss Rose, I'm seventy-two years old. I wanted to live to see it happen." He cast a frightened glance at Thorn. "Now I'm going to hang."

Thorn sighed. "No, you're not, you damned old man. Rose and I are going to get married—"

"What?" Rose interjected.

"—and I can keep your gambling under control if she can't." Remembering that long-ago scene in the stable, Thorn snapped, "You're not like an uncle to me."

"Can't say as you're like a nephew to me, either," Patrick snapped back. Then, remembering his precarious situation, he said, "But that's a generous offer, and one I'll take you up on."

"Wait a minute," Sonny said. "If you're the Texas Ranger you claim you are, how come you're going to let a horse thief go?"

"Because I'm a Texas Ranger—a Texas Ranger who's retiring to get married—and who's going to argue with me?" Thorn stared around at the encircling cowboys. "Hm?"

Shuffling their feet, the cowboys shook their heads and muttered various versions of, "Not me."

Thorn nodded, satisfied. "Some of you men might like to pick the horse thief up and take him into Fort Davis and find him a doctor."

Rose stirred from her place on the ground. "I can take care of him."

"No, you can't." Thorn looked straight at her. "You're going to be busy."

She got that stubborn, huffy, Miss-Rose-Laura-Corey look about her. "No, I'm not."

He ignored that while four of the cowboys hefted the moaning Patrick into the air and carried him away. "And some of the rest of you cowboys might like to gather up Miss Rose's fine horses and take them back to her place where they belong."

"I'll take them back," she said, but she said it to the remaining cowboys' backs as they turned to do as they were told. Clearly exasperated, she pushed some of the hair out of her eyes and appealed to Sonny. "Don't you have any control over your own men?"

"Not anyone gonna stand between a Ranger and his woman," Sonny answered, paying grudging homage both to Thorn's authority and the upcoming marriage.

"I am not his woman." Rose sounded as if she could keep repeating it forever.

"Bad case of the peadoodles," Thorn told Sonny.

Sonny shook his head. "Never expected it from Rose."

"I'll bring her around." Thorn pointed his thumb at the exit to the canyon. "As soon as we're alone."

Sonny shouted at the cowboys, "You men hurry up," then turned expectantly back to the couple on the ground.

Thorn growled, "As soon as we're *alone*."

"Huh?" Sonny checked the progress of the cowboys

again, then, with a start, comprehended Thorn's none-too-subtle hint. "Oh, you mean you want to be alone without *me*."

"Yeah." Thorn wished he'd shot Sonny when he had the chance. "Without you."

"Well." Sonny huffed. "I don't need a house to fall on me. If I'm not welcome . . ."

"You don't have to go." Rose stood with a wince and brushed at the grass stains on her riding skirt. "If Thorn wants to be alone so badly, *I'll* leave."

"You nincompoop," Thorn muttered out of the corner of his mouth to Sonny. "Look what you've done."

"I didn't do anything," Sonny said, instantly defensive. "How come I always get blamed for everything?"

"Obstructing a Texas Ranger, aiding and abetting a horse thief, getting in the way of a Ranger and his woman—"

Sonny raised his hands in defeat. "I'm going, I'm going."

"Leave Goliath," Thorn called to the cowboys. "Rose'll want to ride him. And you, Miss Rose Laura Corey, sit down."

She glared at him, trying to look scandalized, but she only looked hurt, and all over a proposal of marriage.

But he didn't let her know he knew. She wouldn't like his compassion.

And he didn't like her attitude. Where did she get off, blaming everything on him? He was a big man with broad shoulders, but he wasn't spending the rest of his life being the recipient of her choler—or her forgiveness. He taunted, "You afraid to talk to me? You afraid you can't keep your hands off me?"

She sat. "I can keep my hands off you just fine, Mr. Thorndike Samuel Maxwell."

The use of his full name reminded Thorn of that day in court eight years ago, and he flinched. "You sound like my mother."

"Have you been to see your mother?"

She sounded as snotty as she'd sounded when she was six years old, and he responded the same way. "Yes."

"I wondered. I mean, you said you'd been in the county for a while, scouting out the horse thief, and I thought it would be nice if you visited your mother." She paused for a beat. "Like you never did me."

"I told you why."

"Let's see." She pressed her index finger into her chin. "Revenge, wasn't it? Yes, that's right, revenge for sending you to prison. But that doesn't explain the last seven years."

He repeated, "Seven years?"

"Isn't that how long you've been out of prison? Seven years? Isn't that how long you've been a free man? Seven years?" She shook a fist at him, then caught herself. Looking curiously at her hand as if it were someone else's, she straightened her fingers. "Seven years, and you never came to see me or even sent me word. I thought you must be an outlaw. I imagined you shot or sick and dying, and all the time you were riding the prairies and the hills as a Texas Ranger."

"I did come to see you." Thorn glanced around at the wide-open canyon, at the departing cowboys and at that damned gossip Sonny, still dragging his feet and glancing back. Thorn lowered his voice. "I came to see you as soon as I had served my time. I sat up on that hill above your place—you know, the rocky one where we caught the snake—and I watched you. You were working with your horses, talking to your daddy, and you seemed so happy. All the time in prison, all I could remember was the way you looked as you testified against me. That sad look in your brown eyes, the stress in your face. That sorrow was all scrubbed away after a year."

"You came and saw me." She repeated it as if she couldn't believe it.

"Yeah."

"And sat up on the hill and thought I looked happy." She turned her head, and he saw the old lines of strain on her face. "Maybe you should have taken a closer look."

"Maybe so, but I wanted you so bad, Rose. So bad." He pressed his hand to his heart.

"You resisted, I guess." She stared at his chest as if wondering if he had a heart. "You never even let me know you were there."

"What did I have to offer you? I wasn't going to settle down on the family ranch and chase after cows. I wanted adventure and excitement—that's why I got into trouble in the first place." He scooted close to her and stroked her cheek. "You know it's true. Don't you?"

She didn't look at him, but she nodded. "I know it's true."

"I'd already joined the Texas Rangers, and that was right for me."

She slapped his hand away. "But you could have told me you were there on that hill."

"We were going to fight Indians, and I didn't even know if I'd come out alive. Maybe I did the wrong thing—I was pretty young and pretty stupid—but I thought that if I got close enough to you, I'd have to have you, and what would your life have been?"

She came up on her knees and glared into his eyes. "It would have been *my* life. I would have chosen it. I wouldn't be some dried-up old maid waiting for her sweetheart to return. I can't marry a man who doesn't trust me to know my own mind."

"Dang." Astonished, he sat down in the grass beside her. "You're mad because I did the right thing and left you with your parents."

"You left me *alone*."

"And I was feeling noble and honorable and trying to ignore all the sniffles and tears."

"I wasn't crying," she snapped.

"No, I was."

NINE~

Crying? Thorn had been crying that day he'd ridden away from her?

It broke her heart to think of him—young, with prison pallor, facing his first battle—and crying over her. Over Rose, who, until her parents died, had been comfortable and warm and, yes, happy. Maybe she understood, just a little.

But Thorn didn't seem to be interested in her understanding. He looked around the canyon once more, but it was empty now. Empty except for two people sitting and shivering in the strengthening norther. He scanned the canyon rim, then cut a glance at Goliath, anything to avoid her gaze. At last he asked diffidently, "Why didn't you ask about me?"

It was such an odd question, asked with such an odd intonation, she foundered. "Who would I ask?"

It was a stupid question. He knew it and she knew it, but he answered patiently, "You could have inquired of my mama. She knew where I was and what I was doing, and I told her—in a moment of weakness, you understand—that if you ever asked about me, she was to tell you the truth."

"How could I do that?" It seemed that the wind had shifted. For some reason, she thought it blew colder on her now. For some reason, the guilt that had haunted her for so many years returned, and she protested, "I couldn't even look your mother in the eye after sending you to prison."

"Why not? My mama doesn't approve of stealing, you know that. Why, if she'd caught me, she'd have switched me first and *then* sent me to prison."

"I know, but I was just so afraid she hated me, and she'd ask me why you'd taken it, and everybody in the county had already speculated that you'd taken it because I . . . didn't give you what you wanted."

"You didn't want my mother to ask you what happened." He wiped his hand across his mouth as if he tasted something sour. "You were ashamed of what happened?"

"I wasn't at the time. But after Patrick came in, it just seemed . . . dirty."

"Dirty."

She had the feeling she was scrambling to retrieve his good opinion of her, and with more honesty than sense, she added, "Then you went to prison and I didn't dare think about it. Then you got out and didn't come home, and I refused to think about it. Then . . . oh, Lord . . . I couldn't help but think about it. All the time. It was the hottest part of hell, and no one was chained there but me."

"I was there, too. You just couldn't see me, because I was chained to the back of the same scorching rock that held you." He took her hand and attempted a facsimile of his devil-may-care grin. "Actually, sending me to prison was the best thing you could have done for me. It knocked some sense into me." She would have protested, but he continued, "Yes, it did. Knocked me plumb out of my smugness and made me realize what I had to lose. There were men in that prison that didn't know any other life but crime. Men who had gangrene from bullet wounds and men who had consumption because of the damp and dark. It's because of you that I met Major Jones and joined the Rangers. I owe you a debt of gratitude for that."

That seemed so funny, she chuckled a little. "Some debt."

"But I kinda thought, when you never asked about me, that you didn't care anymore. I kinda thought you despised me as a thief and hated me for embarrassing you." He touched her fingers and peered into her face. "That's what I thought."

"I didn't despise you, and I could never hate you."

"I didn't know that." He let go of her hand and stood up. "I'm not some gypsy fortune-teller who can read your mind."

"Well, no, but—"

"I think you were just a coward, Miss Rose Laura Corey, and about the most important thing in our lives."

She still thought he had to be joking, but he was walking away. She called, "You wanted me to go to your mother and ask her to send word to you that I wanted you? You wanted me to chase after you?" Scrambling to her feet, she hurried after him. "I couldn't do that. It would have been too embarrassing for me to . . ." She tried to match his long strides. "Surely you didn't expect that I—"

"I had no reason to despise you. You were the right virtuous Miss Rose Laura Corey. I was just an ex-convict. I was in exile."

"I didn't put you there."

"No, but you were the only one who could get me out. If your parents hadn't died and left you in need, if you hadn't needed a Texas Ranger"—his stride lengthened as if he couldn't be bothered with her—"babe, I still wouldn't be here, because you were too proud to ask for me."

She stopped and stared after him. The nerve! Acting as if their long separation was her fault. He rounded the corner into the other canyon and disappeared from sight, but she couldn't let him get away with the last word. Running, she caught up with him as he led his horse away from the sheltering pine. "Ladies don't ask men to . . . that is . . . ladies wait until they are asked."

"Ladies?" He swung himself into the saddle. "What good does it do to quote etiquette to me? I'm just a rough ol' Texas Ranger. And you're a"—he looked her over—"lady." Tipping his hat to her, he rode away, and she heard him call, "If you'd wanted me, you could have had me."

He galloped away, leaving her standing with her mouth dropped open. Then she raced back to Goliath. The noble stallion was patient as she mounted him using the rails on the corral, and although he wore neither saddle nor bridle, he knew where she wanted to go.

After Thorn, wherever he was going.

She caught sight of him and his stallion in the distance as they topped hills and followed trails, and before too long she realized he was returning to her place.

Why? What was he expecting from her? An explanation? An apology? Because she hadn't chased after him like every other woman in the world? Because she was a lady?

By the time she reached Corey Ranch, she was thoroughly angry and thoroughly windblown, and she slammed into the stable without a thought to disturbing the horses. Finding Thorn feeding the neglected ponies did nothing to improve her mood. Thanking him seemed like more graciousness than she could manage right then. Instead she swung down off Goliath and shouted, "I suppose you would say that ladies don't breed, raise, and break horses."

As quiet as she was loud, he answered, "I would say that it's not horses or proper etiquette that makes a lady, but a kind and loving heart."

Which knocked the indignation right out of her. Was she a lady? She'd always thought so, but right now she wasn't being kind and loving. She was being petty and vengeful.

Leading Goliath to his stall by his forelock, she groomed him before replying, "My mama used to say that ladies do the right thing, whether it's proper thing or not. She said ladies try to see things the way other folks see them before making judgments."

Thorn leaned over the gate. "I always liked your mama. Did she ever say anything about folks who make mistakes?"

"That they ought to learn from them."

Presenting his open, callused palm, he said, "How about we learn together?"

She looked at the hand and looked at him. It wasn't hard to love a man who admitted he'd made a mistake. She hoped it wasn't hard to love a woman who made them, too. Putting her hand in his, she said, "I'd like that."

He tugged her to the gate and helped her out of the stall. They stood looking at each other, half-shy and all hungry.

"Will you marry me?" he asked, plain and simple.

And plain and simple, she answered, "I'd be honored."

Then they were in each others' arms.

The straw crackled beneath them as they sank to the floor, kissing like long-lost lovers.

Which they were, Thorn decided, looking around for a place. The stalls all contained horses, the stable equipment posed a hazard to the wild coupling he imagined. "Someday," he grumbled as he hefted her in his arms, "we're going to make love in this stable. But for now, we'll use your bed."

He stepped outside and the wind took their breath away. In the distance, thunder rumbled, and he tucked her close and ran for the wide porch of the house. He clattered up the stairs before he realized they had company. "Dognation! Rose, those horses are Sonny's and Sue Ellen's."

If anything, Rose looked more dismayed than he did as she saw the pair of horses tethered at the porch, but they had no time to plan evasive action. Sue Ellen had seen them running across the yard, and from the door she screeched, "You-all have an announcement to make?"

"I'll give up drinking and fighting and wild women for you, Rose." Thorn let Rose's feet drop to the ground. "But I just don't know if I can give up swearing."

"Try." Rose patted him sympathetically before she went into Sue Ellen's embrace. "Yes, we're going to be married."

"I knew it. I knew it!" Sue Ellen's wild enthusiasm contrasted with Rose's quieter pleasure. "I feel just like an old-fashioned matchmaker."

"Oh, you are," Sonny said as they entered the parlor. "Did you get your differences settled?"

"We got everything settled." Thorn glared. "Without your help."

"Don't know about that. That was my gun you shot," Sonny said.

"Sonny told me all about it." Thrilled, Sue Ellen clasped her hands at her bosom. "You men are so brave."

Thorn and Rose exchanged questioning glances, but before anyone could ask what Sonny's contribution had been, Sonny asked hastily, "So, Thorn, if you're not a Texas Ranger, how're you going to earn a living?"

"I guess I'm going to dance in Rose's saloon."

"What?" Sonny yelped.

"And Sue Ellen's going to be my first customer in my saloon," Rose said.

Sue Ellen giggled, and when Sonny glared, she giggled again. "I'm only interested in seeing Sonny dance." Cuddling against his rigid figure, she walked her fingers up his shirt buttons. "Won't you dance for me, you sweet thing?"

A flush started up Sonny's neck and flooded his face. For once, he was speechless.

"Come to think of it, Rose"—Thorn stroked his stubbly cheeks—"I guess ladies don't open saloons with dancing boys, either."

"And I suspect I'll be wanting to keep Thorn's dancing for myself, too." Rose sat down on the settee and tugged off her boots. "The saloon will have to wait."

"Well, if I've got no saloon to work in, I guess I'm going to live here with Rose and breed horses," Thorn said, answering Sonny's long-forgotten question seriously. "Horses and . . . maybe some babies. Huh, Rose?"

Rose blushed and looked at her toes. "Yes, Thorn. I'd like that."

"So when's the wedding?" Sue Ellen demanded.

Thorn shrugged. "Tomorrow we'll go down to Fort Davis and find ourselves a justice of the peace."

The two women cried "No!" together.

Bewildered, Thorn looked from one to the other while Sonny laughed. "You dreamer," Sonny said. "You crazy dreamer."

"Why not?" Thorn asked.

"You're not sneaking off and depriving us of the wedding we've been waiting on for years." Sue Ellen sounded determined. "It's going to be the event of the year."

Thorn tugged at the collar of his shirt. "Is that what you want?" he asked Rose.

"No, not that." She smiled shyly. "But I would like to be married by a preacher."

"Oh, yeah."

"And don't you think your family would like to be there?"

"My mother'd skin me alive if she missed it," Thorn admitted.

"There you have it!" Sue Ellen said in triumph. "We'll have a Christmas wedding right here in the parlor. Everybody'll come. You'll see."

"If we wait that long, first baby's going to come early." Thorn sat beside Rose and tugged at his boot.

Sue Ellen grabbed his arm. "Don't you sit down there and make yourself comfortable. You haven't got no cotton-patch license, and you're not staying the night until you two are hitched."

"The baby's still going to be early, Sue Ellen," Rose said.

A mixture of shock, embarrassment, and delight struggled for dominance in Sue Ellen, and being Sue Ellen, delight won. "Oh, honey, I'm so glad." She leaned down and hugged Rose. "It's been a long time a-coming, hasn't it?"

Rose beamed and nodded. Sonny examined the ceiling. Thorn lounged back against the settee and grinned.

"And I told you not to get comfortable." Sue Ellen scolded Thorn as she tried to drag him to his feet. "The whole county will be talking if you move in before you're married. It's scandalous. Now, I can arrange a pretty nice wedding in two weeks—"

"I'm not waiting any two weeks," Thorn said.

"That's as fast as we can make the dress," Sue Ellen insisted.

He planted himself firmly on the settee. "One week, and you can stop digging your fingers into my arm, Sue Ellen. I'm not moving until you promise."

"But her dress!"

"One week."

Thorn was putting down roots, and Sue Ellen could tell. "One week, then. It'll take every woman for a hundred miles working all hours, but you'll have your wedding in one week."

He looked sideways at Rose. "She looks good in that riding outfit. Couldn't she be married in that?"

Sonny hooted, Rose laughed and wiped at the mud that stained the skirt, and Sue Ellen placed her fists squarely on her hips and glared. "Thorn, you stop grinning like a baked possum and get your hind quarters off that settee. You got your week. Now, we women want our wedding."

Thorn appealed to Sonny. "Dognation, you understand. Can't you call off your wife?"

Sonny smirked. "I wouldn't do it if I could. Seeing the almighty Thorn Maxwell with his tail in a wringer does my heart good. You're paying for your reputation now. Face it, man—you're going to be married in a week in one of the biggest fiestas this county's ever seen, and until then, you're going to be with . . . out." He spaced the syllables so clearly, no one in the room was in any doubt what Thorn would be with . . . out.

Especially not Thorn.

His last appeal exhausted, Thorn unfolded himself from the settee. Taking Rose's hand, he asked, "Walk me to the porch?"

Shy as a bride, Rose nodded and went outside with him into the windy evening.

As two self-appointed chaperons, Sonny and Sue Ellen followed them, and Sonny broke off to unhitch the horses from the post by the front porch.

Scanning the clouds, Thorn pronounced, "It's clabbered up to rain. Look, it's flashing in the north. Are you sure you'll be all right by yourself?"

"Just"—Rose glanced guiltily at Sue Ellen—"lonely."

"It's not right to leave you alone like this," said Thorn.

He kept his soulful gaze fixed on Rose, but Sue Ellen answered. "She's been alone before, and she knows how to use her guns."

"Well, that's all, then." Thorn lingered, letting his fingers trace the bones of Rose's face. With a meaningful glare at Sue Ellen, he asked, "Do you think we could have one moment of privacy before I leave?"

Sue Ellen jumped. "I suppose you can. No need to be huffy, Thorn."

Thorn didn't wait to see her leave. Lifting Rose off her feet, he kissed her until he saw flashing lights behind his closed eyelids, until he heard the roar of cannon and felt the ground shake beneath his feet. He would never have stopped, but something pushed him and he staggered. Lifting his head, he realized the wind had grown stronger. The storm burst upon them.

"Come on," Sonny roared. "We're going to get wet anyway."

In a daze, Thorn looked at him, then down at Rose. Her eyes were still shut tight, and the bliss on her face made up his mind. He waved acknowledgment to Sonny, and carefully set Rose on her feet. When he knew she had her balance, when reason had returned to her gaze, he grinned as wickedly as he knew how. In a voice meant for her ears only, he said, "Make sure you leave your window unlatched, darlin'."

ONE RIOT, ONE RANGER

~ *by* ~

Susan Sizemore

ONE~

"Marty, honey, you can't go down to the Black Eye. It ain't proper."

Martha Wirth had two uncles. Unfortunately, Cyrus, the good one, had met his Maker with a bullet a month back. Which left her to deal with Jed, the bad one. And the town of Loon, Texas, to boot. Loon, she'd been told, was named after a bird some hunter had brought back from a trip up Canada way. She was convinced Loon was called Loon 'cause every man, woman, and child in it was a lunatic.

Uncle Jed had gotten himself elected mayor, which made him the head lunatic. He also owned shares of the general store, the livery stable, the bank, and a saloon. But not the Black Eye, or he would have been hollering at her to do something about the riot down the street instead of getting in her way.

Uncle Cyrus had been the sheriff, and Marty had been his deputy ever since she'd learned how to use a Colt Navy revolver better than just about anybody else in town.

Uncle Jed grabbed her arm but she shook him off. Marty was a good six inches taller than Jed Wirth, and a head taller than any other woman in town, not to mention most of the men as well. Height had its advantages.

She looked down her long nose disdainfully. It was what might be called an aristocratic nose, according to Essie. Or just plain big according to everybody else. "I have to go," she said.

Uncle Jed stepped in front of her. "What will Mr. Simpson think? A lady does not associate with the soiled doves down at the Black Eye."

"I'm not going to associate with 'em, I'm going to arrest them."

As for Mr. Simpson, that handsome, preening fool of a banker could lock himself in Uncle Jed's vault and spend his life counting money for all she cared, since it wasn't really her he was interested in, anyhow. Never mind that he came courting her when every giggling, unmarried girl in town—two of 'em, not counting herself—swooned at the mention of Mr. Charles Simpson, fine-looking, educated Easterner.

Marty didn't have much interest in marrying Uncle Jed's bank manager, no matter what Uncle Jed had promised the man in order to get him out here to help run the Wirth businesses. Martha Rose Wirth did not think the word *heiress* meant the same thing as cattle, to be sold to the highest bidder. She wasn't sure, but she didn't think so.

And speaking of cattle, she had better have a talk

with the trail boss whose men had driven a thousand head to the rail yards this morning. Not that it would do any good. His men were probably counting on getting drunk and rowdy as soon as they collected their pay, and once his crew got some bad whiskey in 'em there was no talking to them. They'd start racing their horses up the streets and shooting at anything that moved. There'd be bodies to bury come morning.

Things in Loon were out of hand, and Marty knew it. She would much rather be the sheriff of a reasonably peaceful town. Since Uncle Jed continued to block the doorway of her office, looking stern and stubborn, she decided to tell him.

"I've sent for a Ranger," she said.

His bushy eyebrows furrowed. "A Texas Ranger?"

"Lord, is there any other kind?"

She'd learned early in life that Uncle Jed disapproved of about everything she ever did. He said disapprovingly now, "You'll need a dozen men to clean up this town. I think a vigilance committee would be a better idea."

"One Ranger's all we'll need," she answered shortly. "That's all they ever send." She glared so hard he moved out of her way. "And I *don't* want to hear talk about vigilantes," she added before heading up the dusty street toward the Black Eye Saloon.

Help me, she prayed as she hurried along. She appealed as much to the shade of her beloved uncle Cyrus as to the Lord. *Get that Ranger here quick. Bring me the one man I need to turn this town and my life around.*

Marty prayed hard and loud and felt deep in her soul that somebody—Uncle Cyrus, she hoped, since he always knew what was best for her—was listening.

Somebody was.

Somebody who could shift the stars, make miracles, change lives, and offer second chances. Somebody who had a cosmic sense of humor, and was in the mood for playing games with time as well as answering prayers.

Chris Parris couldn't understand why he was sitting on top of a horse. The last thing he remembered was the sight of an amber glass beer bottle streaking toward his forehead.

Streaking in slow motion.

At the time he'd felt more as if he were in a movie than a bar fight. And there had been laughter. A great cosmic chuckle had filled his head. The laughter had drowned out the background sounds of shouting and breaking glass and Megadeth's song blaring from the bar's sound system at decibels loud enough to cause crop damage.

And now here he was sitting on the back of a horse. A big, blond horse that took no notice of a stranger on its broad back. It just kept walking along a road that wound into a deep valley as if it didn't know it had changed drivers. The horse was heading toward a straggly line of wooden buildings on the bank of a thin silver snake of water. Chris could see that the stream fed a rolling, dull countryside covered in heat-seared grass and a few limp-leaved trees. There wasn't a strip mall or gas station in sight.

He did notice clumps of cattle off in the distance, grazing on the brownish green grass. Then he got his mind off the scenery and back to the question of just what the hell he was doing there. He'd never ridden a horse—he rode a Harley—yet his hands knew what to do with the reins, and his body moved easily with the animal's gait. It felt like something he'd done all his life.

"This is crazy," he said. The horse's ears flicked at the sound of his voice. "What am I doing here?" he demanded. "How the hell did I get here?"

As soon as he spoke the presence he'd felt back in the bar filled his head with the strong impression that hell had nothing to do with it at all, but might, if he didn't learn to watch his language.

Chris didn't like it when anybody told him what to do, even when that anybody was an invisible presence. He considered his crazy current circumstances for a moment, then gave vent to his puzzled confusion by snarling every oath he knew at whoever was responsible for this predicament. Meanwhile, the horse continued on its way at an easy walk, though its ears seemed a little red from the invective it was hearing.

Far from calling forth the wrath of God, or Whoever Was Responsible, Chris got the impression he'd just caused the universe to chuckle and nod approvingly at his stubborn independence. Then the sense of being surrounded by an invisible power ebbed quickly away. He was left feeling completely alone and isolated in an old and alien landscape as the horse reached the outskirts of the ramshackle little town.

"I need a drink," he muttered.

Fortunately, the horse seemed to understand his needs because it came to a halt in front of a peeling sign that read BLACK EYE SALOON.

Marty supposed she'd walk in to find two or more of the girls fighting over Foster Behan again, though

Marty couldn't see the attraction. She'd been told the smug, oily gambler was dapper and gallant, but the dictionary she'd ordered from back East hadn't arrived yet so she didn't quite know what the words meant.

She would find out though, and without having to ask a soiled dove like Essie Harris. Essie, it was well known, had come to town to be the schoolteacher, but had chosen a life of sin when the town council—which was made up of Uncle Jed and anybody who'd agree with him—had decided they couldn't afford to pay a teacher after all. Essie had declared their treatment of her a black eye on the whole community, and as soon as a year of hard work on her back had earned her enough to purchase the saloon, she'd changed its name to reflect her views.

Through Essie's efforts the place had become a proper den of iniquity. Marty didn't precisely know what iniquity was, either, but she knew the cattlemen were sure taken with the girls and whiskey and gamblers that Essie called the amenities of the place. Problem was, the amenities fought with each other when they weren't dodging trouble from rowdy, randy drunks and cowboys.

Marty heard the shouting long before she reached the door. It was, as she'd supposed, coming from shrill female voices. She stopped in the dusty street long enough to check her gun again, not because she thought she'd have to use it against Essie's girls, but because Uncle Cyrus had taught her to be careful before he forgot to be careful himself and went to his reward. She sighed at the memory of her uncle, and went into the saloon, hoping that a few stern words would be enough to quiet the girls down.

Foster Behan, all dressed up in ruffled shirt and

black coat, his hair slicked back and his gold tooth gleaming as he smiled, turned to her and gave a fancy bow as she walked in.

"Oh, Lord, ladies," he declared. "The mistress of our hearts and most of our gold has deigned to grace us with her presence."

Marty checked to see that the man's guns were holstered and then started toward the trio of girls who were clawing at one another in front of the bar. Essie was leaning on the bar, watching the brawl with a grin. "Why don't you throw some water on those shecats?" Marty asked the saloon owner as she grabbed one of the girls by the back of her dress and pulled. The girl let go of the woman she was strangling as she flew backward to land on her rear with a thump.

"Thought I might sell tickets to the fight," Essie answered. "Oh, leave 'em alone, Martha," she added as Marty picked up a second girl and seated her on the bar. "They're just having a little fun."

"Their 'fun' can be heard clear down at the Bible Society meeting," Marty said. "The ladies are complaining. Stay," she ordered the girl on the counter. Marty whirled as the third girl screeched and leapt, aiming her brightly painted nails at Marty's face.

Marty was too busy trying to keep her eyes from being scratched out to pay much attention to the man who pushed open the swinging doors of the Black Eye and walked right in past Foster Behan.

Chris had seen enough cat fights in his time to be unimpressed by the girls going at each other in the space between the bar and the saloon's few scattered tables. He found the long skirts several of them wore kind of puzzling, but he was favorably impressed by the tight jeans covering the trim, heart-shaped rear of the tall girl who was under attack. He didn't let himself be more than momentarily entertained by the fight, though, since he had some serious drinking to do before he could even try to start making sense of whatever was going on.

As he strode up to the bar two other girls joined the fighting women just as they crashed into a table. Chris ignored the shouting and noise of overturning furniture as he spoke to the fine-looking red-haired woman behind the bar.

"Miller Lite," he said.

The woman, also wearing a low-necked long dress, just stared at him.

"Okay," Chris said, as he noticed her puzzlement, "just give me whatever beer you got." He had to shout to be heard above the girls' swearing.

The bartender nodded, and Chris fished into his pocket and brought out money he didn't recognize. Hell, he didn't even recognize his clothes, and he sure didn't know what he was doing wearing a gun belt and a cowboy hat or why everybody but the tall girl was dressed in clothes straight out of a Clint Eastwood movie.

Somebody threw a bottle and glass shattered on the counter as the bartender set Chris's beer down in front of him. The man over by the door laughed and the bartender chuckled while the battle continued across the barroom. Chris took a long gulp of beer and discovered it tasted like moose piss. He'd had worse. He sighed, and turned to watch the show.

The tall girl was holding her own against two of her three assailants, and the attackers definitely looked the worse for wear. "Dammit!" she shouted as the two girls circled her. "Do you want to be off your backs for the next month!?"

The tall girl, Chris noted, was wearing a gun strapped to her long, shapely thigh. He approved of her restraint in not pulling it against her unarmed assailants, even though he knew it was stupid. The world and the people in it didn't play fair. Time and time again he'd expected fairness and had gotten kicked in the head. Still, he admired fair play when he saw it.

"Now, Marty," the bartender called cheerfully. "The girls are just funning you!"

The tall one, who was evidently called Marty, punched one of her opponents in the stomach. The girl collapsed onto the dirty floorboards. Marty whirled to face the bartender. "Call 'em off, Essie, or I'm dragging 'em off to jail. Then there'll be some mighty disappointed cowboys in here tonight."

Essie held up her hands. "All right, all right. It's gone on long enough," she called out to the girls.

The girls, however, weren't listening. Especially not the one Chris saw sneaking up behind Marty with a heavy whiskey bottle in her raised hand. Chris shook his head and put down his half-finished beer. He took a step forward and grabbed Marty's arm, pulling her out of danger just as the other girl swung the bottle. When the attacker stumbled forward, he plucked the bottle from her hand and set it on the counter, pushing Marty behind him.

"Thanks," he heard her say, the word little more than a breathless whisper.

The girl Marty had punched stayed curled up where she was, but the other two turned on Chris. He put his hand on the gun at his hip and looked at the man by the door. Out of the corner of his eye he'd seen him move. "You've stayed out of it so far," Chris said. "Stay out of it now."

The man, dressed like an old-West gambler, gave a slight nod, and went out the door. The girls, who'd turned adoring eyes toward the gambler, looked unhappily back at Chris. He got the impression the argument must have started over the attentions of the man who'd just left. With their audience gone, the girls calmed down instantly.

Chris turned toward Marty. She was leaning against the bar, glaring at the girls. When he turned her gaze met his. She smiled and her hazel eyes lit up, making her rather plain face suddenly very pretty. And he knew what she was smiling at as if he could read her mind.

"So, what are you?" he asked as he looked her up and down. "About six two?"

She nodded slowly.

"I'm six five," he told her. "I'm Chris Parris," he added.

"Well, well," the bartender said sarcastically. "It looks like our Marty's finally met someone she can look up to."

"Chris Parris." As Marty repeated the tall stranger's name, her eyes caught the glint of metal. She slowly looked down until she saw the Texas Ranger badge pinned to his coat lapel.

A Ranger. Her Ranger. And, oh, Lord, he'd caught her brawling in a saloon with Essie's trio of hussies! She swore, but to herself since she was sure a Ranger wouldn't appreciate an officer of the law taking the Lord's name in vain.

Oh, Lord, she thought, reverently this time, but he

was handsome! Tall, wonderfully tall, and broad shouldered, with a square jaw and blue eyes. Blue eyes that were focused curiously on her. His expression urged her on to do her duty.

She looked around and found her bruised and battered opponents standing in a hostile knot over by the stairs leading up to where, she supposed, the iniquity part of Essie's business was conducted. Marty drew her revolver and marched over to them.

"You're under arrest," she said. Before the girls could start a howl of protest she glanced over her shoulder at Essie, who was gaping at her from behind the bar. "Ranger Parris and I are going to clean this town up," she announced, "and we're starting right here."

The girls started to yammer, foully and loudly, and Marty herded them toward the door with nudges from the barrel of the big Navy revolver. Ranger Parris leaned against the bar with his arms crossed and watched her closely as she headed her prisoners out. His gaze on her made her feel big and clumsy and hot all over, but it also gave her the determination to carry on.

"Now you wait one minute, Martha Rose Wirth!" Essie called indignantly. "I've paid my seamstress taxes for this month! You can't take my girls away!"

"That tax weren't my idea," Marty replied. It was Uncle Jed and his council that had decided to impose a tax on single working women, and since it sounded disgraceful to call it a "whore tax," the council had decided primly that all single working women in town must naturally be employed as seamstresses. "Besides, I ain't arresting 'em for sewing, I'm arresting 'em for hittin' an officer of the law."

"Oh, hell, Marty, they were just having a little fun."

Marty was used to Essie and her girls having fun at

her expense. They might be soiled doves, but she was ugly and overgrown, dressed like a man most of the time, and even wore a gun. She shocked the ladies of the Bible Society, and whores—seamstresses—laughed at her openly. Sometimes she wondered why she wanted to save this town from itself at all.

"What am I going to do without the girls?" Essie demanded. "There's drovers in town, Marty. See sense, girl. They'll tear this town to pieces if they don't have some women tonight."

Essie was right, of course. Marty blushed to think of it, but it was true that those cowboys just in off the range were going to go plum crazy if they didn't have something warm and willing to sink their rods into. Essie's girls were a blight, but a necessary one until some kind of peace was restored to Loon.

She sighed. "Oh, all right." She holstered her gun and gestured the girls away. They laughed as they headed for the stairs.

She gave Ranger Parris a look of apology, shyly, from under her lashes. Essie noticed, and snorted with laughter. Marty ignored the crude sound. "I hope you understand, sir."

He lifted his beer glass and shrugged.

The man had to be tired from the long ride, Marty figured, and this was no place to talk. "I'll let you drown your thirst," she said. "We can talk in my office whenever you're ready, Ranger Parris."

The man continued to look at her as if she were crazy. She got the impression that he wasn't sure what was going on. No doubt he'd never seen a woman sheriff before. She'd explain about how there had been nobody but her to take on the job after Caleb Morse shot Uncle Cyrus.

Caleb Morse. She looked at the retreating backsides of the hussies and called out, "Lavinia! Get yourself back down here!"

"What for?" the girl asked, cautiously approaching her.

"I'm taking you to jail." Marty grabbed Lavinia's arm before the girl could get away. Then she spoke to Essie. "Caleb Morse is mighty fond of Lavinia. You tell Caleb where he can find his ladylove when he comes looking for a little comfort."

Essie planted her fists on her thighs. "You're going to get yourself killed, Martha Rose. You know Caleb isn't going to put up with—"

"Just tell him," Marty said as she gave Ranger Parris a polite nod. Keeping a tight grip on the struggling Lavinia, she marched the girl out the door.

Chris knew he should not get involved. What he needed to do was find out just how he'd wandered onto the set of a bad movie and how he could get out, maybe on the blond horse, though a Harley would be better.

He ordered another beer and then asked, "You got a phone?"

Essie gave him the beer but ignored his question. Instead she looked him up and down and said, "I'm fond of that girl."

He took a sip. It wasn't any of his business. "What girl?" he asked when Essie didn't stop glaring at him. "Lavinia?"

Essie laughed harshly. "That trollop? Hardly. Lavinia is an employee. I'm talking about Martha Rose. She's a good girl."

"That's nice." Chris drank his beer and hoped for silence while he pondered his situation. She kept looking at him accusingly. "Didn't look like you cared for her to me," he finally said.

"We've had our differences, but that's her uncle's fault. And now she's going to get herself killed for the sake of her other uncle. Do something."

"Me?"

Why was he even talking to this woman? Why wasn't he out looking for somebody who would explain what was going on? He needed to call somebody, a lawyer, maybe. Or find a clinic. Yeah, that could be it. Maybe he was flashing on some of those controlled substances he'd once enjoyed. Be just like life to play that kind of practical joke on him by giving him hallucinations years after he'd learned better.

"Young man, are you listening to me?"

The woman reminded him of a schoolteacher. "What?"

"If you're going to clean up this town you had better start with Caleb Morse. Or Sheriff Wirth is going to get her pretty head shot off."

"Who?"

"Martha Rose. Marty. The young woman who just arrested Lavinia."

"Right. She's the sheriff." He thought about this while Essie continued to look stern. "It looks like I landed in the eighteen hundreds. I didn't know they had women cops in the eighteen hundreds."

She looked at him strangely for a long time, and finally said, "Martha is an exception to most rules. Besides," Essie added with a slight smile, "when you own half of a county you can be sheriff of its only town if you wish. Actually, it's more like two thirds since

Cyrus left her just about everything he owned. Dear Cyrus, we all miss that man, Martha Rose most of all."

"What's any of this got to do with me? Who do you people think I am, anyway?"

Essie looked significantly at his chest. Chris followed her gaze. He fingered the Texas Ranger badge he was wearing. Texas Ranger? Chris Parris, Texas. Ranger. Texas? "I was in California the last time I looked." At a biker bar in Oakland called Eddie's. "I'm in Texas? In the eighteen hundreds?" Essie nodded emphatically. "How'd I get here?"

"What kind of bad whiskey have you been drinking, Ranger, to make you forget the year?" Essie scratched her chin. "Well, I imagine Marty sent for you."

"Me?"

"Ranger Parris, are you quite all right?"

Chris took off his cowboy hat and ran his hands through his long, dark hair. "No," he said. "I'm not all right." He narrowed his eyes at the woman. "Marty sent for me, huh?"

"She must have. To help clean up the town. It could certainly use it. I wouldn't mind running a respectable establishment. Except that I do so enjoy annoying Jed Wirth."

Chris ignored most of what Essie said. He concentrated on the fact that he was here, wherever here was, because of Sheriff Martha Rose Wirth. He put his hat back on, drained his second glass of beer, and said, "So, which way's the sheriff's office?"

"Caleb's going to kill you!" Lavinia shouted as Marty closed the door that divided the office from the jail's only cell.

No he wouldn't, she thought as she locked the door and slipped the key into her pocket. Not with Ranger Parris on her side. She couldn't help but smile at the thought of the handsome, *tall* lawman who'd just ridden into her life. She wondered what he'd want to start with and how long he would stay in Loon, and she found herself hoping that he'd be around for weeks and weeks. There was so much to do, after all. And the longer he stayed, well, maybe, the longer he'd want to stay. She was smiling when she heard the sound of the office door opening.

"Well, sir," she began before she saw who it was, "where do we start?"

Charles Simpson smiled and closed the door behind him. "Good day, Miss Wirth," he said cheerfully, coming toward her. He took off his hat and held it in his hands. His smile grew wider as he said, "We can start by discussing our nuptials."

Marty noticed that his center-parted hair smelled of pomade, his breath of cinnamon pastilles. She wrinkled her nose. Simpson was always so clean, and half the time she smelled of horse sweat. It weren't natural to be so clean.

"Why would you want to marry me?" she asked, even though she knew the answer.

He took her hard hand in his soft one and said in his high, prissy voice, "For your money, Miss Martha. Pure and simple."

Martha sighed with relief. It sure felt good to hear honesty out of the banker for once. Still she narrowed her eyes suspiciously. "Charlie, you been telling me you love me since you came to town. Why you changing your fancy ways now?"

He took a step closer to her, craning his head over

his stiff collar to keep looking her in the eye. He wasn't a short man, but he wasn't anywhere near as tall as Marty, and certainly nowhere near the fine height and breadth of Ranger Parris. She pictured Chris Parris as he had snatched away the bottle that would have smashed into her head. He'd saved her life, or at least, saved her a nasty knot on the head. She sighed.

"Miss Martha!"

She blinked. "What?" Had he been talking? She hadn't heard a word. Reluctantly she focused her attention on Charles Simpson. He was frowning at her and still holding her hand, too.

He ran his thumb over the back of her hand as he spoke. "Miss Martha, you are in most ways a practical young woman. I've decided to appeal to the practical, responsible side of your nature rather than continue a romantic courtship. The romantic courtship was your uncle's idea, by the way." He put his free hand to his breast. "I would never have attempted such a course of action so distasteful to both of us otherwise."

Marty remembered the time just after Charles had come to town when he'd tried kissing her down by the stream at the Sunday social. He'd thought they were sheltered by the stand of cottonwoods, but half the town had been watching—and hooting and hollering. Fortunately, Jesse Baker had come running up, shouting about rustlers having taken all the horses from the livery stable, so Marty had had an excuse to run off and do something useful.

The town had talked about that kiss for the better part of a month, though. Marty had damn near called out Katie McBride for her wagging tongue, but she figured the woman's darning needle wasn't much use against her revolver. So she'd just bitten her tongue and tried to avoid Charles Simpson. Except Uncle Jed kept throwing them together, and Simpson kept on courting.

At least now he was being honest. "Well, I'm sorry to have embarrassed you, Charlie," she told him, wishing he would go away.

He smiled. "Then make it up to me by marrying me."

"I don't want to marry you, Charlie. I don't want to marry anybody."

He waved her words away. "A woman in your circumstances must marry."

"Why? I ain't in the family way."

He blushed from the roots of his hair down to his stiff collar. "Miss Wirth, such language from a lady!"

"Everybody in town knows I ain't no lady, not that they'd dare say so to my face." She removed her hand from his, and rested it on the smooth wooden butt of her gun.

Charles Simpson cleared his throat. "Lady or not, you are an heiress. Your position and financial situation bring more responsibility than a young woman is capable of dealing with."

"You mean I don't know nothing about business?"

He gave her a smile oilier than Foster Behan's. "Of course you have no head for business."

It was true, she didn't. "So?"

"You own a town, Miss Martha. That town needs to survive and prosper." He pointed at the gun on her hip. "That isn't the solution. Oh, your efforts at law enforcement are admirable, but they are not going to save Loon from destruction."

His words hurt her. Loon was all she had left of her ma and pa, and Uncle Cyrus. It was their dream. Uncle Jed just wanted money, but the rest of her family had had a dream about carving something good and permanent out of wilderness. She was an only child, the only Wirth offspring at all, the only one left to care. Comanches had gotten her parents, and a drunken bastard had taken out Uncle Cyrus. What else was there to do but try to stop the violence?

"I'm doing the best I can," she said. "The Ranger's arrived. He'll get this town peaceful." Or she'd know the reason why!

"Commendable," Simpson said as he nodded. "But protecting the honest citizens of Loon is not enough. It's their prosperity you must consider."

"But protecting 'em's all I know how to do! I ain't smart enough to do anything else. If only I was more like Essie Harris."

"Good Lord! Why? The woman's—"

"Smart. And educated. And good with money. She knows how to do more things than I can think of."

"But my dear, you don't need to be like that—person." He took a step toward her, looking sly and confident, and took her hand again. "You've got me to look after your interests. I promise you that I'll take Loon and make it into the most prosperous town in Texas. I can do it. I can do it for you, for the people of Loon. You care deeply for the people of this fair community, I know you do."

Marty nodded reluctantly. They were a bunch of gossiping, bellyaching, no-account fools, but they were hers. She'd do anything to take care of the people of Loon. The ungrateful snakes in the grass!

"You'd do anything to take care of these people," he said, as if reading her mind. "I know you would. You're a good woman, Miss Martha. Let me help you."

"But—"

"Marry me." He hesitated for a few significant seconds, then went on sternly, "If you don't marry me, I'm leaving my position as manager of your family's property. What with the railroad troubles and all, if I leave, Loon will be a ghost town within a year."

His words sank in, and sent a chill through her. The notion of the railhead moving terrified her, mostly because in her heart she knew it was true. The town would be deserted soon enough if the railroad took its business elsewhere. Never mind the lawlessness, people didn't stay in a place if there was no work for them. The railroad folks were talking about moving up to Kansas just as Loon was on the verge of becoming prosperous. Charles Simpson had promised that he could deal with the railroad. If he left town they wouldn't have anybody who could talk to the railroad men. She couldn't let Charles Simpson go.

Oh, Lord, she was going to have to do it, wasn't she? She'd told Uncle Jed that there was nothing that would get her to marry his bank manager, but she'd been wrong. And Uncle Jed had known it, she would bet on that. She wondered if there was any way she could worm her way out of it. "Marry you? What if I just paid you more money?"

"Money is not the issue here, Miss Martha."

Yes, it was. Why was he trying to confuse her? "You want to own Loon instead of just runnin' it, right?"

"I want to be your husband."

Which was the same thing as owning most of Loon. Why didn't he just come out and say so? Of course, if he was as greedy as she thought, if he owned the town he'd take good care of it.

"Am I so distasteful to you?" he asked.

"I—what's distasteful mean?"

He made a face, but didn't answer her question. "Could you ever care for me, Miss Martha?"

"No," she said honestly, ignoring his frown. She didn't see why she had to puff up Charles Simpson's vanity. She took a deep breath and bit the bullet. "But I reckon I better marry you anyhow."

Simpson's face split in a wide smile. "My dear! You make me ecstatic!" He bent over and kissed her hand.

For a minute Marty just frowned at the spot he'd kissed. "Oh," she finally said. "That's nice." She was distracted, thinking there were some things about kissing and such she should talk to Essie about, if she was going to be a married woman. A married woman. To Charles Simpson. Oh, good Lord, what had she done? "You best be going," she said to him. "I got work to do now."

Simpson frowned. "You'll be giving up your post as sheriff when we're married, of course. It's most unseemly."

"We ain't married yet."

"And you must learn not to use such a rough tone with me, my dear." He shook a finger at her. "A wife is obedient to her husband in all things."

She simply glared, hard enough for him take the hint and make for the door.

"We'll discuss it later," he said.

He put his hat on and opened the door. Ranger Parris was standing there, blocking the doorway, as if he'd been about to come in. "Excuse me," Simpson said as the Ranger moved out of his way. Over his shoulder he said to Marty, "I'll let your uncle know the good news."

Marty gulped. "You do that." She dismissed the banker from her thoughts, making him no more than a bad taste in her memory as tall, handsome, heroic Chris Parris stepped inside her office.

* * *

Chris had overheard most of the conversation before Simpson opened the door on him. He didn't know why he'd paused to eavesdrop on the girl and the man when he'd reached the door. He'd intended to stomp inside as if he were in control of the situation, but instead he had paused to listen. Maybe he'd thought he would learn something about what was going on with this 1800s thing, but he hadn't heard anything useful, even though he'd listened carefully to every nuance in their voices.

He should have walked right in and demanded a ticket out of this crazy place—or a ticket back to the future, since it seemed likely he'd fallen through some kind of time warp. Instead, he had heard Martha Wirth's longing to save her town, and the man's efforts to manipulate her. He didn't know why he should care. It wasn't any of his business.

Then she looked at him. He'd never seen so much trust and hope in anyone's eyes, and it was all aimed at him. *It's none of my business*, he repeated to himself as he approached her. *My job is to look after me, nobody else. Dammit, I wish she'd stop looking at me like that.*

"So," he found himself saying, "you're really going to marry that yuppie?"

"Yuppie? That anything like a yahoo?"

Chris scratched his jaw. "Yeah, something like that. Listen, you don't have to marry anybody you don't want." *It's none of your business, Parris!* he shouted at himself. But he kept running off at the mouth anyway. "He's just out to get your money."

"I know."

"You can do better than that."

"Well, ain't nobody else ever asked me. Besides," she added, "I'm doing what's right."

"Yeah, but . . ." It had to be her eyes that were making him continue. Those big, trusting gold-hazel eyes she was worshiping him with. Nobody had ever looked at him as if he meant anything to them. He liked the way that look made him feel. As if, maybe, he were needed.

Not that he wanted to be needed by anybody. If somebody needed you you'd start needing them and then where would you be? In a *relationship*, that's where. Oh, no, Chris Parris was too smart to get involved with any woman.

Of course, getting involved with a tall, shapely female who seemed to be good with a gun had a certain appeal. She looked as if she could take care of herself, and a woman who could take care of herself was an asset. Well, she might not have been emotionally able to take care of herself, which made him feel as if maybe he should offer her some help. Which was stupid. Really stupid.

"I've got no choice but to marry him," she said. "I just gave my word."

"What's that got to do with it? Call it off."

"That wouldn't be honorable."

"Honorable?" Chris laughed. "Oh, God. Who believes in honor anymore? That's something out of the Victorian era."

Marty frowned. "Essie says Queen Victoria is the reason everybody acts so proper and stiff and all. It's all cause the queen's husband died of cholera or something and now the queen's making everybody in the whole world act like its their fault, so everybody's got to act like they're at a funeral all the time." Marty paused. "I didn't rightly take her meaning, sir, but I know—"

"Screw Queen Victoria!" Chris shouted. "We're talking about you."

Marty blushed. "Oh. Yes, sir."

"Don't call me sir."

Her lower lip quivered. It was a deliciously full lower lip. She had lots of nice features, taken individually, even if they didn't all quite match up to make her pretty. She wasn't ugly, she was just kind of unique looking. Appealing, really.

"Don't cry," he said. "And don't marry that—yahoo—if you don't want to."

"I have to."

"To run your businesses?"

"Yes, si—Ranger Parris."

"Call me Chris."

He leaned against a corner of the desk while Marty stood with her thumbs hooked in her gun belt. There wasn't much in the room—a desk, a couple of chairs, a woodstove with a braided rug in front of it, and a wall-mounted gun rack holding a selection of rifles. Flies buzzed lazily around in the still, hot air. "Why don't you take care of the businesses on your own?" he said.

"Me? Run a business?" Marty asked. "I don't know how. I ain't got no education."

"So? You can go to school."

Her eyes grew even wider. "Me?"

"Sure. Hell, even I've been to college." Okay, he'd taken most of his college courses while he'd been doing time, but at least he had finished school eventually. "Plenty of women run businesses. My sister runs her own business and she's a complete bimbo."

"Bimbo? That anything like what Essie's girls do?"

"No. Not exactly. What I'm saying is, there's no

reason why you couldn't go to school to learn how to manage your own property."

"Really?" The worshipful look on Marty's face deepened, then she looked crestfallen. "Women can't go to college. It ain't proper." She brightened. "But I sent away for a book."

A book. He would bet the town didn't have a library. Or a bookstore. Or even a video rental place. He'd hunted for something even vaguely familiar as he'd walked down the unpaved street. Nothing. Nada. Zip. Not even a McDonald's. What was he doing here?

"Marty," he asked, "what am I doing here?"

Suddenly Martha was all business. "Well, there's that gang of cattle rustlers working out of the Johnson Ranch."

"That's not what I meant."

"Yes, sir—Chris, that's all trouble outside of town. If you want to start in Loon proper, well, there's a shipment of money due at the bank. The Varney gang's bound to come for it, maybe robbing the train, maybe wait and rob the bank after it gets here. Depends on how drunk Virgil Varney is this week. And we've had four murders in the last month, that's murders, sir, Chris, not honest gunfights over cards and such, though we've had a few too many of those what with Foster Behan being too good with a gun and mighty bad at getting caught cheating at faro."

Chris waved a hand in front of her face, trying to interrupt. "Martha—"

She went on relentlessly. "And I've been working on tracking down the varmint that keeps stealing the horses right out of the livery stable. Oh, I'll have your palomino taken to Uncle Jed's stable where it'll be safe enough."

Palomino. Was that what the blond horse was called? "I think I'll name him Harley. Listen, Marty, I meant—"

"Oh, you want to see to something right this minute, I reckon. That'd be those buckaroos in off a drive. We got to get us through tonight before we worry about the regular problems, sir. Chris." She blushed, and gave him a shy smile.

One thing he had to admit, the sheriff of Loon had plenty of troubles, most of them more pressing than being engaged to the wrong man. But none of her problems was any of his business, even if she was looking at him as if he were the answer to her prayers. He'd come looking for answers, and all he'd found were more questions.

"Martha," he said, "you don't understand. I'm not—" What was he going to tell her? That he was from the future? "—from around here."

I'm not here to fight your battles for you, he wanted to say. *Nobody's ever fought any battles for me*. He wanted to say that, too, but the words just wouldn't come out. How was he supposed to be bitter and cynical when she was looking at him like that?

It was a hot day in a dusty town out of the past and he was tired, as well as confused. He didn't know how he'd gotten there, or if he could even get out. Rod Serling was probably going to appear at some point and tell him he was part of a rerun in *The Twilight Zone*.

Chris took off his hat and ran his fingers through his hair. "This has not been a good day."

When a bullet came shattering through the window a moment later it only got worse.

"What the—" Chris yelled as he grabbed Marty around the waist and pushed her to the floor.

She felt him land on top of her as a second shot

came through the window. No one had ever tried to protect her before.

Martha knew she was in love.

"That'll be Caleb Morse," she told the Ranger. "He must have heard about my locking up Lavinia."

"Someone's shooting at us!" Chris said. "You don't have to sound so pleased about it."

But she was pleased at having flushed Caleb out so quickly. Chris's hair was tickling her cheek. He had soft brown hair, and the warm weight on her back was all hard muscle. He smelled like a man, more like dust and sweat than pomade and Sen-Sen. Martha closed her eyes and forgot for a moment that he was holding her because they were in danger. Then more glass shattered as a third bullet was fired, interrupting her brief reverie.

"Martha Wirth, I've come for your hide!" a slurred voice shouted from outside.

Marty lifted her head and shouted back, "You can try to get it, Caleb, but I'm going to—"

Chris's hand came over her mouth before she could finish. "What are you doing?" he demanded.

He slowly took his hand away. Then he rolled off her, which she found kind of disappointing even if she did need to be free to draw her gun. "He's the dirty dog that killed my uncle Cyrus," she said as she cautiously got to her knees.

"Oh." He frowned at her, his narrow eyes making him look tough and dangerous. Of course he was dangerous, he was a Ranger. Between them they were more than a match for the likes of Caleb Morse. "What are you smiling about?" he demanded. He got up off his belly and pointed at the window. "We're being shot at!"

"Where's Lavinia?" Caleb called from outside. "You send Lavinia out here!"

"You come and get her!" Marty shouted back. Caleb fired another shot through the window. Marty and Chris dived for the floor again as the bullet ricocheted around the office.

Once it had embedded itself in the desk, Chris raised his head and snarled, "Don't aggravate the man!"

Marty got up and carefully edged her way to the door, her revolver held tightly in her sweating hand. She knew she didn't have time to let herself feel scared.

"I count four shots," she told Chris. "That means he's down to one bullet." She gave the Ranger a grin, confident that he was there to back her up. "If he don't have a second gun on him, that is," she added, before she flung the door open and rushed outside.

"Marty!" The crazy girl was going to get herself killed! Chris was on his feet and running for the door as he heard two guns firing simultaneously. The air outside was full of sulfurous gun smoke. What was he doing out here? Was he trying to get himself killed?

The next thing he knew he'd shoved Marty to the ground and was standing in the middle of the street pointing a gun at a big red-faced man with an oversized hat and an oversized gun in each hand. Chris didn't know why he was trying to help Marty, and he sure as hell didn't know how, but the weight of the revolver he was holding gave him a certain sense of security. His adversary, who was only a few feet away, looked about as startled at this situation as Chris felt.

"What the hell am I doing?" Chris shouted to the heavens as the man aimed a gun at him.

"Shoot!" Marty yelled as she sprang to her feet. "Damn you, Caleb Morse!"

Her voice caught Caleb's attention, and he immediately swung the gun toward Marty. Chris saw her begin to squeeze the trigger of her revolver, and he knew he had to do something. So he jumped. At Caleb Morse. He didn't know who was more surprised, Morse, himself, or Marty. Instead of firing his heavy revolver he hit Caleb Morse in the head with it.

"Why'd you do that for?" Marty demanded as he eased the unconscious man to the dusty ground. She stomped up to him. "You coulda got killed!"

Chris turned on her. "I could have gotten killed!" He gestured toward the jail, then at the girl, whose eyes flashed angrily at him. "You're the one who ran out to get herself shot at. I was only trying to cover your ass!" *And I don't know why*, an angry, scared voice said in his head. It was stupid. "I could have gotten killed," he went on. "And it would have been your fault!"

Marty looked at the ground, and shuffled her large, booted feet. "Yes, sir. Chris," she corrected, looking up at him through her eyelashes.

He wished she hadn't done that because her look sent a shock of emotion through him that all but canceled out his anger. Damn, but she was—sweet.

Sweet? The woman had been in a gunfight a minute ago. How could he possibly think of her as sweet? "Man," he grumbled, "I have got to get out of here."

Marty nudged Caleb Morse with her boot. "He ain't dead," she pointed out. "Guess we'll have to string him up instead."

"String him up?" Chris stared at her. "You are talking about hanging a man, aren't you?"

"Well, you wouldn't let me shoot him—"

"Without a trial?"

Marty made a face. "I know the law says a man's innocent till proved guilty, but Caleb Morse is guilty as sin and twice as mean."

Chris wasn't sure if what had just happened had been attempted murder or self-defense, or who had attempted to murder or defend whom. All he knew was that he believed in the American judicial system—after all, he'd spent a good part of his life involved with it, and had gotten off more times than not.

"A man deserves a fair trial," he told Marty.

"He killed my uncle Cyrus and he's going to swing."

"Fine, but he gets a trial first."

"Circuit rider won't be here for months!"

"A trial," Chris insisted. "With a jury of his peers."

Marty squinted at him. "What's a peer?"

"His equals."

"Horse thieves and murderers?"

"I'm not going to argue about this, Marty." He bent down to take the man's feet. "Just help me get him into the jail."

Marty would have objected to being fair about anything with a low-down scoundrel like Caleb Morse if Ranger Parris's words hadn't reminded her of what she'd said to Uncle Jed about vigilantes not so long ago. The Ranger was right, of course, she thought as she hoisted Caleb up by the shoulders while Chris took his feet and helped lug the unconscious man into the jail. Of course he was right, he was the representative of law and order, of civilization, of everything she wanted for Loon. And herself.

She gave him a quick look when his head was turned away as he opened the office door, and sighed.

It must have been too loud, because Chris shot her a glance that said he knew exactly what she was feeling. It was a look that made her feel hot all over, but she didn't know if it was with embarrassment or what. She sighed again, to herself this time, as they carried Caleb back to the cell.

Lavinia shrieked as they set the groaning murderer down long enough to unfasten his gun belt. Ranger Parris did a quick pat-down for any other weapons while Marty turned to the hollering soiled dove.

"What's the matter with you, girl?" Marty demanded.

"Is Caleb dead?"

"'Course he ain't dead." She gave Chris an admiring look. "Ranger Parris didn't come to town to kill folks. Caleb here's going to get a fair trial, then we're going to kill him."

"Martha!" Chris snapped.

"If he's found guilty by a jury of his peers," she added quickly. "Being civilized don't come easy, and that's the truth." She unlocked the cell door. "You can go now, Lavinia," she told the girl, who was still staring worriedly at Caleb. "He'll be fine," she assured her. *For a while*, she added to herself.

Lavinia walked out of the cell while Chris dragged Caleb in and left him on the bed. "This town got a doctor?" he asked as he emerged.

Marty shook her head as she made sure the cell door was locked good and tight. "But Caleb's too mean to die from a hit on the head."

Chris looked thoughtful for few moments, then he nodded and said, "I bet."

Marty stepped away from the cell, then gently herded the other two back into the office, where they stood, looking confused. The Ranger looked more than confused; he frowned as if he had the worst hangover of his life. It made Marty's fingers itch to soothe his fevered brow. Or something.

"Go on, now," she said to Lavinia as the girl began to look Chris over. "Essie'll be needing you back at the Black Eye."

Lavinia sidled up to Chris. She put a hand on his arm. "How about you, Ranger?" she asked, voice all low and husky, with a sultry look in her eyes.

Chris looked down at her as if he'd just noticed her. He smiled, a slow, syrupy kind of smile. It would have set Marty's heart to fluttering if it had been turned on her. But it wasn't. Seeing him look at one of Essie's girls like that reminded her that he was just a man after all, even if he was a man with a badge and a sense of justice, and a man who'd saved her twice, and a man so handsome and most especially tall that she just wanted to tie him up and drag him to the preacher before he could draw a breath to shout about it.

Which reminded her that she was promised to Charles Simpson and that she had no business having such thoughts about another man. Not even aTexas Ranger. Especially not a Texas Ranger. She sighed.

"I don't know what I'm doing here," he said. "I don't know how I got here. I don't belong here. Don't look at me like that!"

"Like what?"

"It makes me crazy!"

"How am I looking at you?"

"Like I'm the hero you've always dreamed of. It makes me want to do—things."

"Things?" she asked as Lavinia rubbed up against him like a hungry cat. The girl was acting as if Marty weren't even in the room.

"Things," he repeated, and made a kind of desperate gesture that took in the office and the town and her. "Heroic—things." He swore, and ran his hands over Lavinia. "This is my kind of woman," he told Marty, as if she'd asked him. "I like hookers. I've liked lots of hookers. Well, a couple. Okay, I've never had to pay for it. But I don't like nice girls. Nice girls are nothing but trouble. Even the ones that don't get into gunfights."

"Oh," Marty said, not sure what she wanted, but knowing that she felt hurt because he didn't want to give it to her.

"Come on," he said to Lavinia, pulling her with him toward the door. He threw one more glance at Marty as she watched him go. "I need a drink," he said. "Oh, man, do I need a drink."

TWO ~

"Marty's a nice girl," he said, pulling Lavinia closer. The hooker giggled in his ear, then licked it. He kept on talking to Essie, who was standing stiffly across the bar from him. The mirror behind her reflected the dirty, noisy crowd filling the Black Eye. Chris ignored them, concentrating his attention on the red-haired saloon owner. "A nice girl," he went on. "I don't need a nice girl."

"'Course you don't, darlin'," Lavinia whispered huskily.

"I knew a nice girl once," he went on. "Back in the twentieth century. I stole a car to impress her. Turned out her dad was a cop." He smiled at the memory of the high-speed chase that had ended his escapade with that nice girl. He'd been fifteen.

Behind him, a fight was getting started. He took a

drink of the worst rotgut whiskey he'd ever tasted, and nearly choked. "What's this stuff made from?"

"You don't want to know," Essie told him.

No, he didn't suppose he did. He scratched his ear, having forgotten for a moment that Lavinia was playing with it. Her other hand was attached to his crotch, which might have explained the ache down there, but he didn't think the hooker had much to do with it. "It's Martha," he complained. Essie nodded wisely. "She looks at me with those big eyes and I— "

Chris was interrupted by a body bouncing hard against the bar right next to him. The impact jostled his glass, so he picked it up and finished off the foul liquid. Essie obligingly poured him another out of a squat green glass bottle and told Lavinia to go back to work. The girl patted his crotch once more and flounced off.

Chris watched the fight in the mirror for a few moments. It reminded him of watching a hockey game on the screen at a sports bar back home.

"Back home," he muttered as flesh and furniture collided behind him. There was a lot of shouting, and one of the girls began screaming like a banshee. Chris already had a headache. The whiskey wasn't helping, and neither was the girl's piercing shriek. He leaned his elbows on the bar and glowered at the mirrored chaos for a few more seconds.

His attention was caught by a bald man who'd pulled a big bowie knife out of his boot. The knife seemed like a waste of time since he was pointing it at Foster Behan, who had drawn a gun.

A gun. Chris sighed. Everybody had guns, but Behan seemed to be the only guy interested in using one right now. He straightened slowly and turned, and everyone in the room froze as he moved. It probably had something to do with his size and the shiny star pinned on his coat.

He nailed Behan with an angry look. "If that thing goes off, I'm going to be very annoyed," he announced.

They stared at each other for a while, and all was silent in the room. The man with the knife slunk back into the waiting crowd. Chris ignored everything but the cold, hard eyes of the gambler. Sweat formed on his back and rolled like a ghostly finger all the way down his spine. He wanted to shudder, but didn't; he just kept looking steadily at the gambler. He was aware that Foster Behan's gun was ready in his hand while Chris's own—though he still had no idea how he'd gotten a gun in the first place—was still in its holster. He'd never actually fired a gun in his life, but he knew that, somehow, he was capable of using it. If he could get to it. If he had to.

He didn't have to. Slowly, after nobody in the sweating crowd seemed to have taken a breath for a long time, Foster Behan's gaze and the hand holding the gun lowered.

"I think you'd better leave."

Chris looked behind him, at the woman who'd spoken. "Essie?" he asked, but the saloon owner was looking at the gambler.

"Did you hear me, Foster Behan?" she went on. "I said get out."

It was Behan's turn to say, "Essie?"

"I've had quite enough of your violent, cheating ways, Mr. Behan. Get your carcass out of my establishment."

Behan gaped at her. So did the crowd, including Lavinia and Chris. "But—" the gambler started.

Essie reached under the bar, and came up with a

rifle in her hands. "Right now, Mr. Behan." Her gaze flicked to Chris. "Or Ranger Parris will see you out. We wouldn't want that, would we?"

The woman's voice held a threat Chris didn't think he was up to fulfilling, but he gave a slight, squinting Clint Eastwood sort of smile to the gambler anyway. The crowd began to laugh. Behan looked once more from Essie to Chris, then he holstered his gun and walked out the door.

"Well," Essie said as she put the rifle back under the bar. She patted Chris on the arm as the conversation and carousing started up again. Chris turned to face her. "It looks like you're going to clean up this town after all," she told him.

He was? Him? "Me?"

"Even I begin to see the virtues of virtuous living."

"Glad to hear it." He could have been killed. He could have flat out been killed. It wasn't that he couldn't have been killed plenty of times before, but this time he felt it. "I definitely need a drink," he said. He was shaking. "I need more than a drink." He saw a mental flash of Martha Rose Wirth looking up at him from under her long eyelashes. "No, not that. Anything but a nice girl."

He spotted Lavinia crawling all over a man at the other end of the bar. Lavinia was not a nice girl. He grabbed a bottle of bad whiskey from Essie, then he grabbed her before the other man could hire her away.

"Come on," he said to Lavinia. "Show me the way upstairs."

The Black Eye was quieter than Martha had expected. The second thing she noticed was that there was no faro game going on in the big corner table where Foster Behan always sat. Her third observation was that though the place was crowded and the drinking was heavy, the usual edge was missing; nobody looked ready to start a fight just for the hell of it.

The first thing she had noticed was that Chris Parris was not in the barroom.

Martha tried not to wonder where he was. She told herself it was none of her business how the Ranger spent his own time. Essie was behind the end of the bar close to the staircase. Marty noted that the traffic on the stairs was brisk and she didn't see any of the girls in the barroom. What the girls were doing with the men upstairs reminded her of why she'd come into the Black Eye in the first place. She gulped, but lifted her chin proudly and walked straight up to the saloon owner.

"Evenin', Essie," she said.

"Good evening, Martha Rose. What's on your mind, girl?" Essie asked. "You look like the devil's at your heels." She brought a bottle of ginger beer out from under the counter and poured Marty a glass.

Marty stared at the glass of dark liquid, then smiled her thanks at Essie. The ginger beer was Essie's own personal supply and she didn't share it much. Marty took a long, satisfying drink while Essie kept looking at her in that shrewd way of hers.

When Marty put down the glass, Essie leaned toward her and said quietly, "Tell me about it, Martha Rose."

Marty sighed and came straight out with it. "I'm fixing to marry Charles Simpson and I want to know about things. Woman-and-man things," she added as Essie's eyes went round with surprise. "You got to help me, Essie, 'cause I don't know nothing and I don't like it."

Essie's expression changed from surprised to shrewd. "Simpson's got you scared, doesn't he, girl?"

"'Course he does," Martha blurted out before her pride took over. "Of course he don't," she corrected a second later. "I just want to—" She gestured toward the stairs. "Know."

Essie's eyebrows shot up, then she turned all prissy and schoolmarmy. "Proper young ladies shouldn't want to know about such things."

Marty looked beyond Essie, to her own reflection in the mirror behind them. She was all tall and gawky and scared looking, and she didn't like it. "I don't see no lady in this place." Then, without thinking about it, she reached over the bar and touched Essie's hand. "Help me, Essie Harris," she whispered. "'Cause you're right about Simpson having me all spooked."

"If he's got you spooked," Essie told her sternly, "you've got no business marrying him."

"Yes, I do. Because of business. For Loon. So the town'll . . ." Her voice trailed off as the look on Essie's face grew more annoyed with every word she spoke.

"Business? Girl, what I and those girls upstairs do, is for business."

She knew Essie meant that selling herself to Simpson was just whoring by another name. Well, maybe Essie was right. "We all do what we have to," Marty said. "Loon needs Simpson and Simpson wants me. I don't want him, but that don't matter none and he and I both know it."

"Hmmph." Essie crossed her arms over her lush bosom. "I know wanting when I see it, and I saw you looking that way at Ranger Parris earlier."

"I—" Marty went hot all over, but didn't deny Essie's words. "That don't matter none," she said. "Wantin' don't matter."

"It should." Essie's voice was low and fierce. "Believe me, girl, it should." She touched Marty's hand. "Don't let your uncle Jed turn you into a whore the way he did me."

Marty swallowed hard. "I've always been sorry about that, Essie. I want to make Loon a better place."

"But you don't have to marry Simpson to do it."

"I do!" Marty insisted, pain nearly choking her.

"Oh, Martha Rose, really!" Essie gave a loud huff.

"Just tell me what a woman needs to do in the bedroom. I need to know how to keep a man happy."

"Charles Simpson will only be happy when he's counting *your* money," Essie snapped.

Marty rubbed her hands together while her gaze dropped to the scored wood of the bar. "I know." She looked up at Essie sheepishly. "But I was hoping I could learn a thing or two about distracting him."

"Distracting him? What do you mean, Martha Rose?"

Marty cleared her throat. "Well, I, uh . . . I heard you say once that a man could be led around by his privates if a woman had a mind to learn how to do it." She ignored Essie's sudden deep chuckle. "Well, I've a mind to learn."

Essie clapped her hands together and laughed, hard and loud. *Oh, Lord,* Marty thought as people looked curiously their way. *Oh, Lord, please don't let her tell the world what I just said. Just strike me with lightning right here and now, if that's what Essie Harris is going to do.*

Instead, Essie leaned so close no one else could possibly hear. "So, you want to know how to please a man, do you?"

Marty could only nod.

Essie pointed up the stairs. "You go right on up to the first bedroom on the right side of the hall."

"But—" Well, she didn't suppose Essie could teach her any tricks out in public. "Yes, ma'am."

Essie's eyes were gleaming, with amusement and something else. "You go on up, Martha Rose." She patted her on the shoulder, and gave her a little push toward the stairs. "You'll get expert instruction up in the front bedroom, I promise. You go on up," she repeated when Marty hesitated. Essie winked. "I'll be up directly, soon as I get a few things taken care of."

Marty went, but it worried her that she could hear Essie chuckling after her as she shouldered her way through the crowd on and around the staircase. Everyone seemed to be either getting ready to or just done with their spot of iniquity. At least, she figured as she put her hand on the knob of the first door on the right, she was finally going to learn what one fancy word meant.

Not tonight, Chris had told Lavinia, I've got a headache. He didn't believe he'd actually said it, used the dumbest line in the book, and a woman's line at that, even if it was true. It was definitely true. He was trapped in the past, and his head hurt, and he could have gotten killed at least twice already that day. Besides, Lavinia didn't look or smell any too clean, and he just wasn't ready to risk his life by screwing around with a girl who could have anything from crabs to anthrax on her medical records, no matter how much he thought he needed to get laid to reassure himself that he was still alive.

So he told her he had a headache. After she called him a few old-West rude names she had left, slamming the heavy door so hard it vibrated. He sat on the bed, staring at the steady flame in the glass chimney of the lantern and worrying about his sanity. Occasionally he took a very small sip of very bad whiskey just to see if it would help. He came to the conclusion that the whiskey was more likely to cause hallucinations, if not outright death by poison, than it was to cure them. So eventually he gave up drinking it, even for medicinal purposes.

"I can't get drunk," he muttered at last. "I can't get laid, and I don't know what I'm doing here. What *can* I do?"

As he finished speaking the door slowly opened with a creak. Chris was up, with his gun in his hand, faster than he could think. He didn't know how he'd done it, just that he had and it felt right. Everything about this place felt right, even the hot wash of desire that spread through him as he saw who had disturbed him.

Martha Rose Wirth stood in the doorway, looking surprised. Her gaze flicked from the gun to his face and then to his chest and she slowly turned very, very red. He'd taken off his shirt when he'd thought Lavinia might be a viable option and hadn't bothered putting it back on. He wondered now if he should clutch it to his exposed bosom to protect himself from her roving eyes. Then he chuckled, low and deep, at the thought.

"Uh," she said. "I—uh—That's a mighty fine tattoo," she finally managed to stumble out. She cleared her throat. "I ain't never seen a man with a rose on his chest before."

Chris replaced the gun in its holster, but the adrenaline rush that had come with drawing it kept right on burning. His body wasn't thinking about fight-or-flight reactions, though, but something equally basic and primitive.

He looked down at the three-inch-wide red rose tattooed on the skin of his left collarbone. Then he met her gaze and felt the heat throbbing between them. He traced his fingers slowly over the tattoo. "Maybe I did this for you, Martha *Rose*," he said.

The words were spoken as much on reflex as drawing the gun had been. It was his turn to go bright red, even while desire continued to curl through him. He didn't mean to take a step toward her any more than he'd meant to say what he just had; he was just reacting to that primitive urge.

What was she doing there, anyway? And was he going to let innocent, eager Martha Rose get out the door before his urge to screw her brains out got out of hand?

Marty knew there was some sort of mistake. She had to be in the wrong place. Ranger Parris was alone and she was mighty thankful for that. There was certainly no iniquity going on, there was just a hungry-looking man with his shirt off. Essie must have rented the room to Ranger Parris, and he must have been getting ready for bed when she walked in on him. He'd been in the right to draw on her; she'd have done the same to anyone who opened a door on her without knocking.

She intended to back right on out, but she couldn't take her eyes off Chris Parris. He was the best-looking thing she'd ever seen, but then she knew that already. Whether his shirt was on or off, he reminded her of some big, brown mustang stallion. There was no taming this man, though why anyone would want to she didn't know.

Tame him, no, but why was the idea of riding him so interesting?

Stallion. Marty swallowed hard. Good Lord, but the man's jeans were tight. "I, uh . . ." Her mouth wouldn't work to form the words. 'Course, how could it, when her brain was being cooked by the steam rising off the rest of her, and her mouth wanted to settle long and hard on his? If she felt like that from the sight of his bare chest, she wondered what she'd do if he took his pants off. Melt like butter in the hot sun, probably.

"Essie," she said suddenly as Chris took a step toward her. She meant to back out of the room, close the door, and go looking for the empty room where she was supposed to wait for Essie Harris to come talk to her. She closed the door all right, but she was inside the room when she did. She found herself leaning back against the warped wood and realizing she'd just done the most improper thing a good girl could do. She was now alone in a bedroom with a half-dressed man. Queen Victoria was going to be mighty disappointed if she found out.

"Well, screw Queen Victoria," she murmured. "Charlie Simpson's gonna have a calf."

Chris was staring at her. She expected he'd notice they were alone any second now, then he'd get all righteous about her smirching his reputation as a gentleman and then he'd see her firmly out and slam the door behind her. And he'd want her badge besides, 'cause a body had to be respectable if they were to work alongside a Texas Ranger.

Instead, he took another step toward her and just kept *looking* at her. The more he looked the more the space between them heated up. She took a step closer to him. Since the room wasn't all that big to begin with she figured they were going to bump right into each other pretty quick if they kept on going.

"Uh," she said, then touched her throat, 'cause it felt tight. So did her clothes. And her pulse was all fluttery. His gaze moved down her body, but it might have been his hands that moved over her instead. Things happened, to her breasts and her stomach. Her own hand moved, from her throat to the top button of her shirt. She felt as if she ought to loosen her clothes, just a bit, to get comfortable.

The look in Chris's eyes just got hotter when she unfastened the button. "Oh, yeah," he said, voice real low.

Just undoing one didn't make her feel any better at all, so she undid some more while she and Chris took a step for each button until they were standing about an inch apart. He reached out and pushed her shirt off her shoulders and down her arms, and she shook it the rest of the way off.

She was wearing a lace-edged camisole under her shirt, tied with a pink ribbon. Chris ran his finger across the delicate edging, his fingertips just barely dusting her skin. "Oh," she said, wanting him to do it again.

He did. "Like that?" he asked.

She didn't answer, she just looked down and watched his fingers move over the very tops of her breasts. "Should you be doing that?" she asked, knowing he shouldn't. But she liked it.

Instead of answering he bent down and undid the camisole ribbon with his teeth. Then he kissed the side of her breast!

"Oh, Lord!" she said.

"Oh, yeah!" he said in response.

Then he straightened and his mouth found hers. Marty gasped at the initial contact, then his lips did things to hers and his tongue was all over the place inside her mouth and she liked it more than anything she'd ever felt before. This wasn't at all like the time Charlie Simpson had kissed her. He'd just put his mouth on hers and that had been the end of it, just a little lip smacking, all chaste and acting like they were both supposed to be embarrassed by the whole thing.

With Chris, lips were just a part of it. His mouth was hot and demanding and coaxing and his hands were splayed out on her behind, pulling her against him in a way that made their bodies fit just right. And, oh, Lord, but it was hot and aching where they touched! She'd never known that being hot and hurting could feel so good.

Chris could tell she'd never been kissed. Some primitive, possessive part of him really got off on the idea of being the first man to kiss Martha Rose Wirth.

When he stopped kissing her long enough to look at her, he found that those big golden eyes were regarding him all worshipfully, and he liked it.

Relationship! a voice in the back of his head screamed. *If you screw this girl you're going to get in a relationship with her.*

Shut up, he told the warning voice. *Who says I want to screw her? Maybe I want to make love to her.*

That's worse. Much worse. Doomed! You're doomed!

Marty swallowed hard, then she reached out tentatively and put her hand over the rose on his chest. "Was that—does that—is that the iniquity part?"

"Iniquity?" He ran one hand slowly up her back to

tangle his fingers in her hair. She arched like a cat. "Like in den of iniquity?" he asked. She nodded. "What do you think?"

She swallowed again. "I reckon it is."

He gave her his slowest, sexiest smile. "But you like it."

"I was hopin'—" She looked away, and blushed. "I asked Essie to teach me all about the iniquity part. So I could—well, so I could—"

He stroked her throat and ran a finger along her stubborn, square chin. "You need a man to teach you what you want to know. I think I'm man enough for the job." When she didn't answer he kissed her again. This time his hand found her breast and stroked and teased it, matching the rhythm of what his tongue was doing in her mouth.

Slowly, her tongue and hands began doing things too, and the next thing he knew Chris had flipped her down on the bed. She was underneath him, all lush and curved and willing and he was hard with wanting her. They were both panting and making small, inarticulate sounds while they fumbled with each other's clothing.

It was going to be good, great, the best. Chris could tell. It was going to be the kind of sex they'd both always dreamed of—even if Martha Rose Wirth had never actually dreamed of sex. But that was okay because he'd dreamed of enough for both of them. He was perfectly willing to ignore the shouting and shots just outside the window. What was happening on the bed was far more important to him than any possible riot on the main street.

"No!" he pleaded when Marty raised her head from the pillow and looked toward the open window. "No. It's all right."

"But . . . Chris . . . I—I, oh, Lord!"

He stroked her. "That's right. Concentrate on how I'm making you feel, Martha Rose. You like that?" He moved his hands to a different spot as she nodded. "How about this?"

She squirmed with pleasure and said his name with breathless eagerness, but her gaze strayed back to the window. Her attention was obviously on the disturbance down below. Chris groaned, and got up off the bed to slam the window.

"I was in Los Angeles during the riots," he muttered as he crossed the room, "and it was a lot quieter than this town."

The curtains blew back as he reached the window, and someone in the crowd looked up and saw him. "There he is!" he cried. "That's the Ranger!"

Shots were fired into the air. A cry went up.

"Where's the sheriff?" someone bellowed. "Where's Martha Wirth?" The question was punctuated by rumbling shouts and more shots.

"We want to see her right now, Ranger!" another man called. "We've got business with the sheriff!"

He hoped Marty wasn't listening. He gave her a sharp look and waved for her to stay put, but she was already sitting up, fingers fumbling to fasten her lacy top. He frowned at the idea of her getting dressed since it meant he was just going to have to undress her again. She probably thought she was going outside to face the mob.

"Wrong," he whispered.

He wanted her to stay on the bed, where he intended to get back to her as soon as possible. He could see about a dozen men milling around in the light cast by the open door of the saloon. Their angry faces were all turned up to him. He wanted to just slam the window and ignore them, but if he did they might come charging up to the bedroom. If these turned out to be the more respectable members of the community, he could end up facing a lynch mob if they caught him getting ready to make it with the town's leading citizen.

With that realization in mind he stepped back from the window and quickly buttoned up his jeans. Then he called down to the men still shouting below, "What do you want?"

"Marty!" several called back.

"I know that," he shouted. He put his hands on his hips. "What do you want with the sheriff?" He knew what he wanted with her, and soon. His groin ached with the knowledge of just how soon he wanted her.

"This ain't nothin' to do with you, Ranger," a man shouted at him. "You just tell us where we can find Sheriff Wirth, then stay in your room."

"What you don't know won't do you no harm," another man added.

Chris shot a puzzled look at Marty. She'd gotten up and was putting her shirt back on. Her jeans were neatly buttoned and she had an air of determination on her strong features. She met his gaze briefly, blushed, and went back to dressing.

"You know what they want?" he asked her.

"Yep," she replied. "I surely do. This is your fault," she added as the roaring and gunfire outside got louder.

"What? They know what we're doing?"

Somebody started pounding on the bedroom door before Marty could answer. Then Essie's voice called, "Chris, Marty, there's trouble. Jed Wirth is down here demanding the key to Caleb Morse's cell. He's got a hanging in mind. You two decent?"

"We're decent," Marty called back, her voice tight. She went to the door and yanked it open. "You had no business sending me up here," she told Essie. "But I suppose we can talk about it later," she added with a narrow-eyed glare.

Chris thought it was a far better Clint Eastwood imitation than he'd been able to manage. Of course, with Marty maybe it wasn't an imitation. She might wear lace next to her skin, but she was also tough as nails.

He liked that in a woman.

As Marty stepped out of the room Chris said, "Wait."

She didn't respond. He could tell by the stiff set of her back that she was thinking she was the sheriff, and that she had work to do.

She was crazy. The situation was crazy. He hurriedly finished dressing and followed the women down the stairs anyway.

She ached all over. Marty wasn't sure why her skin still felt as if Chris was touching it, but it did, and half her mind was still in that room, on that bed, wanting the things he did to her. She cast a glance at Essie. She would have hit the saloon owner if she'd looked smug, but Essie wasn't laughing at her.

"Why'd you do that?" Marty asked her as they reached the top of the stairs.

"The Ranger looks like a man to me," Essie answered. "You need a man to teach you the things you want to know."

Marty's jaw tightened. "I want to learn how to pleasure a man, not how to, well, you know." She blushed, her skin growing hotter than it already was.

Essie's plucked eyebrows arched at her. "Do I? What did the Ranger teach you, Martha Rose? That a woman can feel good, too?" She put a hand on Marty's arm. "Charles Simpson will want you to lie still and keep quiet and give him sons. That enough for you, girl?"

Marty could hear Uncle Jed shouting for her downstairs, threatening to come up and find her, and hollering about what kind of business was a good woman doing on Essie Harris's second floor whether she was the sheriff or not. She could hear dark male laughter as well and crude answers to his question. She was going to have to face all that laughter and Uncle Jed's anger. Bracing herself for that, she didn't have time to think about Essie's question right now.

So she just said, "It's enough," and went on down the stairs. Essie muttered in disapproval as she followed her.

Uncle Jed was waiting at the bottom of the stairs, red faced and glaring. He waited until she reached him before he bellowed, "What the devil's going on here, girl?" She could smell the liquor on his breath.

Essie pushed past Marty to confront him. "Martha Rose is doing her duty. Now you leave her alone."

Jed snorted. He and Essie glared daggers at each other for a bit, and it was Jed who looked away first. Essie tossed her head and went back behind the bar with a little smile on her face. She declared a round of drinks on the house, which got all the cowboys' attention off Marty and her uncle right quickly.

"Well?" Uncle Jed demanded. "What are you doing here, Marty?"

"None of your beeswax," she answered sharply. "What are you doing here? What are your friends doing outside?" She asked as if she didn't know already.

"Justice," he answered. "The Vigilance Commitee of Loon is going to see that justice is done."

Marty wanted to spit. "Vigilance Committee? You mean you and George and Mike Brown and Bob Mason and—"

"Hush!" he interrupted her. "The identity of the members is supposed to be secret."

She put her hands on her hips. "Everybody in Loon knows who you and the town council are. A bunch of drunken fools."

"We're not acting as the council, but as the—"

"I don't care what you're calling yourselves," she said. "I told you I wouldn't have no vigilantes in Loon. You go on home, Uncle Jed."

"Give me the key to the jail," he said, holding out his hand.

She shook her head. "Ain't no way."

"Caleb Morse is going to swing."

"That's the truth. But not before he has a trial."

"He's guilty as sin and you know it."

She gave a firm nod. "That I do."

"Well, then, let me have the key."

"No, sir, I will not."

Uncle Jed shook a finger in her face. "I'll take it from you if I have to, girl."

She shook her head, and put her hand on the butt of her pistol. "I'll see him hanged, Uncle Jed," she said. "But Ranger Parris says he's going to stand trial, so he's going to stand trial."

"Ranger Parris!" Uncle Jed exploded on a drunken breath. "I'm your own flesh and blood, girl, you'll do as I say! Give me that key!"

"No."

"Morse killed my brother. Cyrus was your uncle."

"I know what the son of a bitch did, but I ain't having vigilantes in my town."

"Your town? Your town? Girl, I am the mayor of this fair community. You will do as I—"

"Oh, shut up," Chris Parris said from behind her. She'd heard boots coming slowly down the steps, but hadn't paid much attention to them while she argued with Uncle Jed.

Marty risked a quick glance at him as he stopped just a step above her and put his hand on her shoulder. Every inch of her lit up with his touch, but she tried to ignore the prickle of longing. She had business, not a man to think about. Still, it was nice having Chris by her side. For the business part, mind.

"Don't just shut up," Chris said to Uncle Jed. "Go away. I don't want you here."

Uncle Jed must have had quite a snootful, since he just looked angrier at the dangerous sound of the Ranger's voice. "You stay out of this!" he thundered. "You give me that key, Marty!"

"No," she said again. "Do I have to hit you over the head, Uncle Jed? I ain't giving it to you. Go on home."

"You heard her," Chris added.

"I mean to see justice done."

"So do I," Marty assured him. "I ain't letting the man who killed Uncle Cyrus get away." She glanced at Chris again. "But the law's the law."

"You won't give me the key?"

Chris crossed his arms and tilted his head to one side. "I think she's already made that clear."

Marty turned and sighed worshipfully at Chris. Not only was he taking her side against Uncle Jed, he looked good enough to eat while he did it. Lord, but he was a fine figure of a man!

Meanwhile, all Chris really wanted was to get Martha Rose back upstairs. His head was full of visions of doing the wild thing with her long, strong legs wrapped tightly around his hips. Doing it all night long. But Marty was into duty and honor and all that and she wasn't going to bed until this old dude and his friends outside gave up and went away. Chris knew it was all his fault, anyway, for talking her into holding Morse for trial.

I should have let her shoot him, he grumbled to himself. *But that would have been wrong. Since when do I care about right and wrong?*

Marty was looking at him through her lashes again. He wished she wouldn't do that, but he loved it when she did. She looked as if she were hanging on his every word, even though he'd been mumbling to himself.

"Go on home," he said to the angry man. "Right now. I mean it."

Marty's uncle looked him up and down. "Who do you think you are, coming into my town and giving me orders like some kind of—"

"Texas Ranger," Marty interrupted him. "That's who he is, Uncle Jed." She stabbed a finger at her uncle's chest. "He came here to make this town a decent place to live in."

A chill ran up Chris's spine when Marty proclaimed his mission as such. "I did?" he said, more of a whisper to himself than to her.

She went on without paying any attention to him. "We've got real law in this town now. And everybody, every last mother's son, is going to obey it." She poked her uncle in the chest again, and he staggered backward a step. "Even the so-called mayor. You get my drift, Uncle Jed?"

He looked shocked. "Are you threatening me, girl?"

"You want to stay mayor?"

"We could organize a real election," Essie suggested from behind the bar.

"Yeah," Chris said. He put his hand on Marty's shoulder. "You can be replaced, you know. Impeached for obstruction of justice," he added, because it sounded good.

The mayor gaped at him, but Chris was more interested in the hungry look in Marty's eyes. He didn't know if it was because he was defending her against her bully of an uncle, or because he was upholding the law, but whatever he was doing was obviously turning her on. The look she gave him went straight to his head, and his crotch. He had to have her and it had to be soon. But first he had to get her alone.

"Come on, Sheriff," he said. "Let's get back to your office."

"To protect the prisoner," she added.

"Yeah, fine." To hell with Caleb Morse, the office was the only place he could think of where he knew they could have complete privacy—even if he had to set Morse free so he and Martha Rose could lock themselves in the cell. Together. Alone. All night.

He grabbed her arm and pushed her ahead of him past Jed Wirth and through the noisy crowd in the saloon.

Jed followed, complaining all the way, but Chris didn't pay him any attention. He didn't pay much attention to the crowd waiting outside the saloon either, except to notice that there weren't as many angry men milling around as when he'd first looked down from the upstairs window. There were four men left, and they all started yelling at Jed as he stepped outside behind them.

"I thought you said there was going to be a necktie party," one of them complained. "It seems to me all we're doing is standing out here acting like fools."

"It better be soon," one of the others said. "I gotta get an early start at the store in the morning."

"I promised my wife I'd be home afore midnight, Jed."

Marty would have paused to confront the men who were gathering around Jed, but Chris kept going. He only gave her time to call over her shoulder, "Go on home, you fools," before he rushed her along the dark street.

She kept looking back as if she expected the men to follow them to the office. They didn't, but rather stayed clumped around the front of the saloon, complaining about it being too late to get a proper riot started. It was pathetic. The last thing Chris heard before they reached the office door was Essie yelling for them to come on inside and have a drink.

"Say something else," Marty said as the door closed behind them. She suddenly felt nervous, alone in a dark room with the one man she was hungering for.

"I don't want to talk," he said as he leaned back against the door. He pulled her to him. "No way do I want to talk." He buried his face in her hair and kissed her ear, then his teeth skimmed around the rim of it.

It was delicious and distracting, but she was persistent.

"Say something else, something like . . . Obstruction." Lord, what a fancy, fine word! She'd been rolling it around in her mind all the way back. While his hand had been on her shoulder and she'd felt the heat from his body, she'd been thinking about his way with words.

"Obstruction," he repeated after her, but his voice was raw and husky. She shivered and pressed herself to him. Her mouth found his throat, then she worked her way up through the rough stubble on his jaw until she was kissing his mouth, bold as brass. She tried putting her tongue in his mouth this time. He not only let her, but made a deep sound that told her he liked it as much as she did. His hands were all over her for a while then, and she sort of lost track of things, but eventually she said, all hot and breathless, "Talk smart to me, Ranger. Them words sound so good."

He laughed, a soft, teasing sound, but not teasing like Essie's girls. It was a personal, private, friendly kind of sound. And it was right in her ear, all tickling and exciting. "How about," he whispered, "lewd and lascivious behavior? How's that sound?"

"Good," she said. "Real good."

He lifted his head and they looked at each other in the dark. "I've known women who wanted me to talk dirty to them, Martha Rose, but you're the first one who ever asked me to talk smart."

"I ain't like most women," she answered, and for once she was proud of it. Chris Parris's hands and mouth had been telling her he liked her just fine the way she was and it made her feel good, inside and out.

"No," he agreed, his quick fingers working at the catch of her gun belt. "You're . . . unique."

"What's that mean?" She was grinning as she asked

the question, while her fingers inched along the rim of his belt, moving toward the clasp. He had his shirt off already—she kind of remembered doing that—and now she had plans on getting him stripped down to his drawers and maybe further. She didn't even blush as their belts fell at the same time, thunking heavily against the floorboards. His hand went inside her jeans, making her jump and squirm against his busy fingers. Finally it was Marty who pulled Chris over to the rug in front of the black iron stove.

"What's unique mean?" she asked again as they settled on the rug together. She didn't know where her camisole had gotten to but didn't care as his mouth came down on her naked breast. In fact, it was better without clothes coming between them. He'd suckled her like this back at Essie's, but it had been through the material of the camisole. That had felt mighty good, but it was nothing compared to this. He moved to the hard point on her other breast and played his tongue over it and around. When his mouth came down to cover where he'd been playing she grabbed his head and said things she'd heard Essie's girls say to Foster Behan but hadn't known what they meant until now.

"Unique," he said, lifting his head when she didn't want him to, "means that you are one of a kind."

He moved off of her for a little bit, finishing the job of getting undressed. She did the same, hurrying to get out of her boots and jeans and drawers.

She laughed as she tossed aside her clothes. When she caught a questioning look from Ranger Parris, she said, "It ain't even Saturday night and here I am naked as a jaybird. 'Course, mostly, I don't take all my clothes off even to bathe."

"Modesty," he said, sounding kind of confused and distant. "What a strange concept. Where I come from—"

"Concept." She repeated another new word. "That like conception?"

"What?"

"I heard tell of a town down near the Mexican border called Concepcion. Concept sounds like that."

"Let's not talk about conception, okay?" he said as he took her shoulders and lay her back down.

His hands were big; when they covered her they made her feel small and dainty and female. "I like having your hands on me, Christopher Parris."

"Christian," he corrected, and she could detect a hint of surprise in his voice, as if he didn't like his real name or something. It was a fine name, as fine as he was, and she told him so.

Or she tried. He was kissing her all over again by then and she kind of lost track of just about everything but how the kissing felt. Pretty soon she was rolling around like a crazy thing and loving every second of being crazy.

The feel of his rod sinking into her body, hard and heavy and just right, was the best surprise she'd ever had. Lightning had hit just about every spot where he'd touched her during the night, but that sweet fire was the best of all. She let the flood take her. She had no choice, as Martha Rose Wirth was completely lost in pure pleasure for the first time in her life.

When he rode her she wrapped her legs around him and met every thrust, clutching the straining muscles of his back, pulling him to her, into her. When he stiffened and made a low moaning sound, she got lost in the flood completely. She was not alone, for she knew Chris was there, going down with her. And it wasn't like drowning at all. It was like throwing herself into the sun and burning into a happy, satisfied, mixed-up heap of ashes.

"Can't a man get any sleep?" Along with the shout, the sound of a fist banging loudly on the nearby wall filled the office. "Sounds like a couple of wildcats in heat out there."

Chris lifted his head off Marty's shoulder and shouted, "Shut up, Morse!"

Caleb Morse ignored him and called, "That you out there, Lavinia? I could sure use some of the comfort you've been spreading around out there, girl."

"Shut up!"

"Ain't never heard you yowl like that before, Lavinia. All that caterwauling gives me an itch for it, girl."

Chris got to his feet and stomped naked to the door separating the jail cell from the office. He flung it open and shouted, "Shut up!" one more time. "Leave it alone. Go back to sleep. Or I'll stuff one of my boots down your throat," he added angrily as he slammed the door closed.

Morse didn't make a sound as Chris went back to where Marty was sitting in the center of the rag rug. She looked up at him, and he thought he could see her glowing pink with embarrassment in the faint light coming through the barred window.

"Don't pay any attention to that scumbag," he told her.

"At least he don't know it was me," she whispered.

"Your reputation's safe with me." That was the sort of thing he ought to say to a Victorian girl, wasn't it?

"I ain't safe at all with you, Ranger Parris," she answered, with a soft lilt in her voice.

He sank down beside her and put his arms around her. It was a hot night, they were covered in sweat, but he wanted to hold her. He liked holding her, and the big girl fit perfectly against him.

"I'm getting sentimental," he said quietly, to himself, even if he was speaking out loud. "Sentiment is stupid. Gets me in trouble every time." But he was unable to resist the question. "Well, how'd you like it?" She both had and hadn't acted as though it was her first time. He'd loved her combination of innocence and eagerness. A lot could be done with a woman like that—both to and for. "Well?"

She touched his face, resting her palm on his cheek. "I liked it fine," she said, sounding all taciturn and Western again. Stoic. Kind of like Tommy Lee Jones in *Lonesome Dove*, but without the beard.

Okay, so he would have been happier if she was wildly gushing about what a great lover he was, not that he needed her to tell him he was wonderful or anything. "Insecure?" he muttered. "Me? No way."

"What?" she asked.

"Nothing," he answered. "You're beautiful."

"Thank you." She sounded embarrassed, and she obviously didn't believe him.

She lit a lamp on the desk and set about gathering up her clothes. He lay on the rug, propped up on one elbow, and watched her as she started to dress.

"You've got a great body," he said. "And you know how to use it."

She stopped buttoning her shirt and blushed all over. "I . . . but . . . I never—"

"So you're instinctively great in the sack. This is an asset."

She smiled, and did her eyelash look at him. He could see that her breasts and her nipples were getting hard again. "There you go talking again," she said.

"Really turns you on, doesn't it?"

"Turns me—?"

"Gets you hot? Uh, arouses you."

"It makes me all hot and bothered, if that's what you mean."

"You get me hot and bothered." He held his hand out to her. "Let's do it again."

"Well," she said slowly, "I could use all the lessons I can get." She put her hands on her hips. "You're a mighty fine teacher, Ranger." Then she chuckled, a low, wicked, sexy sound that went straight to Chris's groin. "At least there's one thing of mine Charlie Simpson won't be getting."

Inexplicably, her mentioning her fiancé bothered him. A lot. He didn't think it was his conscience. Fooling arround with attached women had never bothered him before.

"Are you really going to marry that wuss?" he asked as Marty joined him on the rug. "You deserve better than that."

"I have to do it," she said. "I'm not going to talk about it."

She kissed him then, distracting him from any complaints about her taste in husbands. Then she did things that heated them both up again really fast. Eventually he rolled onto his back, straddled her on top of him, and taught her a new way to ride.

They were lying tangled up together on the rug, mostly asleep, but still touching just about every spot where they could despite the heat. Then the shooting and shouting started out in the street.

"Oh, God," Chris mumbled. "Not again." He was willing to ignore it, but Marty sat up with a groan. "Oh, come on, baby, it's late, leave it alone."

"It's them damn drovers," she answered. "Party's finally moved into the street."

It didn't sound like a party to Chris, it sounded like a riot. Again. "This town's just one damn thing after another, isn't it?" he muttered as he sat up.

Marty was getting dressed again, and this time she obviously meant to stay that way. "Don't go out there," he said as she reached for her gun belt. "Let them shoot each other if they want."

Her shock and disappointment at his words showed plainly on her face. "How can you say that?" Then she ducked her head and smiled.

Don't look at me, he thought desperately. *Please don't look at me like that*. She did.

"'Course, I reckon you're right. It's your job now to settle with troublemakers," she said. "I shoulda remembered."

So she expected him to go out there and face down a bunch of drunken cowboys. Where had she gotten the idea he was a hero? "Somebody set me up for this," he said. "I'm not who you think. Somebody—you see, I'm from—a different time—or a dream—or—I don't know!"

He shouted the last words so loudly that Caleb Morse started banging on the wall again. Marty was staring at him, her look of adoration wiped off her face and confusion in its place.

"Shut up!" Chris shouted at the prisoner.

Somebody screamed outside. There were more shots,

and the heavy thudding of hooves as whooping riders raced past them and up the street.

"We got to get out there," Marty said. "Before somebody gets killed."

The concern in her voice sent a ripple of guilt through Chris. The fool girl just cared too much about the stupid place. "You brought me here," he said. "Somehow. I know it."

"I sent for a Ranger."

"Yeah, but—" More shouting and shots, accompanied by drunken laughter and cursing. Chris did some cursing himself. "No way I'm going to get a decent night's sleep while this goes on," he muttered.

He got up, pulled on his jeans, strapped on the gun belt, and grabbed a rifle off the wall. "Stay here, this shouldn't take too long."

He heard her romantic sigh as he strode purposefully out the door. The sound was much more frightening than what awaited him out in the street.

THREE ~

"I'm getting out of here, Harley," Chris told the big blond horse as dawn arrived the next day. He didn't know how he knew how to saddle the animal, or how he knew how to ride it. It was like knowing how to use the old-fashioned guns, an essential piece of knowledge that Somebody had put in his brain and reflexes when setting him down in this weird situation.

"Thanks," he grumbled to the Somebody. "Thanks a lot."

As he finished with the saddle the big horse turned its head and nuzzled his shoulder. It liked him, he could tell. He wasn't used to having his transportation like him. He wasn't used to girls loving and then leaving *him* to marry another man; it was against the order of the universe, somehow. And he wasn't going to put up with it, or whatever the hell was going on there, any longer.

"I mean, it's supposed to be the other way around," he said as he got on the horse. "I'm your classic loner type, you know. Ride into town, break some heads, break some hearts, kiss 'em good-bye, get on my bike, and ride into the sunset. That's the American outlaw myth I bought into when I was a kid."

The horse snorted encouragingly as he headed it out of town. It was just past dawn, and the air was cool and beautiful. Loon's streets, such as they were, were empty. Chris had no idea where he was going. West he guessed, toward California, maybe. Away from the problems and the big eyes of Martha Rose Wirth. California was home, such as it was. Maybe when he got there it would be the twentieth century.

"Okay," he went on, "this wild-West Texas Ranger thing, it's like the loner myth. I should never have read Joseph Campbell, with all that hero's-journey stuff. I know too much about the archetypes involved here. This is the original American myth. Why have I been spending my life trying to live in a myth?" he wondered.

"Am I living in the myth now? Or did I die and get sentenced to make Westerns?" He took off his wide-brimmed hat to scratch his head. "This is heavy stuff, you know?"

The horse made no comment, and Chris lapsed into brooding silence as they rode. He got so lost in his own thoughts, he paid no attention to anything until the sound of hoofbeats coming up from behind him shook him out of his perturbed reverie. He had felt it getting hot, but he hadn't noticed when the blond horse had stopped moving.

With his hand on his gun, Chris turned in the saddle to see who was coming after him in such a hurry.

He wouldn't have been surprised to see some bad guy coming up from behind to mug him, but of course he wasn't lucky enough for that. No, it was Martha Rose Wirth, sheriff and hero worshiper, heading his way.

He should have kicked his horse in the ribs and run from her, but he couldn't do that.

"I'm out of here," he said as she pulled up beside him. "I'm gone, you hear me?" She nodded. "And I don't want you following me."

She pushed her wide-brimmed hat back on her head. "That's a fine black eye," she said.

"And don't talk to me in non sequiturs." Her eyes went all dreamy at the sound of the big word. Her look set Chris's pulse racing, a sensation he firmly ignored. He tried to concentrate on the aching soreness around his right eye. Some drunken cowboy's fist had got past his guard in the attempt the night before to quiet down the street party. The cowboy had gotten a broken jaw for his efforts, but Chris's eye and knuckles were reminders of the incident. The fistfight had been at the end, after some rifle fire and threats had pretty much dispersed the crowd. Some horses had stampeded, and somebody had gotten shot in the arm, but Chris wasn't actually responsible for any of that damage. Word that he was had spread through the drunken crowd, though. Eventually, he'd herded them all back to the Black Eye where they sacked out on the barroom floor. Chris had settled next to the door with his rifle at the ready, and had brooded the rest of the night away.

And there was the one thing he'd brooded about the most, sitting on a horse next to him, looking attentive and eager, and pretty. When had he decided she was pretty, anyway?

"There's no getting away from you, is there, Martha Rose Wirth?" he asked as she gave him a hopeful smile.

"I'm a pretty good tracker, Ranger," she answered. "Besides, I figured you'd need some help."

He didn't want to ask, but he did anyway. "Why would I need help?"

"Train's due sometime today."

"Yes?"

"I reckon you plan to catch the Varney gang in the act."

"The act? Robbing the train?" She nodded. Train. She had mentioned a train yesterday. A train was a far better means of transportation than a big blond horse, even a friendly one. The train would be going into Loon to pick up the cows the cowboys had brought in. Maybe he could take the train out of town. Hopefully in a different car than the cows.

He didn't remember seeing any train tracks on the way into or out of town, so he said, "You better show me where the train runs."

He got another one of her curt, businesslike nods. She turned her horse off the road and he followed. He also noticed that she had some heavy-duty hardware strapped onto her own horse.

"You look like a gun runner, babe," he said as he moved Harley up to ride beside her.

She made a face. "I don't have no use for them comancheros," she told him.

Chris decided she was talking about local gun runners, but he didn't pursue the subject. He'd heard enough about the problems of Loon already. He did ask, "What's all the firepower for?"

"Thought you might want to set up an ambush of the Varney gang."

Of course she did. He decided to just follow her without making any comments.

Marty was glad Ranger Parris wasn't talking too much as they rode up the ridge above Cyrus Gully. A narrow set of train tracks ran through it, ending at the cattle pens just north of town. Besides the pens there was a water tower and a sidetrack used for turning the engine. It was not much as railheads went, but this spur line fed into a bigger line that took the beef cattle up to Kansas and the world beyond. Every now and then the train brought in mail and other supplies, which, more often than not, the Varneys stole before the train got to town.

It wasn't much, but that train was the most important thing Loon had, and Marty had every intention of saving it from all comers. To do that she had to get rid of the Varney gang, and then she had to marry Charles Simpson.

Simpson was on her mind a lot as the sky turned a fierce blue and the sun grew hotter. That was a lie; Chris Parris was on her mind. Chris Parris and all the wicked things they'd done the night before were just about all she could think about. What they'd done, and knowing that she wanted to do it again. Soon.

She had to talk to him about it, even if it wasn't proper to talk about such things out in the light of day. She cleared her throat several times as they crested the ridge and headed down a path through scrub and scattered cottonwoods.

"You choking on something?" Chris asked before she could get any words out.

"Uh," was all she could say before she spotted the four horsemen heading toward the tracks from the opposite side of the gully. "Damn!" She turned a grin on the Ranger. "Look at them out in the open like that, just like they was going for a Sunday buggy ride." She laughed as she brought her horse to a halt behind a stand of sheltering trees.

"What? Who?" Chris asked as she dismounted.

She didn't take the time to answer but got down and pulled out first one then the other of the Winchester rifles she'd brought with her.

He got off his palomino and she handed him one of the rifles. "You're expecting me to shoot somebody now, aren't you?"

She didn't know why he sounded so mad about it. Then she realized what she'd done. "You know what you're doing, and you've got a fine rifle of your own. I'm sorry I took matters into my own hands like that."

Chris groaned. Then he took the rifle from her and said, "That's all right. Just don't—uh—do it again."

"Yes, sir," she answered, trying not to look at him or think about being so close to him, and all alone except for the Varney gang on the other side of the ridge.

His hand had touched hers when he took the gun. The touch had sent a hot flash of wanting through her. She had to think about stopping the Varneys from robbing the train, not about dragging Chris Parris down in the grass and getting him to kiss her all over the way he had last night.

That was last night. He hadn't said a word that wasn't business to her today, which was as it should be. He had called her "babe," which sounded like something a man might call a woman he cared for, but it had probably just slipped out. He was Ranger Parris today. Just as it should be.

Chris passed his hand across Marty's face after she'd

stared blankly at him for a while. "You in there, hon? Oh, Martha Rose, talk to me, sweetheart."

She smiled slowly as her eyes focused on him. "Sweetheart," she said. "And hon. Babe."

"Yeah?" He smiled back, responding to the look in her eyes and her sultry tone. *Maybe she doesn't want me to shoot somebody, after all,* he thought. *Maybe she just got me out here in the middle of nowhere so we could fool around.* "It's nice and private around here," he said.

"Except for the train robbers."

"Yeah, them." He peered around the cover of the trees, and Marty pointed. "I see them," he said, and looked back at her. "So?"

"You shoot 'em."

"But they aren't doing anything."

"Then arrest them."

"For what?"

"Robbing the train."

Chris looked down at the empty track. "What train?"

"The one they're fixing to rob."

Chris felt like shaking her. "Marty," he said with the deceptive calm of someone very close to losing it, "you can't arrest someone for a crime they haven't committed yet."

She looked at him thoughtfully for a few moments, passing her rifle from hand to hand. She gave him a smile as her eyes lit up with comprehension. "You're going to catch the Varney gang in the act."

Chris caught a faint hint of smoke curling skyward off in the distance. The train, he supposed. The riders across the way must have noticed the smoke, too, since one of them let out an inarticulate shout.

Chris squinted across the gully. "I need that train,"

he said. "Nobody is robbing it today. And I'm sick of confrontations," he added as he raised the rifle to his shoulder and stepped from behind the trees. He heard Marty move to cover him. "No more confrontations after this," he promised himself.

Marty fired her rifle. The bullet sprayed up rock dust at the feet of the gang's lead horse.

"Marty!"

"You got to get their attention," she replied, keeping her Winchester trained steadily on the riders opposite them.

Guns were drawn, rifles were cocked. There was a shout of, "It's the Ranger!" from across the way.

"What the hell do you want, Ranger?" a deep-voiced man called.

"That's Virgil Varney," Marty told him. "Sounds sober." She didn't seem to think that was a good sign.

Chris could hear the train now, a faint rumbling in the distance. "I want you out of here," he called to them. "Nobody's robbing the train today."

"Oh, yeah?" Varney called back. "Seems to me we outnumber you, Ranger."

Chris felt sweat gathering on the back of his neck, and ignored the drop that rolled down his back. Weird thing was, he was sweating because of the heat, not from nerves. "Go away," he said.

How many times had he said that since coming to Loon? That was what he needed, for all of this to just go away. He cast a quick look at Marty, who was steadfast and stone featured beside him. Damn, but she was brave. Or maybe just plain stupid. No, brave, so damn macho that he'd feel like a real wuss if he walked away from any fight this *girl* was ready to face. Which was every fight that came along. He didn't know how much longer his testosterone level was going to be able to deal with this.

"Something has got to be done about this crazy town," he grumbled. "Just so I can get some rest."

"Amen," Marty responded, her voice a fervent whisper in the still, hot morning, underscored by the distant roar of the approaching train.

"Someone is going to die here, Ranger," Varney shouted.

"Unless you leave, yeah," Chris said. "Get out of here or I'm locking you all up. For—unlawful assembly."

"Locking you up," Marty added for emphasis. "Or shooting you dead."

"Stop that!" Chris whispered fiercely to her.

"He'll do it," one of Varney's men told the gang leader. "I saw him face down Foster Behan at the Black Eye."

"And he brung in Caleb Morse," one of the others said.

"Sent home the mob that was out to lynch Morse, too."

"All by hisself."

Chris was pleased by the awed concern in the voices of Varney's men. He stayed still and quiet, with the rifle poised on his shoulder, and hoped his reputation would do his work for him.

"He's a Ranger, Virgil," the most nervous of the five said. "I don't like messing with a Ranger."

"They take care of their own," another one pointed out. He pushed down Varney's gun hand. "You kill him, the Rangers'll send a posse after you, for sure."

Varney gave the man a shocked look. "After *me?* You in this with me, or not?"

The man shook his head. "Not today, Virgil. No way I'm helping kill a Ranger."

"But—" Varney looked around at his men. They were all turning their horses and heading back up the ridge. "Damn!" He shook his fist at Chris, then put away his gun and followed his gang away from the train.

Chris could smell the smoke from the train engine, and could make out the three cars and caboose the engine towed. The dilapidated train didn't look worth the effort of robbing to him, but he did hope it was worth the effort of saving. Maybe soon he'd be getting on it and getting out of this crazy town.

"Go on back to the office," he said to Marty as they put their rifles away. She looked about to argue that she wanted to stay at his side. He did not want her there when he bought a ticket out of Loon. "I'll see that the train gets safely into town. I want you to write up an incident report."

She stared, then pointed at herself. "Write? A report? Me?"

He gave her a stern look. "That's the official procedure, Sheriff. The junior officer on a case always writes the incident report. We have to send it off to—" Where did Rangers come from? "Headquarters." He softened his voice. "And I trust you to do a fine job, Martha."

She answered him with a nervous smile.

He swatted her horse's rump. "Get going, girl. I'll expect that report to be done when I get back to the office."

It wasn't that Marty wasn't willing to do anything Ranger Parris asked of her, it was just that she didn't write so good. Not that she didn't want to learn how. She'd been real happy when Essie had come to town, hoping the new schoolteacher wouldn't mind teaching a half-grown, all-wild girl a thing or two about reading and writing. Then Uncle Jed had messed up that dream just as he'd messed up everything she ever wanted to do. She was left an ignorant fool, with him in control of her ranches and her share of everything the family owned.

Sitting at her desk, with a blank piece of paper in front of her and a pen held as if it were a poison snake, Marty found herself wondering more about Uncle Jed's reasons for keeping her ignorant than about what words she should write down. The pen had come to Uncle Cyrus from his father, her grandfather, and had sat in this desk the whole time Cyrus was sheriff. She didn't even know if he knew how to use it. He'd taught her everything she knew about practical things, but he'd agreed with Uncle Jed that book learning was nothing a woman needed. She sighed, and tried to stop thinking and get on with writing.

When the door opened she looked up eagerly, happy to put off the task Chris had set for her, even if she felt a stab of guilt for disappointing him. "I'm doing my best, Ranger," she said, before she saw it wasn't him. "Oh, hello, Charlie," she said when she realized it was the banker who'd just walked in.

The man's face looked like a thundercloud and he held his mouth pursed, as if he'd just tasted something sour.

"Miss Wirth," he said, coming to a stop in front of the desk, "I wish to have a word with you. A word concerning your behavior with Ranger Parris."

Oh, Lord, she thought, *he knows*. She wondered why she didn't feel guilty knowing that Charlie Simpson knew what she'd been doing with Chris. She ought to start begging his forgiveness for behaving no better than one of Essie's whores. Ought to, but didn't intend to.

What she did do was push her chair back and stand up so Charlie Simpson couldn't loom over her like a father over some bad little girl. Nobody in this town was going to loom over her but Chris Parris, and he didn't exactly loom. His standing over her made her feel . . . safe.

"May I have a word?" Simpson asked, forced to look up at her.

"You already said more than one." She wished he would go away.

"You've been spending time alone with the Ranger."

If she was blushing she hoped the tan on her face hid it. "I've been helping him with his duties. Ain't nothing wrong with that."

His mighty frown got mightier. "There has been talk."

"I walk down the street and folks talk. You'll get used to it, Charlie," she assured him.

"I will not." He lifted his chin. "You're going to be the wife of the leading citizen of this community. I will not allow a breath of scandal to be attached to your name."

She smiled. "I'm glad you're ready to defend my honor, Charlie. You want me to give you shooting lessons?"

He stamped his foot. Honest to God stamped his foot, like one of Essie's girls in a tizzy. "You," he declared, "will modify your behavior so that no scandal can ever be attached to it. I will not have my good name sullied by your scandalous actions."

Marty looked at him while she digested his words.

"You want me to stay in the house except for Sunday meeting, is that it?"

"If that is what it takes to keep your reputation spotless."

"I'm the sheriff."

"Not for much longer."

She nodded. "When we're married I won't be the sheriff. By then Ranger Parris'll have this town whipped into shape. He'll go his way and I'll live in the front parlor. That suit you?"

"My dear, damage has already been done." He spoke slowly, as if he were going to crack if he wasn't careful. "Your uncle Jed saw the two of you at the Black Eye last night."

"Uncle Jed's lucky he didn't end up in the cell back there. He was out to lynch my prisoner."

"Nevertheless, you were seen in a most inappropriate place with a man. Your reputation—"

"There you go again. It was business. Ask Essie."

His face went from angry red to shocked white. "I would never speak to a fallen woman!"

"I've seen you smile and dip your head when she comes to the bank."

"That," he said, "is business."

"Oh. So her money's good even if she ain't?"

He gave a superior little smile. "Precisely."

Marty scratched her chin. "You don't—consort—with soiled doves?"

"Certainly not."

"I heard that you spend half an hour every Friday night with Essie's new girl. Her name's Maude, ain't it?"

Charles gasped and went all red again.

Marty looked down at her desk and said, "I've got a report to write."

Grateful for the change of subject, he asked, "A report? How can you write a report when you don't know how to write? What sort of work is that for a woman?" He went on before she could respond. "What sort of work is being a sheriff for a woman?" He banged a fist on the desk. "Miss Martha, I insist you put away your gun and put on a dress. I've had quite enough of my fiancée—"

"Put on a dress and do what?" she asked, with a dangerous edge to her voice.

He made a sweeping gesture. "Whatever it is good women do. Bake biscuits, perhaps."

"Biscuits?"

"I'll require my wife to be provide me with three decent meals a day, Miss Martha."

She knew how to cook, but he didn't seem to think so, and she wasn't in any mood to tell him different. "And sewing and cleaning, and such, Mr. Simpson? You'll be wanting your wife to do those things, too, I reckon."

"Of course."

"But no reading or writing?"

"If you need anything read, I'll read it to you. Bible verses, and other such uplifting material."

"But you wouldn't be reading any—well—big, fancy words to me, would you?"

He squinted at her. "What sort of words do you mean?"

"Oh, I don't know. Words like 'lewd' and 'lascivious,' maybe."

His eyes went wide, and his ears and cheeks turned bright red. Lord, but the man could change colors fast. "Where did you hear such filth?"

"Filth?" She couldn't keep from smiling reminiscently. "Are those dirty words?"

"Of course they are. Did Ranger Parris say such things to you? That swine!"

"It's law talk. He's just teaching me law talk, Charlie. Ain't no harm in my learning about the law. I'm the sheriff."

"Not for much longer, Miss Wirth."

It kept coming back to that, her giving up being sheriff. She didn't like talking about it, even if she knew it was coming. Why did he have to rub it in? She wasn't used to taking orders from anybody, and she didn't like being pushed, but she had to admit he was right. Her promise to marry him brought obligations she had to live up to.

She had to grit her teeth to do it, but Marty said, "I'm sorry, Charlie. I've just been doing the best I know how."

He gave her a superior smirk. "You need a firm hand to show you the way, my dear. I've known that from the beginning."

"I reckon you're the man to show me the way." She ignored the twisting pain in her belly from saying such gentle words to him.

Simpson folded his hands across his stomach and looked her up and down. "I'd much rather see you in a modest dress than in your current attire."

Chris had told her last night that he liked the way her sweet, heart-shaped behind looked in jeans. Charlie Simpson would rather have her hide it behind a bustle. She would have bet he'd want her to sleep in high-necked nightgowns and lie stiff and still while he rutted away on top of her, too. Just like Essie had said.

Which was the way it should be, for proper married folks. Queen Victoria would approve.

The thought left such a sour taste in her mouth, Marty wanted to spit. But before she could do such an unladylike thing the door opened again. It wasn't Chris this time either.

"What do you want?" she asked as Uncle Jed came in, carrying a parcel wrapped in brown paper. She shook a finger at him before he could answer. "Not one word about Caleb Morse from you."

Uncle Jed looked the way a man ought to after having a snootful the night before. His eyes were bloodshot and he'd apparently cut himself shaving a few times. He didn't argue with her about Caleb Morse. He just gave one ugly look toward the cell door, then said, "I brought you a present, Marty."

She eyed him, then the package, suspiciously. "What?" Uncle Jed wasn't what she'd call a generous man.

"Open it." The command didn't come from her uncle, but from Simpson.

She gritted her teeth at his tone, and found herself wondering if she was going to wear her teeth down to nubs in the next few years, just to keep from sassing her husband. *Husband. Oh, Lord.*

"Well, go on."

"Yes, Charlie," she said, barely able to move her lips for the clenching of her jaw. She ripped open the paper to find a bundle of blue satin covered in lace and braid and pearl buttons. The bodice was so stiff with boning it probably could have stood on its own.

"What's this?" she asked.

The men were smiling proudly, at the clothes, not at her. "It's your wedding dress," Uncle Jed announced. "It came in on the train. I didn't have your measure, so I sent the dressmaker your Sunday dress to work from."

"So that's what happened to my gray dress. I've

been looking for it for weeks." Weeks. Lord, Uncle Jed had been planning this wedding even before Simpson got to town, hadn't he? Well, she'd known he had at least hoped, but she wished he hadn't been so damn sure she'd go through with it.

She couldn't stand the looks on the men's faces when they remembered to look at her. They were so proud of themselves. "It's pretty," she said. "Thank you." She hoped they wouldn't expect her to praise the finer points of the dress as if it were a shiny new Colt six-shooter. "The Ranger told me to have this report done by the time he got back to the office, so I got to get back to work."

"But—" Simpson began.

"The sheriff said she has to get back to work," Chris said from the doorway.

They all turned to look at him as he stepped into the room. He was carrying a package, too. The look he swept across Charles Simpson and Uncle Jed got them moving. The pair left in a hurry, without so much as another glance Marty's way.

Chris came to the desk and put down his package. "What you got there?" she asked.

"Don't know," he said. "Something that came in on the train. It's addressed to you."

Marty's eyes lit up as he spoke, and her pleased expression was almost enough to make up for his disappointment in finding out that the train wouldn't be leaving town for a couple more days.

As she ripped into the stained brown paper covering what had felt like a book to him, he asked, "So, what is it?"

A moment later she held up what was definitely a book. A thick, heavy book, bound in brown leather with gold lettering on the cover. "My dictionary," she said reverently. "It's my dictionary!"

He'd never heard anyone sound so pleased in his life. He was glad to see that happy look on her face, to see her eyes shining. When he'd walked in she had looked distinctly unhappy. Unhappy and cowed, and the men in front of her had obviously been real pleased about it.

She deserved better than that.

He didn't know what she did deserve. Certainly not him, though that was what a voice in the back of his head was insisting.

"A dictionary?" he said, to get his mind off the possibilities of life with Martha Rose Wirth.

She hugged the book close, and looked at him with desperation in her eyes. "You won't tell anybody, will you? Please?"

He perched on the edge of the desk, took off his hat, and put it down beside him. "Tell 'em what?"

"About my, well, about my book. They'll just—you know—make fun of me."

Chris wanted to hug her, she looked so vulnerable. He couldn't understand why she cared so much for the people in this town. They must have made it awful for her when she'd been growing up so tall and ignorant, and hungry to learn. That was the key to Martha Rose, he realized; she was a smart girl who'd been told she didn't need to know anything beyond the confines of this one-horse town. She'd heard it so much she'd come to believe it. Her uncle Jed had a lot to pay for.

"I won't tell anybody," he promised. He leaned over and pried the book away from her. "And I won't make fun of you."

"No," she said with a shy smile that twisted his heart. "You would never make fun of me."

Right then and there he almost told her he loved her. The words simply showed up on his tongue, and he practically had to bite it to keep them from coming out. He opened the dictionary instead. The big book was heavy in his hands, and the pages were covered in tiny print.

"No pictures," he said. She came around the desk and stood very close to him, peering over his shoulder. "Come on," he said, trying to ignore her warmth and the press of her breast against his shoulder, "let me show you how to use this. Pick a word."

"Iniquity," she said promptly. And laughed. The sound held a combination of eagerness and earthy lust. It set Chris's head spinning. He wanted to grab her and push her down on the desk and get her naked and teach her about more than just words. He was barely able to find the word she'd asked for and help her read the meaning.

When they were done with iniquity she said, "'Wickedness.' I thought that's what it meant. It didn't feel wicked, doing iniquity with you."

"It wasn't wicked," he said. "It was best time I ever had."

"It was?"

He searched for appropriate—big—words. "Fantastic. Magnificent. Sexual gratification on a cosmic scale."

"Oh." Her breath whispered warmly across the back of his neck as she spoke.

She pressed closer, so close that all he could think of was her. "Read me some more big words, Chris."

From her tone it sounded as if she were thinking exactly what he was, that there was a lot to be said for a large, inventive vocabulary.

He was looking to see if this Victorian dictionary had a definition for fellatio when the door opened. Chris looked up while Marty spun around. They both shouted, "What?"

It was Lavinia. She looked at the book, looked the pair of them up and down, and giggled.

Chris slammed the book shut. "What?" he demanded.

"That must be one of them French books Essie ordered from St. Louis," she said, coming forward. "Does it have pictures?"

"No, it doesn't have pictures," Chris snapped. "It's a dic—" Marty elbowed him in the ribs. "Evidence," he finished. He slid the dictionary behind him.

It didn't matter. By the time she'd reached the desk, Lavinia's attention was drawn to the other package. "Oh, my," she said as she held up the blue satin dress. She looked wonderingly at Marty. "Is this yours?"

"I reckon," Marty answered. "I'm supposed to get married in it."

Chris took an immediate dislike to the fancy blue dress. When Lavinia held it up to Marty he saw that it was a two-piece affair, some sort of blouse-and-skirt combination. He'd never seen anything so complicated in his life. Of course, he'd always thought a girl didn't need to wear anything more complicated than lingerie out of a Victoria's Secret catalogue anyway.

"This waist is too short for you," Lavinia declared.

"It was patterned from my Sunday-go-to-meeting dress," Marty said. "The one I've had since I was fifteen, and it never did fit right."

"This will have to be altered," Lavinia said with a critical shake of her head.

"Or burnt," Chris muttered. The women ignored him.

"I'm not much good at sewing," Marty said.

"I could do it for you," the other woman offered. She sighed. "Back when I first came out West I thought I could get work as a seamstress. I didn't know I was going to end up as a *seamstress*."

Marty looked at Lavinia suspiciously. "Why do you want to help me, Lavinia Stuart?"

Lavinia's chin went up. "Because I want out."

"Want out of what?"

"The life I've been leading. I've decided to mend my evil ways. Essie said I should talk to you."

Martha looked puzzled. "About mending? I don't have any—"

"About opening a dressmaking shop." Lavinia shook out the blouse. "I've got some money saved, but if you could loan me the rest I could make a start."

"Money?"

"Essie says you're rich but you don't know a thing about money."

"I don't," Marty admitted.

Lavinia nodded. "Well, Essie does. She said that if you help me set up shop and let me make dresses for you, you being the richest woman in the county, then the respectable women would buy dresses from me. She says respectable women herd like sheep and would do whatever you did, especially if you're fool enough to marry the banker and get all prissy."

"*Prissy?*"

Lavinia ignored Marty's indignant shout and went on. "I could make something of myself as a seamstress. Essie says I could do it." She made it sound as if Essie's word was law.

Essie was one smart woman, Chris already believed that. "Sounds like a good idea," he put in when all

Marty did was stare at Lavinia. "My sister owns a boutique. She does okay." He smiled fondly at memories of some of the skimpy underwear his sister sold. "There was this gold lace bra—"

"You think it's a good idea?" Marty asked him.

He nodded, his thoughts on what Marty would look like in nothing but an inch or so of gold lace. Nice, very nice.

She looked back at Lavinia. "Well, I reckon I could—"

Outside, somebody fired a gun. A woman screamed. The sound of shouts and running feet came through the half-open office door. Lavinia made a nervous, squeaking sound.

Chris and Marty just looked at each other and sighed. "Not again," they said together.

"Does this town ever quiet down?" Chris asked.

Marty just shook her head. "That's why I called for a Ranger."

"You should have called for the National Guard."

"The what?"

"Never mind." He put his hat back on. "Come on," he said. "Let's go see who's shooting at us now."

FOUR~

It was Foster Behan, standing in the middle of the street and glaring his anger from under a slightly squashed bowler hat. He swung his hand up and fired as Marty followed Chris out the door. Marty got one quick glance at him as she dived behind a watering trough. She could see that the gambler's fancy clothes were rumpled and he was unshaven. His gun hand was none too steady, either, or else the bullet he had fired at her would have found its mark before she reached safety. He looked mighty dangerous, she decided as she peered up over the wooden rim of her low shelter.

"I've come for you, Ranger!" the gambler announced in a voice slurred with drink. "You can't humiliate a man and not expect him to get satisfaction. I'm calling you out."

"You're drunk," Chris said as he marched toward Behan. "Get out of here."

"I'm going to kill you!"

Chris waved his hand as if he were shooing away chickens. "No, you're not. Get the hell out of here."

Chris didn't pay any attention to the wild look on Foster Behan's face, but Marty did. "Careful!" she called. "He likes killin'."

"We're going to settle this like men," Foster Behan said. "Right here in the street, all right and honorable."

Chris made a sharp gesture. "I don't need this bullshit, Behan. Get out of my face."

Chris started to return to the office, but Behan called out, "I'll shoot you in the back if you want, Ranger."

Marty stood slowly. "I don't think so." She made sure he saw her big Colt Navy revolver. "You heard him. Git."

"I'm staying," Behan declared. "This is a lawful challenge. I'm not letting the Ranger hide behind your— skirts. This is my town and I want him out of it or dead."

"Your town?" Marty shouted. "Get your carcass—"

"You yellow, Ranger?" Behan taunted.

"No," Chris answered. He looked at his hand. "Sort of brown."

"I'm calling you out."

"Right. Out. Macho crap. I've had enough macho crap in my life, thank you."

But Behan wasn't going to be put off. Marty considered just shooting him like the vermin he was, but she reckoned that might be illegal. Chris wouldn't like it if she did anything illegal. He'd probably make her fill out a report.

"Meet me in the street or I'll kill you where you stand," the gambler said.

Chris hesitated a few more seconds, then he shrugged and muttered, "Shit. All right, let's do it."

Marty had seen Foster Behan shoot men before; he was good at it. He cheated at it the way he did at cards.

Behan holstered his gun and backed into the center of the street, and Chris followed him slowly out into the merciless afternoon light. Marty noticed that Behan made sure to have his back to the sun.

There was a small crowd gathering, curious folk clinging to the shadows near the edges of buildings. Uncle Jed and his friends were gathered outside the entrance of the store; Simpson and his clerks had come out of the bank. Everybody was watching as the men took to the street, but nobody was offering to help, or to stop the violence. Nobody cared.

Suddenly, Marty didn't know why she'd been so damned worried about the people of Loon all those years.

"Fill your hand," Behan said. His hand flashed down toward his holster.

There was a glint of steel in the sunlight.

It was over in less than a moment, with one gunshot. Marty's gasp was drowned out by a howl of pain. Foster Behan was on the ground, clutching his wounded hand. Chris was looking at his gun hand, a puzzled frown creasing his handsome features. He looked as if he didn't believe he'd just shot the gun right out of his opponent's hand.

"Damn, I'm good," he muttered.

Marty came forward slowly, still holding her Navy revolver. Chris gave her a smile, but she didn't pay him much mind. She knew Foster Behan better than that. The man could shoot left-handed as well as right, and he always carried a derringer in his boot.

When Behan squirmed around and went for it she was ready for him.

Chris jumped at the gunshot. At first he didn't know what the hell Marty was doing. Then he looked, and saw the little gun clutched in the gambler's other hand. And the hole in the man's chest. She'd killed Foster Behan.

She'd saved his life. Martha Rose Wirth had just saved his life.

He looked incredulously from Behan's body to Marty as she put her gun back in the holster strapped to her shapely thigh. An overwhelming emotion swept through him. He didn't know what it was—gratitude, adrenaline, lust, some sort of mixture of all of them. Her gaze slowly met his. He didn't know what she saw in his face, but he saw the worry and the worship and the love she was giving him.

She loves me, he thought. *And she worries about me*. No woman had ever worried about him before. And she had killed for him. She honest to God had killed for him. He gulped. What do you say to a woman who's fierce enough to kill for you?

"Thank you."

She gave a slight, embarrassed nod. "My pleasure." Then she looked around and called out to some men in the crowd gathering around the scene. "We got a burying to attend to. Where's Lucas Farley?"

"Who?" Chris asked.

"The undertaker." She put her hands on her hips as a plump man in a black suit pushed his way to where Behan lay. "He's all yours, Lucas," she said. She looked at Chris. "You gonna make me fill out a report on this?"

Chris stepped away from the group, and she followed him. He put a hand on her shoulder and felt her shaking underneath her outward cool. "You want to be alone for a few minutes?" he asked her.

Her eyes lit with pleasure. "I surely do," she told him, grateful for his understanding.

He nudged her gently toward the office. "Then you go on inside and get that report started. Me, I need a drink."

He needed more than one drink, he needed several, but he limited himself to one wretched beer. He was on duty, after all. He couldn't help but smile at the irony of knowing that Chris Parris, ex-con, was thinking of himself as the law west of wherever the hell the place was west of.

Like the good bartender she was, Essie Harris lingered just across from him and waited patiently until he was ready to talk. He could hear the girls bawling upstairs, where they'd fled at the news of the gambler's death. He and Essie were alone but for the flies buzzing around the hot room.

"The train leaves in a couple of days," he heard himself say at last. "And I don't think I'm going to be on it. She saved my life."

"You've still got plenty of work to do here," Essie said. "Duty and honor—"

"Don't have shit to do with it."

"It's Martha Rose," she said, resting her hands flat on the bar. "I think you'd do just about anything for that girl."

"What?" Chris was indignant. "I don't do anything for anybody. I—"

"Of course you're going to have to be man enough to do the one thing she really needs."

What was the woman talking about? Chris finished the beer and set the glass down with a heavy thump. "I'm cleaning up her damn town, all right? Since I blew into Loon I've been shot at, and shot at, and shot at. Don't people in this town ever run out of ammunition?"

"Mostly we make our own," Essie answered, with a note of pride in her voice. "The question is, what are you going to do about Martha?"

Chris stared at his glass. What was he going to do about Martha? "I'm from the future," he said, not caring whether he would be believed. "I don't know how I got here, or why. This seems like some kind of crazy dream."

"And Martha?"

The woman was relentless! Hadn't she been listening to him? Why wasn't she freaked at hearing him say he was from the future? He sighed. "Martha's the only good part about this dream."

"Well, then, if it's a dream, it isn't a nightmare, is it?" She smiled brightly. "Sometimes I think we should just relax and enjoy our dreams, don't you?"

"Yeah, I guess." He still couldn't believe how calm she was about—

"Honey," she said before he could ask, "there isn't a story I haven't heard since I took up this profession. I could write a book."

Chris smiled at her. "In my time you probably would."

"And Martha, what would you do with Martha in your time?"

"Marry her, I guess," he said before he quite realized

the treacherous words were on his tongue. He blanched at the sound of them. "I mean—" *I can't.* He couldn't, could he?

Essie gave a satisfied smile. "I thought so."

"But . . . I . . . she . . . oh, shit." He heaved a weighty sigh. Him get married? Give up his freedom? That was the last thing he wanted. He thought. Maybe. Besides, Marty had made it clear she didn't want him. She was selling herself to save her goddamn town.

"Give me another beer."

Essie nodded, but before she could pour the brew, the swinging doors squeaked open and she looked up. "Martha Rose," she said with a smile, "we were just discussing you."

Marty moved slowly across the barroom, the heavy skirts of the blue satin dress trailing in the dust behind her. When Chris turned and looked her up and down she could tell he didn't like what he saw, except for the bodice that dipped down a bit too low over her breasts. Well, that couldn't be helped. She knew she was ugly, and it didn't matter anyway. He wasn't ugly, oh, no, not even with a day's growth of beard stubbling his strong jaw.

She stopped in the middle of the floor and took a good long look at Ranger Parris. Her last look at him as a man she could commit iniquity with, she told herself. He looked back, but neither of them said anything.

Once she had him memorized she walked up to Essie.

"Well, it's a pretty enough dress," Essie said. "But it could use some letting down in the waist. Do you want me to call Lavinia?"

Marty could hear the girls making a racket upstairs. The last thing she wanted was for them to see her, in the dress, or while they were wailing over Foster Behan. They'd forget about him soon enough, but laughing over her in her wedding dress would keep them entertained for weeks.

Wedding dress. She sighed and put a small cloth bag down on the bar. Chris sidled up next to her, but she ignored his large, interested presence. "There's six hundred dollars in there," she told Essie. "For Lavinia's shop."

Essie fingered the bag as she looked steadily at Marty. "This is a good thing you're doing, Martha Rose."

Marty gave an embarrassed nod. "Time somebody did something for somebody in this town, or it ain't ever going to get better."

"Oh, I certainly agree, but Lavinia won't need quite so much to start her shop."

"Where'd you get the money?" Chris asked. He picked up the bag. "Six hundred's a lot in this day and age. Isn't it?"

"It's a very handsome sum," Essie said.

"The rest is for you," Marty told her.

"Whatever for?" Essie asked.

Marty found it very hard to talk. She felt like such a fool for not having had the gumption to do this sooner. "I know it may be too late," she said, "but I thought maybe you could use the money to open up a school. The town could use a school," she rushed on. "And you're a teacher, so—"

She stopped speaking as Chris put his hand on her shoulder. Essie was staring at her, wide-eyed with surprise, and it took a lot to surprise Essie Harris these days.

"Start a schoo—" Essie started.

"Where'd you get the money?" Chris cut her off.

Martha didn't want to look at him. She felt cheap and dirty, somehow. "From the bank," she answered. "It's my money."

"You've never touched a penny of your money," Essie said. "I'm surprised your uncle Jed allowed—"

Chris put his hand under her chin and made her look at him. "Where'd you get the money?"

"And why are you wearing that dress?" Essie added suspiciously.

She hadn't planned on telling them. She didn't want to tell them. She told them. "Charlie wouldn't let me have the money unless I said I'd marry him today." She jerked her head away from Chris Parris's warm, callused hand. "So I'm getting married today." She put her hands on her hips and glared at Essie, since she still couldn't bear to look at the man she couldn't have. "You got a problem with me getting married, Essie Harris? Becoming a *respectable* woman?"

It was Chris who waved the bag under her nose. "Looks like you're getting paid for it to me."

She flinched at the cold anger in his voice, and snatched the money from him. "This is mine! Mine all legal and proper."

"But not for long," Essie said. "Not after you marry Simpson."

"I know that!" Why was Essie giving her a hard time about using money for a store and a school? "The town needs what this money will buy, but Simpson—"

"Simpson won't invest in the town," Essie cut her off. "He'll take your money and head straight back East as soon as he can."

"No, he won't!"

Chris grabbed her shoulders and hauled her around to

face him. "Are you really marrying this Homer Simpson jerk?"

"Charlie Simpson," she corrected. She made herself look him in the eye. "I have to. I promised."

"Screw that," he growled. "Don't throw your life away on a promise."

Martha's mouth dropped in shock. How could he say such a thing? He looked as if he meant it, too, with his eyes blazing with anger. The look on his face twisted something inside her.

"A promise is a promise," she said.

He laughed, and the sound hurt her ears. "A woman's gotta do what a woman's gotta do. Is that it?"

She blinked. "Of course."

"It's the Code of the West."

Why did the sound of his voice rub against her like salt in a wound? Why didn't he make her a few promises himself? 'Cause he couldn't possibly love her, that was why. She was just a tall, ugly, unfemale thing. She could moon over him until the cows came home, but he couldn't love her. He was just funning her about not wanting her to marry Charlie, that was all. It hurt her like hell.

"Code of the West," she said, instead of saying what she was thinking. "What's that?"

"Something you find in a bad movie," he answered. "And in worse dreams." He let her go and turned back to the bar. "Didn't I ask for a beer, Essie?"

"Why, so you did, Christopher."

"Christian," Marty corrected, and got a dirty look from Chris for her trouble. "I can't help it if I know your name."

He looked her coldly up and down. "Remember how you found out?" he asked as he leaned on the bar.

The way he growled the question sent shocks of memory to every spot he'd touched the night before.

"Simpson gonna make you feel like that?" he went on in a voice that was like a dark purr.

"No." But that wasn't important. She stomped her foot on the floor. "Why are you so all-fired mad at me, Chris Parris?"

He whirled around and shouted, "Because you're marrying the wrong man!"

Then he walked out, leaving Essie and her to stare openmouthed at each other.

"Well!" Essie said after a few moments. "Well! Don't just stand there, girl. Go after him!"

Marty's heart twisted in such a tight knot she knew it would never get untangled. But she left her feet firmly planted where they were. She looked at Essie, at the still-swinging doors, and back at Essie.

"I promised Charlie Simpson I'd marry him," she said, to remind herself as well as Essie. "I don't break promises."

"You," Essie said, "are a fool."

Marty sighed, and refused to cry. "I know. You're the only friend I got, Essie. You want to come to the church and stand up with me?"

Essie's silence filled up the room for a bit, but her anger faded fast enough. She shook her head, clicked her tongue against the roof of her mouth, then said, "I'd be honored to, Martha Rose."

Chris berated himself out loud as he stalked down the street. "Oh, that was brilliant. Very dramatic. Very macho. Go ahead, walk out. Let her marry the dork like she deserves."

He didn't know where he was going, but he walked with such determined fury that what few people were around took one look at him and hurried to get out of his way.

"Good," he grumbled. He didn't want any company anyway. He was a loner. Loners, by the very definition of the word, didn't want anyone around. Loners didn't get involved. They didn't fall in love. They just lived the myth.

"She saved my life. She made love to me. She loves me. I know she loves me. She's just stubborn and stupid and has this Victorian notion of honor that is going to ruin her life. I don't care."

He noticed that he had stopped in front of a horse and that that was who he was talking to. It was all right, it wasn't as if he was raving to a stranger. The horse was his big blond Harley. It appeared that he was in the stable, though he didn't know how he'd gotten there. Maybe he'd been wandering the street mumbling incoherently for hours. This was Loon; who would notice?

Maybe she was already married by now. Maybe he should just get out of town.

Or maybe he should just go back and tell Marty he loved her, needed her, and wanted to take care of her when she wasn't taking care of him.

"Maybe," he grumbled, and the horse nickered encouragingly. It gently prodded his shoulder with its nose. He patted its neck and said, "I wish I had an apple or something for you."

The big horse snuffled, then looked at him from under half-lowered eyelashes with an expression he could have sworn was just like Marty's. Then it tossed its head and pointed its long nose—a nose not unlike

Marty's—toward a burlap bag hanging from a nail on a nearby post. Shaking his head, Chris went over to the bag and came back with an apple for the horse.

"Here you go, Harley. She's better looking than you are, you know, even if you are a natural blond," he said as the horse munched loudly. "She's a lot better built, too. That Simpson jerk is getting the best woman I've ever had." He sighed. "Lucky bastard."

The horse ignored him and kept on eating while Chris found a curry comb and began to brush its sleek gold coat. "I guess you and I ought to get out of town," he said after a while. "Maybe I could take you along on the train."

A picture of Marty in her fancy blue dress popped up in his mind, bringing a wave of regret mixed with annoyance. "If she thinks I'm going to hang around saving her ass once she's married she's got another think coming." *Married.* "I should have said something."

He threw down the comb and looked determinedly toward the stable door. "I am going to say something. Charlie Simpson isn't marrying my woman! Whose dream is this, anyway?"

As he strode from the stable he could have sworn he heard the horse snicker. He wasn't sure if the sound was encouragement, or amusement.

Chris forgot about the horse as he hurried up the street toward the whitewashed building in the distance that had to be the church. He was about halfway there when he heard the gunshots. His steps wavered for a moment. He closed his eyes to keep from looking in the direction of the sound. He was not going to pay attention to this, he wasn't going to be diverted. Let the citizens of Loon kill each other. He was going to stop Martha Rose Wirth's wedding, and nothing was going to stop him.

More shots. Shouting. A man appeared from around the back of the bank building. He looked around frantically, spotted Chris, and headed his way. Chris started sprinting toward the church, but the man grabbed his sleeve before he'd gotten very far.

"Ranger," the man said, panting. "The Varney gang's robbing the bank!"

"Good for them," Chris said. "Everybody needs a hobby. 'Bye."

The man wouldn't let go. "You gotta do something, Ranger. You and Sheriff Wirth gotta do something!"

Chris turned around and looked at the man. "The sheriff," he repeated. A slow smile spread across his face. "The hardworking, dedicated, dutiful sheriff." He rubbed his jaw and nodded. "Yeah. Right." He laughed, and noticed that the worried man was looking at him as if he were crazy.

"You know my horse?" Chris asked. The man nodded. "And the sheriff's?" Another nod. "Good. Saddle 'em and bring 'em to the church. And hurry it up."

The man ran off. A few more shots sounded near the bank. Chris continued to ignore the crime in progress. He laughed again and headed for Marty's office.

Standing in the little entryway in the back of the church Marty could see that most of the pews were empty. She was glad of that. The idea of the whole town turning out to gawk at her going down the aisle chilled her to the bone. It was better this way, with just a few people attending. Uncle Jed was standing up by the pulpit with Charlie and the preacher. Uncle Jed's housekeeper and the ranch foreman sat on one side of the church, and Uncle Jed's head clerk, George, sat on the other side. They were all squirming around in the afternoon heat and fanning themselves with the pasteboard fans provided to the church by the undertaker. None of them glanced back to where she and Essie stood. Nobody but Jed and Charlie, who kept making little, impatient gestures for her to get moving. The preacher kept checking his pocket watch.

The holdup was Essie, who was busy pinning and sewing Marty's shirtwaist to make the dress fit better. Marty didn't care if the dress fit or not, but she appreciated Essie's effort to put off the proceedings as long as possible. Essie had insisted on fixing her hair, too, before starting on the dress. That had taken quite some time since Marty's thick brown hair reached all the way down her back once it was unbraided.

"You don't have to go through with this," Essie said again. "Give me another pin."

"I do," Marty answered. Again.

She figured her words to Essie were good practice for when she finally made it to the altar. She found herself looking back toward the church door. Again. Maybe she was hoping somebody—somebody on a big palomino—would ride in and rescue her.

"Why?" Essie demanded in a loud whisper. She straightened up and looked Marty in the eye. "You don't need Charles Simpson."

"The town," Marty explained yet again. "The railroad."

Essie threw her hands in the air, scattering pins. "Why don't you just buy the damn railroad, girl?"

At Essie's shout there were gasps and questions from up front. Marty saw Charlie and Uncle Jed start to march down the aisle toward her. She ignored them to look questioningly at Essie.

"Buy the railroad?" she asked. "Can I do that?"

"Not the whole railroad, but you could buy shares, enough to keep the spur line in Loon."

"Why didn't you tell me this before?"

"Because I didn't think of it, I suppose."

"Well—I'll be damned!" Marty turned a scornful look on Charlie Simpson as he and Uncle Jed approached her. "Looks like I don't need him, after all."

Uncle Jed grabbed her arm. "You made a promise, girl. I aim to see you keep your word, and mine. A Wirth never breaks their word."

"I never asked you to ask him to marry me. I never wanted to marry him."

"You promised to be my wife," Simpson said. He carefully slicked back his hair. "You should be grateful I want you."

"Well, I ain't."

"No one else does. You'll end up a spinster if you don't marry me."

She wasn't particularly worried about spinsterhood. "I don't want you. Essie says I don't have to have you, so I won't."

"Martha!" Uncle Jed shouted. "Such ingratitude! After all Mr. Simpson's done for me, and for you and Loon."

"What's he ever done for Loon but raise interest rates? And what about all those foreclosures on people's property?" Essie demanded.

Simpson waved a finger under Marty's nose. His expression was ugly, and his tone vicious. "There's such a thing as breach of contract, young woman. If I take you to court you'll lose everything you own."

"That's right, Martha," Uncle Jed put in. "Breach of contract is a serious matter."

"Excuse me," the preacher said, coming up to join the fight. "Is there going to be a wedding today or not?"

Marty looked around her in helpless confusion. Everybody's face wore a look of determination—Charlie's, Uncle Jed's, even Essie's. She didn't know what to do. Breach of contract? It sounded like some fancy law term of Chris's. She wished she had Chris here to explain it. It sounded mighty serious. She didn't know what to do. For a moment there it looked as if she'd found a way out of the hole Uncle Jed and Charlie had dug her into. She guessed not. She guessed she'd have to go through with it.

"The wedding?" the preacher asked again, speaking directly to her this time.

She gulped, and nodded. "I—"

Just then the door banged open and Chris Parris came sauntering in. "Sheriff," he said loudly, heading straight for her. "I've been looking all over for you!" He looked serious, but his eyes had a wild smile in them, just for her.

Just for her. She smiled, inside, and the ice that had gripped her heart began to thaw. "Me?"

Uncle Jed stepped between Chris and her. "What are you doing here?" he demanded of the tall Ranger.

Her Ranger.

Chris pushed her uncle aside with no more than a flick of his hand. He held her gun belt out to her. "The Varney gang just robbed the bank," he said. "We gotta ride."

She grabbed the gun belt and had it strapped on over her fancy dress in seconds.

Chris grabbed her and kissed her, hard.

Charlie and Jed shouted together, "The bank!"

She was glad to see that her uncle and fiancé were far more concerned about their precious bank than her being kissed, in the church, in front of God and the preacher and everybody, by the man she loved.

She kissed him back, hard. Her tongue took his mouth by storm and he was the one who ended up moaning and clutching her this time.

Essie pulled them apart before they sank down on the church floor and began rolling around and taking their clothes off. "Not now!"

"I love you," he said, and he wasn't talking to Essie.

"I love you," Marty answered. "I loved you when you walked into the Black Eye."

"Me, too. Loved you when you were kicking ass in the bar."

"I love it when you talk fancy."

"I love the way you look at me."

"I'd love for you two to shut up," Essie said. "Get out of here."

"What about the Varneys?" Simpson demanded.

"Oh, yeah, right." Chris let her go, then looked at Simpson. "The sheriff and I are on the case. Come on, babe," he added to her. "Let's go get them varmints."

"But Marty!" Uncle Jed pointed at Simpson. "What about—"

"I came here to clean up this town," Chris declared. "Can't do it without the sheriff's help."

"That's right," Marty said. "It's my duty. Wirths do their duty, Uncle Jed. And I *promised* Ranger Parris all the help he needed. You know how you feel about promises."

Essie cackled and hugged herself. "Hoist on your own petard, Jed."

"What's that mean?" Jed demanded.

"If you'd have let this town have a decent school, some education might have rubbed off on you."

While Jed glared at Essie and Charlie Simpson dithered about being robbed, Chris took Marty's arm and ushered her toward the door. "The horses are waiting," he whispered.

The preacher hurried after them, with Simpson in tow, and stopped them just before they could get out.

"But what about the wedding?" he demanded.

"What about it?" Marty asked.

"The wedding!" Simpson said.

Chris grabbed the banker by the lapels of his coat. "There's a train leaving in two days," he told him. "Be on it."

"What? But—" Charlie sputtered.

"Or under it," Chris added with soft menace.

Chris put him down and then gave Marty a quick, fierce, possessive hug. "There'll be a wedding," he said to the preacher. "As soon as we round up the Varney gang. But you're not marrying Simpson," he informed Marty as he shoved her out the door with a teasing swat on the behind. "You're marrying me."

"Yes, Ranger Parris," she said obediently as they headed for the horses. "My pleasure."

"It will be," he said. "Believe me, babe, it will be."

In a partnership with her husband, **Catherine Anderson** has owned and successfully run two businesses. She currently lives in Oregon with her husband and their two sons.

A native Texan since 1982, **Christina Dodd** has immersed herself in ridin', ropin', and romance. Between cattle drives, she pens award-winning novels and shrinks her husband's jeans in the dryer. She's a fan of long-necked bottles, long-horned cattle, and long, tall Texans. When Christina dies, she wants to stay in Texas instead of going to heaven, 'cause Texas is where all the cowboys live.

Susan Sizemore lives in Minnesota. Her first novel, *Wings of the Storm*, won the 1991 Romance Writers of America Golden Heart Award.

AVAILABLE NOW

CIRCLE IN THE WATER by Susan Wiggs

When a beautiful gypsy thief crossed the path of King Henry VIII, the king saw a way to exact revenge against his enemy, Stephen de Lacey, by forcing the insolvent nobleman to marry the girl. Stephen wanted nothing to do with his gypsy bride, even when he realized Juliana was a princess from a far-off land. But when Juliana's past returned to threaten her, he realized he would risk everything to protect his wife. "Susan Wiggs creates fresh, unique and exciting tales that will win her a legion of fans."—Jayne Ann Krentz

DESTINED TO LOVE by Suzanne Elizabeth

In the tradition of her first time travel romance, *When Destiny Calls,* comes another humorous adventure. Josie Reed was a smart, gutsy, twentieth-century doctor who was tired of the futile quest for a husband before she reached thirty. Then she went on the strangest blind date of all—back to the Wild West of 1881 with a fearless, half-Apache, outlaw.

A TOUCH OF CAMELOT by Donna Grove

The winner of the 1993 Golden Heart Award for best historical romance. Guinevere Pierce had always dreamed that one day her own Sir Lancelot would rescue her from a life of medicine shows and phony tent revivals. But she never thought he would come in the guise of Cole Shepherd.

SUNFLOWER SKY by Samantha Harte

A poignant historical romance between an innocent small town girl and a wounded man bent on vengeance. Sunny Summerlin had no idea what she was getting into when she rented a room to an ill stranger named Bar Landry. But as she nursed him back to health, she discovered that he was a bounty hunter with an unquenchable thirst for justice, and also the man with whom she was falling in love.

TOO MANY COOKS by Joanne Pence

Somebody is spoiling the broth in this second delightful adventure featuring the spicy romantic duo from *Something's Cooking.* Homicide detective Paavo Smith must find who is killing the owners of popular San Francisco restaurants and, at the same time, come to terms with his feelings for Angelina Amalfi, the gorgeous but infuriating woman who loves to dabble in sleuthing.

JUST ONE OF THOSE THINGS by Leigh Riker

Sara Reid, having left her race car driver husband and their glamorous but stormy marriage, returns to Rhode Island in the hope of protecting her five-year-old daughter from further emotional harm. Then Colin McAllister arrives—bringing with him the shameful memory of their one night together six years ago and a life-shattering secret.

Looking For Love?

Try HarperMonogram's Bestselling Romances

TAPESTRY

by Maura Seger
An aristocratic Saxon woman loses her heart to the Norman man who rules her conquered people.

DREAM TIME

by Parris Afton Bonds
In the distant outback of Australia, a mother and daughter are ready to sacrifice everything for their dreams of love.

RAIN LILY

by Candace Camp
In the aftermath of the Civil War in Arkansas, a farmer's wife struggles between duty and passion.

COMING UP ROSES

by Catherine Anderson
Only buried secrets could stop the love of a young widow and her new beau from bloomimg.

ONE GOOD MAN

by Terri Herrington
When faced with a lucrative offer to seduce a billionaire industrialist, a young woman discovers her true desires.

LORD OF THE NIGHT

by Susan Wiggs
A Venetian lord dedicated to justice suspects a lucious beauty of being involved in a scandalous plot.

ORCHIDS IN MOONLIGHT

by Patricia Hagan
Caught in a web of intrigue in the dangerous West, a man and a woman fight to regain their overpowering dream of love.

A SEASON OF ANGELS

by Debbie Macomber
Three willing but wacky angels must teach their charges a lesson before granting a Christmas wish.
National Bestseller

For Fastest Service
—
Visa & MasterCard Holders Call
1-800-331-3761

MAIL TO: **HarperCollins Publishers**
P. O. Box 588 Dunmore, PA 18512-0588
OR CALL: (800) 331-3761 (Visa/MasterCard)

Yes, please send me the books I have checked:

☐	TAPESTRY (0-06-108018-7)	$5.50
☐	DREAM TIME (0-06-108026-8)	$5.50
☐	RAIN LILY (0-06-108028-4)	$5.50
☐	COMING UP ROSES (0-06-108060-8)	$5.50
☐	ONE GOOD MAN (0-06-108021-7)	$4.99
☐	LORD OF THE NIGHT (0-06-108052-7)	$5.50
☐	ORCHIDS IN MOONLIGHT (0-06-108038-1)	$5.50
☐	A SEASON OF ANGELS (0-06-108184-1)	$4.99

SUBTOTAL ....$________
POSTAGE AND HANDLING ....$ 2.00
SALES TAX (Add applicable sales tax) ....$________
TOTAL: $________

*(ORDER 4 OR MORE TITLES AND POSTAGE & HANDLING IS FREE! Orders of less than 4 books, please include $2.00 p/h. Remit in US funds, do not send cash.)

Name ______________________________

Address ____________________________

City _______________________________

State ________ Zip ____________ Allow up to 6 weeks delivery.
(Valid only in US & Canada) Prices subject to change.
HO 751